I MARRIED A CATMAN

Prime Mating Agency

REGINE ABEL

CONTENTS

Chapter 1   1
Chapter 2   13
Chapter 3   32
Chapter 4   44
Chapter 5   57
Chapter 6   78
Chapter 7   91
Chapter 8   115
Chapter 9   138
Chapter 10   158
Chapter 11   172
Chapter 12   190
Chapter 13   211
Chapter 14   222
Chapter 15   233
Chapter 16   248
Chapter 17   259
Chapter 18   275
Chapter 19   291
Epilogue   299

Also by Regine Abel   317
About Regine   321

I MARRIED A CATMAN

He was the dream mate she never expected.

When Ophelia seeks the services of the Prime Mating Agency to find her soulmate, she's floored to learn that her perfect match is Gaelec, an intimidating, feline-looking ex-convict. Despite her better judgment, she agrees to the union only to discover that a sweet and cuddly male, with the fluffiest fur, hides behind the stern but sexy mountain of muscle that is her new husband.

She was his anchor in the tempest.

After serving twelve years in the worst prison in the galaxy, Gaelec just wants to go home to a quiet life. But the evil forces that led to his incarceration are once more set on ruining his life. Having a brand-new mate thrust on him—and a human at that— is the last thing Gaelec needs. And yet, he soon finds himself unable to resist the sweet but strong woman, with her adorable freckles and adventurous spirit who makes him want to purr again.

With so many forces conspiring to bend him to their will, can Gaelec finally find the peace and happiness he seeks with his Ophelia, or will they bring him down a dark path again?

DEDICATION

To those who have fallen and gotten back up, learned from their mistakes, and strived to do better for themselves, and for others.

To teachers, mentors, and those who dedicate their lives to training young minds and preparing future generations for the challenges that await them.

Money and power mean nothing as both can be gone overnight. Skills and knowledge are the greatest wealth anyone can possess, and the most invaluable gift you can pass down to others.

CHAPTER 1
GAELEC

Back straight, tail stiff, and my chin lifted, I advanced with an assurance I didn't truly feel under the unusually quiet gazes of the other inmates. Lord Amreth looked even more imposing than usual with his massive bat wings, heavy horns, and silver-white eyes that observed me as I approached with the bag containing my few possessions.

For twelve years, twelve looong years, I served my sentence in one of his Quadrants on the dreadful prison planet Molvi. The Obosian Warden examined me in silence with an unreadable expression. It took every bit of my willpower to keep my own features neutral, despite the wild pounding of my heart.

"Time to go, Gaelec," the Warden said at last with his deep, rumbling voice.

I nearly felt faint with relief. Although he had always been fair and a male of his word, life had thrown too many sneaky blows at me. I now expected foul play at every turn.

"Time indeed, Warden," I replied, proud that my voice sounded calm and steady.

He lifted a wand-like stick from his weapons belt. No words were required for me to know what he wanted. I held my bag before me while he ran the scanning device over it. Although he appeared focused on that menial task, the Hell Lord—as humans labeled them—remained keenly aware of his surroundings and ready to parry any treacherous attack anyone might launch on him while they believed him distracted.

The Obosians—who owned and operated this prison—received that Hell Lord nickname for their apparent resemblance to mythical beings they called demons but with dark gray skin. And this place certainly qualified as what humans described as Hell.

All the worst criminals ended up here.

Although I didn't consider myself as such, the crime I committed guaranteed a first-class ticket to this nightmarish place. For all that, I had been lucky in my demise. Each Hell Lord controlled a sector of the prison planet. Those sectors were divided into four Quadrants ranging from Light to Dark. Q1—commonly referred to as the Light Quadrant—was reserved for those who committed the least grievous crimes and generally could expect to be released at the end of their term. Q4—the Dark Quadrant—was pretty much a death sentence. They regrouped the foulest criminals there. As for Q2 and Q3—the Gray Quadrants—your chances of survival gradually decreased. It all came down to the luck of the draw as to who else you were incarcerated with.

I had landed in the Light Quadrant. Considering how painful my stay here had been, I couldn't imagine surviving the tougher ones.

"You're all good," Amreth said as soon as he finished scanning both my bag and me.

He gestured for me to get inside the shuttle that had landed in the open square in front of the building that served as our dwelling. It was located a short distance from the facilities where we performed the refinement and transformation work on the minerals we extracted in our sector.

My heart soared as I headed towards the vessel. A few other inmates cheered, some of them jeering as they finally came to life. I made eye contact with as many as possible. I didn't care for most of them. And yet, my chest slightly constricted as I teasingly waved or nodded in farewell. For all their faults and flaws, they'd been my tribe for varying durations over the past twelve years.

I wasn't foolish enough to assume the sadness I glimpsed here and there came from actual sorrow over losing *me*, Gaelec. They merely mourned the skills I diligently acquired during my stay on Molvi and put to good use for the improvement of our Quadrant and quality of life.

My mind reeled as I climbed the ramp into the shuttle. I had not left this wretched place since my incarceration. Something akin to a wave of panic attempted to take root, but I clamped down on it. I hadn't fought this long to regain my freedom only to cower back to what had become almost safe in its familiarity. For all its hardships, the Quadrant was a controlled space with clear rules and expectations. Now, I was going right back into the unknown.

I settled in one of the twelve passenger seats of the shuttle. To my surprise, the Warden didn't shackle me. Instead, he sat across from me in the chair reserved for the guard that normally escorted convicts here from the triage center of the spaceport.

He crossed his legs and leveled his glowing eyes on me with a discreet but amused smirk on his generous lips. By all accounts, Lord Amreth—like many Obosian Lords—would be deemed a very handsome male. His skin was on the darker spectrum of gray, his shoulders broad, and his muscles bulging and ropey. In sharp contrast, long, silver white hair, typical of his species, cascaded down his shoulders. But it was his silver eyes that always hypnotized me, the way they stood out against the black sclera.

"You used your time among us well, Gaelec," Amreth said at

last in a pensive tone as soon as the shuttle doors closed, and the pilot got us airborne. "You've learned some excellent trade skills, worked hard, and above all, you behaved. I would have hated to be forced to challenge your release, had you acted otherwise. But now that you're regaining your freedom, please see to it that you do not commit crimes again."

I stiffened and narrowed my eyes at him. Although I expected a similar speech on my way out, something in the way he said this set all my senses on high alert.

"Why would I?" I challenged.

"In too many ways, your culture condones or incentivizes it," he replied in a factual manner devoid of any condemnation. "Once back home, you will face many pressures to go back to the type of activities that got you caught in the first place."

My stomach knotted at the accuracy of his statement. Undoubtedly, my Pride would quickly start putting pressure on me to participate in potentially lucrative missions to benefit our whole community.

I shrugged, trying to keep a nonchalant attitude about it. "That's true. However, as you've stated so well yourself, I've worked hard over the past decade. Every month, I made it a point to exceed the minimum productivity quotas to earn extra credits. After all this time, I have very comfortable savings. If I lead a reasonably frugal life, the interests alone will suffice to cover my expenses."

My heart sank when the Warden took on a commiserating expression laced with a hint of pity.

"What? Why are you looking at me like that?" I demanded, the suspicion blossoming deep within sparking my anger. "You deposited my wages into my savings account, did you not?"

He bristled at the implication that he might have embezzled my credits. That he appeared to decide to let it slide only increased my growing sense of doom. Obosians were almost fanatical in their obsession with upholding the law, which made them the perfect species to run the strictest penal facility in the galaxy. Accusing one of them of committing a crime was the greatest insult imaginable.

"Of course, I did. However, most of it is gone."

"WHAT?!"

In my shock and anger, I shot out of my seat and towered over him. Obviously, it had been an instinctive reaction in no way meant as a threat towards him. However, it could be easily perceived as such. I realized my error in a blink. Although he didn't move from his seating position, the Hell Lord's hands immediately began to glow as the electric tendrils of his Lumiak crawled over them.

They were electric energy that the Warrior breed of their species could summon at will. At low intensity, it zapped the target with a powerful enough discharge to temporarily incapacitate them. At maximum intensity, it would flat out burn you to cinders.

He didn't have to say a word. The hard glint in his silver eyes did all the talking. I mumbled an apology as I resumed my seat. He stared at me a moment longer, his stern expression making it clear he would prove a lot less lenient should I make that mistake again. Duly chastised, I lowered my eyes even as my mind continued reeling about his shocking statement.

"Your savings have been siphoned by your Pride. The Matriarchs considered it as your contribution."

"My contribution!" I exclaimed, crestfallen. "Why the fuck would I contribute to the Pride when I wasn't even there?! Why did you even allow this without my consent?"

"I didn't know," Amreth said in an apologetic tone. "In truth, I only found out three years ago when Argin returned."

I stiffened, and I felt my blood drain from my face. "Argin?! He was arrested *again*?"

Amreth nodded with a grim expression. "Yes. Worse still, he

was sent to another Warden's sector, but this time in a Dark Gray Q3."

My chest constricted with sorrow for the older male. He had become a mentor to me two years into my sentence and for the following seven years before he completed his own.

"That doesn't make sense," I said, utterly baffled. "Argin saved *a lot* of credits. He was the one who encouraged me to learn new trades on top of teaching me everything he knew. He kept repeating to prepare a safer future for when I got out so that I would never return here. Why would he commit another crime?"

"Because your Pride did the same thing to him that they were doing to you," the Warden said, anger audible in his voice. "He returned home to find all his credits gone. But for him to stay, they demanded a steady contribution. As he was too old by then for a Pride to want to keep him otherwise, participating in one of those 'missions' was his only hope not to be expelled. He got caught and lasted less than six months in Q3."

A slow growl rose in my throat. Teeth clenched, I fought the urge to let my claws extrude so that I could tear everything to shreds to vent the helpless fury I felt. The older male deserved—earned even—the right to a peaceful retirement. Our Pride's greed robbed him of countless years of his life in prison, and then killed him by depriving him of his means to survive.

"As soon as I realized what they had done, I intervened," Amreth continued in an appeasing tone. "It was too late to save him, but I did what I could to give you a fighting chance once you were released."

"How did you intervene?" I asked, fighting with my conflicting emotions.

"Seeing what they had done to Argin, I decided to check into your own accounts. As you belonged to the same Pride, I suspected your Matriarchs would behave the same way with you. Sadly, they did. Therefore, I stopped depositing your wages in that account, had your assets frozen, and then transferred into a new account where I added your other earnings from that point forward."

He removed a small object from his belt which I recognized as a credit stick. Feeling numb, I instinctively reached for it when he extended it to me. I stared at it blindly, still in shock. I wanted to mourn the old male, but thoughts of what awaited me back home clamored for my attention.

"I cannot get back what they already stole from you, but this contains the information on that account with all the credits you earned over the past three years," Amreth said softly. "Under the circumstances, I took the liberty of putting those credits in a safe investment account. The capital was guaranteed, and it earned you some respectable interests. It's nowhere near what you would have had without the theft, but it will give you a comfortable enough amount to start off with so that you will not be strong-armed into falling again."

I gave him a stiff nod. He deserved a far more elaborate response. He didn't owe me any of this. In truth, many Wardens likely wouldn't have lifted a single finger had they been in his position when this tragedy unfolded with Argin. For Obosians, the fact that you committed a crime was all that they cared about, motives be damned other than to justify an even harsher sentence.

"Gaelec," Amreth said, the sternness of his voice reclaiming my attention. "As soon as you go home, your people will push you down a dangerous path again. You *must* resist."

Even though he was likely right, I instinctively felt defensive —if not offended—on behalf of my people.

"You don't know that," I countered with a clipped tone.

"I do, and so do you," he retorted more harshly. "I've seen too many of your people in similar situations. It becomes an endless vicious cycle with Nazhrals. You have a nice soul, Gaelec. You're smart, strong, still very young, and with great potential. Do not waste it. Do not allow yourself to be manipulated. I would hate to see you again on Molvi. Be warned that a second offense is a guaranteed sentence at minimum in Q2 but more than likely Q3 or Q4. Do not get yourself killed over this."

I barely repressed a shudder. He didn't have to go into further details for me to know that as talented a hunter and fighter as I was, my chances of surviving another journey on Molvi were slim to none, especially in one of the darker Quadrants. He also didn't have to specify that a second sentence would be far longer than the twelve years I just served.

"Your words have not fallen on deaf ears," I said in a non-committal fashion.

He stared at me quietly for what felt like an eternity, making me want to squirm. A million thoughts were crossing his mind. With a conviction I couldn't explain, I realized the Warden was debating whether to say something else. That piqued my curiosity. Obosians were brutally honest and borderline callous in the way they always spoke their minds.

"The United Planets Organization and the Enforcers are launching a massive campaign to put an end to smuggling, piracy, and slaves trade," Amreth said at last, while appearing to carefully choose his words. "Be aware they're setting many traps to catch anyone participating in these illegal activities. Too many allies are negatively impacted by these crimes."

My eyes widened to hear him reveal such a thing. Granted, it didn't take a genius to know that all galactic merchants and traders fumed at the rampant issues they faced with space pirates. Obviously, my people weren't the only ones involved in these crimes, but we certainly played a huge part in it.

"If anyone even remotely hints at a mission involving the Levendoc Corporation, avoid it at all costs. You *will not* survive it," Amreth warned at last just as the shuttle was entering the docking bay of the spaceport.

"Why are you telling me all this?" I whispered, my confusion audible.

"Like I said, you have a nice soul. Too many decent people get on the wrong side of the law because of bad influences. You've been given a second chance. Don't waste it."

With that, the Warden rose to his feet and headed for the door. Considering how extremely cautious he always was whenever he visited the Quadrant where we were incarcerated, seeing him turn his back to me threw me for a loop. My chest constricted at this extreme display of trust. Granted, he could see my soul and therefore if I harbored any ill intent towards him. Still, he wouldn't have done this inadvertently. He made a deliberate choice to further drill in his message.

He believed in me.

Do I believe in myself enough to do right with the opportunities presented to me?

We quietly walked down the ramp into the large ship hangar. It was a different area than when I first arrived here. Only a couple of guards hung around in a very laid-back fashion, unlike the processing area with countless security measures that could instantly kill anyone foolish enough to attempt a last-minute escape.

A few people briefly glanced in our direction, most politely nodding at my companion. The deference they showed him reminded me that his Lord title stemmed from the fact that he was indeed nobility.

He led me to a medium-sized ship where a few other ex-convicts who had completed their sentences were also boarding. It would transfer us to various bigger vessels that would take us to our respective homeworlds or destinations.

The Hell Lord gestured with his chin for me to proceed. I nodded and started climbing the ramp only to stop at the top. I glanced over my shoulder at the Warden, who was stoically staring at me, waiting for me to get inside for his duty to be completed. For a reason I couldn't explain, my chest constricted again as if I was saying goodbye to a friend. And yet, our interactions couldn't have been farther from it over my more-than-a-decade stay here.

"Thank you, Warden," I caught myself blurting out.

I didn't know what I was thanking him for specifically, but he seemed to sense what I meant. His glowing eyes slightly went out of focus, and his face softened in a way I couldn't recall ever witnessing before. Although he was only a few years older than me, his almost paternal expression struck me hard.

"Safe journey, Gaelec. May you find happiness and prosperity."

I didn't know what peering at my soul just now revealed to him. Whatever it was, it pleased him. With one final nod, I entered the vessel. As much as I hated the Obosians—more on principle because of their self-righteous sense of superiority—I had tremendous respect for Lord Amreth. In a different world, I would have loved to be friends with him.

Contrary to my initial beliefs, I didn't socialize or take advantage of all the amenities offered on either of the two vessels aboard which I traveled during the trip back home. My new freedom felt overwhelming, as was the economy cabin paid for by the Obosian justice system to return me to my people. While most customers would find plenty of faults with the room, from its size to the quality of the mattress, to me, it felt overly luxurious.

And everything was too quiet.

Who would have thought that I would resent proper soundproofing one day? However, spending twelve years with the only guards being some of the foulest creatures that roamed the forest surrounding our Quadrant had taught me to fear silence. When the wildlife stopped making any noise, it meant that something terrifying lurked nearby.

It would take me time to shed many of the survival responses I acquired over the years.

But as the distance closed with my homeworld, the trauma of my incarceration gradually gave way to anxiety about my imminent arrival. What kind of welcome awaited me there? Growing up on Melelyn—the Nazhral homeworld—I'd known too many people who had been arrested and sentenced. Very few ever returned home. The majority died in various painful ways long before they finished serving their sentences. Of those who made it out, many decided to start over elsewhere. And then you had those who, like me, went back to their Prides.

As the majority who did so had sustained grievous injuries, they'd often been turned away by their Matriarchs. After all, what use was a male who could no longer provide or protect?

In my case, I'd done a great job of keeping myself safe. I was in excellent physical shape and had acquired a variety of skills that could make me invaluable to the Pride if they decided to leverage them. This gave me hope that I would be one of the few not to be cast out.

The image of Oluina flashed before my mind's eye. The old pain that I thought long buried came back to the surface. She had been so beautiful, fierce, and wild that I'd been totally enthralled by her. When she chose me as her companion, I'd been over the moon. So few could brag about having the honor of being picked by the youngest female to ever become Head Huntress of her Pride. We'd been so perfect together that I'd foolishly believed we would become bonded mates, a rare occurrence among my people.

However, she discarded me the moment I got arrested. Growing up, I'd seen plenty of females who continued to write and stay in touch with their incarcerated lover or partner. She never wrote to me once. Worse still, my younger brother informed me that the very day my team and I were thrown in jail, she shacked up with Moriak.

That foul male—eight years older than I was—always saw me as a threat. He made no mystery how much he resented Oluina picking me over him. As she was three years my elder, Moriak believed he was a better match for her as a more mature male instead of the young eighteen-year-old cub that I had been at the time. For that entire year, Moriak abused his power as Alpha of the Pride to multiply the ways to try and get rid of me. I was assigned the most dangerous hunts, and he constantly pushed me to participate in the riskiest missions with the prospect of wealth to further secure my position in the Pride.

As he acted in a similar fashion with all other young males who, like me, sought to be invited into the Pride, I merely took it as a compliment and made it a point to accept every challenge for the pleasure of showing off. I'd been such a fool, blinded by love and ego.

Is he still the Alpha?

At the time of my arrest, I had just turned nineteen, while he was twenty-six. Today, he would be thirty-nine. Very few Alphas remained at the head of a pack that long. On average, they lasted six or seven years before a younger, stronger male ousted them. Then again, the longest record belonged to a male from my birth Pride, Aran Sulwyn, who had served for thirty-one years.

If Moriak was still in power, would he still harass me and make my life difficult, or was I now finally old enough for him to leave me be?

The distressing thought plagued me for the remainder of the journey. Regaining my freedom and returning home should have been the happiest time of my life.

Not this.

CHAPTER 2
GAELEC

As I disembarked the vessel upon landing in the Melelyn spaceport, I couldn't help feeling hurt that no one came to greet me or escort me back home. It had been a foolish expectation or hope. A glance at the time on my bracer indicated it was only a few minutes after 1:00 PM. This meant everyone would be working or out hunting. It made no sense for them to deprive the pack of their labor only to come pick up one person when a perfectly fine public shuttle system could take care of it.

As the private shuttle flew me to the Nevian Valley—after which our Pride was named—countless conflicting emotions surged through me. The oddest sense of well-being washed over me as I took in the beautiful rivers gleaming under the sun, the lush forests teeming with life that had been my hunting grounds, and the freedom and endless possibilities they offered. But the warm feeling in my chest cooled gradually as I took in the outline of the village.

Although it clearly expanded by a few new buildings, it lacked the majesty of the memories that sustained me all those years on Molvi. Granted, more than a decade had gone by with me idealizing what it had been. However, time unmistakably left its mark. The buildings looked dated and tired. Even from here, as the pilot began our descent, I frowned at the type of technology still being used for the village's main power source and communication tower.

How did I not notice how antiquated all this already was back then?

I'd been too young, too in love, and too clueless to notice these kinds of things. Fighting for survival, where efficiency meant a modicum of comfort instead of endless hardship, did wonders to whip me into being more aware.

As disappointed as I felt about the fantasy I had built in my head, seeing all these deficiencies gave me hope. I now had the knowledge and the skills to make the improvements this place sorely needed. Surely, the Matriarchs would acknowledge this as proof of my worth?

However, a sharp pain sliced through my chest at the sight of my house by the cliff. Despite the many changes and not particularly nice expansions performed on it by the new owner, I still recognized my original creation.

When I requested permission to build there, everyone thought me crazy. It was a wild and overgrown section of the village with tons of gnarly roots and a rocky, uneven terrain. But I instantly saw its potential. So long as I worked on it in my spare time and with my own materials, the Matriarchs didn't object. They figured I would give up early on once I realized the folly of my endeavor. But in less than six months, I completed the first phase of the project.

To this day, I vividly remembered the look of awe and disbelief on every face as the house steadily took shape. Back then, it only had two bedrooms—each with its own hygiene room—a kitchen and living area. The plan was to expand it by a couple more rooms to shelter all the cubs Oluina and I would have.

Although small compared to other bigger homes, it had been the most modern in its design on top of offering a breathtaking view of the valley and river below. As the Alpha of the Pride, Moriak had been livid that the newcomer that I was, still wet behind the ears, should possess a better house than his own.

Naturally, he appropriated it as soon as I was arrested.

That grovas took my youth, my freedom, my female, and my home.

What else would he take from me now?

The shuttle landed on the pad at the northern entrance of the village. The original founding sisters of this Pride wisely chose the location. The surrounding steep cliff made it impossible for any attacker to sneak up or flank us. They had only one way to come at us, making it easy to push back and fight off a siege—not that such confrontations ever occurred anymore. Granted, aerial attacks remained a possibility. However, the Prides qualified as fairly primitive in their everyday lives, and we closely stuck to old traditions when it came to rules of engagement.

After disembarking, I carefully approached the guard by the entrance of the village. I didn't know him. That didn't surprise me. At a glance, he appeared to be in his mid-twenties. He would have joined the Pride halfway through my incarceration. I nodded as I approached him. He barely spared a glance at my bag, too busy giving me an assessing look. I could tell he was evaluating how much of a competition I could possibly be. It was disheartening to be reminded of that aspect of being a male among my people.

"Are you Gaelec?" the guard asked as soon as I was but a couple of meters away from him.

"Yes. I am Gaelec Sulwyn," I replied politely.

"Good. Rozel will see you in the Great Hall. You may proceed."

Although taken aback, I kept a neutral expression on my face and nodded. As I entered the village, My sense of unease cranked up another notch. Why had he not given me his name in exchange? This was how you treated strangers—namely roaming males—who were not welcomed to stay in the village. Had the decision regarding me already been made? Was that a sign that I was banished from the Pride?

The mostly empty streets only enhanced the sense of doom that I felt, another indication that I wasn't wanted here. As I made my way towards the Great Hall, I tried to enumerate again the list of qualities I could offer to justify keeping my place here. It was the largest building in the village. It served as both a gathering hall and the mansion shared by the three elder females who ruled the pack as our Matriarchs. As the eldest, Rozel ruled the Pride. Although the other two had a say, as well as all the huntresses—especially Oluina as the Head Huntress—in the end, Rozel's word was the law.

I could only hope that the sliver of affection she showed me in the past survived my long absence.

My eyes flicked this way and that, taking in my surroundings. Up close, the village looked much better than it had from a bird's eye view. Although still dated, the place was well-maintained. Despite the streets being made of packed dirt, they were clean and level. The dwellings and shops showed no signs of neglect, many even appearing to have recently received a fresh coat of paint.

The sound of young voices giggling and shouting stirred a powerful sense of longing within me. Seconds later, a clowder of cubs ran across a perpendicular street a few meters in front of me. The even group of males and females appeared to be chasing each other. But even as that adorable tableau warmed my chest, my heart constricted for the little males. In only a few more years, their carefree life would come to an end as they frantically prepared to be cast out.

I stepped inside the small antechamber at the entrance of the building. The large doors granting access to the Great Hall beyond already stood open. Straight ahead, at the other end of the spacious room, the three Matriarchs sat on an elevated dais in the otherwise empty room.

The first half of the room was rectangular while the other portion looked like half a hexagon. The slanted sides flanking the back wall had a few seats upon which the huntresses settled during official and large gatherings. Although also elevated, those two sections, split into two rows of seats, were slightly lower than the Matriarchs' section. At the bottom of the four steps leading up to the dais, three rows of seats framed the left and right sides of the vast open space where entertainment was occasionally held.

Presiding in the center, Rozel watched me approach with an intense look. Her deep blue eyes peered at me with an unreadable expression. At seventy-two, she was still remarkably fit, in no small part thanks to the healthy sheen of her multi-colored fur in shades of white, orange, and black. To her left, Priya seemed a bit uneasy, not to say nervous. That bothered me a lot. Slightly younger by five years, with hazel eyes, and gray fur with black stripes, she always acted as the more moderate voice of the trio.

As for Jilam, her blue eyes—the same color as Rozel's—stood out sharply against her pure white fur. She seemed annoyed to be there. With her no-nonsense personality, I could only presume that whatever outcome would result from this meeting, the decision had already been made. Therefore, this formality was a complete waste of her time.

That didn't bode well for me.

I often thought that Pryia would have made a far better Head Matriarch than her older sister. But in all the ways that mattered, Rozel always proved to be the more dominant.

"Gaelec, welcome home," Rozel said in a friendly tone.

Home!

An instant wave of relief swept through me that she should have used that term, instead of greeting me with something along the lines of 'Congratulations on completing your sentence' which would have established more clearly that she no longer deemed me a member of the Pride.

"Thank you, Rozel," I replied graciously. "It is good to finally be home again."

She openly examined me from top to bottom. For half a beat, I almost expected her to ask that I spin around so that she could get a proper view from every angle. Thankfully, she spared me that ignominy.

"You look extremely well and healthy," she mused aloud, the surprise audible in her voice. "In all my years, of the few who survived, I can't recall seeing one return in such great shape. They were always at least heavily scarred if not maimed."

Is that what you were hoping?

Obviously, I kept the snarky thought to myself and instead maintained a neutral expression on my face as I nodded.

"Life on Molvi can be deadly if one isn't cautious or smart. I stayed out of trouble and watched my back," I replied in a factual manner.

She nodded approvingly while continuing to give me an assessing look. "Well done, my friend. The Pride can always use a new injection of strong blood. We need good providers and fearless protectors. Our young Queens will be quite pleased to see how you have returned to us."

I barely repressed the violent urge to cringe upon hearing those words. There was a time when this would have filled me with joy. After all, being deemed a desirable partner constituted a male's best chance of being welcomed into a Pride. But twelve years in prison made me revisit several of my priorities. More importantly, I didn't want to start butting heads with their current males.

However, the way the Matriarch narrowed her eyes at me hinted that I failed to hide my thoughts.

"Do my words displease you, Gaelec?" she asked, a sliver of a challenge in her voice.

"They don't displease me, Matriarch," I replied cautiously. "But I'm not here to compete with anyone for the females' attention. After the hardships of the past few years, I would welcome a bit of respite."

"Have you forgotten that you need our favors to retain your place in our midst?" she asked, her tone and gaze slightly hardening.

"Not at all," I said in a reasonable and appeasing tone. "I fully intend to prove myself useful to the Pride. As you said yourself, I can help protect everyone after surviving multiple encounters with some of the foulest creatures in the galaxy, which lurked in the forests surrounding the Quadrant we were incarcerated in. During my sentence, I acquired many skills that will greatly benefit the village, with various upgrades that will increase productivity and reduce costs and waste."

She pursed her lips, looking unconvinced. "True though that it may be, our Queens might still take offense to your disdain."

I fought the urge to roll my eyes. "It is not disdain, Matriarch. I simply do not wish to step on someone else's territory. Like I said, I just want to settle back home, find my place again, and make myself useful."

She narrowed her eyes at me. "Is it Oluina? Your feelings for her have not waned?"

This time, I couldn't help a huff. "Not at all. Whatever existed between us ended over a decade ago once I got arrested."

The look she gave me screamed loudly that she did not believe a word I said, which only annoyed me.

"Don't be bitter. As you well know, very few males return from Molvi. And those who do are usually but a shadow of themselves. We all do what we must to survive. She had no reason to believe she would ever see again the prime male that you used to be. But you look spectacular. There's no question Oluina will want you back."

"I do not resent any of the choices or decisions she made," I countered in a reasonable tone. "But you must understand that I'm no longer the nineteen-year-old cub that I was at the time. I do not seek romance, only peace and rewarding work. I thought you'd be pleased that I don't plan on stirring any trouble."

The Matriarch opened her mouth to respond. But before she could even utter a word, I felt Oluina's presence behind me moments before she stepped inside the room. I glanced over my shoulder to see her strutting in, her gait sensual and fluid. She had undeniably matured over the past decade. Her curves were fuller and insanely enticing, likely as a result of motherhood. Her bushy, fluffy tail very slowly swayed behind her. Her luxurious reddish-brown fur—pristine white around her chest and belly—looked insanely soft.

"Well, well! We were just speaking of you, Oluina!" Rozel said with a satisfied tone.

Although protective of all her daughters, the Head Matriarch always had an overly soft spot for Oluina.

As I watched her approach, I had to admit that she had grown even more beautiful than in my memory. And yet, the lascivious way in which her piercing green eyes examined me made me nauseous. To think, there had been a time where I would have perceived it as incredibly sexy and flattering to my childish ego.

No words could express the relief I felt to no longer be enthralled by her charms. On the whole journey here, I dreaded that a single glance at her would bring back old feelings crashing down on me. Contempt would have worried me as it might have indicated that I truly harbored some bitterness over her moving on so quickly. But she only stirred indifference, and the natural queasiness one might feel at persistent unrequited attentions.

"Gaelec!" Oluina said in an overly purring tone. "You have matured nicely, my dear."

"Thank you, Oluina," I said politely as she closed the distance between us. "You look great as well."

She raised a furry eyebrow, surprise with a hint of outrage fleeting over her features.

"Just *great*?" she echoed, clearly expecting me to gush over her.

I smiled, pretending to be too dense to understand what she wanted. She pinched her lips, looking annoyed by my silence.

"I'm assuming you just returned from a hunt?" I asked to stir the conversation towards safer terrain.

"I did," she replied, puffing out her chest, heart face brightening at this opportunity to brag. "And it was an excellent one at that, too. We shall feast for a few days."

"Well done!" I said politely with the appropriate level of enthusiasm without going overboard.

"Food is not a problem anymore," Rozel swiftly interjected as she gazed upon her daughter with maternal pride. "My Oluina has been our Head Huntress for the past nine years now."

"Congratulations!" I said, although not in the least surprised. "You worked hard for this."

She had always displayed great talent and ambition. For all her faults, I couldn't take away the fact that she had trained relentlessly to be at the top of the chain.

"She most certainly did!"

Oluina ran her hand over the fluffy patch of white fur on her chest in a gesture that was far too sensuous to qualify as an absent-minded movement. She often praised my skill at stimulating her with that sensitive spot for her. This less-than-subtle reminder of our previous intimacy bothered me to no end. I pretended not to notice.

"You should come see me hunt one of these days. You will be impressed," Oluina purred.

"If time permits, I will consider it," I said in a non-committal fashion. "However, I expect to be fairly busy earning my place here again."

Oluina's face immediately hardened as she visibly bristled at this gentle rejection. "What better way to secure your place here than to form strong bonds with the Head Huntress?"

I gaped at such a forward statement, if not a semi-veiled threat. My mind raced to find an appropriate response. The large doors opening behind us gave me a slight reprieve.

"Gaelec?" a stunning young female called out.

Tall and slender, she appeared to be the same height of 5'10 as Oluina, or maybe an inch shorter. A discreet blood smear marred her otherwise stunning white fur with dark gray spots. My eyes widened as I took in the large tuft of silver-gray fur on her chest and mischievous blue eyes, allowing me to finally recognize the newcomer. I sniffed the air to pick up her scent and confirm my eyes weren't fooling me.

"Ylis?!" I exclaimed.

She broadly grinned at me, her fangs peeking through her parted lips before she broke into a run. On instinct, I opened my arms and welcomed her as she all but crashed into me, making me take a steadying step back from the force of the impact. She'd been but a very young cub when I was taken away—just a few days shy of her eleventh birthday.

After giving me a bone-crushing hug, Ylis rubbed her temple against mine, marking me with her scent before letting go. I took a step back to give her a proper once over, marveling at the beautiful young female she turned into. Although we were completely unrelated, I felt like a proud big brother, not to say father.

"My dear, you look stunning, and all grown up!" I exclaimed.

She struck a pose in a flaunting manner while waving her tail from side to side a couple of times.

"And she's become one of our most promising young huntresses!" Priya added proudly.

I bit the insides of my cheeks to have her mother thus chime in, singing the praises of her own offspring just like her sister had done but moments prior about Oluina.

"I'm not surprised," I replied, glancing at the Matriarch before returning my attention to Ylis. "You were always talented, even as a very young cub."

"And it's in large part thanks to you!" she said with a mix of gratitude and affection that warmed my heart. She then waved at me. "But you also look amazing! I can't believe you're finally back. And I'm so happy to see you returned to us safely."

"Thank you. It is good to be back."

"Well this is all nice, Ylis, but the meat needs to be cleaned and cut," Oluina interrupted, clearly displeased that I should bestow so much attention to her young cousin. "You know how clumsy the juniors are without proper supervision. You can both babble and catch up later. For now, you have work to do."

The way Ylis's stare hardened as she gazed upon her older cousin hinted at some serious competition between them. I had mixed feelings about it. A part of me rejoiced to see that the female I always considered as the sister of my heart had the backbone to stand up to Oluina. Most people—males and females alike—allowed her to stomp all over them until she got things done her way. Seeing Oluina's unfounded jealousy also amused me tremendously. However, I knew how petty and vindictive she could be. I didn't want her to become abusive towards Ylis because of me.

To think there was a time I mistook her ruthlessness and sense of entitlement as strength and fearlessness.

Despite her obvious displeasure, Ylis gave her cousin a stiff nod followed by a friendly smile my way before she headed back out of the building. The smug smirk on Oluina's face pissed me off to no end. As the Head Huntress, she could issue such commands and expect the other females to obey. The respect of hierarchy was no joking matter.

"They could use your help as well, Oluina," Rozel suddenly added, wiping out the triumphant expression off her daughter's face. "We need to wrap up our discussion with Gaelec."

As much as I loved it, that took me aback. It wasn't uncommon for the Head Huntress to sit in on these types of meetings. Lips pinched, it was Oluina's turn to respond with a sharp nod to be thus dismissed. Tail stiff, she walked out of the Great Hall.

Although relieved to see her gone, tension crawled up my back as I faced the Matriarch. The unreadable expression had returned on her face as she quietly studied me. She didn't need to tell me that she was less than impressed by how the reunion with her daughter went down.

"We reserved a house for you. The dark wood cabin by the forest, if you remember it," Rozel finally said once the silence stretched to an almost uncomfortable length.

"Yes, I remember it," I replied in a neutral tone.

"Unfortunately, we cannot give you your old house back. You can understand that, as we had little reason to believe you would return, we couldn't let such prime real estate go to waste. Not only has Moriak been raising his offspring there, he made several upgrades and expansions over the course of the years. It would be unfair to evict them now."

As much as this entire situation infuriated me, I had known all along what the outcome would be. It just pissed me off that he should have been the one to appropriate it.

"Of course, I perfectly understand and expected as much," I said calmly. "But I'm grateful you provided new accommodations for me."

"Naturally," Rozel replied, seeming relieved I didn't make a fuss. "Take the next few days to relax, reacquaint yourself with everyone, and reflect on how you will integrate yourself and contribute to the Pride."

"Thank you, Matriarchs," I replied, looking at each of the three females in turn.

The gentle glimmer in Priya's eyes gave me hope. She always approved of the fraternal way in which I had mentored her daughter. The genuinely affectionate reunion she witnessed between Ylis and me further played in my favor. Although she didn't have the final say in anything, I didn't doubt she would put her finger on the scale to protect me if it came to that.

As soon as I stepped outside, I deeply inhaled the fresh air as if I'd been suffocating in there. I didn't know how I felt about this entire situation. The part of me that rejoiced at being back home also struggled to readjust to what had previously been normal. Such a long time away, constantly fighting for your survival, made you look at the world with new eyes.

A wistful smile settled on my lips as I spotted a group of huntresses showing off the trophies they claimed from their kills. I remembered all too well that youthful excitement following a particularly successful hunt. While a few names escaped me, I recognized most of them. However, seeing them all grown up reinforced how long I'd been absent.

Shaking the thought away so that I wouldn't start feeling depressed about all those wasted years, I followed the main path towards the southwest corner of the village which bordered the forest. Although it was common for males to live in the dwellings located at the more exposed edges of our settlement, this particular house possessed even less protection than the others.

Technically, it wasn't a problem to the extent that wars between Prides were mostly a thing of the past. Roaming males looking to force their way in always challenged the alpha first, and then the other males should any of them choose to contest his dominance. Wild creatures were the bigger threat, not that too many dared to venture this close to people. But it sent a clear message that I would need to work my way up to a better status among them.

Truth be told, they had given me this humble dwelling expecting to see a broken male. A part of me suspected they would swiftly offer better accommodations now that they saw my current fitness level, and especially once I proved how valuable my contributions could be.

The sudden feeling of being observed snapped me out of my musings. I jerked my head to the left only to see a familiar silhouette a few hundred meters away. The white fur with black spots and the unusual patch of black fur on the chest immediately revealed the identity of my stalker. Even from this distance, I saw Moriak flinch. He likely hated being caught spying on me.

Groaning inwardly, I slowed down and then stopped when he began walking towards me. I shifted the bag containing my meager possessions to my other hand to keep my claws from extruding or my hands from fisting. This day had been unpleasant enough without having to deal with him as well. Then again, getting this chore out of the way now also had its perks.

"Look who's back!" Moriak said with forced enthusiasm.

The same way I was discreetly examining him, he was also assessing me but blatantly so. Despite his best efforts, my appearance had him instantly seething. I had never been small, but I nicely filled up over the past decade, as was to be expected with any cub growing to full maturity. The harsh life on Molvi also forced me to keep fit and build muscle mass. Today, I was slightly taller and noticeably bulkier than our current Alpha.

And he fucking hated it.

He kept himself in good shape as well. However, at thirtynine, he would be deemed past his prime by Nazhral standards. The far more comfortable life he enjoyed also meant he wasn't as lean and well-defined as me. I suspected my speed and strength would easily trump his. There was no question in my mind he was thinking the same.

He narrowed his green eyes at me. "You look surprisingly well for someone who spent over a decade on the presumably worst penitentiary in the galaxy," Moriak said, trying to sound playful. "Ex-cons are usually scarred and roughed up, but you're all kinds of pretty. Were you imprisoned or on vacation?"

I tilted my head to the side and raised an eyebrow at him. "You sound disappointed. Were you hoping to see me come back maimed and disfigured?" I asked in an overly innocent fashion.

"Of course not," he replied, sounding defensive. "I'm surprised, that's all. It is extremely rare for people to return this unscathed. But hey, we can always use a strong fighter. And you visibly became that during your absence. There are lots of roaming Sikkals in these parts of late. With the impending mating season, the males are trying to claim broader territories."

"Gladly. I will be happy to assist with this," I said in all sincerity.

"Good. You were an excellent hunter," he said in a slightly patronizing tone before taking on a falsely concerned expression. "But I wonder if you might have grown a little rusty after all this time."

I snorted, not fooled in the least by his insinuation. "Hardly. I have fought far worse than Sikkals on Molvi. They will require little effort in comparison."

Moriak's face closed off as he tried to hide his displeasure at my comment. "I see."

"I doubt it," I replied mockingly as I resumed walking. "On Molvi, we're not locked up in prison cells or any other such things. We're contained by forests and rivers filled with the type of foul creatures you could not even begin to imagine. Very few survive encounters with them. But I became quite adept at hunting them. They make for fine dining."

"It is good to hear," Moriak replied, tagging along, although he looked as if he just bit into something nasty. "We shall promptly put your new skills to good use. But may I ask where you're headed?"

"To my new home to unpack and settle in," I said mockingly while showing him my bag.

My fist itched to punch him in the throat when he glanced at me with a fake air of guilt and commiseration.

"Ah yes… I'm afraid the one you built is no longer available. Hopefully, you hold no hard feelings towards me for settling inside it with my younglings?"

I clamped down on the anger wanting to resurface, knowing he was deliberately needling me for that very purpose.

I shrugged and looked at him with a nonchalant expression. "Why would I? I was gone for twelve years. Had no one taken residence within it, it would have decayed and then become but a shadow of what I had built."

"Right. It is very understanding of you," Moriak conceded begrudgingly.

"Obviously, I was sad to have had so little time to enjoy it. But then, who would have guessed I would get arrested barely a week after completing its construction?" I added, locking eyes with him.

He swallowed hard and averted his eyes with a slightly nervous smile. "Yes, quite the tragedy that no one could have anticipated. After all, you always returned from your previous missions."

I stopped and turned to look at him, forcing him to do the same.

"Indeed, I did. And I will continue to do so. No matter what hurdles or challenges are thrown at me, I will *always* return home," I said, the intensity of my stare making it clear that should he try to get rid of me again in the future, he would face a truly formidable foe.

"We want nothing more than that, Gaelec. Like I said, we could use an additional strong hunter," Moriak replied, pretending not to understand my underlying meaning.

Obviously, he would never confess to the wrongs he levied against me and other young males, but I would remind him daily that I was no longer an easily manipulated cub.

I resumed walking, and he shadowed me in silence for a short while. I almost told him to just spit it out or piss off as I didn't particularly enjoy his companionship. But I was too intrigued by what else he might have to say to risk alienating him.

"I understand you saw Oluina after her return from the hunt?" he asked at last, although it was more of a statement than an actual question.

I barely repressed the urge to roll my eyes. Was *that* what this was all about?!

"That's correct," I replied in a noncommittal fashion.

"She must have been excited to see you," he continued, trying to sound casual about it.

I shrugged. "You could say that. But I want to believe any member of the Pride would be pleased to see any one of us safely returned home."

"Right. But your case is slightly different," he admitted begrudgingly, his voice hardening that I was forcing him to spell things out. "Therefore, I figured you would want to know that Oluina was in heat not even ten days ago. For all we know, she could be pregnant with my cubs as we speak."

I snorted and gave him a disbelieving look. "If that is the case, congratulations to the both of you. But I'm confused as to why you felt the need to share that information with me."

He gave me a 'Don't be dense' look that made me feel even more amused by how pathetically insecure he was showing himself to be.

"Are you seriously going to tell me this does not upset you?" he challenged.

It suddenly struck me that, as much as he feared competition, his ego demanded that other males should covet what he considered his. Otherwise, if they didn't, it implied that what he thought valuable actually wasn't.

"Why would it upset me? Oluina and I had a youthful fling more than twelve years ago. She moved on, as have I. Life is too short to live in the past. I am looking forward to the future and new possibilities, not to repeat history."

"That's good to hear. But you're a Stellig," Moriak argued, his face taking on a stubborn expression. "Females are drawn to that and to the type of offspring a male like you could sire on them."

Although I shrugged again, I couldn't help the taunting smile that stretched my lips. I was indeed a Stellig. It was a rare genetic trait that displayed as lightning-shaped streaks in our fur and hair. According to legends, Stelligs were supposed to be blessed by the gods. We were bigger, stronger, and faster than the average male. We also possessed an increased resistance to disease and toxins. Obviously, it had nothing to do with any type of gods but merely genetics. Nevertheless, it made us appealing sires. Although females never developed those markings, those sired by one of us tended to show our other traits. It was the surest way to become the Head Huntress of the Pride or even to ascend to the role of Matriarch.

"Be that as it may, females have the right to like whatever they want, but that doesn't mean I am obligated to submit to their wishes."

He pinched his lips, visibly not convinced. I almost asked him why the fuck he was so concerned about where I spilled my seed. Unless something drastic occurred, Oluina was pretty much guaranteed to become the next Head Matriarch. So long as I didn't covet her, and he kept other potential competition at bay, he should encourage me to turn my attention towards other females.

"Very well. As for Ylis—"

"Look," I interrupted, making no effort to show my annoyance, "I just got home from a grueling experience and simply want some peace and to relax. Beyond the fact that Ylis is a sister to me, I'm not looking for a mate right now. So stop fretting. I'm not here to compete with any male."

The pointed look I gave him made it clear I wasn't after his position as Alpha of the Pride either.

"Well, here I am," I added, gesturing at the humble abode they assigned to me as we walked up to its entrance. "I will go settle in now and will see you later."

He clenched his teeth, annoyed to be thus dismissed. This conversation didn't go the way he hoped. The fool apparently expected me to be the same young and easily influenced cub of old.

"All right. Welcome back. I will let you know about the next culling or…"

His voice trailed off as if he caught himself at the last minute. My stomach instantly knotted. I didn't need him to finish the sentence to know he almost mentioned the next mission. There would never be another such thing for me.

He gave me a stiff nod, turned around, and walked away.

CHAPTER 3
OPHELIA

My heart skipped a beat when the chime of the monitor went off. Although knowing what it would display, I stared at it before glancing back down on the ticket firmly held in my hand to confirm the numbers matched.

Yep, it was finally my turn.

I jumped to my feet under the envious stares of the other candidates waiting for their turn and hastened to the temporary office the Prime Mating Agency was using on the Persea Space Station. With it being a very popular entertainment hub for multiple minor planets and moons in the area, it was quite accessible for a great number of people. The agency came here twice a year and stayed for a couple of days during which the most famous empathic matchmaker in the universe tried to help people in the region to find their soulmate.

Despite my usual adventurous nature, I couldn't believe I was truly going for this. Granted, signing up for the PMA did not guarantee a match would be found. In truth, countless candidates waited for years before their match was found, and in some cases they never were. Still, the prospect of being among the lucky ones sent a thrill down my spine.

Before I could rasp my knuckles even once on the door, a masculine muffled voice bid me enter. I complied, my pulse picking up another notch. The small room that greeted me offered no distraction other than the large window that looked down into the plaza below. The other walls were completely bare, the only furniture consisting of a table which served as a desk, and a guest chair across from it.

The Temern, sitting on the other side on what I presumed to be a bench so that it wouldn't interfere with his massive wings, rose to his feet to greet me. He was taller than I had imagined, likely around 6'2. Naturally, I immediately recognized the famous face of Kayog Voln. Knowing that he was in his mid-to-late sixties, it blew my mind how young and fit he looked. Although on the more slender side, he had broad shoulders and chiseled abs beneath the maroon down feathers that covered his body. His chest and face boasted golden feathers, and a long, white, fluffy tail with a spot of gold at the base trailed behind him. He peered at me with gentle silver eyes.

Although I'd never been particularly drawn to bird folks, I couldn't deny finding this one very attractive. It was all the more embarrassing that he was old enough to be my father, on top of being well known for his very happy marriage to a stunning female of his own species.

But hey, there is no crime in appreciating the view.

"Hello, my dear," Kayog said in a warm and friendly tone. "Please do come in and have a seat."

I instantly liked him and felt at ease. A broad smile stretched my lips as I closed the door then headed for the seat offered.

"My name is Kayog Voln, founder and primary agent of the Prime Mating Agency," he said, resuming his seat after I settled in my own.

"Hello, Master Voln. My name is Ophelia Moreau," I said with a nervous giggle.

"Please, call me Kayog. I'm quite informal," he said with as huge a smile as the stiffness of his beak allowed.

"So long as you call me Ophelia," I replied.

"Done! So, Ophelia, how may I help you today?"

"By finding me a mate, of course!" I replied enthusiastically.

"Am I to presume that things have not gone well on the dating scene?" he asked in a sympathetic voice.

I shook my head. "Although things have been very quiet on the romantic front for me for a while now, I cannot complain of the type of horror stories I'm sure you've heard plenty of. I'm single more out of circumstances than actual unfortunate incidents."

"Circumstances?" he echoed with genuine curiosity. "Do tell."

"I'm a bit of an adventurer and free spirit," I said sheepishly. "I grew up an orphan in a refugee colony. The workers there were fantastic and did so much to help the desperate people flocking there to get their lives back on track that I wanted to do something similar for others. As soon as I turned eighteen, I signed up for missionary and volunteer work at similar colonies or with primitive cultures. I mostly work as a teacher, but I also helped in a variety of different fields."

"It sounds like it has indeed been quite the adventure," Kayog said with a smile.

"It has been. I love discovering new cultures and helping people. It's one thing visiting a foreign place for a week or two as a tourist, and a completely different affair when you actually live among them for a few months or a few years. It opened my eyes to so many wonders and various ways of thinking that I don't think I ever could have acquired otherwise," I said wistfully. "Since I also don't mind roughing it out in the wild, and enjoy hiking and hanging outdoors, I've never had a problem living even among the most primitive species."

"It sounds like you love the life you've lived so far. May I ask what changed, which is now prompting you to look for settling down?" Kayog asked in a gentle tone.

"There are no actual changes of heart," I corrected. "My current life isn't quite conducive to finding a mate. As my last mandate just ended, and I happened to be near Persea, I figured I would seize the opportunity to see what miracles you could perform for me. Maybe you could help me find both love and my next career move."

He cocked his head to the side in that way birds often did when observing something. He narrowed his eyes, instantly giving me the inexplicable urge to squirm.

"Why do I feel there is more to it than you're telling me?"

My cheeks heated to be thus called out while one of the motivations that prompted me to seek him out in the first place came back to the fore. With my ridiculously pale skin, my face had to be crimson right now. The corner of his beak quirked with amusement in light of my tattletale physiological reaction.

I cleared my throat and shifted in my seat. "Well, I try to keep abreast of galactic news in various ways during my missions. I've grown quite fond of the work of a reporter named Malaya Velasco."

"Ah yes! Malaya is such a delightful young woman!" Kayog exclaimed.

The almost paternal affection that lit up his eyes did something funny to me. I heard of the Temern's reputation for being a truly caring person instead of the typical business-driven agent. It further fueled my sentiment that I had been right coming to him, even though the chances of him finding me a match were likely slim to nil.

"I read the story of her unlikely marriage to an Obosian Hell Lord. I'm not going to lie, Lord Kronos is insanely hot!" I confessed with an embarrassed giggle that had the Temern bursting out laughing.

"The Obosians are quite appealing to women. Those horns,

bat wings, and piercings seem to work wonders," he added in a gently mocking tone.

My cheeks burned even more as I nodded sheepishly. "It's the whole demon, dark elf, badass justice defender mix that just makes them beyond irresistible."

He chuckled some more while waiting for me to get to the point. I licked my lips nervously, tucked a strand of my fiery hair behind my ear, and went for it.

"In the media coverage of her official Obosian wedding, Malaya's new husband's best friend, Lord Amreth, was prominently featured. To say that I was heavily drooling would be the understatement of the century. Finding out that he's single only had my toes curling even more. So…"

"Are you asking me to introduce you to Lord Amreth?!" Kayog asked, visibly stunned.

Mortified, I pressed my palms to my cheeks. Truth be told, I didn't really know how to answer honestly. In the back of my mind, yes, I hoped he could introduce us, wave a magic wand, and make this scrumptious-looking beast of a male fall madly in love with me.

But of course, that wasn't how it worked.

"Honestly, I would have loved for you to deliver him to me on a silver platter," I confessed sheepishly. "Since that's not going to happen, I wouldn't spit on you finding me my own perfect mate, ideally an Obosian. But I'm open to pretty much anything else."

"I see," Kayog said, rubbing the bottom of his beak as one would their chin while pondering something. "Unfortunately, you are not Lord Amreth's soulmate, nor are you meant for an Obosian."

I stiffened, bristling at such a swift and definitive statement. That he ruled out Lord Amreth, I could see. But Obosians as a whole?

"How do you know that? Maybe you haven't met him yet?" I

challenged before a terrible thought popped into my head. "Or are you sensing something off with me that would make them not want me?"

He snorted and shook his head before giving me an indulgent smile. "No, Ophelia. Not at all. You have a delightful soul, one that an Obosian undoubtedly would appreciate. But I already know who your mate is. I just did not expect it would be him."

My eyes widened, and my jaw dropped. "You already know my mate?!"

He nodded, his silver eyes sparkling with mischief that had me both excited and worried.

"I do. Honestly, I didn't really expect to find his mate. By human standards, he's definitely alien. Although part of his species is deemed advanced, his lifestyle qualifies as primitive. Unlike Lord Amreth, he doesn't have wings or horns. Instead, he has fur and a tail."

"Fur and a tail?" I echoed, my mind racing as I ran various species through my head.

My stomach knotted as I narrowed down the potential candidates. The almost mocking glimmer in his eyes seemed to hint I would not be too crazy about the answer.

"Are you saying he's a Yurus?" I asked with a hint of worry.

In principle, I wouldn't mind too much to be mated to one of them. They had come a long way from their barbaric past. With their half-minotaur, half-orcish appearance, they weren't hard on the eyes. But their genetically violent nature made me a little skittish at the prospect of marrying a Yurus.

Kayog's mischievous smile expanded as he shook his head. "I said no horns, remember?"

"Right!" I replied, feeling silly for forgetting. "Then who…?"

My voice trailed off as I gave him a horrified look. His shoulders shook with barely repressed laughter at my reaction.

"Please don't say he's a Nazhral?!"

"I don't need to since you did on my behalf," he replied teasingly.

"Oh God!" I exclaimed.

Resting my elbows on the table, I buried my face in my hands, crestfallen.

"Aww, Ophelia, don't be so sad," Kayog said in a sympathetic voice. "Gaelec is a good male. And he's your soulmate."

I parted my fingers to peer at him. "So he's not a pirate or a hardened criminal?" I asked in a small voice.

He frowned and gave me a slightly disapproving look. "You know, you shouldn't assume that someone is a criminal just because of their species."

Fighting the urge to further hide my face behind my palms, I dropped them to clasp my fingers on top of the table, my cheeks burning with embarrassment.

"You're right. I'm sorry," I said, mortified.

"Don't be," Kayog said in a much gentler tone. "Nazhrals have a very bad reputation. So it's understandable that you should have that instinctive reaction. Gaelec is not a criminal, but he's *indeed* an ex-convict."

I recoiled and gave him a 'What the fuck?!' look.

"What?! You just shamed me about assuming that he was a criminal only to turn around and tell me that he in fact used to be?!"

He held my gaze unwaveringly. "I chastised you for assuming that every member of an entire species are criminals. The fact that he happened to have committed a crime in his past does not mean that it applies to every single Nazhral."

I pursed my lips and gave him a stiff nod.

"Furthermore, Gaelec isn't an unrepentant hardened criminal either. He was young and got manipulated into committing the act that led to his incarceration," Kayog explained, while typing something on the keyboard of his computer.

"How young was he?" I asked with genuine curiosity, although still not thrilled about that pairing.

The Temern quickly read something on the holographic monitor of his computer. I assumed he had pulled up Gaelec's file.

"He was nineteen and served twelve years. In fact, he was released only two weeks ago! The timing could not have been more perfect," Kayog said enthusiastically.

"Released from where?" I asked. "Where did he serve his sentence?"

"He was on Molvi," he replied in a factual manner.

"Oh, my God! That's just too much for me," I said, unconsciously shaking my head. "They only send the worst criminals there!"

"Don't be too quick to judge," Kayog gently chastised me before blowing up the holographic monitor and setting it so that it would display its contents on both sides, allowing me to read it as well. "Here, take a look at his release report. It just so happens that the very Lord you were fawning over was his Warden."

My eyes widened at this revelation. What were the odds? Still, I greedily read the report. To my shock, it was extremely positive. Obosians were not known to sugarcoat anything.

"And here is what your mate looks like," Kayog added, activating the small 3D holographic projector on top of the table.

I shamelessly examined the rather hot male that appeared. I didn't quite know how I felt about his undeniably feline traits. Granted, he was clearly humanoid enough not to be confused with an animal, but I always assumed I would end up with someone a lot more human-looking, like an Obosian, and the dryad-like species called Edocit, or even a four-armed Zamorian.

"Are we even compatible?" I asked sheepishly.

"Of course. Humans are incredibly adaptable and compatible with a majority of species, which is why most of my pairings involve one of you, man or woman. Although rare, there have been unions between humans and Nazhrals. Their genes are dominant, so the offspring usually look entirely Nazhral."

"I see," I said, scratching my nape uneasily.

My reluctance didn't stem from his appearance or what any children we might decide to have could look like. His body looked phenomenal, and his face attractive. But I didn't know if I wanted to become involved with someone who dabbled in criminal activities. Also, twelve years on the worst prison planet had undoubtedly affected him. What kind of post-traumatic syndromes would he display? Had his stay there hardened him? With him having been released so recently, what were the odds he would go back to his old ways?

"I can see you are worried," Kayog said in a sympathetic voice. "I can almost hear your thoughts. But know this, Ophelia, I would never send you into danger. Gaelec is your soulmate. And frankly, he needs you."

My brow shot up. "Oh? What makes you say that?"

"Nazhrals aren't evil," he explained gently. "Their society is drastically divided between the city dwellers who hold all the wealth, power, and advanced technology, and the Prides who are in many ways comparable to Earth's old aboriginal tribes. It is a vicious cycle that must be broken. They are just trapped in a culture where the rich exploit the poor and especially their youth."

"So I'm guessing Gaelec comes from one of those Prides?" I asked.

He nodded. "Now that he's returned home, there is no question that his people will try to twist him into falling into those old ways again."

"My point exactly!" I said, throwing my hands up. "I can't be married to a potential slaver or murderer. I know that's not what he was arrested for. The report said smuggling weapons on Grubrya—which was stupid considering how strict the anti-gun laws are over there—but I bet he committed other crimes before that he got away with. How bad were they?"

"I can assure you that he was never involved in the slave trade and that he didn't commit any murder," Kayog said firmly.

"How do you know?" I challenged, baffled. "And what makes you believe that specific guy is my soulmate?"

"Because I met him four years ago, after Rihanna's case," he replied matter-of-factly.

"The Yurus Chieftain's mate?" I asked.

He nodded. "After her arranged marriage to Zatruk allowed her to avoid the unfair prison sentence she received, countless prisoners on Molvi reached out to my agency in the hopes that a similar pairing would allow them to be free of their remaining sentence. Obviously, the Obosians swiftly passed laws to close that loophole and ensure any convict would have to serve their full sentence. But it wasn't before I had already met with Gaelec."

"So he tried to exploit the system to dodge paying for his crimes," I said in a harsh tone.

The disappointed look he gave me stung. Fine, maybe I was being overly judgmental, but I found it difficult to get excited at the prospect of being married to an ex-criminal who was likely to commit a crime again.

"Wouldn't you also wish for any opportunity to reclaim your life, especially if you had committed that mistake due to the immaturity of youth?" Kayog asked. "You know, only one other member of his crew was sent to a Light Quadrant with the minimum sentence of twelve years. Everyone else was sent to a Gray or Dark Quadrant, which are the toughest places on Molvi, and a near death sentence."

"Only him and another?" I asked, surprised. "Why is that?"

"Because when they got caught, one of his crewmates tried to murder the guards arresting them. Gaelec intervened and saved that guard's life. He was fine with smuggling, but not killing. I intensely questioned him during our meeting to assess the type of male he was, as I would never risk pairing someone to a potentially evil or abusive partner."

I nodded, mollified by his words.

"Gaelec was an exemplary prisoner. Not only did he stay out of trouble, but he also learned many trades and worked hard to put aside enough savings to give him a good start once he regained his freedom. He's a *good* male," Kayog said with conviction. "Having his soulmate in his life will undoubtedly help him stay the course. Once he tells you the details of that failed mission, you'll see he wasn't a bad person."

I raised my eyebrows and gave him a disbelieving look. "The way you said that, you seem to assume I will accept."

"I do," he said matter-of-factly.

I gasped and gaped at him. "What if I don't?!"

"Then I'll have to insist until you do," Kayog replied with a shrug. "You're unquestionably made for each other. There is no greater gift than to be reunited with one's other half. It would be unconscionable for me to let you throw away your happiness."

"And what if he doesn't want a human?" I countered with a bit of sass.

He huffed. "Then I'll insist until he does. Don't forget that I'm never wrong on that front, Ophelia. Nothing and no one can ever make either of you happier than each other."

The conviction in his voice struck me hard. I stared at him, feeling torn.

"I hear what you're saying, Kayog, but a criminal?"

"An *ex*-convict who has served his time. His debt has been repaid. Should he be punished forever?" he challenged in a soft voice.

I scrunched my face and shook my head. "Of course not. But what if he relapses? Where does that leave me?"

"Although unions through the Prime Mating Agency have a compulsory six-month trial, should he relapse and get back to criminal activities—which I absolutely do not believe he will—then you will be entitled to an automatic annulment, and we will pay for your relocation home or wherever you wish to go."

I continued to stare at him, more conflicted than ever. The wretched male batted his eyelashes at me while making the most adorable face, making me laugh against my will.

"You know I will pester you relentlessly until you give in. In a few months, I promise you will personally message me to thank me for helping you make the best decision of your life."

And against my better judgment, I caved in.

CHAPTER 4
GAELEC

I placed the last batch of cleaned fish in the cooling unit then pulled off my work gloves before washing my hands. The stares of my companions weighed heavily on me. More than two weeks after my return, I felt more like a stranger than ever. The males kept their distance, studying me, a few of them undoubtedly reporting my every move to Moriak.

I didn't know any of them. Males rarely lasted more than five or six years with a Pride. Ten pretty much constituted a record, unless they were among the extremely few who managed to form a permanent mate bond with one of their females.

Aside from Moriak, the other two males I had encountered before were far older and worked in different parts of the village. I foolishly hoped they would rekindle the friendship we once had. However, they were here on borrowed time, their expert skill being the only reason they had not been evicted yet. It made complete sense for them to avoid drawing unnecessary attention by associating with me.

It sucked beyond words to be in my current position. The males didn't want to incur Moriak's ire by befriending me. And the females were growing steadily annoyed with my indifference towards them. Sure, I could force myself to cozy up to one of them. But aside from the fact that I didn't want any of them, doing so would be an all-around lose-lose for me. Any female I pursued would infuriate Oluina, on top of whatever male had previously secured her favors or was working towards it.

The thought of giving in to Oluina made my stomach roil, not to mention that it would cause an all-out war with Moriak. There was simply no winning.

Why can't they just leave me alone?

Despite the gloves and protective clothes I wore to cleanse today's catch, I still reeked of fish, no matter how much I scrubbed. I hated that task. Instead of gutting the slimy things, I wanted to be optimizing our buildings and revamping our infrastructures. But the Matriarchs were too rigid in their desire to keep things just the way they were. My tongue burned with the need to insist, but I didn't want to make myself more of a pest than necessary.

Then again, a part of me believed their reluctance partially stemmed from the fact that they didn't know if they would keep me. Having me begin significant modifications that no one else would be able to finish or maintain would put them in a precarious situation. And that made sense.

Should I just leave?

That question was now a constant companion of mine. Every other hour of every day, I would weigh the pros and the cons of just moving on elsewhere. But where?

I couldn't return to my birth Pride, even though the younger brother I kept in touch with would have been extremely happy about it. But our Matriarchs would not allow it. Anyway, it didn't make sense for a male to stick around in their birth Pride as all that females present had a direct bloodline with him since they were all his sisters, cousins, or aunts. And going to another

Pride would put him in the same position that he was currently facing. The Alpha and other males would feel threatened by him, while the females would want to use him as a breeder.

Maybe I should just go to the city.

Except I wasn't made for it. The short time I spent in similar environments, whether during my journey back here or while on the few missions I performed before my incarceration, the packed population hubs had felt overwhelming to me. Too many people, too many blinking lights and technology shouting for your attention, too many vehicles threatening to run people over from all sides, and above all not enough nature.

Heaving a sigh, I walked out of the fish plant on my way home. I would take an intensive shower to try and scrape off more of the lingering stench and then go for a run through the forest to clear my head. However, as I turned onto the main street, I spotted Ylis chatting with a couple of young huntresses in front of the Great Hall.

"Gaelec!" she exclaimed, waving at me.

After a quick goodbye to the other females, she ran towards me. I stared at her with curiosity, wondering what had her so excited.

"I'm not sure if you're aware, but there's a feast coming up next week. I was wondering if you would accompany me?" she asked with a huge grin.

My stomach dropped. We had not seen each other much since my return as Moriak appeared to conveniently assign tasks to me on the type of schedule that limited my ability to spend time with the females, which suited me just fine. She was the last person I expected this from. Shifting uneasily on my paws, I searched for the most diplomatic way of turning her down.

She snorted and gave me an amused look of disbelief. "By the gods, Gaelec, relax! You may be a Stellig—and a hot one, too—but I'm well aware that you're not interested in me that way. I might have been offended if I didn't also only think of you as a big brother and the best trainer."

My face heated from embarrassment at the same time as my shoulders slumped with relief. I would have hated to alienate the one person I considered a friend here.

"Sorry," I said sheepishly. "But the Queens have been a little intense lately."

She laughed, although I didn't miss the glimmer of commiseration in her blue eyes.

"Yeah, you shouldn't have come back all muscled up like this," Ylis said teasingly. "You've got all the females going into heat. But hey, having me by your side should help keep them at bay."

I snorted. "Are you trying to piss off Oluina?" I asked teasingly.

To my surprise, some of her amusement faded, and her face slightly hardened. "Absolutely. She needs to get over herself. And at the same time, I'll get Moriak to fuck off."

I stiffened, outraged anger immediately surging within me. "He's trying to move in on you?" I ground through my teeth.

"Of course," she said with a dismissive wave of her hand. "Oluina is great but nearing the end of her reign as Head Huntress. She knows it and hates it. Moriak is in a similar position. He's trying desperately to stay relevant but is terrified of you."

"Which I totally do not understand," I said with genuine confusion. "I've made it abundantly clear that I do not want his position or her. Why can that not be enough?"

She glanced over her shoulder at the huntresses still standing outside the Great Hall and gestured for me to fall into step as she started walking towards my residence.

"Because every female is drooling over you, and every male is afraid of you," Ylis said in a factual manner. "You being a Stellig makes you highly desirable to begin with. But you survived more than a decade on Molvi and returned looking fabulous. Although you haven't been on a hunt yet, we can all see that you're even more badass now. Just looking at the way you move, your strength when you pull out the fishnets and carry the crates screams of how lethal you've become. They think you're merely biding your time, assessing everyone before issuing your challenge."

I heaved a sigh, feeling utterly annoyed. "What will it take for them to get it through their heads that I just want peace?"

"Nothing, I'm afraid," she said in a sympathetic tone. "The longer you maintain your distance, the more upset the huntresses will grow at you snubbing us all. So, here I am! I can be your excuse not to pursue the other females, and you can protect me from that old pervert."

I burst out laughing at the sing song way in which she pronounced that last sentence. She was so adorable, I wanted to ruffle the soft mane on her head.

"You know, I'm eight years older than you. People might deem me an old pervert as well if they believe us to be a couple," I said teasingly.

She waved a dismissive hand. "Eight is entirely fine. It beats sixteen years with him!"

"Fair enough," I said with a chuckle. "They all expect you to take over the Head Huntress role at the rate you are going. With you *choosing* me, the Pride will see me as an even bigger threat."

Ylis shrugged and gave me a smug look. "They will, which means better protection for you!"

I snorted and shook my head affectionately at her. "How are you still single?" I asked, genuinely confused.

The oddest expression fleeted over her beautiful features, piquing my curiosity. She appeared on the verge of saying something before shrugging again with an air of disdain.

"All the males here are annoying and too whipped by Moriak. Hopefully, there will be some hot new males attending the feast. After all, its whole purpose is getting new blood into the Pride."

I gave her a sideways glance with a hint of amusement. "But that means I will get in the way of any interesting suitors," I challenged.

"What you will be is protection," she countered with conviction. "Half of the males who will show up will be flat out insufferable. You can send them packing on my behalf. Anyway, it's not like we're going to be all over each other. We can just act the way we always have, close and affectionate, which will keep people guessing."

"As you wish," I said with a smile.

She stopped mid-stride and turned to stare at me. "You truly are the best. I'm really glad you're back."

For the second time since my return, she gave me a bone-crushing hug and rubbed her temple against mine before releasing me. My heart ached. It had been so long since I had been embraced with such genuine affection. I missed how much simpler life used to be.

Just as I was releasing her, we both jerked our heads to the left, simultaneously getting the sense of being observed. My heart leapt in my chest when my gaze locked with Moriak's. He was glaring at us, clearly seething. Next to him, an older male dressed in fancy attire was also looking at us but with a speculative expression.

"Fuck!" Ylis hissed under her breath.

"What is it?" I asked although my gaze didn't stray from the Pride's Alpha.

"That jerk with him is Ranor, the recruiter," she replied, her voice tense. "There's a big mission coming up in the next few weeks. Whatever you do, don't go!"

My stomach painfully twisted upon hearing those words. There was no question in my mind Moriak would put as much pressure as possible to make me participate and hopefully get caught again. What better way to eliminate the competition?

"Don't worry, I have no intention to do so ever again," I said, anger seeping into my voice.

"Good! Remember that the reason he's not taking you on cullings is because he fears and hates you. He cannot allow you to outshine him. Be careful. He will start whispering in the Matriarchs' ears to get them to coerce you to go."

"Thanks for the warning, but I will leave the Pride before I'm conned into throwing my life away like this again," I replied firmly. "Anyway—"

My com going off silenced me. I glanced down at the interface on my bracer only to have my jaw drop in shock.

"Something wrong?" Ylis asked with a sliver of worry.

I shook my head. "No. Just a completely unexpected communication. I must take it. I will talk to you later," I replied absentmindedly.

"Okay, I'll see you later," she said, still sounding both curious and a little concerned.

I accepted the vidcom request, which was to commence in fifteen minutes, and hurried back to my dwelling. How in the world did Kayog Voln have my contact information? What could he possibly want?

All thoughts of scrubbing the stench of fish off me were gone as I frantically paced in front of the couch in the small but comfortable living area of my two-bedroom dwelling. The six minutes remaining before the time of the call dragged on endlessly as I stared at my vidscreen. My mind was running wild with speculations as to why he would reach out to me after all this time.

I still remembered our meeting, four years ago. The prospect of using the agency to get out of prison quickly had been extremely enticing. Foolishly, I had entertained the thought that Oluina would see the error of her ways and present herself as my soulmate—which I stupidly believed her to be at the time—and we would be reunited.

To my dismay, when we met, the Temern informed me that she declined an interview with him, which would have enabled him to confirm whether she and I were indeed soulmates. That crushed whatever lingering feelings I still harbored for her. After the initial pain, I was grateful for it giving me the final clarity needed to move on.

Anyway, shortly thereafter, the Obosians cleverly amended the law. From that point forward, any spouse would have to come stay with us in our Quadrant, if they couldn't wait until our liberation. It had been a devastating blow to all the hopefuls. But as my heart had already been broken for the second time by then, it just felt like further confirmation that we were never meant to be.

I barely swallowed the yelp rising in my throat when the beep of an incoming call went off. I all but threw myself onto the couch before accepting it.

The smiling face of the Temern filled the screen. I couldn't say for sure where he was, but he appeared to be in a mostly barren room, probably some sort of temporary office aboard a spaceship. I speculated about the latter because the clarity and strength of the signal indicated he couldn't be too far from my homeworld.

"Greetings, Gaelec," Kayog said with enthusiasm.

"Greetings, Master Voln," I said cautiously. "I expected you to be shocked to see my face and promptly apologize for calling the wrong number."

He chuckled and shook his head. "Not at all, my friend. You're exactly the person I wish to speak to."

"What in the world for?" I asked with genuine confusion.

"To tell you that I have finally completed the task we initiated four years ago and found your soulmate!" he said with a grin as one would announce wonderful and long-awaited news.

"What the fuck?!" I blurted out after a few seconds of stunned silence.

"I said I found your soulmate," Kayog repeated, looking as if he was battling the urge to burst out laughing.

"Why would you keep looking for her?" I exclaimed, flabbergasted. "I don't want to mate! Truth be told, I didn't really want one back then. It was only a means to get out of prison early. But I am free now."

"All the more reason to enjoy your newfound freedom with the love of your life!" Kayog continued with the same joyful tone. "Ophelia is quite eager to meet you."

Ophelia... That's a pretty name.

But that didn't change my total disinterest in what he was offering.

"I am surprised and impressed by the dedication you put into pursuing this matter," I said in as diplomatic a fashion as I could. "However, I'm in no position to take a mate. Beyond the fact that my current situation is precarious, I genuinely don't want or need a female right now. Anyway, what species is she?" I couldn't help but ask.

"Ophelia is a human," Kayog said with a grin.

"A human?!" I exclaimed, shocked, not to say horrified. "How in the world could a human be my soulmate? Are our species even compatible?"

"Yes, my friend. Humans and Nazhrals are perfectly compatible. Previous unions between your two species have yielded the most adorable offspring," he replied smugly.

"Be that as it may, humans are furless, clawless, ridiculously slow, can't hunt to save their lives without all kinds of equipment, and are embarrassingly weak. Our females are huntresses. How would she even fit in?"

"While you are correct in your brutal assessment of humans, they have many other qualities that compensate for those other perceived shortcomings," he said in a slightly chastising tone.

"They are incredibly adaptable, smart, resourceful, compassionate, and extremely loyal."

"Not all," I immediately argued at that last comment. "There were plenty of them in Molvi, ready and eager to backstab anyone if it could profit them."

"With all due respect to you, Gaelec, the inmates from Molvi cannot be used as reference to assess the morals and personality of an entire people. Every species has their rotten folks."

I begrudgingly grunted in concession.

"But Ophelia is your soulmate, of that I have no doubt. Don't you want someone who will never betray you and stand up for you? Someone who will wish nothing but your happiness for your own sake and not for how they can benefit from you or use you? Someone who will stand by you through thick and thin?"

I crushed the intense longing his words stirred in my heart and shrugged. "Your human doesn't know me. She has no reason to show such loyalty or devotion."

"She doesn't know you yet, but she will. Ophelia cannot love anyone more than she will love you, and the same will apply to you where she's concerned."

"Even if that were true—and I'm not saying it is—I'm not in a good situation. Any day now, I could get evicted from my Pride. I'm still in the process of earning my place here again."

"Wouldn't it be easier to go through this phase with someone willing to support you every step of the way?" he argued.

I narrowed my eyes as a suspicion blossomed in my heart. "Why would she? Humans—and most of the galaxy for that matter—have a very negative opinion of Nazhrals. Why would she subject herself to the hardships I'm facing? What is she running from?"

"Ophelia is not running away from anything," Kayog said in a firm but reassuring tone. "She's running *towards* her soulmate. And you're correct about humans' opinions about Nazhrals. She was quite worried when I revealed your identity and past to her.

Your people have a questionable reputation. As you stated so well, humans are physically weaker and more vulnerable than species such as yours. It is scary for her to put herself in such a situation."

Although I hid it, his words stung my pride.

"Which is all the more reason why her so-called eagerness to give this a try seems suspicious to me," I challenged.

"She is willing to give it a try because I vouched for the honorability of your character. I am a Temern. I can feel your emotions. And in my case, as an Edal, I possess a rare ability among my people which allows me to see and hear the song of your soul. You're a good male, Gaelec. You are worth fighting for. I am never wrong when it comes to reuniting the two halves of a soul. She understands that there can never be another for her but you. Therefore, she is willing to take the risk and get to know you during the six-month trial required by the agency."

I shifted in my seat and swallowed past the lump in my throat. It was a good thing that we were having this conversation through vidcom and not in person. His being able to feel how deeply his words moved me would have made me far too self-conscious.

"Even if I wanted to give this a try, the Matriarchs must approve any newcomer who wishes to join our Pride," I argued. "And females are not allowed to join. The only females in a Pride must be direct blood relatives of the Matriarchs."

"But Ophelia is not trying to join your Pride as one of the new Queens or future Matriarchs. She's merely here to be with her soulmate. Prides never block bonded mates to stay indefinitely with their partner, right?"

"Right," I conceded reluctantly. "However, those bonded mates are always males marrying one of the Queens. The opposite has never occurred before."

"Well, there is a first to everything!" Kayog said cheerfully.

I frowned and shook my head, still unconvinced. The Temern sobered and leveled a serious gaze on me.

"Why such reluctance?" he asked with genuine curiosity. "Have you met someone since your return?"

I snorted and shook my head. "No, not at all."

"Aren't you tired of being lonely, then?" he asked in a gentle, almost paternal fashion that had my throat constricting again.

"It's not that simple, Kayog," I said in a tired voice. "The Nazhral culture is so different from hers... Life here is harsh, devoid of all the comforts she's certainly used to in industrial cities."

He grinned and waved a hand as if I'd said something silly. "Remember the part about humans being adaptable? Ophelia does not care for all the trappings of city life. In fact, she spent the past ten years working on various planets performing missionary work with primitive species, most of it as a teacher but some of it to help with housing projects or disaster recovery assistance. She is used to living in harsh conditions and adjusting to foreign cultures. Life in a Pride is far more comfortable than in some of the places where she has lived."

"The past ten years?" I echoed. "How old is she?"

"She's twenty-eight, three years younger than you are. See? You are perfect for each other in every way."

I scrunched my face, failing to find additional arguments to throw his way. To be honest, I didn't really know that I wanted to find any.

"I still need to obtain the Matriarchs' blessing," I muttered.

"Then you get right on it! I have faith in you. In the meantime, I will tell Ophelia to prepare for her journey to your homeworld," Kayog said in a triumphant tone. "Trust me, Gaelec, you will not regret this."

After exchanging our farewells, I stared blankly at the dark screen, too many thoughts rushing through my mind to properly sort them out. But two of them dominated. I had no idea what my soulmate looked-like, and I didn't know a damn thing about human females.

Glancing out the window at the Great Hall in the distance, I heaved a sigh at the prospect of breaking the news to the Matriarchs. This was guaranteed to go well…

CHAPTER 5
OPHELIA

I hurried out of the humongous cruise line ship that brought me to the Melelyn spaceport, homeworld of the Nazhrals. I hated being late, and our vessel docking more than two hours past our scheduled arrival had me totally frantic. Obviously, it had been beyond my control, but I still felt shitty about it.

We'd been doing so great, too, until a bunch of flipping pirates decided to attack us. The panic that spread through the passengers died down in minutes when our ship's defense squad just swarmed the fools who thought to make bank at our expense. I could see why they would have set their sights on the *Behemoth*. Aptly named, the humongous cruise liner could host more than nine thousand passengers and had its own fighter fleet and military-grade defense systems.

To say that I'd been rattled would be quite an understatement, not only because of the scare from the attack, but also seeing the pirate vessels get obliterated. By all accounts, none of them survived. Finding out that the attackers had been Nazhrals only made matters worse. As we completed the journey here, more than once, I asked myself if this was a sign from the universe telling me to turn back and hightail it the hell out of there.

But my dumb ass had committed to this, and right now it was doing a spectacular job of getting nowhere fast.

The ship had four different exits. Being somewhat directionally challenged, I merely followed the crowd towards the closest one, figuring the signs outside would tell me where to go to reach the meeting room where Kayog and my future husband waited for me.

And they had a billion signs…

The problem was that not a single one even remotely referred to the meeting rooms. None of them resembled the images I consulted before our arrival. Being visual, I often went through virtual visits of locations I would travel to so as to avoid getting lost.

My stomach knotted as I followed the exit sign along the hallway stretching endlessly before me. More than once, I considered asking the people rushing past me, but my tongue systematically got tied. Being the only off-worlder here, I felt even more overwhelmed by everyone's massive size, including the females.

After stumbling into a dead end, I turned around and half ran back the opposite way only to hit a sealed door with a biometric lock.

"*Putain de bordel de merde!*" I hissed.

I only ever cussed in French—my mother tongue—once I was seriously losing my shit. Naturally, now that I had finally grown enough of a spine to brave the funny stares and ask for help, everyone had conveniently vanished.

How the fuck do so many people just go poof?

I backtracked to the ship, taking a couple of wrong turns along the way before finally spotting two males engaged in an intense conversation. I sheepishly approached them, only to have one glaring at me like I had some serious nerve for invading their personal space.

"Sorry to bother you, but I'm lost. Could you—?"

To my dismay, the jerk simply turned his back on me, his huge, fluffy tail almost slapping me out of the way. I gaped at his back in disbelief before glancing at his companion. The wretch briefly made eye contact with me and bared his teeth in a way that clearly said for me to beat it.

"*Espèces d'enculés!*" I muttered under my breath as I turned around and stomped away.

Feeling utterly discouraged, I blinked back the tears pricking my eyes. I hated feeling this helpless. I hated even more that I didn't have a direct com to contact Kayog.

"What are you doing here, human?" a booming masculine voice suddenly barked at me.

I yelped, and spun around, nearly dropping my overnight bag in shock. My eyes felt on the verge of popping out of my head at the sight of the massive Nazhral male, his fur dark as sin, and the bluest eyes leveled severely on me. The scar that ran across the arch of his left eye down to his cheek made him look even more intimidating. He had stepped out of a room accessible through what was otherwise an invisible door.

Pressing a palm to my chest to contain the erratic beating of my heart, I licked my lips nervously and took a tentative step towards him.

"I'm sorry. I'm completely lost. I just arrived on the *Behemoth* and must have taken a wrong exit because I can't find any directions for meeting room 3B where I am supposed to meet my friends," I said anxiously.

He muttered something under his breath. Despite my translation implant, I couldn't make out his words. Not that I needed to. It didn't take a rocket scientist to recognize someone mumbling something about stupid tourists always getting lost.

"You exited on the opposite side. This section is reserved for employees and for high security esteemed guests. You are currently criminally trespassing," the male said sternly.

"Wait, what?! I'm not trying to trespass. I just want to go to a meeting room. I got lost!" I exclaimed, on the verge of panic. "If you just tell me how to get back to the other side, I'll be gone in a blink."

My heart dropped through my body when the pile of muscles started moving towards me. For half a beat, I thought he was going to grab me by the neck and drag me brutally to some dark dungeon where I would never be heard from again. But he just marched past me, stomping his feet—or was it paws?—his bushy tail stiff with aggravation.

"Follow!" he snapped without looking at me.

He didn't have to say it twice. I hastened after him, clutching my overnight bag to my chest. I was half running to keep up, each of his long strides requiring two steps from me. I was slightly out of breath when I finally saw the entrance of the ship.

He walked up to another Nazhral security guard by the ramp. Before the poor soul could say a word, my escort gave him a proper dressing down for allowing a human to traipse around the restricted area. I felt horrible for the poor guard. Once done berating him, he turned to look at me. I nearly melted right where I stood.

"Why are you still here?" he demanded, visibly annoyed.

"You didn't tell me to proceed," I said in a small voice. "I would rather not get lost again."

His whiskers twitched, and the corner of his upper lip quirked up into a snarl. To my dismay, instead of being properly panicked by his exasperation with me, I found myself wondering if Gaelec had whiskers that long or the same type of sharp fangs that poked between the grumpy Nazhral's lips.

"Proceed, human. Straight ahead," he said pointing at the inside of the ship. "Follow the blue line on the floor and exit where it says Concourse."

"Thank you, Sir. You are most kind," I said politely and with sincere gratitude.

Under different circumstances, I would have burst out laughing at his flabbergasted expression. But I had places to be. I rushed inside the ship and hurried across to the other side under the annoyed glances of the cleaning crew racing to get everything ready for the next boarding and departure.

I easily found the appropriate exit following those simple instructions. Even as I hurried down the ramp, I battled between relief at finally recognizing my surroundings based on the photos I previously saw and cussing out the guidelines that omitted mentioning following the blue line.

Movement ahead drew my attention. To my shock, I recognized Kayog waving at me. Feeling flustered, I waved back before hurrying towards him and the imposing Nazhral standing next to him. Where the Temern was smiling with his usual cheerful disposition, the male I immediately recognized as Gaelec—my soon-to-be husband—might as well have been a stone statue.

"I'm so very sorry," I said with a nervous laugh as I reached them. "Our ship got delayed, and then I totally got lost by going out the wrong exit. I'm terrible with directions. I'm like a lab rat in a maze."

Although Kayog chuckled at my attempt at self-deprecating humor, it fell flat with Gaelec. He was staring at me, looking totally unimpressed, borderline horrified. I groaned inwardly, both embarrassed and mortified. This was not the first impression I wanted to give him. I was likely sweaty and flushed from my ordeal.

It was all the more embarrassing that he looked good enough to eat. Despite his undeniably feline traits, that male was sheer perfection. His body was hot as fuck. Every muscle was deliciously defined and covered with the tiniest coat of grayish brown fur in just the right amount. The more generous patch of fur around his chest and neck vaguely reminded me of the collar of a Maine Coon. It looked so soft and fluffy I wanted to sink my fingers into it and scratch and then rub my face all over it. But more fascinating still were the unusual streaks, shaped like lightning, scattered artistically over his body and parts of his fur. He could have passed for the God of Lightning. His mane swished to the side, almost in a retro style hairdo that I found super cute and that had me itching to play with his locks. His lips were sensuously plush, and his whiskers long but barely visible.

I felt tiny as he stared at me with stunning, piercing blue eyes. Wanting to break the ice, I forced a nervous smile, to which he stiffly responded.

This was not going well.

"Don't worry, my dear Ophelia," Kayog said in a reassuring tone. "We heard of the unfortunate incident that detained you. As for being directionally challenged, I will have to find a moment to tell you about my countless mishaps over the years. But all that matters is that you are here now."

I gave him a grateful smile before glancing sheepishly at Gaelec, who continued to silently study me. *Bordel*! I needed him to relax a bit. I never considered myself the superficial type, but that male genuinely had me drooling. The thought that he might not like me seriously stung.

"Ophelia, meet your mate, Gaelec Sulwyn. Gaelec, this is your bride, Ophelia Moreau," Kayog said, seemingly oblivious —or deliberately choosing to ignore—the tension between us.

"Hello, Gaelec. It is a pleasure to meet you," I said, relieved that my voice sounded a lot steadier than I felt.

"The pleasure is mine, Ophelia," he replied in a polite tone.

Cue exploding ovaries. *Dieu du ciel!* The voice on that male was out of this world. My toes curled, and my skin erupted in goosebumps. His pupils narrowed into tiny slits as he looked at the phenomenon on my arms, left bare by the sleeveless maxi dress I was wearing. My cheeks burned with embarrassment as an air of worry descended over his face.

"What's happening? Are you unwell?" Gaelec asked with concern.

I shook my head and rubbed my palm over my forearm. "No, everything is fine. This is a natural phenomenon with humans," I said sheepishly. I cleared my throat and gave him a shy look. "We call it goosebumps. It normally happens in reaction to something pleasant. Beautiful music will often do that for us. In this instance, it was your voice. It's quite stunning."

He gaped at me, speechless. I felt the heat on my cheeks cranking up another notch, and I shifted on my feet, not knowing what to do with myself. His shock gave way to the most incredible air of timidity that I never expected to see on such an imposing male. He seemed flattered, touched even by my clumsy but honest compliment.

"Thank you, Ophelia," he said at last, regaining his composure. "I'm glad the sound of my voice pleases you."

Both of his feline ears twitched as he spoke those words, turning slightly forward as if to better listen to his own words. The sudden urge to scratch him behind the ear struck me hard. I once again groaned inwardly at my ridiculous reactions. I tended to have no filter, which occasionally got me in trouble.

"Well, if you are both ready, we can proceed to the meeting room where Isobel awaits us to conclude your union," Kayog said, sounding particularly pleased.

I wouldn't go so far as to say that I was pleased, too. But that little glimpse of Gaelec's softer side intrigued me. Maybe we could patch up this bad start.

I happily followed the two males through too many corridors until we reached meeting room 3B. It wasn't that I was clueless when it came to following directions, but more that I suffered some sort of sensory overload when surrounded by big crowds and all the disturbing flashing signs, monitors, and other displays that they constantly crowded public places with. My eyes no longer knew where to look and struggled to process all of it. So my brain just went into protective mode and started blocking out certain things, flat out ignoring they were there.

While I genuinely loved roughing it out in the outdoors, this issue also played a large role in me not being too keen on life in the big cities.

As we closed the distance to our destination, Gaelec took the lead to go open the door for us. With a will of their own, my eyes flicked to the long, poofy tail that trailed behind him. It had that same beautiful grayish-brown color with more of those white, lightning streaks.

I wonder if its size is proportional to...

I gasped, shocked by my own highly inappropriate thought. To my relief, a feminine voice announcing the imminent departure of some random flight helped bury the sound, sparing me from having to explain to my companions how I had traumatized myself by entertaining lurid musings about Gaelec.

To be honest, I obviously wondered about what Nazhrals were packing down there. Considering that the PMA expected newlywed couples to consummate their wedding the first night, it was only natural that I would educate myself as to what I could expect. To my dismay, some research confirmed one of my concerns regarding his naughty bits. Like a feline, Nazhrals had spikes on their peens. It wasn't triangular-shaped like a cat's but was fairly similar to a human's. However, right below the head, one third of the upper part of the shaft was slightly recessed and covered in a few rows of spikes all around the circumference.

I couldn't deny that it freaked me out a bit.

At least, everything I read about it reassured me as to the fact that they weren't sharp or hard and therefore wouldn't inflict any type of damage. Still, I would remain a little apprehensive about the whole deal until I got to experience it first-hand... pun intended.

As soon as Gaelec opened the door, Kayog gestured for me to enter first. Horror washed over me when our eyes locked and I finally noticed the mischievous glimmer in his eyes and slight smirk at the corner of his beak. Mortified, I realized that, although he couldn't read minds, he had at least perceived some sense of the emotions coursing through me as I ogled my future mate. I averted my eyes and hurried inside while fighting the urge to kick that bratty Temern.

A medium-sized room with white walls and dark floors greeted me. A large oval table With enough seats for eight took up most of the space. Atop a console propped against the left wall of the room, a few basic pieces of meeting equipment could be found including a desktop holographic projector and a 3D printer. A single impressive vidscreen filled up most of the back wall.

But it was the slender, older human female sitting at the head of the table that retained my attention. Isobel Biondi had become a semi-permanent fixture by Kayog's side. In many photos and videos about the services offered by the agency, she could be seen presiding over weddings. Per the Prime Mating Agency's rules, both partners had to be legally wed according to their respective cultures' laws and customs, and in accordance with the United Planets Organizations guidelines for the union to be registered in the Galactic Hall of Records. Without that legally binding contract, the partners could not claim the benefits and protections they provided.

With me being human, this first union would follow Earth's traditions. However, as Nazhrals didn't have official wedding ceremonies, I wasn't quite certain how that part would be handled.

Kayog proceeded to make quick introductions between the priestess and me—since she already met Gaelec—then immediately moved on to the wedding. Considering how many cases he handled all over the galaxy, I suspected the substantial delay due to the pirate attack and my stupid self getting lost significantly derailed his busy schedule.

The priestess directed us to move to the front of the large window, setting the pleasant view of the Plaza below as a backdrop.

"Please stand face to face and hold each other's hands," Isobel said.

We did as instructed. He suddenly felt even more massive, especially seeing how my hands got swallowed in his much bigger ones. They were soft and warm, aside from the strange feeling of the rougher patches at the tip of his fingers. I immediately cast out the highly inappropriate thought that tried to worm its way inside my mind again as to how that texture would feel in unmentionable places.

Bordel! When did I become such a horn ball?

"We are gathered here to celebrate the union of this woman, Ophelia Moreau, and this Nazhral male, Gaelec Sulwyn, in the sacred bond of marriage. Such union must be entered into freely, with honest intentions, a genuine commitment, and not for financial gains or deceptive purposes," the priestess said in a gentle but solemn voice. "Ophelia Moreau, do you freely and willingly take this Nazhral male, Gaelec Sulwyn, to be your lawfully wedded husband, for better or for worse, through good times and hardships, in sickness and in health, until death do you part?"

"I do," I said, surprised by the sincerity with which I spoke those words.

For a reason I couldn't explain, and despite his lukewarm reaction towards me, I felt a powerful connection with this Gaelec. That Kayog affirmed that we were soulmates only strengthened that feeling. I would do everything in my power for this union to work, for better or for worse.

"Gaelec Sulwyn, do you freely take this woman, Ophelia Moreau, to be your lawfully wedded wife, for better or for worse, through good times and hardships, in sickness and in health, until death do you part?"

"I do," he replied with a determination that did funny things to me.

You didn't need to be a rocket scientist to realize he had some serious reservations about me. I didn't give him the best first impression. Yet, something in his demeanor told me that he was ready and willing to brush that aside and put the necessary effort to make this work. I couldn't ask for more.

"Kayog Voln, do you bear witness that this human female, Ophelia Moreau, and this Nazhral male, Gaelec Sulwyn, freely committed to be legally married to each other in accordance with human and galactic laws?"

"I do," Kayog said with an enthusiasm that almost had me snorting.

I couldn't remember ever meeting anyone who eternally seemed to be in as high spirits as this Temern was. And his happiness was contagious.

"By the power vested in me by the Clerical College of Earth and the United Planets Organization, I declare you husband and wife. Gaelec Sulwyn, you may kiss the bride," Priestess Biondi said.

I lifted my face towards him expectantly, a timid smile settling on my lips as my stomach fluttered with anticipation. However, his hesitant look took me aback. Kayog clearing his throat reclaimed our attention.

"As I understand it, kissing is not naturally practiced by Nazhrals," the Temern said factually. "It is a common act between humans to mark a range of emotions from affection to passion."

"Yes, Master Voln. I am aware of what a kiss is," Gaelec said, gently interrupting him. "I did some research about human culture so that I would not be completely clueless when it came to understanding the needs and expectations of my future mate."

"Oh! Excellent!" Kayog said approvingly.

That pleased me tremendously, and I made no effort to hide how touched I was that he would make such efforts. He turned his attention back to me and gave me an uncertain look that I found incredibly adorable.

"That said, I have never kissed anyone before. So I hope you will forgive my clumsiness on that front," he said, a sliver of nervousness seeping into his voice.

Putain! It was so cute!

"Don't worry. We're going to have the rest of our lives for you to practice," I blurted out, right before my face turned crimson.

Kayog's barely repressed snort had me giggling nervously. Looking unsure how to respond, Gaelec settled for an awkward smile then clumsily leaned forward to press his lips against mine.

It was brief. Much too brief. Sadly, I couldn't even evaluate how pleasant it might have been, because his nose and whiskers began twitching almost immediately, prompting him to pull away. For half a beat, he looked on the verge of sneezing as his nose continued to twitch for a couple of seconds.

"Sorry, it tickled," he said sheepishly when I just stood there staring at him, confused.

I snorted, and Kayog wrapped his right hand around his beak in that typical fashion bird folk often did to repress their laughter or to express mortification. A sideways glance at the priestess indicated that she, too, was biting the insides of her cheeks to keep from smiling.

"It's okay," I said reassuringly. "You did pretty good for a first time."

Although unconvinced, he gave me a grateful smile. Still, it bummed me out a bit. I loved kissing. But my gut said he was thoroughly unimpressed by this first experience.

"Before we take our leave as we have another appointment elsewhere, let me remind you of the very basic rules new couples are expected to follow," Kayog said in a friendly tone. "Normally, you would have a Nazhral wedding according to your customs today as well. But as your people do not have formal rituals for bonded mates, that requirement is waived. The human wedding will suffice for the Galactic Hall of Records."

Despite being relieved to have him clarify this aspect, it still saddened me that we wouldn't be married according to their culture. For some silly reason, it felt as if I was making a bigger commitment than he was. But then, it would make no sense for him to invent some sort of ritual just for things to be even.

"As I mentioned to you before," Kayog continued in the same factual manner, "you are expected to consummate your union tonight. I know many find that a huge pressure, especially since you've only just met. But trust me, it does wonders to help bring the couple together faster Instead of dragging the tension and uncertainty of that first night for days and weeks."

This time, I couldn't help shifting on my feet. As I'd been celibate for a while, I was more than ready to get back in the saddle on that front. That my new husband was extremely lickable didn't hurt. But as I wasn't the type to get down and dirty on the first date, I expected plenty more awkwardness once we got around to it. However, the subtle but undeniable way Gaelec's back slightly stiffened at that seriously stung.

Granted, he had a bigger burden. If he couldn't get it up for me, we would have a major problem. Was he even half as attracted to me as I was to him?

He merely gave Kayog a stiff nod, and I quietly imitated him.

"You are both expected to give this union a genuine try for six months. If at the end of the trial period, either one of you truly believe it cannot work between you, then the PMA will handle the dissolution as well as handle your relocation wherever you wish to go, Ophelia—not that it will be necessary," he added smugly, making us both smile.

To my relief, Kayog didn't bring up the part about me being

able to leave the marriage before the end of the trial period if Gaelec fell back into a life of crime. The PMA contract already outlined a series of events and behaviors that would automatically make the contract null and void, especially anything related to violence or that would put one of the partners in physical, mental, or legal jeopardy.

"Last but not least, as per tradition, the Prime Mating Agency will give you a wedding gift. However, there will be a slight delay before you receive it," Kayog said in a mysterious tone. "But expected in the next few weeks."

"Oh, it's not necessary," I said with a smile.

"I know, but I promise you will be happy about it. And with this, I bid you both farewell and all the happiness in the world."

We exchanged our last goodbyes and watched them exit the room. I peered at Gaelec to find him staring at me. It wasn't intimidating. He looked like someone who just got home after a shopping spree and now wondered what the heck to do with all that stuff they shouldn't have bought in the first place.

"Well, we should head back to the village. Your belongings will have been loaded in the shuttle by now," he said in a polite tone.

"Okay," I replied in a subdued voice.

We walked in an awkward silence back to the docking bay and straight to the section where all the small and personal shuttles were parked. He made a beeline for a dark-grey, four-passenger vessel with a respectable amount of storage at the back. Although well-maintained, it wasn't a high-tech or recent model. As Kayog mentioned he'd been released from prison less than three weeks ago, I assumed he bought or rented a used model to be able to move around.

"That's a very nice shuttle," I said as we settled inside to break the silence.

"It's not mine," Gaelec replied, sounding slightly apologetic while taking flight. "It is collectively owned by the Pride. Our people do not travel all that much away from the village, so it's not really required. Or at least, we couldn't justify everyone having their own."

"I see," I said with a frown, my curiosity piqued. "But don't you visit other Prides?"

He snorted and gave me an amused look. "As a male? No, never. That is unless you are trying to join them, or you want to get hunted down."

"Oh wow!" I exclaimed, stunned. "I couldn't find much information on the life of Prides. Most of the articles and videos about your people focused on life in the main cities."

He nodded. "City life and Pride life are extremely different. We are more comparable to your human tribes than your industrialized countries and cities. You will not find off-worlders living among us. They come to work or do business in the cities."

He hesitated and cast a sideways glance at me, a frown marring his forehead. "Although we possess every basic comforts one requires, we do not have all the conveniences of a city or some of the more advanced technologies. You might find life in a Pride to be difficult."

I smiled and shook my head with confidence. "Nah! I'm not worried about that. In case Kayog didn't mention it to you, I'm used to rougher conditions. I lived with many tribes over the years and love learning and adapting to new cultures. In truth, big cities feel too overwhelming and cold to me. Everyone is a stranger, just rushing left and right instead of enjoying the moment. There's something wonderful about the sense of closeness and community found in smaller tribes."

To my surprise, instead of appeasing him, my words appeared to trouble him further. And then it struck me.

"You mentioned that no off-worlders live with the Prides. Is that your way of saying that my presence might be a problem?" I asked carefully.

My heart sank when he once again hesitated and seemed to search for his words before answering.

"Every member of a Pride is expected to contribute in some way and pull their own weight. Females are our primary hunters. You..."

"I can't fight my way out of a wet paper bag," I concluded for him in a self-derisive tone when his voice trailed off. "But I'm sure that I can contribute in other ways. I'm a hard worker and a quick learner. I may not be able to hunt, but I can help process the meat and the skins or assist with any other trade, including farming."

He gave me a strained smile meant to be reassuring that failed miserably. That didn't bode well.

"Hopefully, we will find something appropriate for you," Gaelec said in a soothing tone. "Otherwise, I will make sure to contribute enough for the both of us."

"Thank you," I replied in a soft voice before allowing my gaze to roam over the beautiful landscape sprawling before us.

If not for the two moons hanging low in the clear blue sky, this place could have easily passed for a tropical forest on Earth. Although some of the tall trees looked as if they indeed came from Earth, the shape of the leaves on some other ones as well as the darker color of the bark made it clear we were on a different world. A part of me was excited at discovering this new planet, and all the wonders of its wilderness. But another was increasingly sensing that making my marriage to Gaelec work would be a bigger challenge than I expected, and not purely because of the two of us.

I discreetly studied his handsome profile and the short fur around his chin that almost acted like a beard. Once again, my fingers itched to sink into their softness and properly sample how it would feel. But it was the lingering concern on his face that he still tried to hide that bothered me.

"How disappointed are you with me?" I blurted out.

He stiffened at the same time I flinched inwardly. My wretched mouth had no filter. As much as I didn't regret putting the question out there, I could have handled it a bit more smoothly.

He frowned and looked at me with genuine confusion. For some reason, that made me feel a bit better.

"Why would I be disappointed? I do not know you well enough yet to establish such a thing."

I nodded. "Right, but you certainly had some expectations or hopes. It's obvious that I'm not what you wanted. Don't worry, it's all right for you to be honest. I prefer that."

His frown deepened. But the absence of shame or guilt on his features appeased me far more than a strong denial might have. Most people would be embarrassed to admit they had terrible thoughts about someone else. That he didn't seem guilty hinted that maybe he didn't have such a bad opinion of me just yet.

"No, Ophelia. I cannot say that I'm disappointed. The fact is that I don't know you. Only time will tell," he said gently but firmly. "What I am is concerned. I worry as to how you could possibly fit in with us. Based on the incident at the spaceport, you do not seem to have adequate situational awareness or orientation skills. As a human, you lack natural self-defense skills, and you do not possess the speed and strength that are important for survival. Our females are strong. You're not."

I nodded again as I weighed his arguments. "Everything you have stated is fair. But do not underestimate humans' ability to adapt. What we lack in natural abilities, we compensate for with technology. I may break my hand trying to punch someone, but give me a blaster instead, and good luck avoiding getting shot. I am one badass shooter."

He chuckled, his eyes sparkling with amusement as he probably tried to imagine me shooting the hell out of someone. I loved how it softened his features. My husband was truly an attractive male.

"It is good to hear. And I will help however I can to make it easier for you," he replied.

I beamed at him. "You're sweet."

He snorted as if I said something completely outrageous. Considering the rough life he led over the past decade, I could see how being referred to as 'sweet' would sound ridiculous to him. And yet, he truly seemed sweet under his guarded and a little distant demeanor. My gut told me that as we got closer and knew each other better, this softer side of him would emerge more and more. I was just grateful his incarceration hadn't made him bitter or aggressive.

His amusement suddenly faded, and he gave me an assessing look that immediately had all my senses on high alert.

"And what of you, Ophelia? How disappointed are you with me?" he asked.

The sudden timidity seeping into his voice as he asked that question threw me for a loop. There truly was something adorable about that man, and I couldn't wait to see more of it. However, my wretched mouth once again decided to run away with me.

"Disappointed by you?! Not at all! You're super hot!"

I flinched, and heat crept up my cheeks even as the words spilled out of my mouth. Gaelec blinked with an air of confusion.

"Hot?" he echoed.

I couldn't help but chuckle when he pressed the back of his hand to his cheek as if to check if he was feverish.

"Hot is a term humans use to refer to someone who is very attractive," I explained sheepishly.

His jaw dropped. He gaped at me for a few seconds before realizing he was doing it and closed his mouth with an audible sound before shifting in his pilot seat. That he seemed so completely stunned that I would find him handsome made me wonder how much of the same insecurities I was feeling about how he perceived me he also worried about my thoughts regarding him.

Throwing all caution to the wind, I decided to go all out.

"Even though you're not human, your body is absolutely amazing. Men would kill to have a muscular chest and chiseled abs like yours. Your face is very handsome, and your eyes are stunning. I was worried about how I would feel about fur, but yours is so lustrous and fluffy, especially the one below your neck and around your chest, it's just gorgeous. And then there's those white streaks almost like lightning on your body and your tail. It makes you look like a God of Thunder."

By the time I stopped talking, that paler skin on his face had darkened. He was gaping at me again and started shifting uneasily, looking increasingly self-conscious and yet flattered.

"I… I… err… Thank you, Ophelia. Those are very kind words. Males like me with those white streaks are called Stelligs. It is a rare trait among my people. It appears later in life, towards the end of our teenage years. We tend to be bigger, stronger, and faster than the average male," he declared shyly.

"That's awesome!" I said enthusiastically. "And it looks really nice."

He cleared his throat and averted his eyes in the cutest fashion while his mind was still racing. Gaelec opened and closed his mouth a couple of times before glancing back at me.

"You are also attractive," he said clumsily.

I burst out laughing and gave him an indulgent look. "It's okay, Gaelec. You don't have to lie to make me feel better."

Despite the gentle way in which I spoke those words, he frowned, looking slightly offended.

"I do not lie, Ophelia. To be honest, until Kayog contacted me about you a few days ago, I never thought of humans in that way. But now, I can say that your features are quite harmonious. The green shade of your eyes is stunning. Your hair looks very soft, and I like the way the sun catches in it. It almost looks like it's ablaze. I cannot wait to see it directly outside and not filtered through the windshield. And then you have all those face spots that are truly charming."

The warm fuzzy feeling that had been swelling through me at each of his words came to a screeching halt upon hearing that last sentence.

"Face spots?!" I repeated, disbelievingly.

I burst out laughing. My freckles had been called many things, but face spots were a first. He peered at me in confusion, uncertain as to whether he inadvertently said something wrong.

"These things are called freckles," I said, still chuckling. "And they're annoying as hell. The worst part is that they're not just on my face. I have those damn things everywhere, even on my lips, chest, and arms," I grumbled waving at them on my exposed forearm.

"On your lips?" he repeated with curiosity while glancing at my mouth.

I nodded. "You can't see them because my lip gloss does wonders at hiding those wretched things. But if I stay under the sun too long, and without proper sunscreen, aside from the fact that I will burn, even more freckles will come out. It's like I'm pockmarked," I concluded in an overly dramatic fashion.

Instead of the amused response I expected from him, Gaelec frowned at me with a disapproving expression.

"Do not say that. Your... *freckles*... are not wretched things. To me, they look like our Luen Constellation. It is only visible in the winter or in early summer mornings."

My eyes widened. "Luen? Isn't it the sea of red stars?!" I exclaimed.

He nodded with an approving smile that I should know of it. "Yes. Luen is a sign of good luck and is considered a blessing of the Gods. The more stars are visible, and the greater the blessing. You are touched by a higher power. Embrace your stars. They are beautiful."

My chest constricted as my hand found its way to my face with a will of its own.

"Wow! That's the nicest thing anyone has ever said to me," I whispered as I gazed at him.

He smiled, visibly pleased, the soft glimmer in his eyes melting me from the inside out. In that instant, I realized that I made the right choice listening to Kayog. I didn't know this male, but we were going to make it work.

He was my soulmate.

CHAPTER 6
GAELEC

I didn't know how to feel about my human. As all the women of her species, Ophelia was rather tiny. She was clearly fragile and seemed easily frazzled. She was the exact opposite of our Queens and huntresses. But that difference also applied to her personality and behavior.

My mate seemed really nice.

I perceived no deception in the awe she expressed towards me. My chest still warmed at the deluge of compliments she showered me with. Without boasting, I could say with confidence that I was an attractive male by my people's standards. More than once, our females complimented my appearance. However, with Ophelia, it felt different... not objectifying.

And that made me feel quite guilty for not sharing a similar awe where she was concerned. The kind words I shared with her about her hair, face, and freckles had been honest. But that was the extent of it. The rest of her appearance would take quite a bit of getting used to. Obviously, I had seen humans before. After all, a few humans served their sentences with me on Molvi. But they had all been men, and I never thought of them in romantic terms.

I always found the humans' straight legs strange not to mention limiting. The three segments of our digitigrade legs allowed us to run faster, jump higher, and better absorb the impact of high falls. Ophelia didn't possess a tail, fur, or whiskers. Her small, rounded ears couldn't rotate like ours to better identify the location where sounds emanated from. Her pointy nose looked like it wanted to run away from her face. When we kissed at the end of our wedding, it bumped against mine, making that experience even weirder.

The thought of that kiss had another wave of unease surging deep within. I couldn't label it as unpleasant, but it didn't feature high on my list of most delightful experiences. It felt odd to press one's mouth to someone else's. Just remembering how it tickled my nose and whiskers made me want to sneeze. Sure, with time, I believed I could grow used to it. I couldn't tell whether I would ever develop a taste for it, but if it was something my mate enjoyed—and I strongly suspected she did—I would find a way to adapt.

But kissing was the least of my concerns where physical contact with my mate was concerned.

On top of looking into human culture to better prepare for Ophelia's arrival, I obviously investigated human anatomy. My initial shock at seeing their female had a miniature cock above their slit quickly gave way to confusion once I realized it was actually their clitoris. Our females possessed one as well, but it was located inside their slit, which made a lot more sense. This way, it was automatically stimulated through penetration.

Out of curiosity, I checked the human males' reproductive organs to see if maybe they had an additional appendage or bump near the base of their cock or on their pelvic area meant specifically to cater to that external clitoris. But there was nothing. In fact, their shaft didn't even possess our spikes that enhanced our females' pleasure on top of being highly erogenous for us.

So why in the world had human females anatomically evolved in such an irrational fashion? Or was it the males who had somehow evolved the wrong way that they weren't designed to guarantee their females' satisfaction?

Further research confirmed that men needed to actively work on stimulating their women instead of it being passively taken care of during coupling. I also discovered that I wouldn't be able to trigger my mate's ovulation simply through penetration, as was the case with our females. Human women ovulated on a preset timeline instead of almost on demand with Nazhrals.

That had been the good news out of all of this. Us getting pregnant on our first night would not be ideal. We needed a bit of time to get to know each other first but especially to sort out our situation. I wanted cubs. My entire life, I'd always felt a strong paternal instinct.

But do I want to have my offspring here?

What I read about human family units blew my mind. All genders were afforded the same opportunities. Unlike us, human parents didn't sever the ties with their male offspring after casting them out. I couldn't imagine what it would have been like to have my sire by my side through my teenage years and into adulthood. Would I have made different choices with his guidance?

Assuming we went ahead and remained here with our cubs, would the Matriarchs accept them? Would they even fit with the Pride?

I had too many questions and uncertainties about our couple and our future. A part of me wondered if I made the right decision embarking on this journey when I already had so much to juggle. But another figured now was in fact the perfect timing as it could help guide some of the decisions I needed to take anyway in the upcoming days.

As I began our descent into the village, I stole a discreet glance at my mate. She was feasting her eyes on the beauty of the landscape. No, I couldn't say that I was physically drawn to her, but something about Ophelia felt good.

It was the way she looked at me with sincere admiration. The way her skin colored whenever she was shy. But it was especially that moment she touched her face when I compared her freckles to Luen that shifted something inside me. The self-deprecating way she poked at herself stirred my protective instincts. Seeing her so deeply moved by my words, and the joy it brought to her made me feel good. Her grateful smile and the way it lit up her face could become addictive.

Even as that thought crossed my mind, a shudder coursed through me.

Nazhral females could be so callous and manipulative. Were human females the same? Could Ophelia be playing me right now?

I immediately felt ashamed for unfairly suspecting her. Nothing in her actions or body language even remotely hinted at deception. However, the past twelve years taught me to trust no one.

As I settled the shuttle on the landing pad, I cast a worried glance at my woman. I hated that I wasn't bringing her home to a warm welcome, but potentially to some rude and brutal rejection.

"Ophelia, before we settle home, I must take you before the Matriarchs for their blessing," I said cautiously.

Judging by the instant worry that settled over her alien features, I did a terrible job of hiding my own concerns.

"What if they don't want me?" she asked, her eyes flicking between mine.

"They cannot banish you without banishing me first," I said in a reassuring tone. "I'm in good standing with the Pride, so it would surprise me if that happened. But should that be the case, we will go to the city and then decide where we want to settle going forward."

Her shoulders slouched, and she looked at me with a guilty expression. "I'm so sorry!"

"No, my mate!" I said firmly. "You have nothing to apologize for. You did nothing wrong. Regardless of your presence, I already had many decisions to make about my future. There's a reason I pushed for you to come swiftly once I agreed to go through with this. As my decisions will also impact you and our lives together, it is best that you be involved in the process. After all, we're soulmates."

"Yes, we are," she replied, a timid smile blossoming on her lips. "Then I guess the timing is perfect. So… you believe that we are, then?"

The nervousness with which she asked that question, and the glimmer of hope in her stunning green eyes made me realize she needed some reassurance from me. I had not shown much enthusiasm about us since her arrival. I needed to do a better job of making it clear to her that once I committed to something, I didn't renege on it. In our wedding vows, I pledged to be by her side through thick and thin, and I never broke my word.

"Yes, Ophelia. Kayog is never wrong. Therefore, I believe we're soulmates, even though we do not know each other yet. Whatever the future holds, we'll see it through together."

She beamed at me in a way that once again hit me straight in the heart. She was truly adorable when she smiled like that.

I shut down the engine, hopped out of the shuttle, and circled around it to help my mate down. Naturally, many members of the Pride conveniently happened to be loitering nearby instead of working as they should be. They ogled my mate in a less-than-subtle fashion. I wanted to hiss and roar at them for such rudeness. At the same time, I couldn't blame them for it.

For our members, Ophelia was a true oddity, especially for our females. Off-worlders never came here, and our people hardly ever traveled. Nazhral females only spent time outside of the village to hunt in the neighboring forests. Our Alpha—and on extremely rare occasions our Matriarchs—were pretty much the only people who went to the city from time to time to acquire new equipment, find upgrades for the village, or perform other administrative tasks I had no idea about.

Males who went on missions, and the few who moved to the city naturally would have met off-worlders in the flesh, but probably never a woman. That she was a female made it even more extraordinary—not to say scandalous—as no outsider females were normally ever allowed in a Pride, unless they came warring to take over the village.

So yes, as much as their behavior infuriated me, I could understand. If, like them, I'd only seen a human on screen in vidplays and documentaries, I too would want to get an eyeful in the flesh.

Clenching my teeth, I quickly led my female to the Great Hall. To my pleasant surprise, Ophelia seemed completely unfazed and unbothered by the intense scrutiny she was subjected to. It dawned on me then that, having worked as a missionary with countless primitive species—she'd likely been in a similar situation more than once with her being a curiosity among the people.

This stoicism could prove quite beneficial once she stood before the Matriarchs.

My stomach knotted with apprehension as we stepped into the building. To my dismay, many of the people outside followed us within. It was all the more infuriating that I couldn't do a thing about it. Only the Matriarchs could kick them out, if they so chose.

As we made our way towards the dais, the crowd quietly took a seat on the side benches lining the left and right walls of the front area of the room. But I paid them no mind, too focused on the people sitting on the dais and on each side. On top of the three Matriarchs, all the huntresses had taken their seat on the left and right sides of the semi-octagonal section at the front.

That included the seething Oluina, and a gleeful Moriak right at the edge of the huntresses' section. Ylis's curious and amused expression gave me hope.

I shifted my attention to Rozel, our Head Matriarch. As I feared, she looked unimpressed as she slowly examined Ophelia from top to bottom.

"So that's the female you are shunning our Queens for?" Rozel snarled in lieu of a greeting.

I immediately bristled at the contempt audible in her voice as she continued to glare at my mate.

"I didn't shun anyone!" I snapped.

She shifted her gaze to me, anger burning in her eyes. "You refused them all!"

"I just got home after twelve years on Molvi," I retorted, exasperated that she would force me to rehash the same thing all over again. "I'm trying to find my bearings, not to compete with other males for the Queens' attentions."

"Are our females not worth competing for?" Rozel argued.

I barely repressed the urge to roll my eyes and took a deep breath to keep my cool. "Obviously, the females of the Nevian Pride deserve every honor. But like with every hunt, rushing at the first enticing sound only gets you killed. I wanted to take my time and assess my situation."

"And yet you rushed to the human," Oluina interjected with a disdainful gesture towards my mate.

I cast a glance towards Ophelia, concerned by how such aggressive behavior was affecting her. To my utter relief, she was observing the situation with phenomenal stoicism. I could only pray she would not make any outburst that could complicate matters further. I silently berated myself for not preparing her better for the fierce opposition we might face. But then, never in a million years would I have expected this level of rage.

"I didn't rush to anyone or anything," I replied in a

controlled voice. "I wasn't looking for a mate. Fate brought Ophelia to me when I least expected it."

"Semantics!" Oluina spat out. "You still took her, an off-worlder, while shunning the rest of us!"

"She's my soulmate!" I snapped. "*You* never were, and never will be!"

I flinched inwardly to have allowed my anger to get the best of me. Humiliating her publicly was the last thing we needed. Oluina recoiled while multiple muffled gasps resonated in the room. She bared her fangs at me, and a low growl rose from her throat.

A single hard stare from her mother sufficed to silence her. Rozel then shifted her attention back to me, her own anger almost palpable.

"I already explained how this union came to be," I continued in a reasonable tone, this time addressing the Head Matriarch directly. "The Temern reached out to me unsolicited. Kayog Voln is *never* wrong. Even here in the Prides, his reputation precedes him."

"Be that as it may, you're a Stellig," Rozel said dismissively. "It is unfathomable for one such as you to waste your seed on *her*."

The need to extrude my claws burned my fingertips. Who would have thought someone could put so much contempt in a single word? The fury I felt at their disrespect towards my female had my blood boiling. But for Ophelia's sake, I needed to keep a cool head. For the first time, I genuinely worried. I never expected things to get this ugly. Although it occurred rarely, huntresses were known to slaughter any person they deemed a traitor to the Pride or a threat to its stability. And right now, both the Head Matriarch and Head Huntress seemed to be entertaining that thought.

"My seed would not be wasted on my mate," I said calmly. "I did my research before entering into this union. Although humans and Nazhrals are compatible, our genes are dominant. Any offspring she and I have will exclusively possess Nazhral traits."

"Whatever the case may be, the human is not welcome here," Oluina hissed. "The only Queens allowed in a Pride are blood relatives."

"My Ophelia isn't trying to be a Queen," I countered in a clipped tone before looking back at the Matriarch. "Frankly, I do not understand what all of this is about. When I first informed you of the good fortune that befell me, you agreed to allow my mate to stay here at least for the remainder of my grace period. Granted, you did so with much reluctance, but you nonetheless agreed to it. I wouldn't have brought her otherwise. So what is this all about?"

"And then what? What happens at the end of your grace period if we still feel she's unwelcomed?"

"Then if you banish my mate, I shall leave with her," I said matter-of-factly.

This time, loud gasps—some of them shocked, others outraged—resonated through the room. Moriak looked on the verge of having an orgasm he was so enjoying the spectacle, whereas Oluina seemed ready to commit murder.

"You would abandon your Pride for a human?!" Rozel asked in a dangerously low voice.

"I would leave any place where my soulmate is not wanted. You, better than anyone, know what a rare gift it is among our people to find the other half of our souls," I said in a reasonable tone. "It would be a crime against the Gods to turn my back on Ophelia."

"Then leave now!" Oluina hissed.

"That is not your call to make," Ylis interjected in an icy tone. "We honor that mate bond. As Gaelec said, too few people receive such a blessing. Would you dare spit in the face of the Gods after they bestowed it upon one of us? So long as they contribute their fair share, there's no reason why they shouldn't stay."

I could have hugged her right this instant. Her words resonated well with the rest of the Pride as a few people nodded and whispered their agreement.

"Her? Contribute?" Oluina exclaimed in disbelief. "That *thing* can't hunt!"

"Careful, Oluina," I hissed in a low voice, while taking a threatening step forward. "You do not disrespect my mate."

"Or what?" she demanded in a provoking tone. "You will attack me?"

Ophelia gently ran her palm over my upper arm in an appeasing gesture. Obviously, I would never attack a female. However, that soft touch both calmed me in a way I never expected, but also shamed me that I would have allowed Oluina's taunting to get under my skin.

"*He* won't, but *his champion* will," Ylis replied in a way that made it clear she would gladly answer the challenge.

A sliver of fear flashed through Oluina's eyes. I had not seen Ylis in action since my return. But I remembered how insanely talented she was before my arrest. I could only imagine how much more formidable she became over the years. With her being younger than her cousin, Ylis had a good chance of getting the upper hand. Losing to another huntress would be a devastating blow to Oluina's standing.

"No female attacks other females in the Pride, whether physically or verbally. You have crossed that line many times already," Ylis said sternly.

"She's *not* of our blood. She is *not* one of ours!" Oluina exclaimed in outrage, her tone making it clear it should be self-evident.

"Ophelia is one of ours until such a day as Gaelec leaves or is expelled," Ylis retorted in a tone that brooked no argument.

"He still has the remainder of his grace period for us to decide what to do with his case and hers."

"Ylis is correct," Rozel said stiffly, visibly eager to calm things down before they deteriorated further.

Having her favorite daughter and Head Huntress possibly be dethroned by her younger cousin was the last thing she wanted or needed. She turned her attention to my mate, her eyes cold and resentful.

"You have not made your case, human. Have you no tongue?" Rozel asked.

My heart skipped a beat as I waited to see how she would respond.

"I do, Matriarch," Ophelia responded in a polite voice with an appropriate level of deference. "However, as I had not been officially invited to speak, I decided to hold my peace. I wouldn't presume that I was allowed such a right or to act in a way that might be deemed disrespectful."

"Your mere presence here is disrespectful," Oluina hissed.

I growled again, only for Ophelia to once more soothingly rub my upper arm.

"You're upset that such a fine male as my Gaelec is off the market," Ophelia said in a reasonable but firm tone. "I get that. In your stead, I would be as well. But I would respect the fact that he found his soulmate. I will not apologize for existing or for being the one that Fate meant for him."

Oluina huffed and opened her mouth to spew more nonsense. However, her mother raising her palm in an arresting gesture silenced her. Taking this as a sign that she was not to be interrupted, my mate pursued her response.

But my mind remained stuck on the way she claimed me by calling me *her* Gaelec. How could something so simple feel so wonderful?

"When I approached Kayog, I never imagined that the other half of me would turn out to be a Nazhral, just like there is no question Gaelec never pictured himself with a human. Given a choice, I'm sure he would have picked one of you instead. But Fate chose us for each other. I won't spit on that blessing."

A few more people nodded and muttered their agreement with her statement. While their opinions ultimately didn't matter as the decision rested in the hands of the Matriarchs, their support would undoubtedly help tip the balance in our favor.

"The concerns you expressed, Head Huntress Oluina, are quite valid. Gaelec himself mentioned them," Ophelia continued with the same poise and eloquence. "I can't hunt, and I'm nowhere near as fast or strong as any of you. But I also have no ambition to compete or attempt to replace you. I just want to lead a happy and prosperous life with my husband."

She paused to glance at me with that air of wonder that did the funniest thing to me. She smiled, and I found myself instinctively responding in kind. She turned her head back to look at Rozel, who was staring at us with pinched lips laced with a begrudging air of resignation.

"So while I may not be able to contribute the way your females normally do, I have much to offer from my many travels across the galaxy. I have a broad range of experiences, extensive knowledge in multiple crafts, I'm not afraid of hard work, and I'm eager to learn. I just hope that you will give me that chance after Gaelec's remaining grace period is over. If not, I will respect your judgment. I crossed half the galaxy to be with Gaelec. Wherever he goes, whatever he decides, I'll follow and support him. As per the human vows we exchanged, I chose him for better or for worse, until death do us part. So whether here or elsewhere, I will stand by him."

A wave of affection swelled in my heart for my mate. In my entire existence, no one so steadfastly stood by me. I didn't know this woman, and yet everyone with eyes and ears could see and hear the sincerity of her words.

"Well then, Ophelia, you and your mate will have two weeks to prove yourselves," Rozel said in a clipped tone.

She waved her hand in a dismissive fashion, indicating the audience was at an end. I didn't have to be told twice. As offended as I felt by the callousness with which my mate had been received and then sent away, I was simply relieved the worst had been averted.

Still, today's events confirmed I had much thinking to do and serious decisions to make. My new priority was the welfare and safety of my mate. I no longer felt confident she could find it here.

CHAPTER 7
OPHELIA

We walked in silence back to the shuttle. My blood still boiled from what felt like a brutal assault. On more than one occasion over the years, I faced some initial hostility when I first showed up for a mandate with a new tribe. Only once had I felt compelled to leave as the entire prep work before our arrival had been utterly botched. I believed in missionary work, but only if the locals actually wanted and welcomed it.

That one had been an attempt by the organization to coerce that primitive tribe into adopting their ways and allowing them to appropriate their resources. I not only hauled ass out of there but also reported them.

While the UPO usually did a good job shutting down such exploitative so-called charitable organizations, some still managed to slip through the cracks and do a lot of damage—on top of enriching themselves—before they were stopped. And most tribes and refugee camps did welcome the assistance that we provided. We just had to follow many strict rules to respect their culture and their right to self-determination.

A couple of cultures had been more challenging to adapt to than others. Their societal structure, religious beliefs, or general values severely clashed with my own. At the same time, they provided a wondrous training in learning to look at things through someone else's eyes, casting aside my own customs and belief system.

But the level of vitriol I faced here today took it to a whole other level. I was used to rejection because my foreign presence was seen as a threat, because females were deemed unsuitable to act in any kind of management role, or because a woman unwed and childless at my age was not only a negative influence but also perceived as proof that something was terribly wrong with me.

Getting this amount of hatred because some chick was mad my man didn't want her seriously took the cake.

I couldn't blame Oluina for being every shade of jealous for seeing the fine specimen of masculinity that was my brand-new husband slip through her grubby claws. But damn, you'd think she'd have a bit more self-respect than to throw herself at a male who clearly didn't want her and force him to once more publicly reject her.

I never wanted to be the other woman. Once I realized what had crawled up her butt to make her this angry, I feared for a moment that there had been an ongoing relationship between them abruptly ended because of Kayog informing Gaelec of my existence. I nearly wept with relief once I found out he soundly refused her long before I even came into the picture. He and I had enough challenges to get our relationship going without us also having to deal with him potentially pining away for an old flame.

However bitchy and aggressive as she might try to be, Oluina's entitled bullying didn't faze me. It took a lot for me to throw in the towel and concede victory. So long as I believed Gaelec wanted us and was fighting for us, I'd be firing right back, all guns blazing.

Still, our ability to remain here felt more precarious than

ever. In truth, I wasn't certain I wanted to live among people who clearly hated me, not because of any wrongdoing on my part, but merely for existing. That those people also happened to be at the top of the hierarchy made it even more complicated.

Ever the gentleman, Gaelec helped me back inside the shuttle. While I didn't believe opening doors for females was a matter of courtesy here, it still displayed his attentiveness to me and my needs. The Nazhrals' digitigrade legs made it easier for them to hop onto higher steps. The ship's design was clearly made for their people and not overly friendly for humans. Granted, I wouldn't need a ladder to get in on my own, but each step was nearly double the height of a regular one based on galactic standards. Therefore, I appreciated his help, especially since he offered without me even having to request it.

As soon as we settled inside and closed the doors, Gaelec glanced at me with a concerned and guilty look.

"Are you okay?" he asked with a hint of worry.

I smiled reassuringly. "Yes, I'm fine, thank you. But I won't lie. This was an… interesting first meeting."

Despite the slightly teasing way I spoke that last sentence, Gaelec took on a defeated expression heavily laced with guilt.

"I'm truly sorry, my mate. I didn't expect them to react so strongly."

"Please, do not apologize," I said with a sympathetic smile. "You did nothing wrong and cannot be held responsible for the way they chose to act. It would have been a different story if you had just sprung me on them out of nowhere. But they knew I was coming. If they had such a problem with it, they should have addressed it before I even set foot here. That said, is there something I should know about Oluina?"

He groaned, and the right corner of his mouth corked up in a snarl exposing his fangs as he got us airborne. The aggravation and contempt that the mere thought of that female stirred in him crushed any lingering concerns I might have had about her being any type of competition. My mate had no love or even respect for that female.

The malicious and triumphant glee that instantly triggered deep within should have shamed me, if only a little. But I couldn't—and didn't really want to—muster the slightest compassionate thought for the obnoxious female.

"Before my arrest and incarceration on Molvi, Oluina and I had been paired for nearly a year. The same day I got caught, she moved on to Moriak. That was the big male you probably noticed sitting at the right edge of the huntresses," Gaelec said grimly.

I gasped, my eyes bulging in shock and outrage on his behalf. "*Putain!* She moved fast!"

"She most certainly did. Obviously, once I found out, I was furious, hurt, and feeling utterly betrayed. It especially hurt that the male she rushed to was also the one who sent me on that doomed mission to begin with and who then appropriated the house I finished building but a week prior."

I whistled through my teeth at their brazen ruthlessness. The immediate thought that popped into my mind was that they colluded to eliminate him and steal his property. Oluina didn't need to be involved with him to achieve that. But then, doing so would have given her more leverage to exert pressure on him to go on the mission that condemned him to begin with.

However, I had too little information for now to truly draw an accurate picture of what transpired. If nothing else, it confirmed her position at the very top of my shit list, with Matriarch Rozel and Moriak currently sharing the second place. The upcoming days would help better refine their ranking.

The worried look he cast my way silenced my wandering thoughts.

"Please know that I no longer have any such lingering feelings for her. Her betrayal and all those years apart killed whatever feelings I thought I ever had for her," Gaelec said, tension filling his voice.

I smiled reassuringly. "You don't need to convince me. Your interactions with her and body language made your dislike abundantly clear. I'm not worried about her."

All tension drained from his shoulders, and he gave me a grateful smile before turning back to look at where he was flying. To my surprise, we'd only been in the air for a couple of minutes than he was already descending towards that far edge of the village. In my mind, it would have been a far longer journey. But considering the number of bags and a couple of crates containing my personal belongings, it would have been too long a walk from the ship hangar to our destination while hauling all of this, even on a hovercart.

"Oluina is mad that I didn't chase after her immediately upon my return," Gaelec said with disdainful incredulity.

I snorted. "I could see that."

He snorted as well. "That female is so incredibly entitled. She's self-centered and a user. I was too young and naive back then to see her for who and what she was. If nothing else, my time on Molvi helped me become a much better judge of character and of assessing what motivations drive people. Oluina is no competition to you. Never will be. Since my return, my dislike for her has only increased."

I smiled again, another wave of relief flooding through me. "And what about Ylis?" I asked, my voice bubbling with curiosity.

His face instantly softened as a smile stretched his lips. Despite the obvious affection splattered all over his face, it screamed of fraternal love, not lust.

"Ylis is a wonderful female and like a baby sister to me. Growing up, she was always a little rebellious. She convinced me to help train her in hunting and combat."

"Is that so?" I asked, eager to learn more.

He landed the shuttle in front of a small wooden house, his face taking on a wistful expression as he nodded.

"Males do not train females as we have very different hunting and fighting methods," Gaelec explained. "But Ylis wanted to learn every style as she felt it would make her a much more rounded huntress."

"Is she good?"

The way he puffed out his chest like a proud father and grinned were answers enough on their own.

"She's the best. So much in fact that she is increasingly undermining Oluina's position as Head Huntress."

"That could be a really good thing," I mused aloud. "She seems to like you a lot. She would make a great ally."

He nodded. "A very good one, and she stated as much."

"I'm going to be a problem, aren't I?" I said in an apologetic fashion.

He frowned and firmly shook his head. "No, not you. It's all of them. What you said about standing by me meant a lot to me," he said, that vulnerability I'd witnessed before fleeting over his handsome features again.

"I meant it, Gaelec," I said with conviction.

He gave me a gentle smile. "I know. And all could see the honesty of it."

"That's good, right?" I asked, hopeful.

My heart sank when he snorted and shook his head.

"Actually, it might have the opposite effect. The Queens are all loyal to each other, not to males," he explained in response to my confused look. "All the females within a single Pride are mothers, daughters, sisters, cousins, or aunts. Males are welcomed in at the height of their prime, used for their labor and their seed, and then cast out in favor of newer and younger males. If other females start thinking like you, it will undermine the dominance of the Matriarchs."

My stomach knotted with a nauseous feeling at the matter-of-factly way he described such a horrific culture. And yet, the same had been true for women in ancient times on Earth. Where the Nazhrals treated their males like nothing more than stallions and laborers, women had been broodmares and servants.

"Is that what you want?" I asked carefully.

He snorted. "Absolutely not. I don't want to be used anymore, and I want males to have better prospects than to only have worth during their prime years. But come on, let's get out of here and get you settled in. We can continue this conversation later."

I nodded with an apologetic smile. I didn't doubt people were still spying on us, wondering what we were doing just sitting inside the shuttle parked outside the house.

He hopped out of the small vessel and circled around to help me out. I picked two of my bags from the hold, and in the display of strength, Gaelec lifted one of the three crates with a single hand, carrying it effortlessly back to the house. I couldn't help but chuckle when he further made a show of unlocking the door and opening it wide for me while still holding the massive crate with that one hand. I likely would have strained my back just trying to move it from the hold onto a hovercart.

He put it down inside the cozy little living area right at the entrance and hurried back out to fetch the remaining two crates, which he carried stacked upon each other in a single trip.

Yep, my mate was a beast.

He closed the door behind us while my eyes were still flicking this way and that, as I waited for him to give me the tour. At a glance, it struck me as the typical bachelor pad. It was clean, with basic furniture and no actual decor giving it a personal touch. Although it didn't qualify as a primitive dwelling, it also wasn't high tech or particularly modern. At least, the giant vidscreen on the wall across a comfy looking couch indicated that we weren't cut off from the rest of the universe.

I lived among tribes that were completely off the grid. While it was great in terms of living in the moment instead of vicariously through various media, it also made us quite isolated. By the time we found out what was happening in the rest of that world—and more broadly throughout the galaxy—some truly shocking things had occurred or radically changed the course of entire peoples with us remaining clueless.

He gave me a quick tour of the small two-bedroom dwelling. In large cities where they packed as many apartments as they could to maximize the credits they could squeeze out of a single building, this would be deemed quite spacious. Although it felt cold and a little impersonal, it was in good condition and could easily be turned homey with a bit of love.

The main bedroom had a massive bed with a hand carved wooden frame and what looked like a very comfortable mattress. It only had a pair of nightstands and two large dressers. A closet appeared to have been recently added. Although it was stained to match the rest of the dark brown furniture, it looked a little too pristine without the natural wear and tear one would expect from something older. The second bedroom was set up as an office. It made me quite curious what type of work Gaelec used it for. However, the computer, 3D printer, holographic projector, and large vidscreen hinted at far more than just casual usage. I would have to poke him more about it later.

The full hygiene room contained all the necessary amenities, aside from a tub. I often enjoyed just soaking in a warm bubble bath while reading some steamy romance on my tablet. Recently, I'd fallen down the rabbit hole of monster romance—which had been renamed exophilic romance to be more politically correct. After all, races like the Yurus and Ordosians would undoubtedly take offense at being described as monsters.

Old classics like the Spider's Mate series by Tiffany Roberts and the Duskwalker Brides by Opal Reyne spiced up quite a few of my single nights. At the time they wrote them, humans had not yet achieved warp jumps allowing for intergalactic travels. I often wondered how those prolific authors would feel today if they knew that species very close to the fictional beings they created actually existed, and that some women had in fact mated with them. By human standards at the time, I would now be labeled a monster fucker, due to my union to Gaelec.

That immediately reminded me that I would officially earn that title in just a few hours once I fulfilled that compulsory part of the contract. My stomach did a couple of back flips as conflicting emotions swirled through me. After so many years of abstinence, I was more than willing to get that itch scratched. Considering what a godly body Gaelec possessed, getting down and dirty with him didn't strike me as any type of hardship. But at the same time, I didn't really know him or how smoothly things would go with our different anatomies.

Has he ever even seen a woman's vagina?

Their females weren't quite made like us. I mentally prepared for him to be as challenged as human males in remembering the location of the little nub between my thighs, and the fact that it served an important role during spicy times.

Him luring me back to the kitchen allowed me to temporarily cast out those thoughts. Although I wouldn't call it a gourmet kitchen, it had enough workspace and all the basic equipment necessary to whip up a fine meal.

The somewhat embarrassed look he gave me as we concluded the tour back in the living area took me aback.

"As I mentioned previously, I had a much better home, with a breathtaking view of the river below and far more spacious. But I can expand and improve this one specifically to your liking overtime to make it more suitable," Gaelec said apologetically.

"Oh, my God! Don't be silly. This house is great!" I said in all sincerity. "In truth, I would call it rather fancy."

Gaelec blinked, baffled by my comment.

I smiled and gestured at the luminous room around us.

"When I was a missionary, I stayed on quite a few primitive planets where their dwellings didn't have a comfortable couch like this, and in some cases not even a bed. I spent over a year sleeping on a floor mat, washing in the river, and relieving myself in a hole dug in the ground in the forest. This is luxury."

"By the Gods, I can definitely offer you much better!" he exclaimed.

"And you already are," I said in a reassuring tone. "Please don't fret about that type of stuff. I'm probably one of the lowest maintenance women you'll ever meet."

"I'm happy to hear it," he said, clearly relieved before gesturing at my crates. "Do all of these go into the bedroom?"

I nodded. "These are all my clothes and personal accessories. The only other stuff I brought are a portable computer, my tablet, my blaster, and some of my basic camping gear."

"Perfect. I will bring them into the room for you," Gaelec said, simultaneously picking up two of the crates.

I grabbed my bags again and followed him into the bedroom.

"I built this dresser and closet for you," he explained pointing at each in turn. "If you need more space, I will build a bigger closet or another dresser. In the meantime, feel free to remove any of my own clothes from the other dresser by the window. It is half empty anyway as I don't have too many things. As you can see, us Nazhrals wear very little clothes," he added, waving at himself.

With a will of their own, my eyes glided down the length of his muscular body. They lingered a little too long on the black and gold leather loincloth that dangled in front of his naughty bits. It obviously was merely decorative as he wore a very snug pair of black shorts underneath it. It was cut low at the back to allow his fluffy tail to hang freely.

I quickly averted my eyes as my wretched mind once more attempted to take a deep dive into the gutter and wallow in every shade of speculations as to what lurked behind that fabric.

"Thank you. That's very kind and generous of you," I said, casting a pointed look at the second dresser. "But I will try not to take over everything."

He waved a dismissive hand. "This is your home now, my mate. Whatever you need, you take. And if it is not available, just tell me, and I will see that you get what you require."

"Careful, you might turn me into a spoiled brat," I said teasingly.

To my surprise, instead of the amused response I expected, Gaelec studied my features with a serious but soft expression.

"No, my mate. That is one thing I am convinced I will never have to worry about with you."

Putain! Why did that cause my ovaries to do a couple of backflips? I just gaped at him, words failing me before I shyly lowered my eyes and smiled. His own smile broadened in a gentle way that had my toes curling.

I still didn't know how much or how little Gaelec appreciated me so far, but I was clearly starting to develop a crush on him.

"I must return the shuttle to the hangar. Will you be fine on your own for a short while?" he asked hesitantly.

"Absolutely, I'll be okay. I'll start unpacking in the meantime," I added, waving at the crates.

"Good, I'll be back soon," he said with a smile before heading out.

I stared at his receding back until the door closed behind him. Yeah, my man was fine.

So fine that bitch is still thirsting something fierce over him.

That female was going to be a problem. I knew vindictive when I saw it, and this one was a particularly sore loser with a massive ego. She also struck me as the type to think if she can't have what she wants, then no one else can either. With Oluina being in a position of power within the Pride, I needed to tread carefully. As I loved a good challenge, I had no problem standing up to her. In fact, the aggressive way she came at my man and at me made me even more determined. I might not be as strong and fast as she was, but I was no pushover.

The way Gaelec stood up for me and for himself truly impressed me. For his sake, I hoped we could work things out somehow. Another part of me genuinely wished we would simply leave. This place felt toxic as hell. But, as I was no quitter, I would give it a fair try and put my best foot forward. For starters, I needed to figure out how to contribute. With luck, Gaelec and Ylis could point me in the right direction.

A smile settled on my lips as I thought of the younger female. She had a fire in her that commanded respect. The way she put Oluina back in her place still had a pleasant shiver running down my spine. As much as I didn't want her to get in trouble over me, I wholeheartedly welcomed any support she could provide. I would also like to develop a friendship with her. It would suck to have no one but my husband here, should we end up staying with the Pride.

Just as I was finishing putting the rest of my clothes in the drawers, the sound of the front door opening announced Gaelec's return. The flutter of excitement that prompted took me by surprise. At least, it was encouraging that I should have a positive response to him instead of already counting the days until I could bail out of this contract.

The delicious aroma that wafted to me had my stomach grumbling. I had been too nervous to eat anything during the last leg of the flight here. And now it was catching up to me. I hastened back to the kitchen where I found Gaelec laying out a variety of dishes on the table. He grinned and gestured for me to take a seat in one of the wooden chairs.

I gladly complied.

Contrary to many species with tails, the chairs here actually had a backrest. However, the lower half was completely open, allowing them to tuck the tail in so that they could sit comfortably.

That pleased me a great deal.

"As it's close to the evening meal, I took the liberty of bringing food for us," Gaelec explained while setting down the last few covered bowls. "Our people often share a communal meal in the Great Hall. But it is also perfectly fine to eat privately in our own homes or outdoors."

"What's more common?" I asked.

"It's pretty much mixed," he said with a shrug before going to fetch a couple of plates and utensils in the cupboards. "In the Great Hall, you will almost always find the Matriarchs, the mothers and sires with their younglings, some of the elders, the huntresses, and every non-mated male."

I frowned and gave him a curious look. "Isn't that everyone?" I asked.

He chuckled and shook his head. "No. Most of the bonded mates—who are few—and those who are currently courting or newly paired will want time alone together. The males like me who also aren't actively looking for a mate will avoid eating in the Great Hall. In those times, it is best to avoid drawing unwanted attention."

"I see," I said, my wheels spinning.

He didn't have to spell out that us eating here in private was not only to give us a chance to get to know each other better, but also—and probably mainly—to avoid drawing further attention to either of us.

"As I previously mentioned to you, here, females do the hunting while males handle most of the butchering and cooking. Our females feed and educate the younglings, while the males handle discipline for misbehavior as well as handling most of the cleaning and maintenance around the village," Gaelec explained.

"That sounds like a pretty good setup," I said approvingly as he started removing the lids from the multiple containers on the table.

The delicious aroma had my mouth watering in anticipation

as I got a first glimpse of the generous portions within. It mostly appeared to be different meats with a limited number of sides. I was aware of the Nazhrals being mainly carnivores. But I hoped their meals accounted for enough vegetables and starch for me to maintain a healthy and balanced diet.

Gaelec proudly nodded as he reached for my plate to start putting small samples of everything.

"Life in a Pride is really good in principle. There are many things that we do right, but also far too many that are bad," he said pensively. "Too many things are rooted in fear."

"How so?" I asked, tilting my head to the side.

"Males are constantly reminded that they are replaceable. The smallest mistake or a single bad performance after months of excellence could suffice for us to be cast out. If you're a newcomer hoping to join, it only takes one of the Queens to deem you unfit for the rest of the females to side with her and cast you out."

"Whoa!" I said, a frown creasing my brow. "What happens then?"

"You hope that a different Pride will welcome you," he replied casually, while piling some of what looked like vegetables in the tiny spot remaining on my plate.

I should have told him not to put so much on it so that the flavors wouldn't overlap and mix with each other. That would have allowed me to more clearly identify what I liked versus what I possibly didn't. But he seemed so happy to be feeding me that I didn't have the heart to tell him to stop.

"But what if you're not? What if every Pride rejects you?" I asked with genuine curiosity.

"Then you remain a nomad, or you group up with other roaming males for mutual protection and for convenience," he said while setting the plate in front of me.

My grateful smile froze on my lips before giving way to shock as I got a close look at the food presented to me.

"Errr…"

"Is something wrong?" Gaelec asked, the worry in his voice reflecting the one on his face at my reaction.

I gave him a sheepish look before glancing back down at the plate. "That meat is much too raw for me. Humans need certain foods, especially meat, to be cooked up to a certain temperature, not only for taste but also for health reasons."

He looked horrified.

"My apologies, my mate. I was not aware of this. I will fix it at once," he said as he swiftly picked up my plate and turned around towards the cooking unit on the left counter.

I felt horrible. He'd been so proud to serve me only for me to rain on his parade. I loved good sushi and didn't mind the occasional tartar. But the different meats on the plate literally looked like they had been freshly carved off the carcass and merely sprinkled or rubbed with some herbs and spices. One of the red meats seemed to have been slapped on a hot plate for half a sneeze on each side, just to say it had a taste of heat. The white meat was the one that freaked me out the most. Thoughts of *E. coli* and other bacteria just ran circles in my mind. It was surprising that I didn't see them soaking in a pool of mixed blood at the bottom of the plate.

"Don't be sorry," I exclaimed, rising to my feet. "You couldn't know. I didn't even know how you prepared your meals or what your dishes were. But you don't have to do it. I can take care of it myself."

Gaelec recoiled. The hurt look in his stunning blue eyes took me aback.

"I can properly provide for you, Ophelia," he said, sounding as if I'd just ripped his heart right out of his chest and stomped all over it for fun. "I made a mistake, but I will make sure to learn your human needs. I won't fail you again."

My chest constricted at this strong reaction from him. The words he spoke only moments ago about how Nazhral males lived in constant fear of being cast out for the slightest mistake came back with a vengeance. Did he think I would consider a divorce over something so trivial?

"You did *not* fail me, Gaelec," I said forcefully, making no effort to hide how outrageous and ludicrous I thought that assumption to be. "You're not human. I'm sure that by Nazhral standards, this food is perfect. Normally, I make it a point to try the traditional recipes of every new culture I get the honor to visit. The only exception is when it can jeopardize my health. Raw meat is a lot harder for humans to digest and significantly increases the risk of us suffering from food poisoning. And cooking makes meat taste better to us, especially when it is properly spiced."

"We do spice our meat," Gaelec said, some of the tension bleeding out of him. "We just barely cook it or don't cook it at all. Please teach me what is suitable for you so that I can provide appropriately."

I hated the lingering glimmer of worry in his eyes. With a bone deep conviction, I realized that refusing to let him cook for me would be a crushing blow to him. He would not only deem it a brutal rejection but also proof that I considered him a failure, or at least incapable or unsuitable of catering to my needs. I loved being pampered like the next person, but only because they wanted to, out of affection and not because they felt compelled to as a proof of their worth.

I would make sure he realized that, to me, he was worth far more than his ability to cook meat and build furniture.

"Of course," I said with a smile. "But just so you know, it is normal for humans to cook for each other. That task is not gender specific. For us, it is a way of showing affection. For example, I can't hunt. Does that make me a failure as a female?"

He recoiled and looked at me as if I'd said something silly. "Of course not. You're human, not Nazhral. You cannot be expected to share the same physical attributes as my people."

"Exactly. And it's the same way that you cannot be deemed a failure as my mate for not instinctively knowing how humans eat their food. You're a Nazhral. But I'm happy to show how we like our meat and maybe even show you some of my favorite recipes."

My chest constricted further at the way his shoulders slouched with relief, and he beamed at me. He was so big, muscular, and almost intimidating with that barely constrained strength and power that seemed to radiate out of him, that seeing this vulnerable side of him wrecked me.

"Fair warning, we have all kinds of varying cooking times and temperatures for meat," I cautioned. "As I do not know these specific meats, don't be surprised if I mess things up while trying to figure it out," I added sheepishly.

"I brought plenty," Gaelec said with a smile, seeming pleased by this turn of events. "We can test it together then until we find what pleases you."

"That sounds like a wonderful plan!"

He fired up the cooking plate, and we began trying out small samples of the various cuts. I would start off with the so-insanely-cooked-it-might-as-well-be-leather level then worked my way backward until I found the right one for each. It turned into a hilarious game with Gaelec bemoaning how I was slaughtering the meat. That didn't stop him from tasting everything I did. His horrified expression at the near burnt ones had me in stitches.

It didn't take long for me to realize that some of his over-the-top responses were deliberate, specifically to make me laugh. My man was trying to entertain me.

After a few experiments, I ended up with my brand-new favorite.

"*Oh, Putain!* That tastes just like Wagyu beef!" I exclaimed with a delighted moan as I chewed.

Gaelec chuckled before greedily picking up a piece to taste it as well. The intense look on his face as he explored the texture and flavor didn't go unnoticed. Through the playfulness, Gaelec was paying close attention and filing away information as to what I did and didn't like. Tasting the meat served as a way for him to better understand what kind of tenderness and juiciness resonated the best with me.

"See?" I said, pointing at the piece we had taken a bite of. "This to me would be the perfect prep for this meat. A nice sear outside, and the right level of pink inside."

"Duly noted, my mate," Gaelec said calmly. "I will remember how you like your Sikkal steaks."

After cooking a few more portions of the various meats in a way that was suitable for me, we settled at the table so that he could also enjoy his mostly raw food. While the atmosphere significantly relaxed during our little experimentation, I couldn't help but bring the focus back on what happened in the Great Hall.

"Should I expect us to always have our meals here?" I asked in a soft voice. "I don't mind it. But I'm trying to get a sense of what the next few days will be like."

I immediately felt guilty for upsetting him by stirring things up again. But I needed to know where I stood, especially if he was to go back to work in the morning. Would I have to stay locked up inside the house in his absence for my own safety?

"I'm sorry you had such a harsh welcome," he responded, making me think that he didn't know yet if or when it would be a good idea for us to share a communal meal with the rest of the Pride.

"Don't be. Like I said before, none of this is your fault. Both you and Kayog warned me that there might be some friction. This is not my first time experiencing something like this, although I admit this was one of the highest levels of hostility I have faced," I said pensively. "With the fundamental matriarchal structure of your society, I'm honestly not sure that they will ever accept me. Especially seeing how quite a few of them appear to want you."

Gaelec huffed and waved his hand. "They don't want *me*, Gaelec. They just want my seed because I'm a Stellig. It bruises their ego that I am not groveling for their attentions, especially Oluina. So what you said about following me wherever I decide to go means a lot to me. My stay on Molvi truly opened my eyes."

"How so?" I asked, intrigued.

"I finally understood what it was like to be valued," Gaelec said, his eyes slightly going out of focus as he reminisced. "The Wardens offer some fantastic improvement programs for free. I studied most of them in my spare time. We do not have access to so much education here. So this was a golden opportunity on top of keeping me in a safer space, and therefore out of trouble with the other inmates."

"That was clever and beneficial," I said in an approving tone.

He smiled. "Extremely beneficial. It allowed me to repair a lot of our stuff, upgrade our sector, and generally improve our dwellings, and our lives as a whole. When I left, many of the inmates were genuinely sad. Their lives will get more difficult without me as time goes on. They valued what I had to offer, and they repaid it by whatever means they could to keep me happy."

"It makes sense. You want to take care of the person who makes your life easier," I mused aloud.

He nodded. "Many wonder how come I'm not maimed or scarred like so many ex-convicts. It was largely because no one wanted to mess with the one person who knew how to optimize our generators and the efficiency of our production units so that we had a lot more power throughout the month at a lot lower cost, on top of increasing our mineral output."

I frowned, confused. "I'm not sure I understand what you mean by generators and production units."

"Prisoners on Molvi must earn their keep. The Warden gives

us a set amount of energy every month that we need to use wisely to avoid running out. We can buy extra energy by pooling our resources from the credits we earn through our work. Every Quadrant has certain resources that we can extract in exchange for payment. We're not obligated to do it, but the more we produce, and the more credits we receive that we can then spend on additional energy, comfort items, or to put in a savings account for when we come out. So the quality of our lives is directly linked to how much work we are willing to do."

"And the optimization you were able to do significantly improved your comfort levels as well as the amount of credits everyone pocketed every month!" I said with sudden under-standing.

Gaelec nodded. "The work I accomplished will last them a while, but the equipment requires frequent maintenance. Unless they properly train someone else to take over where I left off, they will need to pay a technician hired by the Warden to perform the repairs instead. That will not be cheap. But none of those fools wanted to put the effort required to learn it."

"That's on them, and their loss. They will feel the sting of your absence in due time. But I'm really impressed by what you accomplished," I said with sincere admiration.

He smiled and lowered his eyes in that timid way I found so unbelievably adorable, and his whiskers twitched.

"So upon my return here, it hit me really hard to realize that I was right back where it all started before this whole mess. Here, I'm expected to always give more and more and be grateful for whatever crumbs they throw back my way or for the right to stay. The Matriarchs keep us in our place with the constant reminder that we're here by their grace. Being paired with one of the Queens or huntresses only grants a temporary reprieve. Our status remains precarious. The sad part is that males keep thinking that they will be the exception. But there will always be a younger, stronger, and more attractive candidate that will swoop in and take your place."

"You have no idea how much I understand what you're saying. Although not as pronounced today as it was a few centuries back, it is a lingering problem on Earth. But it's mostly men doing that to women."

Gaelec's ears perked up in surprise. "Really?!"

I nodded. "A woman's fertility and physical appearance play a large role in her appeal. Men love young women between the ages of eighteen to twenty-five. It's usually also when we're at the prime of our beauty and fitness. But it's stupid since the ideal time for a woman to get pregnant is between twenty-five and thirty-five. And now, thanks to medical advances, women can bear children all the way up to age sixty, but there are a lot more chances of complications the older she gets."

"It sounds like here," Gaelec says pensively, but in reverse. "Our females covet males between eighteen and twenty-five. And we usually get discarded by our mid-thirties."

I shook my head with disgust. "Yep, same thing. Older women have been devastated by their partners of many years suddenly abandoning them for a younger female. But the fools soon learn the hard way that many of those younger women are only in it for their credits. And once they've sucked them dry, the old idiots are left penniless and womanless. Then they have the nerve to try to crawl back to the one woman who had been loyal to them and who would have stood by them in their twilight years."

"I hope those women do not take those men back!" Gaelec growled.

I laughed. "Thankfully, most of them don't. Their ex-husbands should have recognized their value while they were by their sides. Now they can just eat their hearts out while watching the woman they foolishly spurned live her best life without them.

But my question to you is why not just move to the city if you are not treated well in a Pride?"

"Because Pride members are treated like second rate citizens in the cities. To them, we are peasants, borderline savages," Gaelec said with derision laced with contempt. "Most of the nomads who tried their luck in the city get terribly exploited because they don't know the laws. They end up trapped in dead-end jobs making barely enough to scrape by. They're too poor to leave again, so they just work themselves to death trying to survive. And when things get bad enough, they jump on the first mission offered to them, only to end up getting killed if it fails or to land in jail as I did."

"But aren't there placement agencies and other programs that could help them secure a much better job?" I asked, my heart filling with sorrow for those poor males.

"There are placement agencies," Gaelec conceded. "Sadly, we do not have the types of qualifications they seek. Our education within the Prides is severely lacking. Females learn a lot of the more advanced classes, which would allow them to fare much better in the cities. But it doesn't make sense for them to leave the comfort that they enjoy within the Pride. They're the dominant gender here and have full autonomy over their lives and fate. And our government respects the sovereignty of Prides."

"Right. Why live by someone else's rules when you're basically the queen of your own domain?" I conceded.

"Exactly. Whereas males are only trained in basic trades related to those supported by the Pride. The male cubs here in the Nevian Pride learn about everything related to the fishing industry, from catching and preparing the fish, to crafting the various tools relevant to that industry, as well as sailing and ship maintenance."

"But don't males do all the construction work? That would require some physics and engineering training, no?" I argued.

"We don't study that. The females do. They just teach us how to lay bricks, erect walls, and paint them. We learn how to do the grunt work, not the intellectual one," Gaelec replied, sounding dejected.

"Damn," I whispered.

I almost commented about how women spent a few millennia facing a similar treatment. By denying them any form of advanced education that would allow them to have better control of their future, they were kept under the thumb and at the mercy of men.

"I wish I could start my own Pride," Gaelec said wistfully. "Males would get diverse and advanced training, which would open the door to them for better opportunities. They wouldn't live in the constant fear of being cast out or with the knowledge that they remained there on borrowed time."

"Why don't you?" I asked, instantly perking up.

He snorted and gave me an indulgent smile. "Because it would be doomed from the start. There would be no draw to such a Pride. Without females, there's no future. We need offspring to prosper. What female would want to settle in a place that sought to empower males, therefore taking away from their dominance?"

"What about Ylis?" I asked. "I don't know her, but she struck me as the type who might be open-minded enough to consider such a thing. I'm sure we could find a few if we set our minds to it. Anyway, don't females also have to leave the Pride once there are too many of them?"

"Yes," he conceded. "Once there are too many females, it is usually a group of ten to fifteen sisters and cousins who will leave together to start their new Pride. For all that, I don't know that Ylis would want to do that. While she never really displayed a thirst for power, she'll likely take over the control of our Pride. Why would she throw all of that away to take a gamble on such an unlikely project?"

I pursed my lips and slowly nodded. "I guess one can dream."

He chuckled. "One can indeed dream. But for now, my focus is to get you properly integrated within our Pride. Tomorrow, we will hold a feast. You will finally get to see our fun side. And then we'll have a couple of weeks to see how things evolve and where we go from here."

"Sounds good."

CHAPTER 8
GAELEC

I washed and put away the dishes while Ophelia showered. I still struggled with my feelings about the task ahead. Before meeting her, the word dread dominated. Now, nervousness would be a more adequate term.

I actually liked her.

Ophelia was smart, kind-hearted, and seemed sincerely interested in my thoughts and feelings. My chest still warmed at her reaction to my blunder with the food. Not only was she not upset at all with me, but she turned the whole thing into a rather fun experience as we tested the appropriate preparation for her. My mind still reeled at the thought that she wanted to cook and do other things for me.

Unless a male was critically ill or severely incapacitated, females didn't cater to our needs. And even then, they would normally assign another male to that chore. Younglings were the only exception to that rule. That didn't mean females never cooked, or repaired weapons and tools, or performed any other labor necessary to the good functioning of the village. However, them doing things for us was not expected and rarely occurred.

Things could really work out between us.

A spark of hope and excitement filled my heart at that prospect. I wanted to believe that the person Ophelia was showing herself to be so far was genuine, and not just a front. I could see myself falling in love with someone like that.

I just needed to make sure not to make a mess of things tonight.

My innards twisted painfully with preemptive worry. I'd been celibate for the past twelve years since my incarceration. Had she been a Nazhral female, this whole thing would be a breeze, despite me being rusty. You had to be beyond pathetically incompetent to fail at satisfying our females. Even if you tried, you couldn't miss their clitoris. In fact, our partners usually achieved multiple orgasms before we even got a first one, thanks to our penile spikes further enhancing their pleasure.

But what if she finds that freaky?

I looked into their males' reproductive parts. Although our cocks shared similarities, the spikes and under ridges significantly differed. To me, human men were lacking. What kind of pleasure could they possibly give their women with that smooth, unfinished thing?

My people also didn't do that thing humans called foreplay. We just got straight to business. The fact that both our males and females self-lubricated spared us the need for initial preparation. In a way, you could say that we did things in reverse. Only once sated did Nazhral couples proceed to cuddle, which included gentle caresses and grooming. That was my favorite moment.

Is she a cuddler?

I would be heartbroken if she wasn't. Being wrapped up into the arms of our partner, surrounded by their heat and the softness of their fur was sublime.

But she doesn't have fur.

None of the various breeds among her people did. A few men possessed a lot more body hair than others, but it was a minority. The things most human males seemed to share included facial hair called a beard, as well as patches under their armpits and around their pelvic area. Depending on their breed —which I believed they called ethnic groups—they had varying amounts of hair on their forearms and legs. Strangely enough, for those with hairy patches on their chests, if it trickled down their abdominal muscles towards their groin, humans called it a happy trail.

What was so happy about it?

But the real concern was that many articles I read implied that women were not too fond of hairy men. In fact, they had entire trade skills devoted to ensuring the removal of any pilosity they could. Men had countless tools to shave their beards daily. I was still mentally scarred by the visibly painful method involving hot wax to yank their hair right off their bodies. If you really did not want those natural features, why not use the less brutal methods such as a laser?

I almost went into a full-blown panic at the thought Ophelia might request I do the same. As determined as I was to please my mate in every way reasonably possible, this was where I would draw a hard line.

She said my fur looks nice and fluffy.

That thought alleviated some of the worry twisting my insides. I knew that I was way overthinking the whole thing. Considering how stoic I normally was, this level of nervousness couldn't have been more out of character. Then again, I'd never been only moments from my wedding night with a species foreign to me.

My stomach did a couple of backflips when the sound of my female exiting the hygiene room reached my ears. My mind began racing about possible ways to further delay the inevitable. I washed and groomed before picking her up at the spaceport a few hours ago. Would she expect me to wash again even though I was still clean?

Let me shower once more.

If nothing else, it would grant me some extra time to mentally prepare.

Stop acting like it's a fucking chore!

The force with which the little voice at the back of my head chastised me both took me by surprise and shamed me. I was seriously being overly dramatic about the whole thing. Mating with my wife was bound to be a wonderful experience that would bring us closer. Even though we barely knew each other, we were soulmates. Despite being completely different species, our bodies were meant for each other. We would find a way to harmoniously come together.

It was as if a switch flicked on in my head. Saying that all anxiety about it flew right out the window would be a lie. However, it did seem like a weight had been lifted off my shoulders. I quickly washed, dried myself, and brushed my fur.

As I stood in front of the hygiene room's closed door, I debated what to do about my nudity. Technically, putting clothes back on didn't make much sense as I would be stripping right out of them. At the same time, it felt quite presumptuous to just strut right in with my cock on full display.

My limp cock at that.

I flinched and groaned inwardly that I would have allowed that wretched thought to perk its head up. I wouldn't feed it any energy by dwelling on the possibility of such a horrendous turn of events.

Forcing my mind back onto the issue at hand, I realized how limited my options were as all my clean garments and loincloths sat inside the drawers in the bedroom. So unless I wanted to don the same breeches I previously wore, I would either have to enter the room fully bare or get creative.

Annoyed to drag this whole thing longer than necessary, I emitted a frustrated growl and grabbed a clean towel from the shelf. I wrapped it around my waist and tucked the back below my tail so it wouldn't make my rear look twice its size on top of risking an absent-minded movement of my tail pulling open the towel by accident.

Taking a deep breath, I walked out of the hygiene room and crossed the couple of steps into the master bedroom. My breath hitched upon catching the first glimpse of my mate. She was sitting cross-legged on the right side of the bed. Her long mane cascaded down her back some of it in front of her shoulders, draping her in its fiery strands. It contrasted sharply with the paleness of her skin. Beneath her lustrous hair, a sheer green fabric drew my attention. It appeared to be one of those semi-transparent garments that women wore to seduce and entice their partners.

It both flattered and shamed me that she would have taken the time to plan to make herself more attractive for our wedding night, and I couldn't even have planned for a change of clothes after showering. To be fair, Nazhrals didn't have such rituals. And as far as I knew, human males also didn't wear special outfits to make themselves more appealing in bed. But I could have inquired further about it instead of just what their genitals looked like.

She jerked her head up from the tablet she had been reading on to look at me. The abrupt way she did so implied she had not heard me approach. Her light surprise faded almost instantly. Without averting her eyes from me, Ophelia blindly put the tablet down on the nightstand to her left. She gracefully slipped off the bed and stood facing me with a smile.

Although timid, it contained no fear. That did the craziest thing to me. On top of all the other things my stupid mind kept panicking over, I had also worried that Ophelia might need me to reassure her about being safe with me.

I returned her smile and caught myself scratching my nape, unsure what to do or say next.

"Do you want to talk?" Ophelia asked in a soft voice.

I blinked. "Talk?" I repeated, my confusion audible.

"About this," she said, gesturing in turn between me and her. "As there's a bigger burden on males, I figured you might wish for us to discuss this whole thing. We're kind of getting thrown in, headfirst," she added with a nervous giggle.

My cheeks burned with embarrassment. Did she think me impotent? Did I give off such strong vibes of lacking attraction towards her that she felt the need to give me an easy way out in case I couldn't perform?

But what if I indeed can't get it up?

To my undying shame, I wasn't feeling hard at all right now. My cock didn't even remotely seem in the mood for venturing anywhere, least of all into foreign territories.

"Hmmm, yes. Sure," I said, fighting the urge to squirm.

Her smile broadened, and her shoulders dipped with what I could only interpret as relief. It suddenly struck me that this whole time I was selfishly worrying about a potentially disastrous performance on my part, my poor mate had likely also been worrying about this moment. After all, I was significantly bigger and stronger than she was. It had to be terrifying for her to find herself halfway across the galaxy, among strange people who had not shown her the warmest welcome, and to be expected to lie down with an ex-convict she'd only met a few hours prior. I couldn't begin to imagine finding myself in such a vulnerable position.

And yet, she was still displaying that impressive stoicism that screamed of great inner strength and character.

She circled around the bed to its feet and sat down at the edge. Still smiling at me, Ophelia patted the mattress next to her. Without hesitation, I joined my mate and settled beside her. I wasn't so close that we touched, but enough to feel the heat of her body.

Ophelia examined my features for a few moments, her expression soft even as she clearly searched for her words before starting to speak.

"You're not overly attracted to me, right?" she asked in a gentle voice.

I flinched, instantly angry with myself that my reactions towards her might have made her feel unwanted. Simultaneously, a powerful urge to protect and reassure her swelled within me.

"It's not that, my mate. It's just that…"

My voice trailed off, and it was my turn to look for my words. Ophelia raised an inquisitive eyebrow when the silence stretched.

I cleared my throat and scratched my nape again. "It's just that I have never been with a human before."

She smiled, her beautiful green eyes sparkling with a mix of understanding and amusement.

"I get it. I've never been with a Nazhral either."

I snorted and nodded in concession, before shifting uneasily. "There's also the fact that it has been a little over twelve years for me since I've been with a female."

The words nearly scorched my lips as I spoke them. I nervously glanced sideways at her to find her gaping at me. The air of uncertainty that descended on her features took me aback.

"Did… did something happen?" she asked cautiously.

My mind went blank for half a beat as I tried to make sense of what she meant. And then it hit me.

"Oh, no! Nothing of the sort. I mean, everything works as intended. If that's what you were asking…?" I added hesitantly, suddenly wondering if I had misunderstood.

"Oh, good!" she said, her cheeks taking on that crimson color that was seriously growing on me.

"There were only two females in my Quadrant during my incarceration," I explained sheepishly. "Neither of them appealed to me, nor were they drawn to me. Anyways, both were Raitheans who also happened to be mated. In case you are unaware, Raitheans mate for life. It is physically impossible for them to cheat on their partners."

"Yeah, I can see that," she said with sympathy.

She opened her mouth as if to ask another question before appearing to change her mind. I suspected it was to ask me why I had not slept with one of our females since my return. Considering three weeks had gone by, it was a fair question. I wanted to believe she remembered the issues I listed earlier during our meal, and which basically turned me off getting involved with anyone.

Back on Molvi, males held recurring discussions about how much sex they intended to get once they were back home, and all the traditional food they desperately missed that they would gorge on. I expected to behave in a similar fashion. But it was strange how once something became accessible again, it lost a lot of its mythical appeal. Having so much of it openly thrown at me had in fact the exact opposite effect.

She licked her lips nervously and cast another uncertain look my way before going for it.

"You know, we don't have to do anything tonight," she said carefully.

I recoiled and stared at her in shock. A part of me felt outraged by that suggestion, while another feared she was in fact so reluctant to be intimate with me that she was trying to wiggle out of it. That hurt my feelings. But at the same time, I could never force myself on a woman who wouldn't be with me willingly.

"The contract states we must, as Kayog clearly reminded us before his departure," I argued, my voice tense.

Ophelia shrugged dismissively. "I don't care about the contract, Gaelec. This is about you and me, and hopefully the rest of our lives. Anyway, it's not like they have hidden cameras here or that they're going to send an inspector in the morning to make sure we did the deed."

I snorted. For a ridiculous reason, I pictured the Temern

hanging on to the windowsill to try and peep into our room through the night to make sure we honored our end of the deal.

Although she couldn't possibly guess what absurd thought flashed through my head, Ophelia relaxed at my reaction and gave me a shy smile.

"I like you, Gaelec. I like everything that I've seen about you so far, and I want you to like me as well. Above all, I want you to feel comfortable with me. Our first time together should be something we both want, not some chore, not something we're stressing over or feeling coerced to do," she explained calmly. "Kayog makes a valid point about early intimacy helping to quickly tighten the bond between a couple. But intimacy doesn't have to mean sex. Maybe we could just snuggle and cuddle? Then we wouldn't be so awkward around each other."

My heart leapt upon hearing her words. "Snuggles are nice," I said with a bit too much enthusiasm. "I do love cuddling," I added shyly. "So you will never get any complaints from me on that front."

By the way Ophelia's eyes widened, she had not expected such an eager response from me. As I had pretty much made it a point to keep my hands to myself around her, she had no reasons to believe I could be the affectionate type. Quickly recovering from her shock, my mate beamed at me. My chest filled with warmth. She truly looked lovely when she smiled like that.

"I'm happy to hear it!" she replied. "I'm a big hugger and snuggler as well."

"It pleases me tremendously to hear it," I said in all sincerity. "I was hoping it would be the case. That said, just so you know, I do not mean to appear distant or reluctant. The past years have made me quite guarded. In this instance, I admit that I'm over-thinking the entire situation. On the shuttle from the spaceport, you said that you weren't disappointed by me. But I do worry you might be... distraught by the parts of me you haven't seen yet. We're quite different from human men."

Ophelia snorted. Her green eyes sparkled with amusement even as her cheeks reddened. "Yes, I'm aware. You're not the only one who did a bit of research. I read up on your people... about *everything*... if you know what I mean."

I burst out laughing, the face she made being both hilarious and incredibly adorable.

"Well, since we are in confession mode, I also read about *everything* regarding your people, especially female anatomy."

It was silly, but we were grinning at each other like two teenagers witnessing something raunchy for the first time. I liked the complicity it created between us.

"So... it's true that you guys have spikes down there?" she asked, her cheeks so red they seemed on the verge of bursting into flames.

I nodded, surprised to find my smile broadening instead of fading with the anxiety I previously felt regarding that.

"We do. There are usually three or four rows of them all around the circumference," I said with a hint of amusement.

"Are they hard?" she asked, looking half guilty, half worried.

I laughed again and shook my head. "No, Ophelia. They are not hard. You are not going to get torn to shreds by them. Our spikes are hard enough to provide a pleasant sensation to the female, but soft and flexible enough not to cause any pain or discomfort. The tips are also rounded, not pointy. I assure you, that while their sight might be unnerving to you the first time you see them, they will procure you nothing but intense pleasure."

The way she shifted at the edge of the bed lit a strange spark in the pit of my stomach. At a visceral level, I knew with unshakable certainty that she just imagined how those spikes would feel inside her. That subtle response from me to her reaction boded well.

"I'm happy to hear it. We're pretty soft inside, so the thought of spikes had me a little nervous. Those websites have a way of showing the most intimidating pictures. Even the spikes on your tongue look like a bunch of claws ready to shred even the hardest material to pieces."

I chuckled. "You are correct. Close up imagery of both our penile and lingual spikes can appear terrifying. But… hmmm… I understand that women have their clitoris outside instead of within, like our females?"

"We do," Ophelia replied before her face took on a grumpy expression. "And despite that, men pathetically fail at finding it."

"By the Gods, so it's true?!" I exclaimed, flabbergasted.

Ophelia burst out laughing before shaking her head. "It's not true. Well, let's just say that it's partially true. Too many men fail to give it the proper level of attention. Many women struggle at reaching their climax purely from penetration. A lot of us absolutely need clitoral stimulation to achieve it."

I bit back the instinctive urge to say that such an unfortunate outcome wasn't surprising considering how pathetically unimpressive and ill adapted the human males' cocks were compared to their women's sex.

"I promise that I will give your clitoris an abundance of attention," I pledged with a confidence that bordered on smugness.

This time, my mate didn't only squirm where she sat, but her scent also shifted. Although it differed from our females, I instantly recognized the subtle hints of her blossoming arousal. To my pleasant surprise, the enticing, spicy scent resonated straight in my loins. At long last, I felt the first stirring in my nether region.

"Remember you offered when I hold you to your promise," Ophelia replied, her eyes darkening.

"I will expect you to do just that, not that it will be required. I'm a male of my word, and I will be damned before I'm ever accused of leaving my mate unsatisfied."

Something had shifted in the past couple of minutes. I

couldn't quite put my finger on the cause, but I was finally becoming the one more assertive while my mate was the one becoming shy. The more dominant side I miserably failed to display since this whole conversation began sure took its sweet time to join the party.

"But what of your teats?" I asked before immediately cringing, even as my female snorted. "I'm sorry, I meant your breasts. From what I read, it says women like for them to be given some attention as well."

Ophelia nodded, her gaze flicking down towards her chest for a few seconds before she looked back at me.

"Yes. Breasts are quite erogenous for us humans—including our men—but especially for women. We like to get them fondled, pinched, and even bitten. But not too hard," she amended quickly. "A little sting is exciting, pain not so much, unless you're into the whole sadism kink, which definitely isn't one of mine."

Although I nodded slowly, my eyes remained locked on her chest. By Nazhral standards, my woman's breasts were humongous. Our females had four teats on their chests, two on each side—that were just slightly bigger than my own. Technically it wasn't so much the very narrow areola, but rather the size of the nipple itself. It was a bit plumper and longer to make it easier for our younglings to latch onto them. But each teat was merely more than a slight bump on their chest. You couldn't grab a handful with our females unlike with my mate. And those generous bulges on my woman's chest looked like each would fit snugly in my large palms.

Her words replayed in my mind. I couldn't wait to see how she responded to the rough texture of my tongue on her nipples. I read they hardened the more aroused the woman became. I couldn't wait to witness that phenomenon.

"You're staring," Ophelia mumbled after a while.

My eyes snapped back up to lock with hers, and I felt as

embarrassed as she seemed. I had not meant to ogle her breasts. But seeing their impressive size up close had completely derailed my train of thought.

"Apologies. I was just thinking how fascinating our anatomical differences are."

Not wanting to allow any type of awkwardness to ruin the momentum we had gotten going, I considered bringing up the other things I had looked up so far then thought better of it. Several of them felt a little too edgy to be addressed now. Instead, I settled for something a little safer.

"From what I've seen, kissing appears to occupy a prominent place in human relationships and intimacy," I said carefully.

The way Ophelia perked up immediately felt like instant trouble for me.

She nodded, an air of wariness creeping onto her features. "Yes, kissing is a big deal to us, at least certainly to me."

I tried to force a neutral expression on my face as I responded. "It is a strange ritual."

Ophelia's crestfallen expression struck me hard. "You didn't like it," she said, her shoulders drooping.

"I wouldn't say that," I cautiously replied. "In truth, it had been much too brief to get a good sense of it, not that I was really focusing on it," I admitted sheepishly. "Not to mention that it made my nose twitch and tickled my whiskers. But judging by your reaction, I'm guessing it means you enjoy it?"

My mate nodded frantically. "I'm a huge kisser," Ophelia said firmly.

"I see," I replied in a noncommittal fashion. "In that case, I will learn to enjoy it."

My female stiffened and frowned. "No, Gaelec. Intimacy cannot be forced. Kissing should make both people participating feel good. I don't want you to ever do something that you don't like or that makes you feel uncomfortable merely out of a sense of obligation. Whatever happens between us must always be because we both want to. There are plenty of other ways for us to show affection."

"I hear you, my mate. And I thank you for showing such consideration towards me. However, if something gives you pleasure, I will feel the urge to do it for that specific outcome. So don't be surprised by how things will evolve over the upcoming days as we get to know each other better."

"Fair enough. But what of you? I couldn't find anything about ways to please a Nazhral," Ophelia said, scrunching her face.

I chuckled. "Because there is nothing to be listed. Like I said, Nazhrals don't do preliminaries. As our females self-lubricate, and so do males, then whenever we choose to couple, we simply move to penetration. We cuddle after the fact."

"Ugh," Ophelia said with a distraught expression. "We don't self-lubricate. A woman needs those preliminaries, or at least to be heavily aroused for her to get wet. Otherwise, penetration can be quite painful and more difficult, especially if the male is well endowed."

The subtle but wary glance she discreetly cast towards my groin almost made me laugh again. And yet, worry should have dominated over amusement. I was indeed well-endowed. Hopefully, our first coupling wouldn't be too challenging in spite of that. I would have to put extra effort into making sure she received the proper amount of preparation.

That, too, made me chuckle. "Fear not, my mate. I will give you all the preliminaries you require. And please, do not hesitate to correct me if I do it the wrong way, like with the meat."

Ophelia gave me that shy smile again that was seriously growing on me. The way her gaze darkened also indicated that her mind went right back to imagining things happening between us. I truly loved how she seemed aroused at the prospect of intimacy with me, despite our differences. She made me feel wanted, for me, not just what she could get out of me.

"Okay," she said with a nervous giggle. "So long as you promise to also be open with me about the things you like and don't like, and if I'm messing things up."

"Deal. Now, the last topic I think we need to address—unless you have something else in mind that hasn't been brought up yet —we should discuss the matter of offspring," I said carefully.

Ophelia stiffened. The wariness on her face immediately had my own anxiety spiking. For Nazhral females, having offspring ranked high in their main priorities once they reached maturity. From what little I gathered about humans, it wasn't uncommon for them to choose to have very few or no younglings at all. Did she share those preferences?

"Why?" she asked, her voice tense. "You don't want kids?"

Kids was a strange word to refer to cubs, but I was too focused on trying to interpret her body language to dwell on such a superficial matter.

"Actually, I hope to eventually be a father in the future," I said, in a neutral and cautious tone.

"Eventually?" she repeated, although some of the tension drained from her back, which struck me as a good sign.

I nodded. "Assuming you also want offspring, I think we should wait until our situation is a bit more stable before we bring in younglings into the equation."

To my delight, Ophelia beamed at me and nodded vigorously. "I fully agree. I wouldn't want my children to be in a precarious situation, not knowing if we're coming or going. And above all, I want to make sure they will be in a safe environment where they will be welcome and accepted just the way they are."

I smiled, fighting the sudden urge to draw her into my embrace and rub my temple against hers to mark her with my scent. That impromptu wave of possessiveness took me by surprise, but I welcomed it.

"Our females' ovulation is induced by penetration," I explained. "There is a natural juice they consume when they want to prevent pregnancies, as they are very picky about which male they want siring their offspring."

Ophelia waved a dismissive hand. "That's not necessary. I have a contraceptive implant. It's still valid for four years. So there is no possibility for me to become pregnant. Once we are ready to start our family, I'll just have it removed and then within the next couple of weeks, I'll be fertile again."

"Excellent. Hopefully, you will be able to remove it long before it meets its expiry date," I replied.

She smiled and nodded. "Until then, we just get to practice lots and lots."

The way her eyes widened, and her face reddened as soon as she spoke those words indicated she had not meant to blurt them out. I was beginning to realize that my mate tended to let her mouth run away with her. It surprised me considering what impressive control she displayed during our audience with the Matriarchs. But I suspected this occurred when she was in what she perceived as a safe environment, and when she felt relaxed.

If my assumption was accurate, it pleased me that she would feel this way in my presence.

She emitted a nervous giggle to which I responded with a shy smile. And then the most awkward silence settled between us. I could see her wheels spinning as she was furiously looking for something to get the conversation going again. My own mind was going blank. It was truly pathetic.

By the Gods, Gaelec! Get a grip! Act like the Alpha male you're supposed to be!

I cleared my throat and gave her another sideways glance before going for it. "So, about the cuddling you were mentioning earlier, should we proceed with that?"

Looking relieved, Ophelia grinned, and her eyes flicked to my chest with a covetous expression that rekindled that spark that had started fading in the pit of my stomach.

"I would like that. Your chest fur looks so soft and fluffy. Can I touch it?"

The hopefulness in her voice made me snort. "Of course, you can. I'm your husband. That gives you the right to touch me whenever you want, and however you want. My body is yours."

The greedy way in which she licked her lips turned that timid spark into an open flame.

"Don't mind if I do," she whispered, slightly turning to the side to face me.

She carefully lifted her palm to my chest and sank her fingers through my chest fur. I studied her face as it took an air of pure awe. She gently scratched my chest, before running her palm over it, and slipping her fingers through it.

"*Putain!* It's so soft!" she whispered to herself.

There was that word again. We all spoke to Ophelia in Universal, as she did with us, since she didn't speak our language. But there were a few small words like that 'pootain' she had just said which I'd never heard before. They struck me as expletives. Living with a variety of species on Molvi, I'd been exposed to a plethora of them. None of them sounded anything like that one or that other word 'boardell' she also used a few times. I wanted to question her about it, but felt the timing wasn't quite appropriate to have a foreign language discussion.

It had taken us long enough to finally get to some sort of physical contact, I wasn't going to allow my stupid over analytical mind ruin the moment. Anyway, her touch was driving me to distraction. It was incredibly pleasant, making my stomach flutter. Then, to my shock, Ophelia leaned forward and rubbed her face over it.

A bolt of desire struck hard, deep in my belly. My cock jerked in response beneath the towel still wrapped around my waist. I barely managed to swallow back the purr trying to rise in my throat. To my chagrin, my mate stopped and lifted her head to look at me.

"You do realize that, from this moment forward, your chest has officially become my new pillow, right?"

I burst out laughing and nodded in concession. "As I said, my body is yours. But as that also implies cuddling and snuggling, then I am even more for it."

Her smile broadened, then her eyes sparkled with excitement and something else I couldn't define. It didn't matter. I just loved the way it made me feel.

My breath hitched when she resumed her exploration of me. This time, she didn't limit her touch to my chest fur, but her palm glided down slowly over my abdominal muscles, her fingertips tracing each crease. I couldn't decide if it tickled more than it turned me on. Either way, I didn't want her to stop.

"Your body is really amazing," she whispered more to herself than to me before glancing back up and locking eyes with me. "Men would kill to have chiseled abs like yours. I often wondered what it would be like to be married to a man with the physique of a fitness model. I never imagined that it would actually happen."

"I'm glad my body pleases you, my mate," I replied, my voice sounding a bit more gravelly from my own growing arousal.

Her palms resting on my stomach, Ophelia continued to stare at me for a silent moment. Something passed between us, some kind of connection or unspoken understanding. My mate stretching her neck and leaning forward to kiss me broke the magic.

Knowing how it had gone down the first time, I mentally braced for it, intent on focusing on the nicer aspect of that odd practice. However, her lips no sooner touched mine than my nose began to twitch. It tickled, and I couldn't resist the urge to chuckle against her lips.

Although disappointed, Ophelia chuckled as well and slightly pulled back to give me a sympathetic look.

"I'm sorry. It tickles. I think it's because of the way your nose brushes against my whiskers," I said sheepishly. "But aside from that, your lips are really soft. The sensation is not unpleasant."

With a will of its own, my hand settled on her nape, and gently tilted her head back. My mate's eyes widened in surprise, which quickly gave way to excitement when I leaned forward. I tilted my head at a light angle before pressing my lips to hers. This time, although her nose once again slightly brushed against my whiskers, the tickling wasn't as intense, allowing me to properly savor the experience.

It was indeed strange, but also nice. Nazhrals were familiar with kissing, just not mouth to mouth. The smoothness of the cushion of her lips made it unlike anything I'd ever tried before. Whether consciously or not, Ophelia leaned into me, and I found myself wrapping an arm around her body, drawing her closer even as I pressed my mouth a bit harder against hers. She slipped the fingers of one hand into my mane, her blunt nails gently scraping my nape. After a few more moments, I broke the kiss and locked eyes with her.

Something shifted between us, and that odd connection seemed to deepen. I absent-mindedly caressed her back. A violent shiver coursed through my woman, and her skin instantly erupted in those tiny bumps that freaked me out at the spaceport. This time, knowing it was a display of pleasure in response to something I did, I smiled and effortlessly picked her up to settle her in my lap, facing me, her knees on each side of my legs.

To my surprise, Ophelia appeared emboldened by this. Fisting my mane on my nape with both hands, she began brushing her lips over my right cheek in a gentle caress, then peppering soft kisses on every inch of my face. My chest vibrated with an approving sound. Yanking my head back, she pursued her ministrations, down my neck and my chest while I slipped my hands beneath the flimsy and sheer fabric of the sleeveless top of the lingerie she was wearing. As a single ribbon kept it attached between her breasts, it gave me no challenge in accessing her bare skin underneath.

By the Gods, she was so warm and incredibly soft. I never imagined anything could be silkier than perfectly groomed fur. But this exceeded anything I could have imagined. She shivered again as I greedily caressed her back, feeling so bold as to let my hands glide all the way down to the round curves of her behind. The underwear she wore was but a tiny string that disappeared between the seam of her rear, leaving the entire softness of each plump cheek exposed for me to explore.

Then my mate straightened and pushed against my shoulders. On instinct, I initially resisted before giving in when she insisted. She rewarded me with a smile as I lay down on my back, flicking my tail to the side to avoid crushing it under me.

The hungry way with which Ophelia's gaze roamed over my body awakened a dull throbbing between my thighs. My mate was truly drawn to me. I never realized what a potent aphrodisiac it could be. She caressed and kissed every inch of my chest and stomach. When she lingered around my nipples, licking and nipping at them, my blood instantly rushed to my groin. No one had ever done this to me. I didn't know if this was her subtle way of showing me the type of attentions she wanted in return, but it certainly showed me how pleasurable having one's breasts fondled could be.

My stomach knotted when her dainty fingers started fiddling with the knot I made to secure the towel around my waist. It took her a little longer than normal because she wasn't looking at what her hands were doing as her face was still pressed against my stomach while her tongue tickled and teased my navel.

I fleetingly considered stopping her and taking over. After all, as her mate, I had a duty to see to her pleasure first. I almost did just that before it dawned on me that, as much pleasure as I derived from her attentions, this was a necessary step for Ophelia to familiarize herself with my body. In turn, it would help alleviate the remaining fears she no doubt still held.

My breath hitched, and my spine stiffened as the thick fabric of the towel parted, leaving me exposed. My mate, who had been crawling backwards as she kissed a path down my body, gracefully slid down the bed and knelt between my parted legs. Heart pounding, I studied her expression as she examined my cock with a look that equally screamed shock and wonder.

Although I was still nowhere near erect, my cock was no longer fully flaccid either, thanks to how her caresses and kisses stirred me. But before worry could have it go limp again, Ophelia licked her lips in a way that whipped the fire in my loins back into action.

"Putain!" she whispered with awe.

There's that word again. Does it mean 'Wow!' or something else along those lines?

Ophelia reaching for my cock with one hand slapped any such thought right out of my brain. My abdominal muscles constricted painfully when the tip of her index finger started tracing one of the two vertical ridges that framed the underside of my cock from the base up to two thirds of my shaft. But the moment she brushed it over the row of spikes right below the head of my cock, I emitted a low hiss through my clenched teeth.

My mate immediately yanked her hand away, her eyes darting towards mine with a glimmer of panic.

"Sorry!" she exclaimed with an air of guilt. "Did that hurt?"

"No," I said in a grumbling voice as my cock throbbed. "It's just sensitive."

"Sensitive as in painful?" she asked hesitantly, while I felt the urge to grab her hand and put it right back on my needy length.

"No, not painful at all. It's very pleasant," I said in a controlled voice.

Ophelia instantly relaxed, her smile returning and illuminating her lovely face.

"Oh, pleasant is good! Very good!" she said before doing it again.

I clenched my teeth as blood rushed to my groin. My mate's grin broadened as my cock hardened in seconds as she continued to stroke my highly erogenous spikes.

"*Houlà!* Pleasant indeed," she said triumphantly.

In that instant, whatever tension still lingered faded away. Although my excessively long period of abstinence could have been the cause for me having such a strong response to that intimate touch, I didn't believe it was the case. Ophelia was the one turning me on. The way she touched and looked at me made me crave more… from her and no one else. The strengthening scent of her own arousal was also whipping my blood into a frenzy. And watching her nipples pebble and then poke against the sheer fabric of her lingerie only made me even harder.

I inhaled sharply as her hand closed around the base of my shaft, and she slowly started stroking me. A blissful growl tumbled out in me from the delightful warmth of her palm, and its insane softness against my length. I fisted the blanket on top of the bed to help me remain stoic as my mate had her way with me. As pleasure built in my loins, I closed my eyes to will myself to refrain from giving in to the intense pleasure her touch gave me, especially when her hand ran over my spikes.

Big mistake.

The darkness only seemed to enhance every sensation, which nearly had me spilling. I snapped my eyes open again at the same time a silky sensation caressed my thighs. To my shock, I lifted my head just in time to see Ophelia leaning over my groin. The long strands of her hair brushing against me felt like rolda— the most luxurious and softest fabric in the land.

Poking her tongue out, my mate licked my spikes. A sharp

cry escaped me as a bolt of fire exploded in my loins. I nearly lost all control.

"Ophelia," I growled, my voice sounding almost beastly to my own ears as I battled to restrain myself. "You must stop. I won't be able to—"

The rest of my sentence died in a strangled shout, halfway between a growl and a cry. As if fearing I would stop her, Ophelia opened her mouth wide to swallow as much of my cock as possible. An endless string of moans and growls tumbled out of me as she began to bob over me. My entire body was on fire as the lava in the pit of my stomach spread down my legs and up my chest. Despite her hand being too small to fully wrap around my shaft, she closed it tightly at the base, stroking me in counterpoint to the movement of her mouth on me.

I needed her to stop even as I prayed that she wouldn't. My brain stopped functioning from the insane pleasure crashing over me. I felt on the verge of combusting. The little voice at the back of my head trying to shame me for being on the receiving end instead of catering to my female's needs was buried by the sound of my blood pounding in my ears and the endless flow of bliss sweeping me away.

And then Ophelia raked her teeth on my spikes.

My spine seized, and a blinding light exploded before my eyes. I roared. And in a split second of lucidity, I yanked my woman's head away from my cock as liquid ecstasy shot out of me.

CHAPTER 9
OPHELIA

Although my husband took the expression 'being hung like a horse' to a whole new level, I was actually having a blast going down on him. I'd always been rather lukewarm about fellatio. Aside from hygiene—or rather the lack thereof—a man's inability to restrain himself once things got a little heated could be quite the buzzkill. Getting my tonsils smashed in by a guy getting a little too excited and thrusting into my face was not exactly my definition of fun.

Considering Gaelec's insane girth, I was surprised to have even been able to take any parts of him in my mouth. In truth, after seeing the tree trunk between his thighs, I initially ruled out any possibility of doing that. But the incredibly delicious aroma that wafted from him made my mouth water too much not to at least give it a try.

Had he not mentioned self-lubrication, I would have wondered if that intoxicating scent wasn't some kind of pheromone. Maybe it acted as both. Either way, the spicy sweet smell that drew me in ended up tasting like the perfect blend of pomegranate and ginger. The only thing missing was a dab of vodka and some crushed ice to have me sipping on him all day long.

Merde! My man tasted gooood!

Even though I couldn't take too much of him in my mouth, it was enough to have him going wild for me. Each of his growls resonated straight in my clit. The texture of his spikes was just the perfect level of hard yet pliable against my tongue. Imagining how it would feel inside me had my inner walls contracting in anticipation.

Even should his self-lubrication not act as some sort of pheromone, I was pretty convinced it was at least some form of aphrodisiac. My tongue and lips slightly tingled from the light spiciness. But the longer I bobbed over him, the stronger the throbbing grew between my thighs. My nipples were so hard, they actually started hurting. Even my clit felt insanely swollen. I could almost feel my pulse beating down there.

To think I feared the lack of attraction between us!

Watching him get hard for me had been insanely intoxicating. As he growled and moaned under my ministrations, Gaelec was gripping the blankets so hard that he was nearly shredding them to pieces. It made me feel like a freaking sex goddess. I wanted to see him fall apart for me. I took him as deep as humanly possible—which sadly was only past his spikes—and compensated by stroking the rest of his length with my hand. I accelerated my movements as his legs began to shake and the muscles of his thighs and abdomen contracted spasmodically.

Wanting to increase his pleasure, I decided to rake my teeth along the sensitive spikes right below the head of his cock. I barely even finished the movement before he yanked my head back with brutal force. The savage roar he emitted completely drowned my yelp of surprise. It quickly gave way to a startled gasp when his seed shot out in powerful spurts, splattering all over my chest.

Although that outcome had been predictable, I remained kneeling there, gaping with a mix of shock and awe. But it was mostly the look of pure bliss on Gaelec's face that claimed all my attention.

My man was hot!

Seeing his eyes all but rolling to the back of his head as he struggled to regain his composure did crazy things to me. To think my touch had made him fall apart like that!

Gaelec blinked and half-groggily pushed himself up on his elbows to look at me. The look of horror on his face upon seeing me drenched in his seed would have been hilarious if it hadn't been so stinking adorable.

"By the spirits! I'm sorry!" he exclaimed, shooting to a sitting position.

He yanked the towel he'd still been half sitting on and quickly proceeded to wipe the mess off me while multiplying the apologies. I giggled while telling him all was fine, but he still looked mortified. Considering most of it actually landed on my babydoll, it wasn't like I personally was soaking in it.

"Stop apologizing, you silly goose," I said with a grin. "You climaxing for me is the best compliment. I would have been devastated had I failed to pleasure you."

"Be that as it may, I should have pleasured you first," he growled.

He tugged on the string tying it between my breasts and carefully pulled the sullied garment off me, and then realized there actually only were a couple of spots on me, which he quickly wiped.

"The night is young, Gaelec. I'm sure we can get to that soon enough. But first, we need to get you back up," I said mischievously while casting a meaningful glance at his partially deflated cock.

I loved how bold and carefree I acted around him. Normally,

I tended to be a lot more reserved and follow the man's lead. But with Gaelec, I felt inexplicably at ease, like I could be the true self that too often I reined back in to meet expectations or to avoid making waves.

"Oh, no you don't," he snarled in a menacing fashion that had my girly bits standing to attention when I tried to reach for his length.

He grabbed my wrist, shoving it aside, then picked me up by my waist as if I weighed no more than a toddler, and tossed me on top of the bed. I laughed some more, excited to have him take charge in such a commanding fashion. Gaelec had this wonderful duality within him, shy and gentle on one end, dominant and fearless on the other. Both of which had me tingling in all the right places.

He climbed on top of me, holding his weight on his forearm, then leaned down to kiss me. My heart leapt in my chest to see him so determined to grow comfortable with something he knew pleased me. His nose still twitched a little, but once again not as much as the first couple of times. He was quickly figuring out which angle to use for it to be less ticklish for him.

I was also taking notes.

Obviously, I wouldn't push for deepening the kiss anytime soon. But hopefully, we'd eventually get there. For now, I gladly gave myself over to my husband's gentle exploration of me. His hands were everywhere at once, caressing and fondling every inch of my body. The slightly rougher texture of the pads at the tips of his fingers further enhanced each sensation, sending delicious shivers down my spine.

As I had done with him, he brushed his lips over my face. But he didn't just cover my cheeks and forehead with kisses, he also occasionally tilted his head to the side and rubbed his temple against my face, marking me. When his mouth followed a path down to the crook of my neck, he inhaled deeply. The way he purred in approval at my scent had my toes instantly curling. He licked me in that spot, right below my ear, at the corner of the jaw. It was as if he'd known how sensitive it was for me specifically. The rough texture of his tongue had me moaning with delight.

I didn't know if he had read up on preliminaries, was following the general example from how I had explored him, or if he was just naturally gifted, but Gaelec was doing a wondrous job of touching me in all the right places and with the perfect devotion and intensity to have me soaking wet and needy.

The wretched male nearly had me climaxing just from his tongue paying homage to my painfully hard nipples. Feeling the sharp tips of his fangs grazing over my left nipple sent a thrill down my spine. A part of me wanted to keep his head right there while his hands continued to boldly caress my body. But when the left one ventured between my thighs, my mind went blank.

I couldn't process the intensity of the sensations he was stirring within me. A strangled cry escaped me when the rough pad of his thumb grazed over my engorged little nub. My hips jerked, and my hands in his mane tightened. He stopped kissing my stomach to look up at me, his thumb on my clit pausing its movement as he studied my reaction.

Lips parted, eyes hooded, I stared back at him with what I knew would be a lascivious expression. Visibly reassured, Gaelec gave me a smug smile laced with something a little dangerous, like a predator preemptively enjoying the feast he was going to make out of his prey. Eyes still locked with mine, my mate gently flicked his thumb over my clit, studying my responses to his touch. I closed my eyes and threw my head back, my body jerking with blissful spasms as each stroke sent a lightning bolt up my spine.

He gradually increased the pressure as well as the speed of his movements. Simultaneously, one of his fingers began probing my slit. It no sooner found its way inside than I cried out, swept away by my orgasm. I had not expected to fall apart this quickly, but then I never thought he could have gotten me so insanely aroused. In a way, it was almost surprising I hadn't gone off right when he first touched my clit.

Even as I flew high, I felt his lips resuming their journey down my body while his thumb pursued its wondrous assault on my little nub. He only relented once I finally started coming back down. Still partially dazed, I opened my eyes, my eyelids weighing a ton as I peered at my husband. My stomach did a somersault when I found him staring at my crotch with a mesmerized expression.

Just like I had done, he examined me with fascination, but thankfully with an expression that did not hint at any type of revulsion or unease. His flat, feline nostrils flared. I immediately felt self-conscious that he should be inhaling my scent down there. But the starved look that descended over his features, accompanied by a grumbling sound of approval had my inner walls contracting again.

Leaning forward, he rubbed his face against my inner thighs while inhaling deeply. An even louder growl rose from his throat as he caressed my legs with both hands. He slipped them behind my knees and then parted me open wider. I couldn't remember ever feeling this exposed and vulnerable. But any urge to squirm died in a voluptuous moan when Gaelec dove in and gave me one long lick from the bottom of my slit all the way over my clit.

"My mate," Gaelec growled, his voice so deep and gravelly his words were barely intelligible. But it was the hunger in his voice that had my toes curling again.

It was as if something had broken inside him, and he began to devour me in a frenzy as if he were famished. I cried out, my hand fisting in his mane, and my hips gyrating beneath him. The roughness of his tongue was driving me to the verge of insanity. It was too good, too intense. An inferno was raging inside me, threatening to send me spiraling down another chasm of endless bliss.

He slipped his finger back inside me, soon adding a second one. Moving them in and out of me, he scissored them on their way out stretching me in the process. Just as I was nearing the edge again, my mate inserted a third finger. It was a tighter fit, and yet my body shouted for more. Even with his hand making love to me, I was aching to be properly filled, for him to wreck me with that alien cock of his.

He crooked his fingers, hitting my sweet spot just the right way. I couldn't tell if it had simply been that perfect timing as I was already about to topple over, or if the rough padding of his fingers brushing against my G spot—or maybe a combination of all of the above—was responsible, but I went off like a rocket.

I shouted his name, and my head rolled from side to side. I was burning from within, waves upon waves of ecstasy crashing over me as he continued to make me see stars. I vaguely felt him inserting a fourth finger. I was too far gone to fully assess any discomfort that it caused but by the time I came back to reality, Gaelec was now kneeling between my thighs and licking my essence off his fingers with an almost menacing look in his stunning blue eyes.

My pulse picked up with a mix of fear and excitement. The moment of truth had finally come. He settled on top of me spreading my legs wider as he did so. It took me a moment to understand why it felt a little awkward. And then it dawned on me. Nazhral normally coupled doggie style, with the female on all fours.

My chest warmed with affection and gratitude for how attentive Gaelec was in his efforts to please me. He had likely read that missionary was the standard, comfortable position for humans. It meant the world to me that he would put my needs first.

"Do you accept me, my mate," Gaelec asked, his eyes locked with mine.

That he would take the time to confirm my consent even now turned me upside down. How was he so fucking perfect? I smiled and nodded.

"Yes, Gaelec. I accept you," I said, my throat constricted.

I melted further when he kissed my lips even as he began pushing himself inside me. As expected, it was a tight fit. He didn't have to tell me that the kiss was meant to distract me from the inevitable discomfort. As wet as he had gotten me, and in spite of his self-lubrication, my body resisted his invasion after only a few centimeters. With shallow thrusts, he gradually worked his way in.

Breaking the kiss, he buried his face in my neck. I could feel him clench his teeth as he bunched up his muscles, his entire body tense undoubtedly from his effort to rein himself in. Seeing how sensitive his spikes were, it had to be torture for him right now having them so tightly squeezed by my inner walls as they continued to deny him full access. I caressed his back while silently willing my body to start cooperating.

Moments later, it finally complied.

I gasped at the sudden burn as he went from halfway in to fully sheathed. His face still buried in my neck, Gaelec emitted a long and drawn out, almost feral growl. It was terrifyingly sexy. I could almost feel him shaking in my arms as he continued to force himself to remain still as I adjusted to his girth.

He mumbled something unintelligible, the sound too muffled for me to make out his words before he finally started moving. I thought that first stroke would kill me. Lord almighty, those spikes were wrecking me. It wasn't just the amazing added sensation they provided, but it was the way they wrecked the hell out of my G-spot both on the way in and out as they brushed against it with deadly accuracy.

In no time, Gaelec had me writhing beneath him. Liquid

flames coursed through my veins. Each thrust wrested one voluptuous moan after another from me. My nerve endings were ablaze as he took me to new heights. Seeming to struggle with his own overwhelming pleasure, my mate picked up the pace, taking me harder and deeper. His heavy breathing in my ears, the sound of our moans mingling and of our flesh meeting quickly had me drowning in an ocean of ecstasy. It didn't build slowly and gradually, but it came at me like a tidal wave, ready to destroy everything in its path.

And destroy me, it did.

My orgasm slammed into me with a violence that left me reeling. I cried out, my inner walls clamping down on his massive cock even as he pounded into me. Gaelec roared. For a brief moment, I thought he had also given into his own release, but he continued to wreck me as I tumbled down the endless void of bliss.

Before I could fully recover, my mate suddenly pulled away from me. The room spun as he flipped me onto my stomach. With one swift movement, he pulled up my hips, my face still pressed against the mattress, and he rammed himself in from behind with one powerful thrust. I cried out again, feeling full to bursting.

He immediately set a punishing pace. I tried to push myself up to be on all fours, but Gaelec pushed me back down. To my shock, I felt the heat of his chest settle over my back, and then his teeth clamped down on my nape. They didn't pierce my skin, but I instantly understood the unspoken command for me to stay still and submit.

I gladly complied.

Even as he fucked me senseless, Gaelec continued to caress my body and to fondle my breasts. When the rough pad of his fingers found their way to my clit, I fell apart once again. This time, he joined his voice to mine. His seed shot out into me in what felt like even more powerful spurts then when I had gone down on him. He continued to rock in and out of me, his move-ment a bit erratic while his hands on my hips tightened almost into a bruising hold as he filled me to the brim.

Once fully spent, he collapsed on top of me before turning us to the side. With his cock still buried deep inside me, his chest pressed against my back, my mate held me tightly into his embrace, his tail wrapping possessively around me.

My throat constricted when he once again rubbed his temple against mine, marking me with his scent. Too wrecked to move or otherwise react, I snuggled against him, feeling safe and shel-tered, surrounded by his strong body.

I woke up the next morning feeling wonderfully sore. The fact that we had a couple more rounds that night certainly played a part in it. I would have to send Kayog a thank you note about his insistence the couple should have sex on that first night.

Although sad to find Gaelec already up, the wondrous smell of food silenced any thought of an encore this morning. I hurried to the hygiene room for a quick shower. After swiftly brushing my hair, I returned to the bedroom to get dressed. I hesitated for a while as to what I should wear. My mate took a couple of days off to help me settle in. Now, I couldn't decide between some-thing comfortable to go on the tour of the village he'd planned for us today, or something coquettish to further seduce him.

In the end, I settled on a black skort and matching crop top with some sexy cutouts on the side. Naturally, I slathered a thick layer of sunscreen on my skin, as turning into a lobster squealing in pain at the slightest contact didn't feature anywhere on my to do list anytime soon. Oluina would derive far too much pleasure from my misery on top of using this as more proof that I was inadequate as both a woman and as Gaelec's mate.

Thoughts of the wretched female immediately dampened my

mood. Refusing to grant her that kind of power over me, I cast her out of my mind and made my way to the kitchen. My jaw dropped at the sight of the massive feast my husband had laid out on the table. It qualified more as a brunch with enough food to feed eight adults with hefty appetites.

"Good morning, my mate," Gaelec said with a wide grin that had me instantly melting.

I made a beeline for him and gave him a hug. To my delight, he returned it, his tail wrapping around my legs as he rubbed his temple against mine. He tilted his head to bury his face in my neck and deeply inhaled my scent. I didn't know what I smelled like to him, but I loved how it made his chest vibrate with an approving growl.

I called it a growl because it didn't really match a purr, which was quite disappointing. For some reason, I was fixated on that need to hear him purr in that deep, rhythmical fashion cats normally did. Considering he wasn't actually a feline, it was a little bit narrow-minded and cliched of me to want that. But I couldn't help it. At a visceral level, I knew a proper purr from my husband would be beyond epic.

His arms loosened around me. Although I could have stayed in his embrace for hours, I reluctantly pulled away from him. To my surprise he leaned forward and pressed his lips to mine. It was brief, but although subtle, I still noticed the tiny twitch. I bit the inside of my cheeks not to chuckle.

"I have prepared breakfast for you," Gaelec said proudly, as he waved at the table. "I have thoroughly verified the cooking temperatures for everything. As we do not have many of the human ingredients for some of these dishes, I found the equivalent or at least what the recipe sites have deemed the closest thing to it."

"Oh, Gaelec! You're too sweet, but you didn't have to go through so much trouble," I said feeling both moved and guilty that he did all that work for me. "That's *a lot* of food! Usually, I only have a toast with some jam, a cup of coffee, and some fruits."

"Have no fear, my Ophelia. Whatever you cannot consume, I will take care of. But I also seized the opportunity to see which dishes you liked or not to get a better sense of what to make for you in the future. I also added some Nazhral recipes so that you could try them. As for coffee, it appears to be of importance to your people. There is none in the village, but I got confirmation that we can buy it in the city. I already placed an order, and it will be delivered in the morning."

"Wow! You really are the best," I said as we settled around the table. "I brought a bag just in case. But it wouldn't last me too long. I'm relieved to know I can get a steady supply right here."

As I took in the bounty before me, I couldn't believe how much work he managed to accomplish in record time while I was still zonked out in bed. The man truly went all out with his spin on a traditional continental breakfast with eggs, bacon, and hash-browns. The pancakes—both plain and another version with something similar to blueberries—were absolutely perfect, light and fluffy just the way I liked. Their spin on porridge wasn't exactly my cup of tea, but I'd never been a fan of porridge to begin with. He also provided a variety of breads, cold cuts and spreads as well as some fruits.

We enjoyed our meal in an amiable atmosphere. Too full to take another bite, I sipped on a glass of some sort of fruit juice while observing with awe my husband polish off everything else. How was he this lean and sexy when he so easily chowed down this insane amount of food?

To my relief, he didn't challenge my desire to help him clean up and wash the dishes, even though he clearly expected to do it on his own. While I loved getting pampered like anyone else, I also strongly believed in a couple being equal partners, not one person acting as a servant to the other.

We began our tour shortly thereafter. With people at work and the children in school, we enjoyed relatively quiet streets without me once again being subjected to everyone blatantly ogling me. As was often the case in the various tribes that I lived with, Nevian Village didn't have paved streets or sidewalks. They built the houses on each side of properly packed dirt roads. The nice leveling of the streets implied the involvement of some engineering instead of merely frequent use making it that way.

The buildings themselves offered an interesting mix of basic and modern. They made many of them out of wood, stone, and bricks. A few boasted what resembled some kind of processed siding. It vaguely reminded me of old school vinyl. The houses all possessed a single floor, aside from the occasional taller building—the majority of which appeared to have a commercial purpose.

"We're called the Nevian Pride," he explained as we casually strolled down the street under the shining morning sun and a gentle breeze softly blowing past us. "It's standard for a Pride to take the name of the region it settles in, and that it claims as its territory. We're currently in the Nevian Valley, which includes a large section of the forest to the east all the way to the beginning of the mountain range, a small part of the forest to the west, and extensive fishing rights to the Nevian River which you can see from the southern edge of the village."

"So does that make you more of a fishing or hunting Pride?" I asked with genuine curiosity.

"Mainly fishing," he replied before pointing at a tall building to the right. "This is the fish plant where we clean, process, and then ship most of our catches to the neighboring tribes and to the capital city. There's a pathway farther ahead that allows us to go down to the docks when we go fishing. That entire responsibility falls squarely onto the males."

"Your females do not fish?"

He shook his head. "Our females hunt in the forest. In truth, we are not as fond of fish. We prefer real meat from warm-blooded animals. Fish is simply an addition to our diet, and it's a steady source of income for the Pride. For a male, it is a great opportunity to earn the right to stay long past their prime when they proved to be the best or most efficient worker in one of the specialized side trades, like fishing, crafting, construction, tanning, smithing, and anything else you can think of to help meet the basic needs of the village."

"So females do not work in any trade or craft?" I asked as we walked past what resembled a convenience store.

"They do, but mostly older females. A lot of it revolves around things such as weaving, sewing, pottery, and various other low-intensity crafts that they will have no problem performing up to their retirement. At which point, the Pride will look after them until they pass. Females are the only people who always remain with their Pride until they die, unless their numbers become excessive, which is rare."

"Why is it rare?" I asked.

"The size of a Pride varies between one hundred to four hundred individuals. The average usually hovers closer to one hundred and fifty. The standard distribution is one third females, and one quarter males for adults, and the rest are younglings," Gaelec explained as we made our way in the general direction of the Great Hall. "Births usually result in two-thirds of male cubs, who leave around the age of eighteen."

"Wow, that's a surprisingly high percentage of males," I said pensively. "On Earth, the gender ratio also skews in favor of male births versus female. But it's barely a couple of percent higher. It's about 51% males."

He nodded. "Our females regulate the births to maintain a healthy population based on their needs and the availability of resources in the region. When we get close to the maximum population, the Queens only reproduce with the most prime males in the Pride in the hopes of getting the finest females possible, who will also be sent on their way to start their own Pride elsewhere, as soon as they reach maturity. On average, it requires at least ten to fifteen females to start a Pride."

"Damn. So they just go off like the queens of a hive and hope to find a new safe place to settle in on their own? Isn't that brutally hard?" I asked, flabbergasted.

He gave me an indulgent smile. "They're not just kicked out with nothing but their loincloths. Over the year leading up to their departure, they will start scouting the land for a suitable territory to claim. They will also start gathering resources and even begin construction. The Matriarchs will often dismiss some of their older, skilled males, who will eagerly offer their services to the young Queens."

I scrunched my face. "The younger Queens are saddled with older males as initial partners?!"

Gaelec burst out laughing. "Not at all. Those young Queens want nothing but the finest males to sire their first litters. The older males coming with them are usually their sires. It is the best possible situation for one of us to find ourselves in. The fathers of the Queens and Matriarchs of a new Pride usually get to stay with their daughters until their passing, unless they decide to leave to find themselves a new partner."

"I see. So does that mean that pregnancies are a group decision among your females?" I asked, disturbed by that prospect.

He smiled and shook his head. "The huntresses and Queens are free to mate with who they want and have offspring whenever they want. It only becomes a group decision once they get close to maximum population, or if the population drops too low. Speaking of which, this is the school."

"*The* school? As in there is only one school in the entire village?" I asked while eyeing the tall stone building, which appeared to have an impressive courtyard at the back.

He nodded. "There's only one school where cubs of both

genders study together until the age of ten. At that point, the males switch to learning crafts and trade, which they do directly through apprenticeships at the various specialized establishments."

I barely repressed a frown and forced a neutral expression on my face. "And what of the girls?"

He smiled at my use of the word 'girls' as it specifically referred to young human females. But he understood my meaning well enough.

"*Girls* will pursue more advanced education with regards to sciences like medicine, architecture, engineering, and general administration to make sure they will have the knowledge needed to keep their Pride prosperous and efficient. In both cases, males and females will also have hunting training in parallel."

"I see," I replied.

Although I understood their rationale for operating the way they did, it still troubled me how trapped and restricted their children were purely based on their genders.

"That said, some young males leave the Pride early," Gaelec added, his expression hinting that my own was revealing my discomfort with their customs.

"Why?"

"If they show a strong passion or interest for trades we're not specialized in, they will be redirected to other Prides who might be willing to take them in and teach them those trades," he explained.

I recoiled at that thought. "And the mothers are fine with that?!"

I instantly kicked myself for my failure to rein in my stupid mouth. Although he tried to smile with a nonchalant expression, I didn't miss the sad glimmer in his stunning blue eyes.

"Females do not get too attached to their sons. They treat us well and give us the best possible training before we set off. But as they know we will part ways sooner than later, never to see us again, there's no point in forming strong bonds."

"Never? You haven't spoken or seen your mother since you left your Pride?" I asked in a gentle tone.

He shook his head. "My mother likely thinks I'm dead. My younger brother, who's still with the Pride—at least he was when I last communicated with him—might have told her of my survival. But I somehow doubt it. As we usually have a short lifespan once we set off on our own, many prefer not to know what has befallen us. It's easier for them to grieve our loss the very moment we leave."

I stopped walking and turned to face him with a deep frown. He stopped as well and gave me an inquisitive look.

"The day I have children, I'll want to keep my son for however long he wants to stay, and for him only to leave once he's ready, not because some third party demands he does. I want my children to be able to come visit me whenever they want. We humans love and nurture all of our children. They're our babies forever, even after they're married and have a family of their own," I said with far more passion than I expected.

He nodded, his expression serious but also unreadable. "So I have read. It is in part for this reason that it is best we delay having offspring until our situation is properly sorted, and we have a better understanding of the future we will have."

I hated that his automatic response had not been to concur with me and clearly state that no one would force our children out of our home or prevent them from returning whenever they needed or wanted to. At the same time, I appreciated that he didn't try to make promises he potentially couldn't keep just to mollify me.

We resumed walking.

"With so many Queens going off to start their own Prides, don't you guys run out of land?" I mused aloud.

Gaelec shook his head. "There is tons of unclaimed land.

Some may be more challenging to develop than others, but I doubt we'll ever run out. Keep in mind that not all new Prides survive. In fact, many fail due to poor management, power struggles, their inability to stave off local predators, or a variety of other issues. On rarer occasions, long-standing Prides will gradually die off as they exhaust the local resources or become too stale to draw in new blood. There's a natural balance that occurs."

As we approached the intersection, increasing noises in the distance hinted at some intense activity nearby. As soon as we cleared the corner building, a large park I hadn't noticed upon our arrival opened before us. Multiple males moved about, setting things up as if in preparation for a concert or some sort of big outdoors event.

"They're putting the final preparations for tonight's feast. Within the next hour, they will start roasting three whole Sikkals to feed everyone, on top of a handful of other side dishes and meats," Gaelec explained as I stared in awe at the whole setup.

However, the males' serious—not to say grim—expressions clashed with the enthusiasm one would expect people to display when preparing for this type of festivities.

"Why do they all look so tense?" I asked as we kept walking past them.

"Because, as we speak, there are approximately thirty young males who have set up a camp at the edge of our territory with the intent of visiting us tonight," Gaelec said, matter-of-factly.

I cast a worried look at him. "Does that mean we should expect trouble?"

He snorted and shook his head. "No. They're not coming here to cause trouble but are hoping to be invited to join us." He gestured with his chin at the males in the park still working on the preparations. "They're worried about their position here. If enough fine candidates show up tonight, a few of these males will be asked to leave to make room."

"Does that include you?" I asked.

He shrugged. "It could. But you and I still have two weeks of my grace period remaining. Regardless of the outcome of tonight's feast, we will have to make a decision about our future."

Even as he spoke those words, three young huntresses arrived with a huge animal on a hover cart in tow. They headed towards one of the large barbecue spits the men were setting up.

I gave Gaelec a sideways glance. "They granted you a couple of days off to welcome me. But does it play against you that you're not helping them right now?"

He shook his head. "I made sure to perform more than my fair share in preparation for tonight ahead of time. It wasn't required, but it felt wiser to not give them any grounds to find me lacking."

"Smart male," I said with an approving smile.

"Let's go further down near the western edge of the village," Gaelec said, pointing in that general direction. "We have small farms there that are mostly operated by the males, but also by some of the females who can no longer hunt."

"You said that females are always looked after once they grow older and can no longer contribute. But do any of them ever get cast out?"

"Only for an extremely serious crime," he replied.

"Like what?" I insisted.

"Anything that threatens the safety or prosperity of the Pride is guaranteed expulsion," he explained.

"The safety of the Pride only? They've never come to blows over a male?" I couldn't resist asking in a slightly teasing tone.

He snorted. "For Nazhral females, no male is worth that much trouble. Don't forget that our Queens and Matriarchs are all close blood relatives. They will always choose each other over a male."

We spent the following couple of hours completing the tour

of the city before taking a stroll in the nearby forest where Gaelec showed me the places that were safe to visit on my own, and what limits to stay within. Although I made sure to mark the safe perimeter within my GPS, I had no intention of venturing outside the village on my own anytime soon.

CHAPTER 10
GAELEC

We made sure not to arrive too early or too late to the festivities. The Matriarchs and Oluina—as the head huntress—were sitting on the temporary dais put together for the occasion. The other females sat directly on the ground or on soft cushions in a half circle on each side of the platform. A large bonfire in the center of the area in front of the dais illuminated the space, as well as electric torches around the edges of the perimeter.

I led my mate to a spot at the end of the left half circle. The closer one sat to the dais, the higher their rank in the Pride's pecking order. As the Alpha, Moriak was the only male to settle right at its edge, next to Oluina.

I barely repressed the urge to snort as I took in his appearance. He donned his finest hunting armor. Even from where I sat, I could tell he oiled his fur to make it look shinier. I would bet a hefty amount of credits that he also applied some dye to make himself look younger. It was laughable. In a way, I felt pity for him and the desperation with which he clung to his position. His time was running out.

A smarter male would spend his remaining time endearing

himself to the young Queens who would soon leave us to form their own Pride. Granted, he could never hope to become the Alpha over there. But at least, it would spare him the uncertainty of becoming a nomad.

A loud squeal startled me out of my less-than-charitable musings about Moriak. I jerked my head towards the direction it emanated from, the sound having drawn the attention of most of the other people already present. My jaw dropped upon seeing Ylis running towards a male and throwing herself into his arms. That embrace screamed of a level of familiarity—not to say intimacy—that had everyone looking as stunned as I did.

"Whoa! Ylis has a boyfriend?!" Ophelia asked in a whisper, her eyes wide as she ogled the couple.

"I don't know," I replied in all sincerity while stretching my neck to get a better look at the newcomer.

From this angle, I could only see part of his side and his tail. But he looked tall and strong, the flickering and glare of the bonfire making it hard to see any proper details about him. Ylis released the male at last and took a couple of steps back to exchange a couple of words with him.

My back stiffened, and I did a double take, wondering if my eyes weren't playing tricks on me.

"Kazaer?!" I called out, my voice filled with disbelief.

The male jerked his head towards me. His initial curiosity upon hearing his name gave way to an affectionate smile once he recognized me.

He knew I would be here!

On instinct, I shot to my paws and ran towards him. His smile broadened as he also ran towards me. We collided with enough force that most people would have fallen over. I gave him a bone crushing hug, my heart filling to bursting as he reciprocated. I held him for a few moments, then slapped his back twice before releasing him. Both my hands still clutching his upper arms, I examined him from top to bottom.

"Look at you, little brother… all big and strong! And a Stellig, at that!" I exclaimed, an irrational sense of pride swelling within me as I took in his appearance.

Where I possessed grayish-brown fur and blue eyes, my younger brother was pure black with gray accents, and the same lightning-shaped stripes as I did, marking him as a Stellig. It had been nearly a year since I last communicated with him. It was normal as, having just turned eighteen, Kazaer would have freshly been evicted from the Pride. As a nomad searching for a new home, access to the type of com allowing him to send me messages all the way to Molvi would have been limited.

Now nineteen, if not for the difference in our fur shade, he could have been a copy of the young male I had been back then.

"Of course, I am. Just like my big brother," he said affectionately before stealing a glance at Ylis.

Could it be?!

It took every ounce of my willpower to maintain a neutral expression on my face. Instead, I forced myself to turn towards my mate. She was still where I had left her, although she was now standing, looking both curious and uncertain as to what to do. I smiled and gestured for her to approach. Ophelia immediately relaxed and returned my smile as she complied. Guilt gnawed at me to have abandoned her so abruptly like this. But seeing my brother, this unexpectedly after over thirteen years of separation, had blown me away.

"Ophelia, this is my younger brother, Kazaer. We share our mother from the Sulwyn Pride," I gently said to my mate, before glancing back at my brother. "Kazaer, meet Ophelia Moreau. She's not just my mate, but my soulmate, found for me, halfway across the stars, by the Temern Kayog Voln."

For the briefest instant, I feared my sibling might have a negative reaction to her. That thought had not crossed my mind when I first began the introductions. After so many years apart, I couldn't say how Kazaer evolved or what influences might have affected his perspective on the world and other species.

To my relief, although his eyes burned with obvious curiosity with a hint of awe, he gave her a friendly smile. "It is an honor to meet you, Ophelia Moreau, even though Kayog is quite a few years late in finding you. But good things always come when they are meant to arrive."

My mate's cheeks heated as she gave him a shy but grateful smile.

Kazaer returned his attention to me, this time with a mischievous glimmer in his blue eyes so identical to mine.

"Your mate is a good omen, Brother. It appears you have brought us one of Luen's daughters."

I burst out laughing while my mate unconsciously touched the freckles on her cheeks with that same adorably timid smile.

"I most certainly have. But you haven't told me how the two of you know each other," I asked, glancing in turn at Ylis and him.

"After your arrest, I came to recover some of your personal items I believed you would want to keep when you returned, like your Obsidian knife. Ylis gave them to me," Kazaer said, sounding like he was trying too hard to be nonchalant. "She and I kept in touch afterwards so that I could give her updates about your welfare."

To give her 'updates'? Yeah, right.

I bit my tongue not to say it, but I suspected my eyes spoke volumes judging by the way his nose twitched, a telltale sign for him of embarrassment.

"So are you only here to come see your big brother, or are you wishing to join our Pride?" I asked.

"Seeing how picky you are, I figured Nevian Pride might be a good place for me to settle… if they would have me."

The subtle way he glanced at Ylis when he added that last part confirmed my suspicions. My heart swelled at the possibility that two of the people I cared about the most might end up together. I couldn't have wished for a better female for Kazaer.

"That would be wonderful! See that you do our bloodline proud," I said, slapping his shoulder. "But come, sit with us before we get chastised for hogging the floor."

He smiled and fell in step with us. To my pleasant surprise—and to everyone's general shock—instead of taking a seat at her official place on the right side of the Matriarchs on the dais, Ylis sat down with us, next to my brother.

Ophelia's pleased smile confirmed she also perceived the chemistry between the two of them and approved of it. Feeling shameless and eager to help move things along in the right direction, I turned to my brother with a mischievous expression.

"I was supposed to run interference for Ylis tonight, in case some undesirables pestered her. But since I have a mate, that responsibility now falls onto you, Brother."

"A duty I am more than happy to tackle," he replied with a bit too much enthusiasm.

To my delight, the young huntress took on a demure expression I'd never seen on her before as she smiled timidly at my brother.

"You're most kind," she said softly.

"You can always count on me for anything you require," Kazaer said. "Never hesitate to ask."

I couldn't wipe the stupid grin off my face. It made no sense that I should feel like such a proud father, and yet I couldn't help it. This was turning out to be a wonderful start to an evening I dreaded since my return.

My eyes flicked to the other young males who were trickling in. I caught myself assessing the competition that Kazaer might face, although he clearly had a great head start on the others. Quite a few of the hopefuls had great potential. Throughout the night, our females would talk with the ones who piqued their interest to evaluate them. Those who successfully passed the personality test with enough females would be invited to return over the next few days to pass some skill tests. This not only involved their ability to fight wild beasts, but also their trade and crafting competences.

With everyone now gathered around the bonfire, the festivities began with a brief speech by the Head Matriarch welcoming everyone and reminding them that any misbehavior—especially from the visitors—would be met with a swift and harsh response.

And then our younglings took the central area to present a performance, the show including a mix of dance and battle choreographies. Although fascinated, my mate seemed confused by the intensity of some parts of that spectacle. It didn't take a genius to see it went beyond mere artistic expression. But she didn't understand the purpose.

I leaned in to whisper to her. "Males are not the only ones having to sell their worth. Our females must also demonstrate the quality of their Pride. This first part is to show what strong and healthy offspring they can birth, what great mothers they are, and the excellence of the education and training they can provide. At the end of the evening, you do not want a prime male to walk away to seek a different Pride because they were not impressed enough by what we have to offer."

Ophelia's eyes widened at this revelation. She had not considered that aspect. It wasn't surprising considering most of what she had heard and seen about us so far presented the males as being completely voiceless and helpless in all of this. While we undeniably enjoyed far less rights and opportunities, we were not entirely deprived of choices.

The cubs concluded their performance under loud cheers as their mothers—and the few sires still among us—puffed out their chests with good reason. For all my gripes with our Pride, I could never take away the great care and devotion every female showed the younglings. They were happy, healthy, and given all the tools they required for a bright future based on what our society deemed ideal—flawed though it was.

A few of the elder females herded the younglings back to the sidelines, a handful running back directly to their parents. Simultaneously, the Queens and huntresses—Ylis and Oluina included—took the stage. The tension Moriak failed to hide as Oluina made her way towards us gave me no small amount of malicious glee.

The rhythm of the drums and haunting melody of the flutes filled the air as the females launched into their own version of the dance and combat choreographies. It had an undeniably more sensuous and erotic edge to it as the females flaunted their assets. My joy at seeing Ylis exclusively perform in front of my brother was quickly dampened by Oluina nearly shoving Ylis out of the way so that she could dance in front of Kazaer and me.

Gasps and shocked murmurs reached my ears despite the loud music. As outraged as I felt by such shameless behavior, it pleased me that so many noticed and disapproved of such disrespect, especially towards my mate and me. Making a seductive spectacle in front of me implied that she did not recognize or respect my formal union with Ophelia. Doing the same in front of Kazaer was a bit more questionable.

The Queens and huntresses usually showed unspoken deference to each other by not pursuing a male one of them already clearly expressed her interest for, unless that male didn't reciprocate—which made him fair game again. Anyone with eyes could see that something was brewing between Ylis and Kazaer. In fact, quite a few of the Queens cast envious glances in my brother's direction but kept their distance as he had undeniably been claimed, and he gladly welcomed it. Oluina should set her sights elsewhere unless Kazaer blatantly rejected her cousin.

On top of that, the age gap was significant enough to raise eyebrows in a negative way. At thirty-four, Oluina was fifteen years older than my brother. So long as the youngest party had reached maturity, such a pairing was not forbidden. But as the general guidance recommended a gap no greater than five years, this specific instance stirred many disapproving frowns.

To my delight, although knowing that Oluina was the Head Huntress—Kazaer made it a point to ignore her. He ostensibly turned his body sideways to face Ylis. She had been forced to move slightly to the right to make room for her cousin rather than openly fighting Oluina over such rudeness. Most males would be beside themselves with excitement to have caught the eye of the Head Huntress. Unless they committed some kind of unforgivable blunder, winning her favors pretty much guaranteed their acceptance into a Pride.

Not wanting to grant her the attention she absolutely did not deserve from me either, I made a show of also turning away from Oluina to stare at my mate. She smiled at me in that way I was quickly growing addicted to, her green eyes flicking between mine. I smiled back and caressed her lips with my thumb before leaning down and kissing her. I didn't know if my aggravation with the wretched Head Huntress had dulled the extreme sensitivity of my whiskers, but this time, no itching or tickling ruined the moment.

Yes, my wife's lips felt wondrous against mine. I could get used to this and even crave it. I broke the kiss only to have Ophelia's gaze flick towards my nose. When it didn't twitch, her smile broadened even as her eyes widened in joyous surprise. I chuckled then leaned forward to rub my temple against hers, marking her with my scent. She beamed at me and then snuggled against my side. I wrap my arms around her, drawing her closer even as I wrapped my tail possessively around her waist.

An angry hiss reclaimed my attention. Her eyes throwing daggers at us, Oluina turned away in anger before stomping to another area where more of the young visitors were gathered as they enjoyed the show. Although I initially meant ignoring her as a clear message, kissing my mate had genuinely wiped Oluina from my thoughts. I could only hope, for her sake, that she would soon come to terms with the fact that whatever had existed between us was long dead and would never return.

As strange and mostly unappealing as I initially found Ophelia, I no longer doubted that she was my soulmate. The speed at which she had me melting for her was mind-boggling but also incredibly thrilling. I was falling for her, and finally seeing her beauty despite our differences.

With the females' dance finally ending, it was now the males' turn to prove their worth. Their performance had a clear battle focus to it. It was mainly a show of dexterity, strength, flexibility, and speed.

The young visitors couldn't have gotten up quickly enough, many of them making a beeline for the females who had caught their attention the most. Despite how she had shamed herself, Oluina still had a respectable number of candidates crowding in front of her to try and gain her favor. Yet it remained far less than how many her cousin attracted. Older males, already members of our Pride, but who feared imminent expulsion, also joined the dance to prove that they compared and maybe even surpassed some of the newcomers.

For all that, Kazaer crushed any potential competition. He was so insanely impressive that even Ophelia gaped at him in awe. The silly insecure part of me almost regretted not taking part in it to show off my own skills to her. But it might have sent the wrong signal that I was open to other females' attentions, which would have been a slap to my mate.

"He's magnificent, don't you agree?" Ophelia asked Ylis, who was all but drooling at my brother.

A silly grin settled on my lips when the young huntress nodded vigorously.

"The best we've seen since I've been old enough to actually care," she admitted timidly.

It was a relief considering how many other males came

around where we sat to try and catch Ylis's attention. But she only had eyes for my brother. Moriak was livid. A part of me was surprised he chose not to perform, especially seeing how Oluina was openly expressing her willingness to pair with someone else. At the same time, considering the fitness level of the new candidates—particularly my brother—the Alpha would have been put to shame. The last thing he needed was to further draw attention to the fact that he was no longer in his prime, by Nazhral standards.

With the last dance concluded, food was finally served during which males and females mingled and engaged in discussions that could lead to some formal invitations.

"I'll be right back, my mate," I said, caressing her cheek before heading towards the table near the spits where meat was being cut off the Sikkals.

I grabbed one large piece from it, and a raw steak from the bowl of pre-cut Padag. After rubbing some spices on the latter, I brought them over to one of the skillets sitting near the multiple small cooking pits. People could use them to sear some of the seafood and other slabs of meat for a few seconds before consumption. Seeing me slap the 'already cooked' Sikkal steaks drew countless bewildered stares my way.

My ears flicked this way and that to better listen to the growing murmurs around me. I repressed a smile at the countless dismayed whispers as people wondered if I had lost my mind. When they saw me put the steaks on the plate and proudly stroll back to my mate, their disbelief cranked up another notch.

Kazaer frowned as he looked at the contents of the plate before gaping back at me.

"Isn't that a little burnt, Brother?" he asked cautiously.

"It appears Gaelec is trying to murder his human mate!" Moriak exclaimed loudly enough for all to hear, before I could answer.

"No, *Alpha*," I said, pouring as much disdain and mockery as

I could in his title. "I'm merely catering to my mate's specific human needs when it comes to cooked meat."

Paying him no more mind, I extended the plate to Ophelia, who accepted it with a smile.

"I studied cooking temperatures this morning. This Padag meat compares to Earth's lamb. I rubbed on it the closest mix of the herbs and spices your people deem preferable for it."

Ophelia nodded with an air of gratitude before reaching for the piece of Padag and taking a bite from it. She closed her eyes and emitted a moan that resonated directly in my cock.

After chewing for a few moments, she opened her eyes to look at me with awe. "Wow! That cook is perfect!" she exclaimed before taking another voracious bite.

I puffed out my chest while smugly glancing at the crowd. Their stunned looks failed to please me half as much as Moriak's livid expression.

This truly wasn't his night.

To my surprise, a cub named Armiss came sniffing around, his little nostrils flaring even as he stared at the meat with an air of confusion.

"Do you want to try?" Ophelia offered in a gentle tone.

"It's burnt?" the youngling asked hesitantly.

My mate smiled. "It's not burnt. It's just cooked in the perfect way for humans. Here, taste it."

Despite his suspicions that it would likely taste foul, the young male leaned forward and took a tiny bite. The slit of his pupils dilated as his face took on a pleasantly surprised expression. The hesitant way he'd begun chewing gave way to enthusiasm as he quickly swallowed.

"Whoa! It's not burnt, even if it looks like it. That's not bad!" the little one exclaimed.

He then went for another bigger bite.

"Hey!" I exclaimed with false outrage. "That's my mate's food!"

The little brat stared at me with an unrepentant expression as he happily chewed the large piece he just bit off.

"I don't mind," Ophelia said with a chuckle while looking tenderly at Armiss.

"Yes, you do," I grumbled, with playful displeasure. "Or at least, you will once you realize what a bottomless pit he is."

The young cub made a face at me as he swallowed his mouthful. Then, to my utter shock, he snuggled against my mate's side. The way her face melted from a powerful emotion at this unexpected gesture turned me upside down. She caressed the top of his head before scratching the back of his ears. A loud purr vibrated from his little throat as he snuggled deeper against her. She smiled at me with an air of pure joy. At that moment, I realized she was picturing our own offspring cuddling with her.

It awakened an intense longing in me.

We will have a family of our own.

"How come you never purr like that?" Ophelia suddenly asked.

I glanced at Armiss before looking back at her. "I'm not a cub."

"That shouldn't prevent you from purring. I'm sure it would sound amazing with your deep voice. Won't you let me hear it?" she asked, shamelessly batting her eyelashes.

It struck me then that I truly never purred anymore. It hadn't been a conscious choice, but one dictated by my survival instincts. Considering the therapeutic quality of that sound—since its frequency promoted healing—you'd think I'd use it more often. But our people also only purred when they felt in a safe enough environment to put their guard down and give themselves over to that self-healing. It broadcast to the world that you were in a vulnerable position but trusted that no harm would come to you here.

I had not felt safe enough for that in the past twelve years.

As much as I wanted to please my mate, the prospect of

purring made my stomach queasy, especially in such a public setting, and surrounded by so many hostile people.

"Purr," I said in a neutral voice.

Ophelia gaped at me. Although I managed to keep a stoic expression, I inwardly also gaped at myself. I couldn't believe I'd just blurted that out instead of coming up with a clever way of worming my way out of doing it.

Recovering from the shock, my mate burst out laughing before giving me a playful tap. "That's not a proper purr, you cheater!"

Her amusement helped dampen my embarrassment, which in turn allowed my brain to start functioning normally again.

"That's the only one you shall get for now," I deadpanned. "A purr must be earned. Not provided on demand. You'll need to figure out how to draw one out of me."

Ophelia's eyes widened for a split second before her gaze darkened. Although my comment held no lurid undertone, the lascivious expression that descended over my mate's face clearly indicated she interpreted it that way. It instantly sent my blood rushing to my groin.

"Challenge accepted," she whispered in a voice full of promise.

I shifted, my breeches suddenly feeling a little tight. Clearing my throat, I got up to release some of the pressure.

"I will go cook more meat for you and bring some of the sides while I fetch a plate for myself," I said.

She nodded with a mischievous smile, visibly aware of how her comment affected me. It broadened when I scrunched my face, and she resumed eating as I headed back to the spits. By the time I returned, at least seven more cubs—mostly males—were piled up against my woman. Many eyes were stealing approving glances her way, including Rozel. Being accepted by the cubs was primordial. They were the heart and future of any Pride.

Their strong survival instincts naturally drove them away from threats while drawing them towards those who were safe.

A wave of affection swelled within me as I settled back down next to my woman, careful not to inadvertently squish one of the countless little tails.

But the sound of a shuttle overhead broke the magic of the moment. Seeing Moriak perk up before hastily rushing towards the landing pad had my insides immediately twisting with apprehension. Anything that made him happy was a bad sign.

Minutes later, my fears were confirmed when he returned with Ranor, the recruiter.

CHAPTER 11
OPHELIA

The moment Moriak returned with a fancy-looking older male, my husband immediately tensed. I studied Gaelec's face for a few moments, as if it would reveal the source of what almost looked like anger before shifting my gaze back to the newcomer.

I didn't know Nazhrals enough to be able to evaluate their ages for certain, but I estimated that male to be in his mid-fifties. Aside from his age, he seemed much too rich to possibly be a candidate. Unlike the other males who wore skin-tight shorts to the middle of their thighs with a loincloth over it, usually adorned with some kind of pattern or symbol, Moriak's companion had donned a much looser set of trousers with a silky dark fabric that fell right to his knees. The silver embroidery on both the hem of the pants and on the even fancier loincloth with a gem encrusted belt screamed excess and a propensity to show off his wealth.

His tri-colored fur made him look like a calico cat with the patches of white, orange, and black. His yellow eyes peered with an excited and almost calculating glimmer at the people in attendance. Something about him immediately felt slimy. The first thought that popped to mind was con artist. For some reason, the fact that he appeared to be on such great terms with the Pride's Alpha reinforced the distrust he inspired.

What can he possibly want with us?

Whatever it was, Gaelec appeared to know, and it pissed him off to no end. He seemed even angrier than when Oluina pushed his buttons yesterday after I first arrived.

"Dear members of the Pride and guests, for those of you who haven't met my esteemed friend before, please allow me to introduce you to Ranor Dolmen," Moriak said with the excessive enthusiasm of the host of some major event as he introduced the special guests to the crowd. "He is one of the highest-ranking recruiters in all of Melelyn. Because of the deep friendship he and I have developed over the years, he has agreed to come give you an exclusive first notice of a few highly lucrative missions that will take place in the next few days."

My stomach dropped as I finally understood the reason for my mate's simmering anger. A wave of panic swelled within me. What did that mean for him? As a member of the Pride, was participation in these missions compulsory if the Alpha demanded it? There was no doubt in my mind that Moriak would attempt to send Gaelec on the next one, likely hoping he would get caught or killed in the process.

I wanted to believe my man's palpable fury was a sign that he had absolutely no intention of allowing himself to be lured back into this mess, whatever punishment or threat they might levy against him.

To my dismay, Kazaer perked up, and leaned forward with an air of excitement.

"This could be good," he whispered to himself.

Gaelec gasped and jerked his head towards his brother with an air of complete outrage and disbelief.

"Absolutely not!" Gaelec snapped at his brother. "Are you insane?!"

Sandwiched between the two males, I felt myself wither as the cubs still snuggling against me began to stir. Kazaer recoiled, stunned by his older brother's strong reaction. Next to him, Ylis looked extremely troubled. But I couldn't say whether it was my husband's outburst that unsettled her, the news of the imminent mission, or a mix of both.

"What's wrong, Gaelec?" Moriak called out in a mocking tone. "Is that panic I hear in your voice? Would you happen to be suffering from PTSD from your failed mission?"

To my relief, instead of going completely berserk on that taunting idiot—as I personally wanted to—Gaelec reined himself in and simply leveled the most contemptuous stare at the Alpha.

"It's not panic but complete stupor that you would be so gullible or careless as to once again jeopardize the welfare and future of the Pride by taking the first bait of your so-called *recruiter*," my mate retorted, gesturing with disdain at the fancy male as he pronounced that last word. "Tell us, Recruiter Ranor, would that excessively lucrative mission involve the Levendoc Corp?"

The extreme shock on the older male's face—too slowly hidden—and the way his body stiffened confirmed Gaelec had hit a nerve.

"You've already heard?" the recruiter asked in a tone that he tried hard to keep nonchalant, even though it was more of a statement.

He struck me as someone trying to buy time and to find out how much Gaelec knew before he tipped his own hand.

"I have. And I can tell you that this highly lucrative mission is in fact the biggest trap ever set among a series of countless others," Gaelec snarled, eliciting shocked gasps from everyone in attendance.

"What are you talking about?" Ranor asked, in a tone that implied my man was mentally unwell.

But the sliver of nervousness in his voice—subtle though it

was—had every single one of my senses on high alert. The fact —or at least the possibility—that this mission could indeed be a trap was not news to him.

"What I'm talking about is the fact that the members of the galactic alliance are beyond fed up with the epidemic of pirate raids against their ships and merchandise. The Enforcers are launching a massive crackdown against all criminal activities linked in any way to smuggling, hijacking, piracy, and slave trading among others. All those attacks are costing corporations and individuals way too much, making traveling and their businesses unsustainable, not to mention the innocent lives lost on all sides."

Moriak huffed and cast a contemptuous look at Gaelec as if he was some weak and sniveling little boy.

"Why do you care so much about the woes of some random off-worlders?" he asked in a haughty tone. "Their inability to protect their goods is on them. Ever heard of survival of the fittest? Have they brainwashed you into looking after their best interests instead of those of your Pride? That would explain why you returned looking so pretty from Molvi... assuming you even actually served your time there."

It took every ounce of my willpower not to give that son of a bitch an epic tongue lashing for such spiteful and snide remarks. It infuriated me when quite a few people narrowed their eyes at my husband, the seed of suspicion having been planted.

"I cannot decide if you truly are this stupid and narrow-minded to actually believe the nonsense you just spewed, or if you're so desperate to paint me in a bad light for fear I might supplant you that you would stoop to such ridiculous conspiracy theories," Gaelec replied with an air of pity rather than the righteous anger he would be entitled to.

"See how he avoided answering the challenge?" Moriak said triumphantly, glancing at everyone in attendance to take them as witnesses.

"I indeed give a shit about the off-worlders' woes to the extent that their logical responses to the constant losses they sustain will directly ruin or destroy the lives of our people. But you're too dense to realize that. Although I think it is specifically what you're counting on," Gaelec said, his tone hardening.

"What the fuck is that supposed to mean?" Moriak hissed.

"Simply the fact that most of the missions offered by the recruiters are guaranteed jail time for the males foolish enough to sign up for them, especially this one," Gaelec snarled.

"You don't know that!" Ranor interjected, sounding defensive. "I have excellent sources."

Gaelec snorted with disdain. "I most certainly do know it is a trap. Your sources are so excellent that my own sources warned me more than three weeks ago that this fake mission would soon be making the rounds. How do you explain *that, Recruiter* Ranor?"

"Ranor never failed us," Moriak argued.

"He and others like him certainly failed me!" Gaelec snapped. "He failed Argin, Lomar, and countless others. But if you're so confident about his reliability, does that mean you will join in on that mission, Moriak?"

I bit my lip to keep myself from blurting out the 'Take that, *Enfoiré*!' comment that burned my tongue. But I couldn't stop myself from grinning maliciously at his shocked expression.

"I'm the Alpha!" Moriak immediately countered. "My place is here, watching over the Pride."

Gaelec shook his head with an air of pure disgust. "How did I know you were going to spew such a weak argument? You always let us take the risks while you hide behind our females."

"I do not hide behind anyone!" Moriak shouted angrily. "Your past traumatic experience made you skittish, and now you're seeing danger everywhere. Do not unload your burden on the rest of us."

"I'm not being skittish, merely no longer being stupid. You

boast about your friend Ranor being so reliable, but has he informed you of how the new anti-piracy laws directly impact every Pride now?"

"What laws?" Rozel intervened with a hint of concern.

Gaelec turned to look at her. "Convicted pirates now automatically go to a Gray or Dark Quadrant, with a minimum sentence of fifteen years. Where before, the sector in which you were captured influenced which prison you would land in, it is now a guaranteed trip to Molvi. I was in a Light Quadrant for the past twelve years, and it was a nightmare. Gray Quadrants are nearly impossible to survive, but a Dark one is a guaranteed death sentence."

He turned to look at the young males visiting the village for the feast, making eye contact with as many of them as possible.

"If you cubs want to die, then by all means join this doomed mission."

"Stop being dramatic!" Rozel exclaimed in a harsh tone.

"I WAS THERE!!" Gaelec shouted.

The Matriarch took a deep breath and forced herself to take on a sympathetic expression as if addressing a child being difficult.

"We know, Gaelec. And although you may not believe it, we do empathize with the hardships you endured. But whatever the outcome, every Pride needs for our people to go on those missions. Obviously, we want each one of them to succeed so that our males can come home with their full wages. However, even in the case of a failure, the Pride still benefits from their contribution."

"I know that all too well," Gaelec snarled, which had the Matriarch lift her chin defiantly. "It is shameful that it should be deemed acceptable to use these so-called missions as a means to sell us off as slave labor."

"Tread carefully, Gaelec Sulwyn!" Rozel warned.

"Or what? Is truth to be silenced now as well? How about

you ask your Alpha's friend how that exploitation of our youth and labor is at an end now? Sacrificing us will no longer benefit the Pride. The Obosians have seen to it."

Every eye turned towards the recruiter, who shifted uneasily on his paws...

"What do you mean?" Ranor asked with an air of pretend confusion that fooled no one.

"Are you pretending that you haven't heard of the new laws recently passed regarding prisoner wages?" Gaelec asked with an almost cruel smile.

When the recruiter failed to respond quickly enough, my husband addressed the entire audience.

"For those of you who do not know, Argin was a member of this Pride long before I joined you. He was arrested during a mission and served his time in the Light Quadrant of Lord Amreth's sector. I ended up going there as well after my incarceration. He became both a mentor and a friend. It is to him that I owe surviving my ordeal over there and returning unscathed, against all odds."

"We're not here for tales!" Moriak interrupted.

"Silence!" Gaelec snapped, his muscles bunching as if he was readying to go on the offensive.

"We would hear what he has to say," Ylis intervened when Moriak opened his mouth to respond. "Go on, Gaelec."

Despite his obvious desire to challenge the young huntress, the Alpha wisely kept his mouth shut. I could have given her a freaking bone crushing hug. Anyway, judging by the expressions on every face, the rest of the Pride also wanted to hear what was going on. As was often the case with species living in more of a tribal setting, learning what was happening outside of their closed circuit could be quite challenging, even with connectivity.

Gaelec cast a grateful look at Ylis before continuing. "He was released three years ago and returned home. Some of you may remember him," he said, eliciting a few nods from both males and females. "Less than a month after his return, he was forced to participate in another mission because all the credits he earned over more than a decade of hard labor on Molvi was appropriated and spent by the Pride. He had nothing to live off of or to use over time as his contribution, now that he was too old for the types of work expected of him here."

My chest constricted for the poor older male. After surviving Molvi, he deserved a peaceful retirement with the credits he earned. It was criminal that they just took everything and then expected him to provide again or face expulsion.

Judging by the expressions of the people around me, there seemed to be conflicting emotions on that topic. Some of them, especially the younger females, appeared to find it normal. They were undoubtedly raised to think that way, while some of the elders better related to how their bodies slowing down would set an unfair burden on them had they been in his situation.

"As you know, that mission failed. For a second-time offender, the sentence was automatically a Gray Quadrant—although that is now changed to the Dark Quadrant. Argin died within a month of his new incarceration. This never should have happened. He had more than paid his due. But the Pride condemned him in the hopes of continuing to receive his wages while he suffered."

"That was not the intention!" Rozel exclaimed with outrage.

"No, but it was an outcome you were very comfortable with, if it came to that. So long as the Pride got its cut, you were fine with it damning him, thinking it would simply be the same as before. But that time is over," Gaelec shouted, taking us all aback.

"Are you threatening us?" Rozel asked in a dangerously low voice, that had everyone—including me—suddenly feeling extremely nervous.

"I'm not making any threat, Matriarch. I'm simply informing you of what your so-called Alpha and that sorry excuse of a recruiter are hiding from you and everyone else," Gaelec replied with a disdainful gesture. "Following this incident, Lord Amreth proposed a new law that has now been instituted to make sure Prides will no longer have access to any of the wages earned by the prisoners. Although exceptions can be made for those who have younglings and spouses to help, a maximum percentage will need to be authorized after proper validation of such a need has been established."

"That's a lie!" Moriak exclaimed. "We're still receiving wages for incarcerated members of the Pride."

"Not for long, and certainly not from Molvi," Gaelec retorted with contempt. "In case your tiny brain didn't register it, I mentioned that going forward, all pirates will go straight to Molvi, regardless of which sector they were captured in. And every other galactic penitentiary that is part of the UPO is in the process of implementing a similar law. But don't take my word for it. The law was implemented on Molvi three years ago, which is when you stopped receiving my wages, which led many of you to believe I was dead. But for the record, Lomar and Gulan are still alive in Lord Kronos's Light Quadrant. Have you seen any of their wages?"

"My son lives?!" one of the elder females exclaimed, her palm pressed to her chest.

It was my first time seeing one of them actually express concern for males who had left the Pride. I had begun to believe they truly didn't see males as people, but merely tools. This gave me hope that things could eventually change for the better.

"He does. And from what I understand, he's faring decently well and—like I did—seizing the opportunity to learn new trades and acquiring new skills that will give him a chance at a better future once he regains his freedom. The funds being safely set aside will give him the extra leg up needed for success."

My chest constricted further upon seeing that female's eyes misting and her lips stretching into a quivering smile. However messed up I found their society to be, this mother loved her child.

"These new laws are meant to be a deterrent by making sure Prides will no longer profit from crimes, even when they failed," Gaelec continued before turning his attention towards Moriak with something akin to hatred. "Therefore, Alphas will need to come up with new ways to get rid of their competition since selling them as slave labor to prisons will no longer work."

"This is slander!" Moriak hissed, taking a menacing step towards Gaelec.

My back stiffened, and the tension in the park became palpable. To my dismay, too many people perked up, looking almost as if they wanted this escalation. My heart skipped a beat when Gaelec also took a menacing step forward. I almost reached out to grab his hand and pull him back. But I knew better than to interfere. I only prayed that the amazing restraint he'd displayed since my arrival would prevail.

"Is it?" Gaelec challenged. "Am I the only one who finds it funny that most of the missions with the biggest failures only occurred right after a feast with particularly promising candidates, or when a young male started becoming a significant threat to your position?"

"Tread carefully, Gaelec," Moriak threatened, echoing the Matriarch's earlier words.

"Or what?" Gaelec repeated, like he had with Rozel. "Will you challenge me to a duel? Right here and now?"

"Gaelec!" I exclaimed in a whisper, panic settling in.

I didn't fear that he might lose. Although I'd never seen either male in battle, I knew with an inexplicable certainty that my husband would make mincemeat out of his opponent. But I also believed it would open the biggest and stinkiest can of worms possible with consequences I doubted we wanted to deal with.

"Gaelec, are you challenging Moriak as our new Alpha?" Rozel asked.

To my utter shock, instead of being outraged as she asked the question, Rozel seemed almost eager for it to be the case. The calculating glimmer in her eyes didn't bode well. Despite how much she was clearly butting heads with my husband, I was getting a strong impression that she still wanted him to become their new Alpha, or at least to use him to get rid of the current one.

Moriak visibly blanched. Even though he tried to hide it, it was clear to me that he also believed he couldn't win. Judging by the expressions on multiple faces, the Pride believed it as well.

I held my breath as the silence stretched. A cruel smile settled on my husband's lips as he stared down his nemesis. Although I couldn't blame him for enjoying watching the foul male sweat, it nevertheless unnerved me. More disturbing still were the hopeful looks from both Kazaer and Ylis. My mind raced as I tried to assess how it would change our lives if he battled Moriak and won. I couldn't see him and the Matriarch ever seeing things eye to eye. Was I just being pessimistic? After all, I had been here less than forty-eight hours. Maybe once I got to know her better—assuming I ever got the opportunity—she might turn out to be far more flexible than she appeared so far.

"Despite Moriak's constant fear that I will challenge him, I have never held such ambitions," Gaelec said at last, contempt dripping out of his voice. "But I will no longer stand by while we're sacrificed and taken advantage of."

"Your place among us isn't secure that you should be stirring so much trouble," Oluina said, her voice filled with bitterness and anger.

"It isn't," Gaelec conceded, totally unfazed. "But while I am still a member, I will not be silent. I owe our youth a truth I wished I could have benefited from. Other mature males may be content to accept whatever fate throws at them, but I believe in shaping my own future rather than being a victim to it."

In that instant, I realized my mate had made his peace with the likelihood that he would leave. A part of me rejoiced at that prospect while another struggled with it. Leaving felt like a failure.

"We hear your words well, Gaelec," Rozel said with a hint of reluctance. "But a Pride cannot survive without the resources and credits derived from missions."

"They do not have to be illegal or involve piracy!" Gaelec objected. "There are tons of legal options out there. I've done my research. Countless traders and other businesses are constantly on the lookout for hired hands for temporary work. Why are these not the missions being brought to us by the Alpha? These would provide the extra revenue needed without putting our lives in jeopardy. Just like every female wants to come home after a hunt, we want to do the same after a mission. Is that too much to ask?"

Murmurs of approval greeted his words.

"Gaelec makes a good point," I blurted out, my mind racing upon hearing his words.

I hadn't meant to inject myself in a debate that could fundamentally reshape their society, but my damn mouth had a will of its own. With every eye now locked on me, I just decided to go for it.

"As you may have heard, I've spent the past decade performing charity and missionary work alongside various primitive species. I worked alongside the Sangoths for a couple of years. They are a Yeti-like species. They are big, furry giants who live in the mountains and cold areas," I specified in response to the confused glances they gave me upon hearing that name. "Nazhrals would be perfect for performing deliveries or assisting with construction work over there. As I understand it, your people can heat cold air through your noses and can with-stand intense low temperatures."

Many heads nodded in response. Seeing them raptly attentive to my words spurred me on.

"With your claws, dexterity, fantastic hunting skills and swimming abilities, you exceed the minimum requirements for countless temporary work opportunities. Few people want to take on those jobs because they lack too many of the necessary attributes that you naturally possess. Therefore, wages tend to be on the higher end to lure potential candidates."

Ranor huffed, displeased by my intervention. "Those are month-long missions. Some of them can even drag for an entire year. The pay over the period comes down to a lot less than what they would earn over a couple of missions that would only last a few days."

"Assuming they actually survive that mission," I retorted harshly. "I would rather let my husband and the sons I hope to have one day be gone for three months to a year in exchange for the certainty that they will return safely home to me, even if that means with a smaller pay. No amount of *possible* higher wages justifies gambling with their lives and the likelihood that they could be killed or jailed for more than fifteen years. And now, with the new law making sure their prison wages will be untouchable, it makes even less sense to play with their lives."

"There's no pride or glory in this menial work you're trying to push on us," Moriak snarled.

Gaelec opened his mouth to tear into the Alpha, but I clasped his forearm to stop him, my gaze still levelled with contempt at the despicable male.

"Because there is pride to be gained in jumping headfirst into a mission that was doomed to fail to begin with? Because there is glory in stealing and killing? Sending your youth to waste away in a prison is a bragging right to you?" I challenged. "I find you extremely callous to be pushing for such dangerous practices while putting the lives of others on the line even as you remain safely tucked away here."

"I have done plenty of missions of my own, human! Your presumptions scream of your ignorance. I have earned my position," Moriak snapped.

"Do you even remember what it was like to be in their place? Because from what I've seen and heard so far, you appear to have either forgotten or stopped caring. What shame would there be in doing the kind of work I mentioned? How is it any different than the work males perform here for the Pride? You build, hunt, cook, fetch and deliver goods to and from the village. It would be the same! The difference is that instead of gambling on risky missions that randomly come up, this would be a far more reliable, safe, and steady source of income. As the Alpha, isn't it your duty to protect *all* the members of your Pride, including the males?"

"You do not know our ways, human," Oluina snarled.

"But she is learning them," Ylis interjected. "And above all, she's bringing a fresh perspective regarding markets we know nothing about. If Gaelec is right about those new rules—and I do not doubt his words for a moment—then our Pride must adapt to ensure its survival. Why should we keep sacrificing our males in vain?"

My heart soared when many heads nodded their agreement, with quite a few assessing glances flicking between my mate and me. I didn't know these people enough yet to accurately interpret their reaction, but they seemed to be warming up to these ideas.

"The reality is that the last few missions have indeed been catastrophic, and not just for us," Ylis continued in a somber tone. "Gaelec and Ophelia made very good points. Why wait for recruiters to come to us with missions we know nothing about and that cause us to lose our sires, mates, sons, and siblings? Why should we leave our fate in the hands of others instead of reclaiming that control? We could seek out potential hiring partners ourselves and get some variety."

"That's absurd!" Moriak exclaimed. "We know nothing about such things. There are complex contracts involved that we wouldn't even begin to know how to negotiate."

"Recruitment is a specialty profession for a reason," Ranor concurred vehemently. "You try to handle it yourself and could end up selling these males into permanent indentured servitude!"

"Isn't that what your own missions are already doing to us, except sending us to the worst prison in the galaxy?" Gaelec growled. "You both only oppose this because you get a cut for all the males you help recruit. We're no longer your easy source of income. If you want to continue benefiting from us, find safe missions."

"Enough!" Rozel snapped, visibly exasperated. "You have raised some valid questions and provided great insight. We shall investigate the matter later at a far more appropriate time. For now, we are here to celebrate and mingle. Let us eat, drink, and be merry."

Although my mate looked like he itched to pursue the debate, he wisely bowed his head in concession. Careful not to squish the cubs who still surrounded me, he sat back down next to me. Reassured that the conflict was over, the little ones snuggled with each other again.

The festivities resumed, although some tension lingered. We spent most of the remainder of the evening with Kazaer and Ylis. He turned out to be an absolute delight. The chemistry between them was undeniable and filled both Gaelec and me with joy. If things worked out, I would love to have this couple with us.

However, I didn't miss the speculative glances many of the visiting males cast our way, and in particular at my husband. His words had not fallen on deaf ears. They also realized Moriak was not necessarily the Alpha they should try to cozy up to. The next few days would be quite interesting.

To my shock, as we prepared to go home, Gaelec informed me that his brother could not come stay with us until a verdict was rendered as to whether he would receive a formal invitation to join us. All the visiting males were escorted back to their temporary camp at the edge of the Pride's territory. They would remain there for approximately a week or two as they went through the vetting and admission process.

In retrospect, it made sense not to want to have potentially problematic people freely roaming around their village, putting their younglings at risk of harm.

We waved goodbye to him while promising to make time for visits. To my delight, Gaelec took my hand and held it as we walked back home. He'd seemed so grumpy and distant in that space port that I never would have pictured him as the type to be cool with public displays of affection. I loved how proudly he displayed our relationship, despite the obvious reservations from his people. It touched me all the more that his gestures always struck me as spontaneous and not calculated. He wasn't putting on a show to placate anyone, but simply allowing whatever was happening between us to flourish.

We made the short trip home in silence, each of us lost in our own thoughts. For all that, there was no tension or awkwardness. At the same time, I believed we both unconsciously realized the kind of conversations we might want to have would be best left to a more private setting.

As soon as we entered our house, and he closed the door, I turned to face him. He held my gaze unwaveringly, his face telling me to go right ahead and speak whatever was on my mind.

"You've decided to leave, haven't you?" I asked in a soft voice devoid of condemnation.

He pursed his lips and gave it a moment of thought before responding. "I wouldn't say that. Had you asked me that question before the feast, I might have said no. I can't quite swear to it, but I was heavily leaning that way."

"What changed? The recruiter?"

He shook his head. "His presence plays a part in it, but he's only one of the symptoms, not the root cause of the disease eating us from within. Kazaer changed everything. I must protect him. You saw his enthusiastic reaction when Moriak introduced Ranor. Like every young male, he's been brainwashed into believing that running a few successful missions is your ticket to earning the favors of the most desirable Queen or even a Head Huntress. I can do for him and other young nomads what no one did for me before it was too late. This cycle needs to end."

Closing the distance between us, I smiled as I slipped my arms around his waist. He drew me into his embrace and gazed at me with affection.

"I love the ideas you proposed, and I want to help you make it happen. With my experience in charity and missionary work, I can reach out to my contacts to help us find legitimate recruiters once you go back to work. They could provide us with a list of solid, safe, and well-paying missions that could further help you make the case with the Matriarchs."

"That would be wonderful, my mate," Gaelec said gratefully. "I've been looking into some of the rehabilitation resources for ex-convicts and hoping to find assistance from their crime prevention services."

My eyes widened. "That's a great idea, too! There's no question they would want to help, especially with programs targeting the Nazhral youth. I think you're onto something big!"

The look in his eyes wrecked me. It was this mix of gratitude and another powerful emotion that I couldn't put into words. I just knew that my response deeply touched him.

"You truly are my Luen," he whispered while caressing my cheek. "A blessing and a guiding light in the darkness."

"*You* are the guiding light, Gaelec," I said in a gentle but firm voice. "These are your ideas. And I will do my best to help you make them come true because I believe in their merit. You could make a huge difference for your Pride and in the lives of countless young males. And tonight, a lot of people realized it as well. It amazed me how badass you were, standing up to those two idiots. You're a true leader. Not only by your authority and charisma, but because you put the people before yourself. And everyone saw it. I'm so proud of you."

"As I am of you, my mate," Gaelec replied with a fervor that made me weak in the knees. "You handled this entire mess and Oluina's rudeness with such grace. You speak of my charisma, but you do not realize the extent of your own. Our younglings are instinctively very cautious and suspicious of strangers. They didn't just approach you unbidden, but they also piled around you. A couple of them even fell asleep. It is the greatest sign of trust. You welcomed my brother like he was your own, and above all, you stood by me unwaveringly. You will never know what it meant to me that you should have my back like that."

"Always, Gaelec. Always. For better or for worse, until death do us part, I will stand by you," I pledged.

"My mate..." he whispered, before leaning down and rubbing his temple against mine.

Without another word, he picked me up like a bride and carried me to our room.

CHAPTER 12
GAELEC

The flame of desire didn't so much spark as flare up with surprising intensity as soon as I rubbed my temple against my woman's. The irrational need to mark her with my scent, to brand her as mine took hold of me with the strength that left me reeling. Throughout the evening, the possessiveness she stirred in me increased with every passing minute.

I didn't understand how she gained so much power over me in such a short time. It was especially confusing since she hadn't used any of the tricks other females usually did. Obviously, the fact that she hadn't listed any demands or conditional promises made her even more enticing to my eyes. But there was just something about her, about the way she smiled, looked at me, and made me feel simply with her presence that had become incredibly addictive.

Every time she brushed against me, whether by accident or intentionally, I immediately began craving her embrace. Even as I carried her to our bed, memories of the previous night had blood rushing to my pelvic area.

By the Gods, it had been so insanely good with her!

To think I had found her appearance strange and mostly

unappealing. And now, I couldn't stop thinking about all the little things that made her so perfect. From the incredible softness of her furless skin to the impromptu way it covered itself in those ridiculously cute little bumps for no apparent reason, to those magical spots she called freckles and that I wanted to lick one by one, my mate was a treasure trove of wonders that fascinated me. I loved how she wrinkled her strange pointy nose whenever she was embarrassed or annoyed. The intensity of the redness of her skin as she blushed would never stop making me want to both laugh and squeeze her in a tight hug.

And those eyes… those stunning green eyes that always seem to peer into the very depth of my soul just mesmerized me.

However, as I lay her down on the bed, it was a different wonder that I wanted to feast my eyes—and my mouth—on.

Ophelia kicked off the flat shoes she'd been wearing while I was leaning down to kiss her. That reminded me just how fragile humans were. She needed clothes to protect her skin from the elements and keep her body warm, and shoes to shelter the insane softness of her sole from rocks and other sharp objects on the ground. Another wave of protectiveness flared within me thinking of how ill-equipped humans were to survive in the wild.

Nazhrals were naturally designed to thrive in most environments and against many dangers or predators. We only wore clothes to hide our genitals. But that was a relatively recent thing, dating a few centuries back after we made first contact with off-worlders. We always had loincloths, but they were more a fashion statement that people randomly elected to wear, mostly to display wealth and status.

However, as much as I found the outfits she wore flattering, right now, I wanted her fully bare.

Still standing at the edge of the bed, I bent forward and licked her navel, left exposed by the short, formfitting top she was wearing. Throughout the day, that little button relentlessly taunted me. Remembering how she shivered and squirmed last night when I licked and nipped at it, my tongue twitched to see if I could get a similar reaction from her again.

And I did.

I loved how responsive Ophelia was to my touch. During our multiple, unbridled couplings, I inventoried each of her sensitive spots and made certain to give them all the attention they deserved. A couple more licks and nips had my woman's legs jerking, which made me chuckle with quite a bit of smugness.

But the blossoming scent of her arousal urged me to get down to business, as humans liked saying. I climbed onto the bed, my knees on each side of her legs. Slipping my hands beneath the hem of her top, I lifted it up in a bold caress, my lips following in their wake as they exposed her breasts. They fascinated me. Considering their massive size—compared to a Nazhral female's—and how perky they were, one could have expected them to be firm, almost hard. And yet, they couldn't have been softer and more pliable.

I fondled them with both hands, reveling in the strange texture of her areolas and nipples as they began to harden. It was such an odd phenomenon. But knowing that arousal prompted that reaction fanned the flame burning in the pit of my stomach.

While my thumb continued to tease her right breast, I released her other breast so my mouth could take over giving it some much needed attention. Its texture on my tongue made me instantly hard, as did the way her body jerked in response, accompanied by the sexiest throaty moan. I licked and laved her nipple a while longer before resuming my journey upward.

I finished lifting her top while peppering soft kisses around her chest area and neck. She raised her arms to allow me to rid her of the garment.

I leaned forward to kiss her. It still felt a little strange to me, but no longer in an unpleasant fashion. This thing was growing on me, which was a good thing as I knew my mate enjoyed it. She immediately responded, pressing her lips against mine while wrapping her arms around me. By the gods! It did the most wonderful thing to me that she truly seemed to crave proximity with me. I loved her eagerness and passion.

As I continued to caress her body, I felt emboldened and licked the seam of her mouth. Ophelia froze and slightly pulled her head back. Eyes flicking between mine, she studied my face with an inquisitive look, as if to make certain she hadn't misinterpreted my intentions. Suddenly feeling uncertain, I gave her a nervous smile. My mate's face lit up, and she returned my smile with the loveliest mix of encouragement and timidity.

When she lifted her head back towards mine, I gently reclaimed her lips. This time, as soon as I poked my tongue out, her lips parted, welcoming me in. Despite my apprehension about such an unusual thing, I carefully made her tongue's acquaintance. It was the strangest and yet most fascinating sensation.

Humans didn't possess a raspy tongue like we did, but never in a million years would I have imagined such softness. It was smooth, warm, and silky as it danced around mine. In retrospect, I shouldn't be surprised considering how impossibly soft her mouth had felt around my cock.

A needy moan also escaped me at the memory of the insane pleasure she'd given me that way. Clamping down on the wave of lust surging in my loins, I focused on that kiss. Savoring my female's sweet taste, my exploration grew bolder in tandem with my confidence.

Who would have thought licking the inside of another person's mouth could be this pleasurable?

The look of wonder on my woman's face when I ended the kiss wrecked me. She smiled, gratitude, lust, and something else I couldn't define warred for dominance on her features. All that mattered was that I wanted her to always look at me like that. In that instant, I realized I would do anything and everything to make this woman as happy as any person could be... whatever the cost.

For the next eternity, I worshiped every inch of her body. I would never tire of the feel of her soft skin under my tongue, its slight saltiness, and intoxicating scent. My mate loved being licked and nipped. To my surprise, she also enjoyed when I carefully raked the tips of my claws or fangs on her, obviously without breaking skin. I was starting to suspect Ophelia liked flirting with danger, and I would gladly oblige.

Her stomach quivered in that sexy way of hers as my mouth traveled down her body to my prize. The scent of her arousal had my cock throbbing with need. Humans didn't have pheromones in the traditional sense, and yet my mate's musk acted on me like the most potent aphrodisiac. The slightest waft sufficed to make me burn with the urge to put her on all fours and unleash my passion on her.

Even now, it took every bit of my willpower to keep me from doing just that.

Ophelia's breath became a bit faster and shallower as I stared at her treasure. It already glistened with her essence for me, and her little nub was perking its head up, clamoring for my attention. Her slit was the most adorable shade of pink. A part of me deplored that it was cleanly shaven. I had looked forward to seeing tight curls, the same fiery red as her hair, framing her slit.

Although slightly disappointed, finding her completely bare had not surprised me. From what I'd read about humans, removing body hair was a common ritual among them, especially for women. In fact, except for the nearly invisible, extremely fine short hairs on her forearms and the long locks on her head, my mate had no other hair anywhere, including under her armpits or the length of her slender legs.

A pity, truly. But that didn't stop me from reveling in the extreme softness of her skin.

Ophelia's stomach quivered when I deeply inhaled her intoxicating musk. My chest vibrated with a hungry growl before I dove in for my feast. Nazhrals didn't perform oral sex on each other. This had been another first for me. What a shame it would have been to have missed out on something so mind-blowingly blissful.

The tartness of my female's essence exploded on my taste buds. It made me even harder and hungrier to devour her. Encouraged by my woman's moans and by her hands gripping my mane, I greedily licked and sucked on her clit. As much as I initially thought a woman's body to be poorly designed that her most erogenous part would be located on the outside, I now finally saw its value.

With our females, there was no pleasure in them without penetration. As it triggered their ovulation, unless they took active measures to prevent unplanned pregnancies, you couldn't really mate just for the enjoyment of it. But this little wonder would allow me to pleasure my mate whenever, wherever, on a whim.

A practical trait I intended to make extensive use of.

Slipping two fingers inside Ophelia—their entry eased by how wet she already was for me—I zeroed in on the sensitive bundle of nerves right at the top, a short way in. Her body instantly jerked in response. It felt amazing knowing exactly where and how to touch my female to send her over the edge.

I fleetingly wondered again why human males were so ill-designed to satisfy their women. They should have had an external appendage devoted to stroking their mate's clitoris with each thrust, and they required either similar spikes on their shaft to massage what they called the G-spot or have a recurved cock to make sure it wouldn't just shoot past it.

The Gods did human women dirty.

But not this one. My mate would never want for orgasms.

As if she'd read the thoughts crossing my mind, Ophelia suddenly cried out, her back arching as ecstasy swept her away.

My mouth still latching on to her clit to keep her flying high for as long as possible, I tilted my head up to peer at her. At first, I could only see the delectable hard buds of her nipples until her back relaxed onto the mattress.

By the Gods, she looked stunning!

With her pale complexion, her face, neck, and chest were flushed, giving the impression her freckles were bathed in a reddish glow, just like the red stars of Luen. Her green eyes were darkened with passion, her lips parted as voluptuous sounds flowed out of her in an endless stream, and her face was dissolved in an expression of pure bliss... Bliss that *I* had given her.

As soon as she started to come back down, I yielded at last to the demands of my painfully hard cock. I kissed my way back up before settling on top of her. Although she parted her legs wide to welcome me, that position humans called missionary would take a while for me to get used to. My legs didn't find it natural. Technically, it wasn't all that different from kneeling, but it required for me to mostly sustain my weight on my arms rather than on my knees.

But I couldn't deny this human position offered far more intimacy than the standard Nazhral one. Nothing compared to being face to face with one's soulmate as our bodies became one. With a single smile laced with an equal measure of passion and tenderness, my mate expressed her consent, reinforced by the possessive way in which she wrapped her arms around me.

Like I did on our first night, I willed my cock to self-lubricate then pressed my lips to my woman's as I began pushing myself inside her. It was meant to distract her from any discomfort she might feel. Considering my girth, it was almost a miracle she could receive me. Even now, despite the multiple rounds we'd enjoyed last evening, her body once more resisted my invasion. My loins burned with the need to just ram myself in and give in to the insatiable hunger Ophelia awakened in me.

I forced myself to stick to shallow thrusts and deepened the kiss.

Lost in the softness of her tongue and the sweetness of her taste, I was almost startled when her body suddenly yielded to me. Ophelia hissed against my lips, no doubt from the burn. The tightness of her sheath squeezing me from all sides had me on the verge of spilling.

Nothing should feel this good.

Summoning all the self-control I possessed, I continued to kiss and caress my woman as she adjusted to me, until her inner walls started contracting around my length. As soon as I began moving, a nearly feral growl rumbled in my throat.

It was so fucking good!

My spikes were already highly erogenous, but the way she gripped me, her searing heat stroking every sensitive nerve ending both on the way in and out, had me on the verge of erupting. I could barely think. My entire world narrowed down to the inferno raging in my loins. Each thrust sent lightning bolts coursing through me. Ophelia's hands and mouth on me, the exquisite feel of her feverish skin against mine, and the voluptuous sound of her moans in my ears soon had me drowning in a maelstrom of sensations.

I didn't know when I picked up the pace. One moment I was trying to rein myself in, and the next I was pounding into her. I wanted to fuck her raw. To brand her, break her, have her as insane with desire for me as I was for her. She was writhing beneath me, whispering my name between two moans, her breathing labored as she began to crest.

She fell apart with a sharp cry. Her inner walls clamping down on my cock nearly had me come undone. Grinding my teeth through the urge to surrender to my own release, I pursued my relentless assault, taking her even harder, deeper, and faster. I still wanted her too much, even if it killed me.

For a brief moment, I considered pulling out of her and flipping her onto her stomach. Not only was that a more comfortable position for me, but there was something incredibly erotic about firmly gripping a female's waist, the plump curves of her behind slamming against your pelvis as you ram your cock into her, over and over again. Another bolt of lust exploded in the pit of my stomach at the memory of how my female rocked in front of me, last night, meeting me thrust for thrust as I wrecked her.

But I couldn't bear the thought of no longer being one with her for the merest second. Instead, I slipped my arms behind her knees and folded her legs up towards her chest even as I spread them wider. She was pinned down and fully opened to me.

I went feral as I gave in to the lust and passion she stirred in me.

Ophelia never got a chance to come down from her current high as I ravaged her with unbridled fury. Having her trapped beneath me, helpless but to take all that I had to give, and still begging me for more only fueled the madness that had my mind on the verge of fracturing.

As waves upon waves of pleasure almost too much to bear threatened to overwhelm me, I released my mate's right leg and slipped a hand between us. I wouldn't last much longer, but I needed my woman coming all over my cock as I gave in to my orgasm.

The rough pad of my fingers no sooner touched her clit than Ophelia's body seized, swept away again. This time, I surrendered with a powerful roar, followed by a long stream of feral grunts. I continued to rock in and out of her, my movements erratic as spasms of ecstasy shook my body. My seed shot out of me in endless spurts of pure bliss.

Fully spent, I collapsed on top of my mate, before turning us around so that she would lay on top of me. My cock still buried inside her, my tail tightly wrapped around her waist, I let the spinning room settle around us, along with the frantic beating of my heart.

Even now, our bodies still bound as one, I couldn't seem to get close enough to my woman. She was mine, and I was hers. In that instant, I knew no one could ever own me more fully than she did.

Ophelia was my soulmate.

~

On my way to the boat for today's fishing expedition, I mentally sorted out the plans Ophelia and I had for later tonight. We would meet my brother in his temporary camp and take him on a tour of some of the landmarks in the area. My mate shamelessly hinted that we should invite Ylis to tag along, which I wholeheartedly agreed with. We could even bring some food to have a meal under the stars or hunt something fresh on the way.

The sound of an unpleasant voice to my left interrupted my musings. I stopped walking and braced as Moriak closed the distance with me. Seeing his two favorite minions, Latsa and Olmar, following him had my eyes narrowing with suspicion. I hadn't spoken to him since that fateful night of the feast. I couldn't say whether he'd been avoiding me, or if he'd been too busy doing damage control with the Matriarchs and convincing them to proceed with the mission.

To say that I'd been disappointed by the total absence of follow-up from anyone in a ruling position would be quite an understatement. I wanted to believe that the females were taking this time to do their research and reach some sort of consensus before they reopened the debate for the rest of the Pride at large.

"Gaelec, you won't be fishing today. We need you to come with us for a hunt," Moriak said in a commanding tone. "Several Sikkals roaming nearby must be culled."

"Very well," I replied in a guarded tone, my eyes flicking to his two companions. "It will only be the four of us? None of the candidates will join us?"

Moriak waved a dismissive hand. "No. We will test the younglings another time. These Sikkals threaten the females' hunts. They're males in heat going on a rampage. Now is not the time to train or mentor inexperienced newcomers."

"All right. Give me a moment to go warn my mate," I replied, forcing myself to maintain a neutral expression despite my continued suspicions.

While I didn't disagree with his reluctance at bringing people whose performance might be questionable during a culling, it made little sense that he would pick me instead of the other available males not currently on duty, and with whom he hunted regularly over the past few years of my incarceration.

"That won't be necessary," Moriak replied in the same dismissive manner. "We don't have time for this, and the Matriarchs will handle it."

"The Matriarchs?" I echoed, my back stiffening. "Why? They summoned her?"

He gestured for me to follow and began walking towards the entrance of the village. "Relax. They only want to get to know her."

That made me even more suspicious. The urge to run home and make sure all was well burned in my gut. But I couldn't justify it purely based on my insecurities. Whatever my current feelings about the Pride and its leadership, I didn't fear any physical harm would come to my woman. On that front, even if dealing with an off-worlder, Nazhrals had extremely strict rules of engagement whenever a female was involved. You never attacked a female unless under an agreed upon duel between opponents of matching skills. If someone wanted to challenge my Ophelia, they would have to face off against her appointed champion.

"I still need to get my weapons," I argued.

Without slowing down, Moriak shook his head. "We have a spear for you."

"Only a spear? No blaster?" I challenged, my sense of unease cranking up another notch.

"They cause too much damage to the pelt," he replied as if that was self-evident. "They are in high demand right now, so we want to minimize any burns. Cuts can be easily stitched. But fear not. I have a stun gun with me just in case, not that hunters of our caliber should have any need of it," he added, patting the weapon hanging on his belt.

I nearly demanded why he could have one but not me. A quick glance at the other two males accompanying us showed they didn't possess any blaster either. Although that somewhat pacified me, it only underlined what double standards our so-called Alpha operated under, multiplying the ways to keep himself safe while putting the rest of us at risk.

Four speeders already waited for us by the guard post. A pretty sturdy and respectable spear leaned against my vehicle. A quick inspection reassured me there was no foul play afoot, at least as far as the weapon they had given me was concerned. Latsa and Olmar seemed to have similar weapons on their respective speeders. Long and narrow, the hovering vehicles could comfortably carry two adult passengers, with the second one sitting in the back. However, it surprised me that no one tagged along aboard a shuttle or hovercar to carry back the massive beasts we would slay.

After a little over a fifteen-minute ride, Moriak slowed down and dismounted, leaving his speeder in as secure a position as possible in this wild environment. Without a word, we imitated him.

"I will head west," Moriak said. "We will herd them towards the rocky formation, corner them there, and then take them out."

I frowned. "Why not push them straight north? Don't we still have traps over there?"

He shook his head. "That's still too far. The beasts could stray and further scare away the fauna.

I fought the urge to argue. Whatever fauna was going to be scared by the roaming Sikkals had already been. With the other two males keeping quiet, it felt wiser not to make waves.

By the look on Moriak's face, he expected me to do just that. The sliver of disappointment he displayed hinted he'd been hoping I would have done so. That would have allowed him to take little jabs at me, implying that I was too scared to face them using my own skills rather than relying on traps to do the work for me.

"Latsa, you will go south, and Olmar, you will go east," Moriak ordered before turning to me. "You keep heading northeast, towards the stone range."

I gave him a stiff nod, and we all parted ways. It felt like a silly approach to me, but I wouldn't give him any grounds to find fault with anything I did. All my senses on high alert, I kept my eyes peeled, looking for safe spots, cover, and vantage points that could be leveraged once things got heated. It troubled me to have been sent directly towards the dead end where the battle would take place rather than have me assist one of them into herding our potential prey here.

In more ways than one, I felt like I'd gone right back to my early days on Molvi, and we went out into the forest to catch some extra meat to supplement our meals. As a Nazhral, my diet consisted mostly of meat, and the standard portions provided by the Warden had to be rationed over each week to make sure we wouldn't run out before the next supply came in. To my dismay, some of the other inmates sought to do me in, planning on claiming it as a hunting accident. I quickly learned that the convicts weren't too keen on having an extra mouth to feed or potentially a new threat. The idiots failed to realize that their provisions increased with new arrivals.

Back then, it placed an unnecessary additional stress on me

knowing that my companions represented a bigger threat than the creatures that roamed out there. At least, as I proved my worth and value, that threat waned and then faded altogether. But what remained was my growing proficiency as a hunter, skills that now perfectly served me.

As I neared the edge of the forest which opened on a small clearing in front of the rock formation, my nose twitched as it caught a strange scent. It was extremely subtle and easily over-looked. It didn't qualify as fruity or vegetable, and instead had a musky undertone to it. It baffled me as I couldn't figure out what creature it might emanate from. Nothing on the ground or the tree bark indicated the recent passage of whatever might have produced it.

I almost shrugged it off then decided to investigate it. Following the scent, I was shocked to realize it grew more potent closer to one of the areas I had filed away as a perfect spot to take refuge in if one of the beasts charged me. More suspicious than ever, I carefully approached the area, surveying every centimeter of both the ground and the large trees from whence it seemed to emanate. My jaw dropped when I finally noticed the very discreet trap trigger.

Why the fuck didn't he warn me?

No one would have set up this trap without his knowledge. If not for listening to my instincts and seeking out the source of this odd smell, I never would have known its presence. If chased by a Sikkal, I would have run straight for this tree and fallen into what appeared to be a simple pit. Without seeing its actual depth, I couldn't say for sure how much damage I would have sustained. In the best-case scenario, I would have been stunned or maybe broken a limb. But the most likely outcome would have been for me to be stuck with no way out while the creature devoured me.

A seething anger burned deep within me as I began exploring the area, searching for more traps. A short distance away, the same subtle scent tickled my nose, leading me to a second, and then a third trap. The former was clearly a net trap, whereas the latter was a spiked pit. That *grovas* denied me a blaster for fear the creature's fur would be damaged but then elected to hold the battle near spiked pits?

That scent clearly was some sort of pheromone meant to draw the beasts towards the traps. We used similar techniques in the past, but this specific scent was unknown to me. The question was whether it became their new standard during my absence, or if Moriak deliberately changed it to something he knew I would likely not pick up or pay any attention to.

The sound of incoming creatures cut my investigating short. One moment, I heard the muffled sound of some stampeding beasts. The next, a massive male shot out from the tree line and came charging straight at me. In the distance behind it, my three companions were running to catch up.

Judging by the span of the Sikkal's four, heavy, recurved horns, it was a fully mature male. Big, angry eyes stared at me from its long face. Three additional horns lined each side of its face, from the temple to the corners of its mouth, which appeared deceptively small. It tilted its head and aimed the bone ridges lining its long forehead at me as it surged forward. The damn things acted like a battering ram. A direct blow at full force would shatter every bone in my body.

I bolted towards the tree with the net trap, pursued by the thundering sound of the beast giving chase. With its huge torso and massive front legs, each step sounded like a giant hammer bashing an anvil. Despite their imposing size, Sikkals moved at dizzying speed. Although extremely fast myself, I could hear it gaining on me. Without slowing down, I jumped over the trap and onto the tree behind it and used my claws to latch onto the bark before scrambling onto a branch.

A second later, the startled and angry scream of the creature filled the clearing as the trap closed around it. The rope immediately yanked up the net, dangling the caged beast from one of the limbs. The ancient tree shook, rattled by the sudden addition of such tremendous weight on a single branch, thick though it was.

The creature thrashed savagely, aided largely by the fact that the net was too small to properly contain it. Even as it dangled upside down, it tried to stab me with the sharp horn-like spike at the tip of its tail. I barely managed to jump onto a different branch to avoid getting impaled. Without pause, I immediately tried to spear the creature, but the branch broke right as my weapon would have made contact. The Sikkal plummeted a short distance to the ground and fell into the pit below. It was too small for the beast's considerable size, but it still got partially stuck.

To my utter shock, instead of closing in to finish it off, my companions just stood there at a safe distance, observing the scene.

With the claws of my left hand digging into the bark of the lowest branch, and the claws of my left paw sinking into the trunk for support, I leaned over the scrambling beast and stabbed my spear at it. The wretched thing turned just at the right moment to cheat me from giving it a fatal blow. The blade of my weapon found its mark in its flank instead. The Sikkal screeched and blindly swiped its tail at me. I narrowly escaped getting lacerated to oblivion by the sharp bone spikes, which lined its upper side by yanking myself back onto the branch.

I cussed under my breath when that movement appeared to give the creature the jolt required to get it unstuck. It shot out of the pit, stabbing the tip of its tail at me even as it began to ram its forehead against the tree to break it. The creature would then violently swipe it from side to side so its huge, recurved horns would further jolt the tree. Despite its thickness, my refuge would eventually break from the repeated assault. But the tail's attacks forced me to move to weaker branches, which shook too much under each impact.

Running the length of the branch I was currently standing on, I leapt onto the next tree. Before I landed, the angry scream of another beast resonated behind us. A smaller Sikkal came rushing into the clearing. As one, Moriak, Latsa, and Olmar shifted their attention to the calf, leaving me to deal with the mature male on my own.

I cussed again as my stalker charged the new tree I was in. Waiting until the last minute, I jumped down as soon as the beast rammed it. Legs and arms pumping, I ran towards the third trap, praying that the spiked pit would be wide enough to engulf the Sikkal. If not, I would be in serious trouble as it was located at the foot of the rock formation that sealed off the clearing. Heart pounding, I could almost feel its breath on my nape as it gave chase.

For one horrible moment, I feared I wouldn't make it. One meter from where I believed the pit to begin, I leapt towards the stone wall. I hissed at the sudden burn in the back of my calf as three vicious claws swiped at it. Had I been half a second slower, it could have done serious damage and severed both muscles and tendons.

Mid-air, I threw my legs forward, as one would do to perform a long jump. The startled scream of the Sikkal resonated at my back followed by a loud ruckus as it fell into the pit. As soon as my paws touched the wall, I bent my knees to absorb part of the impact before pushing back with all my might. I back-flipped, landing just behind the creature. Once again, the pit was too small, but a few spikes still managed to pierce through the front left leg and shoulder.

Without missing a beat, I dashed forward and jabbed my spear at its back. I missed the spine by barely a couple of centimeters. It swiped its tail at me, and the sharp points of the bones lining it rushed straight at my face. I dropped to the ground, and the underside of its tail grazed the top of my mane.

Before I could fully recover, the beast spun around, almost

tearing its front leg off on the spikes. Maw open impossibly wide —belying how small it looked when closed—the creature lunged at me to bite my face off. On instinct, I thrust my spear into its gaping mouth, jamming it through its throat and into its brain. The Sikkal emitted a sharp, gurgling sound, almost stunned, its entire body stiffening for a brief second before it shook with a series of dying spasms.

Only then did the quickly approaching galloping sound register in my brain. My blood turned to ice when I glanced over my shoulder to see the calf, only a few meters away, charging me. I yanked my spear out of the defeated Sikkal and jumped on top of its carcass a split second before the younger one rammed into it, sending both of us crashing against the stone face of the mountain.

My teeth rattled in my head, but I pushed past it, jumped onto the ground, and ran. Behind me, the calf had resumed its pursuit. Although younger, the beast still stood close to five foot high and over six foot long, with a weight of no less than three hundred pounds. The mature male I'd slain had been a third bigger.

Being smaller and lighter, that calf was also a lot faster. But I had nowhere to take refuge in. He was pushing me towards the barren side of the clearing, away from the trees, and directly alongside the impassable stone wall.

He was trapping me the same way we'd intended to trap them.

Searing rage flooded through me at the total absence of intervention from my companions. Where the fuck was that stun gun Moriak had brought? Why weren't they running interference or taking shots while it was focused on me?

But now wasn't the time to dwell on this.

As I would never outrun the Sikkal like this, and with it only a couple of meters behind me—and quickly gaining—I leapt with all my strength, nearly ten feet high, and twenty feet forward in the direction of the rockface. For half a beat, I feared I might have miscalculated the distance, but thankfully, my paws hit the wall, and I kicked off of it again. Twisting mid-air, I stuck my spear between my teeth, and landed a few meters away, first on my hands, then on my paws to help dampen the impact.

I immediately pushed off the ground, using my front and back claws to propel me farther as I ran on all fours. I didn't like running that way, but it doubled my speed as I raced alongside the mountain cliff. If I could make it back to the first trap that hadn't been set off yet, it would give me the break I needed to finish off that damn creature.

Just as that thought sparked in my mind, the now familiar musky scent wafted to me. In my frantic escape, I nearly missed it. It was close. Too damn close. But I couldn't see any of the barely visible markers delineating it. In desperation, I jumped at the wall, kicked off of it at a ninety-degree angle, away from the trap ahead, and pivoted to face the incoming beast.

My heart skipped a beat to find it right there, already on me. I barely had time to yank my spear from between my teeth and raise it in front of me to counter the swipe of its massive, clawed hoof. The staff snapped in half under the force of the blow, provoking a painful shockwave through my arms, and sending me crashing onto the ground.

Although I contorted my body to land on all fours, the much too short distance didn't allow me to properly absorb the shock. The impact had pain radiating up my arms and legs, and my limbs nearly buckled under me.

But I had no time for pain.

I rolled out of the way as the calf lunged at me again. The damn thing was too fast. I slammed my knee under its jaw half a blink before its teeth could take a bite out of me and thrust the bladed right half of the spear towards its neck. With the beast recoiling, the blade buried itself under the jaw instead and through the mouth, only to be stopped by a bone. The calf reared back, screeching. As I held on to my half spear still embedded in its maw, the beast's movement yanked me forward with it.

Using that momentum, I savagely swiped my claws at its underbelly, spilling its guts while kicking it backward. It toppled over, thrashing. With one swift movement, I yanked my spear free then stabbed it into its skull, putting an end to its misery.

Breathing heavily, my lungs and muscles burning, I stared at the dead calf before glancing towards the other pit where the adult male lay still. Behind me, the discreet crunching sound of rock and dirt announced the approach of the other three males. Teeth clenched, I wiped some of the blood and gore from my kills matting my fur and turned to face the newcomers.

I leveled a hard stare on Moriak as he and his goons stopped in front of me.

"Next time, just tell me to go on the hunt on my own… *Alpha*," I hissed, putting as much contempt as I could on his title.

He lifted his chin defiantly, failing to hide his anger and disappointment that I survived this ordeal.

"You've been gone twelve years, Gaelec. We needed to assess if you were still fit," he said in an unrepentant tone.

"I'm sure that's all it was," I said, my voice dripping with sarcasm. "Then I would suggest that you mark hidden traps when you run these little *tests*. Otherwise, one might interpret it as deliberate sabotage or even a murder attempt."

Moriak bared his teeth and took a menacing step forward. "Careful, Gaelec. I will not tolerate such slanderous insinuations."

"Did that hit a nerve, Alpha? And what are you going to do about that insinuation? Are you going to lure more beasts in the hope they will kill me, or will you request the assistance of your companions to finish the job?" I taunted.

It was a cocky move on my part to provoke him with these two males by his side. However, with his back turned to them, Moriak couldn't see their expressions as I could. Taken aback by that comment, he suddenly seemed to remember their presence. The moment he glanced back at Latsa and Olmar, he visibly blanched.

He had made a serious miscalculation.

In their eyes, any trace of respect had vanished. Although he still had the title, they were looking at *me* as the Alpha. I didn't have to ask why. He never would have survived what I just did. And he knew the word would spread.

"I performed both the kills on my own. You can clean all of this up and bring the meat back to the Pride," I said in a tone that brooked no argument.

Ignoring Moriak's outraged expression, I stomped back into the forest towards my speeder and returned home.

CHAPTER 13
OPHELIA

Over the past two days since the feast, I'd been hard at work reaching out to potential headhunters and browsing through various off-worlder listings for seasonal and hired hands work. Some were hit and miss but many were turning out to be quite promising.

Gaelec and I wanted to have a foolproof plan that even Oluina and Moriak would have no leg to stand on should they want to challenge it. While my mate was getting increasingly aggravated that no new meeting had been called to discuss the matter, I seriously welcomed the reprieve. On top of giving us a bit more time to strengthen our case, it also gave me an opportunity to better understand the dynamics, politics, and culture within the Prides. The goal wasn't to change their ways, but only for them to pursue the lifestyle they wanted in a safe way for all.

A sudden beep startled me. It took me a moment to realize it came from my com. It had been quiet since my arrival here. It wasn't exactly like I had a whole bunch of buddies to message, day in and day out. To my surprise, it was a summons from the Matriarchs, requesting my presence in the Great Hall.

Why the fuck do they want to see me now?

They undoubtedly knew that Gaelec was off fishing. Was it an ambush? Were they hoping I would stumble and somehow stick my foot in my mouth in a way that would justify them casting me out? Or were they planning on using some sort of pressure tactics to get me to force Gaelec into behaving the way they wanted?

Too many questions swirled in my head. As I obviously would never find the answer by making myself sick by speculating, I ran to the hygiene room to make sure I was presentable, then headed for the door. I hastened down the side road onto the main one leading to the Great Hall. As expected at this hour of the day, the streets were empty with everyone working.

My stomach fluttered with nerves as I reached for the door to the antechamber of the Great Hall, only for my heart to sink when it opened on Oluina. A single look on her face indicated she'd been waiting for me.

Putain de merde! Just what I do not need!

Even knowing that it was pointless, I started marching towards the heavy doors leading into the Hall only to have Oluina park herself in front of me, blocking my way. Obviously, I could try to circle around her and keep going, but that would be pointless and juvenile.

Annoyed, I stopped and locked eyes with her, making no effort to hide how much her presence displeased me.

"Little human," Oluina said in a haughty tone in lieu of greeting.

"Big Nazhral," I replied in a similar fashion.

"It's Oluina," she said, in a clipped tone.

"And for me, it's Ophelia," I said in an obnoxiously polite voice.

She scoffed, irritated that I didn't seem intimidated or destabilized by her little games.

"Whatever you have to say, your time is poorly chosen. I'm expected," I said matter-of-factly.

"I'm well aware," she retorted with a shrug. "But you and I will speak first."

I rolled my eyes and sighed heavily, making it clear I was not only uninterested but quite annoyed by her insistence.

"What do you want?" I asked, my irritation audible in my voice.

"I thought you should know that Gaelec is only using you to make me jealous, to punish me for moving on back when we all thought he had no chance of surviving his incarceration," she said with a smugness filled with malice.

I burst out laughing, her shocked and confused expression at my reaction making me laugh even more. Did the stupid female really think I would fall for these schoolgirl bullying tactics?

"No, Oluina, he doesn't. Gaelec moved on from you years ago. You may still be clinging to the past, but he's not. Frankly, your behavior is quite embarrassing. You should have far more self-respect than trying to force yourself on him," I said with a mix of pity and contempt.

"I'm doing no such thing!" she hissed.

"You most certainly are! Since my arrival—and apparently even before that—you've repeatedly thrown yourself at him despite him clearly expressing both in action and in words that he doesn't want anything to do with you. That's not going to change. He rejected you before he even knew about me!" I said, unable to comprehend how anyone could be so stubborn, border-line obsessive.

"You say that. And yet, he chose you, a pale copy of me," Oluina said in a superior tone.

I recoiled, failing to see how in the world she came to such an outlandish conclusion.

"What the hell are you talking about? You and I are nothing alike!" I exclaimed.

"My name is Oluina, and yours is Ophelia. My fur is reddish-brown, your hair is red. I'm 5'10, and you are about the same. I have green eyes, and so do you. You are my human copy, just weaker."

My eyes widened, and my jaw dropped. Even though I believed this was an incredible stretch, I had to admit that I never paid attention to those similarities.

"Now you see it!" Oluina said with an air of triumph, interpreting my reaction as shock and devastation.

I snorted and shook my head at her. "Wow, are you truly so desperate to cling to any straw? You're right, we do have a few similarities. But that only confirms that Gaelec has a type when it comes to females. It isn't uncommon for people to have certain preferences. He happens to like tall redheads with green eyes. Big deal. Twelve years ago, my husband was looking for *me* when he *settled* for *you*."

"He did not settle," she snarled.

"Oh, but he did. You were the closest thing—and a pale imitation at that—to what he truly wanted. You see, Gaelec didn't pick me as a copy of you. In fact, he didn't pick me at all. Kayog paired us before either of us ever even met or knew of each other's existences. So you were never a factor in what brought us together. And you still aren't today. Do yourself and us a favor. Just move on."

I almost felt sorry for her as she fisted her hands with anger. I couldn't begin to imagine what it must be like to be so desperate to have something you never could. It boggled my mind all the more that I knew deep in my bones that she wasn't even in love with him. She just had this sick need to win. The fact that anyone could reject her simply didn't compute. In her mind, it meant she needed to fix us until we saw the truth that she exclusively held. Otherwise, it could only mean that somebody was conspiring against her to steal what was rightfully hers.

"If you think to make him Alpha and take my place in this Pride, you are sorely mistaken!" she snarled in a menacing tone.

I burst out laughing again and shook my head at her with

genuine pity. "You poor girl! Seriously, look at me," I said, spreading my arms wide, glancing down at myself and then back at her. "I'm not as big, as strong, or as fast as a Nazhral female. I can't hunt like you do, nor do I want to! Like I've said before, the only thing I care about is Gaelec. And he has stated time and time again that he has no interest in becoming the Alpha. All he wants is safety for himself, for other males, and for the entire Pride."

I ran my fingers through my hair, feeling both discouraged and overwhelmed that we were seriously still rehashing this nonsense. Why was it so hard to get through to them?

"You're possibly the next Head Matriarch of this Pride. If Gaelec is right—and we both know he is—then your Pride will steadily decline and risk facing extinction. Instead of fighting him at every turn and making his life difficult, you should leverage the knowledge and experience he's acquired during his time on Molvi. He's ready, willing, and eager to put all of it towards the improvement of this village. If you all keep pushing him away, then it will be your loss and someone else's gain. Don't let others benefit from the treasure you currently have in your midst because you're too blind to see it. Now if you'll excuse me, I am expected."

I circled around her and pushed the heavy doors open onto the Hall.

My stomach knotted as I entered the room to find Rozel, the two other Matriarchs, Ylis, and a handful of other young huntresses sitting on the elevated dais at the end of the spacious area. It felt like standing in front of a jury without a lawyer during a trial for murder.

At least, Ylis's sympathetic gaze made me feel a little less alone. I could only pray she would run interference if the others became a little too belligerent.

"Come in, Ophelia Moreau," Rozel said in a solemn voice while waving me in.

Although not ominous in and of itself, the absence of warmth in her tone, and the cold glint in her eyes didn't bode well. The way her gaze followed her daughter coming in behind me before she hastened to her seat near Ylis on the dais had me even more nervous. Had she known Oluina was going to corner me outside? Had she instructed her to do so?

"I will get straight to the point," Rozel said, putting an end to my wandering thoughts. "Your presence here defies our rules. We've been debating at length without coming to an agreement as to how we can possibly justify letting you stay among us."

That hit me hard. On my way here, I mentally rehearsed answers to the hypothetical questions I expected that would be thrown at me, all of them revolving around how I could contribute to the Pride and Gaelec's ideas for missions. This specific question had not been in the cards.

I pursed my lips, not wanting to rush into an answer before I fully comprehended the root cause of their problem with my presence.

"Before I answer, I would like to ask a couple of questions to better understand the issue," I said carefully, and proceeded when she gave me a stiff nod. "If one of your Queens or huntresses had fallen in love with a human, would you ask her to leave or forbid her mate from coming here to live with her?"

Rozel waved a dismissive hand. "That situation isn't comparable. All the females here are of our bloodline. In any Pride, the only females allowed are all closely blood related."

My stomach knotted, but I kept a stoic expression as I nodded slowly. "If that is an immutable rule, then I fail to see the point of this conversation. However, if it is not immutable, then I would like to discuss what you feel could be done to mitigate your discomfort about something that no one can change. My blood is my blood."

"It is a golden rule that is strictly enforced by every single Pride on Melelyn," she insisted.

"Then it sounds like your decision is already made," I said with a sliver of annoyance that she kept circling around the answer instead of just being blunt. "In which case, I would respectfully submit that it is a little narrow-minded. All laws and rules evolve with time."

"Rules are made for a reason," Rozel countered, sounding a little miffed, no doubt due to my comment about narrow-mindedness.

"They are," I conceded. "But they're always based on the circumstances of the time they were established. Back when your people first created these Prides, you didn't know of the existence of off-worlders. Therefore, the chances of a female of another species marrying one of your people was never even a possibility. Times have changed. If I'm here today, you can be certain that more will come. There are already countless humans in your capital city. I bet if we do a little digging, we'll find out that some of them are married to Nazhrals. And more of your males are likely to meet their off-worlder mates, especially if you adopt the safe missions Gaelec suggested."

"We never consented to go that route," Rozel immediately said, sounding defensive.

"Rozel," I said in a reasonable tone as if speaking to a difficult child, "you saw Ranor's reaction when Gaelec named the company involved in that lucrative mission he was coming to recruit people for. If a Warden informed my husband of the fact that it was a trap, then you know it is true. Sacrificing your males will give your Pride nothing."

I glanced around the room to assess how hostile my audience was. To my relief, aside from Rozel and Oluina, the others seemed receptive, although a bit guarded.

"You may not be aware of this, but my arrival here was delayed because Nazhral pirates attacked our vessel and failed. Our cruise ship had a literal defense fleet onboard. They swarmed the pirates and obliterated them."

"What ship?" a female I didn't know asked, her voice tense. "What was the name of the vessel you arrived on?"

"The Behemoth," I replied carefully.

The female took a shuddering breath, and her face contorted with a sorrow she failed to hide. She shook her head as if in denial while blinking away the tears that threatened to surface. One of the females next to her gently rubbed her back in a soothing fashion.

"Did any of the Nazhrals survive?" the Matriarch named Pryia asked—Ylis's mother.

I cast a hesitant look at the younger female still struggling to rein in her emotions, before looking back at the Matriarch.

"Hmm… Unfortunately no. The Nazhral vessel was obliterated. There were no survivors."

The younger female emitted a choked sob and ran out of the room.

"Andrane!" Ylis called out after her.

But she left without looking back. The female who had been trying to soothe her cast an apologetic look at the Matriarchs before going after Andrane.

"Her brother was part of that mission," Ylis explained in a tired voice. "He turned eighteen two months ago, so he had to leave our Pride."

My heart ached for him. The poor boy never even had a proper chance to live. He'd likely been sent on that mission as a requirement to join whatever Pride he had approached. What a pointless waste.

"You must understand that more and more ships like the one I traveled on are doing the same now. Piracy will soon have no chance of succeeding at all. If you pursue this, you'll only be sending these males to their deaths," I said in a pleading tone. "I've researched the law changes on Molvi that Gaelec mentioned. He's right. They won't allow Prides to receive a single credit from the prisoners' work. And right now, the United

Planets Organization members are so fed up, they have begun applying sanctions on your planet."

Rozel shrugged. "We have nothing to do with those sanctions. What happens in the capital has little impact on the Prides."

"That's partially true, but you need credits to buy all the things that you cannot create here from the capital, especially equipment," I argued. "If Melelyn starts facing multiple embargos, you will feel the pain from it. It always trickles down to everyone."

"Which is why we need the credits from the missions," she retorted stubbornly.

"But that's not viable!" I exclaimed, my annoyance seeping into my voice.

"It has worked for generations during all of which we also heard the same threats that you are mentioning now," Rozel countered dismissively.

I narrowed my eyes at her. "That may have been true in the past, but it won't be any more with all the crackdowns. Tell me, how many successful missions have your people accomplished of late?"

She didn't have to answer. The uneasy looks that multiple females exchanged told me all that I needed to know.

"You have the potential to chart a new way for the Prides," I said pleadingly.

"You ask too much from us," Rozel snapped.

"I ask for nothing," I replied stiffly. "All I'm doing is making suggestions on a safer way forward. At the end of the day, I'm here for Gaelec. I will do whatever I can to help him and his people. But I promise you that if you continue down your current path, you *will* suffer extreme losses. The Enforcers are and will continue to crack down hard on this. What would it cost you to give this a try and establish yourself as a leader instead of trying to play catch up after everyone else has finally wised up to what they need to do?"

"It is not our way," Oluina argued.

"But it could be, if we so chose," Ylis interjected. "The Osuan Pride does something similar."

Oluina huffed and made a dismissive gesture. "They're a bunch of weirdos!"

"Weirdos who prosper," Ylis retorted harshly. "Unlike other Prides, they do not evict their males, who get to leave in their own time to seek out a mate. Those males are extremely sought after but are very picky."

"What you mean is that most of them are self-righteous snobs who think themselves too good for the Prides and end up just going to the city instead," Oluina said with disdain.

"They're not acting as snobs," Ylis said with a hint of irritation. "They simply avoid Prides in order not to be used and then discarded the way we do with our males. Can you blame them?"

"Whatever their motives, it is neither here nor there," Rozel interjected, annoyed. "In the end, safe missions are not lucrative enough. Like you, we have been doing our research into Gaelec's statements. We would not be able to survive on the meager proceeds from your safe missions."

"That's only because your males are untrained!" I argued. "Their education is far too basic as it entirely revolves around trade, hunting, and crafting. There are tons of virtual mentoring programs available that could be provided here. Gaelec benefited from it on Molvi. Better trained males could secure better paying missions. I can't hunt, but I can definitely help you with that."

"That is if we allow a human to remain among us, which is against our rules," Oluina said snidely.

"If you—"

A sudden ruckus outside interrupted me, drawing our collective attention. Moments later, the heavy doors to the antechamber burst open as a female ran in.

"Gaelec returned from the hunt!" the female announced, her voice filled with excitement.

"What hunt?!" I exclaimed. "Gaelec went fishing this morning."

Oluina burst into a malicious laugh. "There was a change of plan. He went on a Sikkal culling. Didn't he tell you?"

"Where are the others?" Rozel asked. "We would hear their report."

"He's alone and covered in blood," the female replied.

"WHAT?!" I shouted.

I didn't wait for her response and bolted out of the room.

CHAPTER 14
GAELEC

The muffled sound of Ophelia's voice calling my name reached me even before the main doors of the Great Hall burst open. She jerked her head left and right, looking for me.

"Gaelec!" she shouted, her voice laced with panic, when she finally spotted me.

I didn't need a mirror to know what a mess I looked like. When I eviscerated the Sikkal, its blood sprayed all over me. As much as I felt guilty for worrying my mate, I deliberately chose to come straight to the Great Hall specifically so they could see the state I was in. Moriak set out to kill me. While I did not intend to openly make that accusation, an image spoke volumes. I wanted there to be no question that I had seriously been put in harm's way under his watch, while the other three males who should have supported me returned without so much as a speck of blood on them.

"I'm fine, my mate," I said in a reassuring tone as Ophelia ran towards me.

She stopped straight in front of me and immediately began pawing at my arms and chest, looking for any sign of injury.

I chuckled, my heart melting to see how much she cared about me.

"I'm fine, my Ophelia. Most of this is not my blood. I only got a superficial cut on the back of my calf," I said softly.

"Then whose blood is this? Why so much of it? What happened? And where are the others?" she asked, stretching her neck to look over my shoulders before glancing back at me, worry and confusion still audible in her voice.

"Slow down! One question at a time," I said, amused before sobering.

A small crowd was gathering around us, including the Matriarchs, Oluina, and Ylis.

"What happened? Where are the others?" Rozel asked, echoing Ophelia's words.

This time, all warmth faded from me as I stared coldly at the Matriarch. "They're coming. They are bringing back my two kills."

"*Your* two kills?" she repeated in a dubious tone.

"Yes, *mine*!" I retorted, baring my teeth. "Your Alpha and his companions lured the beasts to me then watched as I fought them on my own."

"WHAT?!" Ophelia shouted.

My eyes still locked with the Matriarch, I gently caressed my mate's hair in a soothing fashion.

"Apparently, he felt I needed to be tested again after a twelve-year absence."

A strange glimmer fleeted through Rozel's eyes. I couldn't say if she was troubled by Moriak's actions, disappointed I'd prevailed, or feeling guilty that she might have condoned any of it. The lack of shock she displayed upon hearing my words confirmed she'd either been aware of his intentions or highly suspected them. Either way, to me, it made her an accomplice.

"It's fair for the Pride's Alpha to evaluate the fitness level of the males who join us," Rozel said in a non-committal fashion.

"By luring two wild beasts on a single male to fight on his own?!" Ophelia exclaimed, outraged.

"It's okay, my mate. He wanted to prove a point, and I proved mine," I said, staring at the Matriarch as I spoke those words to make my underlying meaning clear. Then I turned to my mate, my face softening as I smiled at her. "All that matters is that I came back home to you unscathed."

A powerful emotion crossed her delicate features, and she threw herself into my arms, hugging me with near desperation, seemingly unbothered by all the blood covering me. I returned her embrace and kissed the top of her head.

"Let's go home, my mate. I need to wash."

She nodded, her face still pressed against my chest. Giving me one last squeeze, Ophelia reluctantly let go.

I wrapped my arms around her shoulders, and she slipped hers around my waist. Before heading back to our house, I glanced at Oluina with a mocking expression.

"By the way, there's no need for you and the other females to go hunting today… or the next few days for that matter. My kills will suffice to feed the entire village for the week, with leftovers."

She scrunched her face as if she'd bitten into something foul, while a few of the other huntresses that had followed her out of the Great Hall—including Ylis—bit the insides of their cheeks not to laugh. But I also didn't miss the speculative way in which they observed me.

I had no time for the power games they wanted to play.

Without another word, I led my mate back to our dwelling. She remained oddly quiet the whole way there. A part of me wondered if it was to keep any discussion safe from prying ears, or if she needed some time to process what she just heard.

As soon as we entered, Ophelia boldly took the lead, all but dragging me to the hygiene room. To my shock, after she helped me remove my loincloth—or rather did it herself, even slapping my hand aside when I tried to unbuckle my belt—my mate quickly stripped out of her own clothes so that we could shower together.

Despite the instant arousal I felt at seeing her naked, I behaved, allowing her to take charge. On instinct, I understood she needed to get some sense of control in this entire situation as she undoubtedly felt she had none since her arrival here. Whatever effort she made to influence her future within the Pride, in the end, her fate mostly rested in other people's hands.

She turned the water on and pushed me underneath it for a first quick rinse.

"Was it a murder attempt?" she asked at last.

"Yes," I replied without hesitation, raising my arms to give her better access as she continued to rinse the blood off me with the retractable shower head. "Or at the very least, he wanted to maim me and demonstrate that I was useless enough to be banned."

"Will he try again?" Ophelia asked, putting the shower head back on its hook and then reaching for the soap.

I shook my head. "Although not impossible, I highly doubt it. Moriak seriously hurt his cause today."

"How so?" she asked with genuine curiosity while working up a lather and then rubbing her soapy hands all over me.

An approving moan rumbled in my throat at the delicious sensation of her hands on me, the soap making each motion feel like an even silkier caress. Ophelia chuckled smugly which had me playfully glare at her before becoming serious again.

"Moriak elevated me today. However they feel about him, Latsa and Olmar won't lie about what they witnessed. In truth, I wouldn't be surprised if they start pushing for him to step down," I mused aloud.

"Seriously?!" she exclaimed, stunned and slightly confused. "Why? Because he tried to get you killed?"

I shook my head. "The fact that they stood back and

observed without interfering proves that they didn't truly have a problem with him testing me. I can't say to what extent they were distraught by how bad it got, or if they even considered intervening with him stopping them. I was far too busy trying to stay alive to pay attention to their interactions with each other. But they saw my performance, and the fact that there were hidden traps he had not warned me of. That went a little too far into slimy territory."

"Trying to get you killed is okay, but hiding the existence of the traps that would help him achieve that is not?" Ophelia challenged with disbelief.

I snorted and turned around so that she could wash my back. "Correct, because there is no honor in such underhanded practices. He wouldn't have won by being stronger and smarter, but essentially by cheating. That he used such questionable tactics, even using some sort of pheromones, which I believed further enraged the creatures, screamed of desperation. And the fact that I prevailed under those conditions, with two beasts against me and nothing but a spear, earned their respect and admiration. Now, they're comparing the two of us and finding him lacking in comparison."

"Of course, he is," Ophelia said, her voice dripping with pride. "Anyone with eyes can see that you're the better male. But if they do push for you to become the new Alpha, are you going to reconsider now?"

"No," I said.

She turned me around and studied my features in an inquisitive manner, taken aback by the finality in my tone.

"Why?" she asked softly. "Do you find ruling too much?"

I shook my head. "I'm extremely confident that I could do it and even better than he ever could or would. But this entire Pride is broken. In his twisted sense of self-preservation, Moriak has been crippling our defenses for years by culling and sacrificing any male who might have threatened his position."

I took the soap from her and began washing her in turn. She smiled and willingly yielded to my touch. I tried to ignore the way her nipples pebbled as soon as I ran my soapy hands over them.

"We have weak males," I continued. "Our infrastructures are dated, and they won't let me upgrade anything. And all that is due to Rozel's bone-deep fear of change."

Ophelia pursed her lips and slowly nodded. "I noticed that during my meeting with them right before you arrived. She understands everything that we're saying, but she stubbornly refuses to budge. The only explanation I can come up with for such an irrational behavior is that she wants to cling to what is comfortable and familiar to her."

"Yes and no," I replied, turning her around to start washing her back. "It is power that Rozel is clinging to. Based on what Ylis told me, her sisters—the other two Matriarchs—have increasingly been questioning some of the decisions she's been making over the past few years."

"How does doubling down on things that are unpopular help her retain power?" Ophelia argued, confused.

"Because the Head Matriarch must master everything within the Pride. Any job the males perform, she must be able to perform as well or at least have a very strong functional understanding of it," I explained. "She knows all the systems we have implemented. She would have to learn the ones I want to introduce. Unfortunately, instead of seeing this as an opportunity, she got stuck on the idea that she would technically be at my mercy during implementation, and likely for a while afterwards. How does she know I wouldn't keep some information secret from her? What if I tried to leverage it to somewhat blackmail her into giving me more power?"

"You would never do that!" Ophelia immediately exclaimed, outrage audible in her voice and visible on her face as she turned to look at me over her shoulder.

My heart instantly melted with affection for my woman. I leaned forward and kissed her lips.

"You are correct, I wouldn't. But she has become too paranoid. In many ways, she's like her daughter and Moriak. They're all past their prime, but cling to what they have to the detriment of the Pride. Oluina's and Moriak's behavior is not surprising. It's merely a symptom of the trickle-down effect from Rozel's own actions."

Ophelia turned around to face me, her eyes brightening as if in sudden understanding.

"You've officially decided to leave, right?" she asked softly.

I nodded, my eyes flicking between hers to get a sense of how she felt about it. "Like I said after the feast, I was increasingly thinking that it was likely the way to go. But today sealed it. Are you okay with that?"

She snorted and made a dismissive gesture. "I told you already, wherever you go, I go. I'm always up for an adventure. And starting one with my mate sounds thrilling."

Although delighted by her response, I continued to study her, my tone serious. "An adventure, yes. But it's not going to be a joy ride," I warned. "Things will be harsh at first. We won't have all the comforts and conveniences that we have here."

"So?" Ophelia asked, raising her eyebrow as if to dare me to continue implying she wasn't tough enough for the challenge that awaited us.

I couldn't help a smile, my chest warming some more for my woman. "You know, I'm really starting to like you."

She chuckled and pressed herself against me. "You had better, because I like you lots."

I kissed her lips again, the tender emotion that had been taking root in my heart growing further.

"Are we going to start our own Pride or just live like hermits?" Ophelia asked softly as we began to rinse each other.

"Just the two of us will be difficult," I conceded, "unless we move to the city, which I would rather not. Some of the older males here would gladly follow me if I wanted to start my own camp."

"Not a Pride?" Ophelia asked. "You wouldn't want some females to tag along?"

I hesitated. "To be honest, I doubt any of them would want to come. But it's not going to be an issue for what I have in mind."

"All right. But where would we go?"

"There's lots of land available," I said with confidence. "It is open for any Pride or nomads to claim. Most people avoid certain areas because there is no infrastructure, and they do not possess the skills to develop them. I learned a lot on Molvi. And thanks to the credits Lord Amreth sheltered from Rozel's greedy hands, I have enough of a starter fund for us to acquire the basics that we will need."

"I have my own savings and many contacts among intergalactic charitable organizations who could help us find affordable stuff. We could build a dream Pride! Or camp, however you want to call it," she amended sheepishly.

I smiled, a spark of hope and excitement I had not felt in a long time surging within me. "Yeah, I think we can create something amazing."

Her eyes flicked between mine with a sliver of suspicion. "You've been planning this for a while, haven't you?"

It was my turn to give her a sheepish expression. "I fantasized about it many times over the years, and even more so since my return. To me, it was just that, a wild dream that I had fun trying to sort out the details of, even knowing that it would never come true. And then you came into my life. It was the final push I needed to make the jump."

"Me?!" she exclaimed, stunned.

I nodded. "You made me realize that I really don't want to live in a place that tries to dictate who I can be with, how I must live, and whom I may love. I refuse to stay somewhere I'm not valued or wanted for who I am instead of just what I have to offer. You make me feel worthy of love and respect."

"Because you are," she said with a conviction that messed with my head.

"My beautiful mate," I whispered before claiming her lips.

She wrapped her arms around my neck, her fingers sinking into the wet strands of my mane as lukewarm water continued to rain down on us. Her lips parted beneath mine, and my tongue immediately answered the invitation. The arousal that had abated during our conversation came back in force. My cock hardened as my hands began roaming over her again, but this time with a much different intent than when I was washing her.

Ophelia moaned against my lips and pressed her pelvis against me. But our height difference had my shaft pressing against her stomach instead. I lifted her up and she instantly wrapped her legs around my waist. To my surprise, keeping herself propped up with one arm around my neck, my woman slipped the other one between us to stroke me. I hissed against her mouth as intense pleasure immediately built in my loins. My mate quickly realized that she only had to start twisting her wrist as she stroked the spiked section of my cock to have me cresting in no time.

Refusing to let her one up me, I took a couple of steps towards the tiled shower wall and pressed her back against it for additional support. Holding her with one arm under her bum, I also snuck my fingers between us to rub her clit. Finding her already wet for me had me burning with too much impatience to settle for long preliminaries.

To my shock, Ophelia appeared to be on the same wavelength as I was. I'd barely given her little nub a few rubs before she was pushing my hand aside with the back of hers and then aligning my head with her slit. A part of me wanted to argue that she needed more preparation, but the other was more than happy to oblige.

I barely started pushing myself in before my female brutally jerked her hips down, impaling herself on my cock. We both cried out at the burn, and Ophelia buried her face in my neck and then bit me with her blunt teeth. It was hard enough to sting, but not enough to break skin.

However, it broke something else in me.

I didn't give her the time to adjust to me. I willed more of my self-lubrication to exude to help compensate a little for the lack of proper preparation, and immediately began to move inside her. My pace quickly picked up as I thrust deeper into her. Ophelia clawed at my back, spurring me on with her moans and the throaty way she whispered my name.

In no time, I was pounding into her, my blood boiling with an insatiable passion, as she squeezed my length from all sides, electric sparks steadily firing off from each of my sensitive spikes. Feeling myself nearing the edge, I slightly shifted my angle so that my head would strike her sweet spot first on the way in, before my spikes gave it another rub both going in and out.

Moments later, Ophelia cried out. Her inner walls clamping down on my cock wrested my own climax out of me. I roared and slammed myself in deep as my seed shot out in a blissful flow. The searing heat of her tight sheath continued to contract spasmodically around my length, squeezing every last drop out of me.

Breathing heavily, I pressed my forehead against hers, as our pulses slowly settled down. Lifting my head, I kissed her lips before locking eyes with her. We smiled, the tenderness and a deeper emotion too early to give a name to shining brightly between us.

Not ready to end the deep intimacy of the moment, I buried my face in her neck, and we remained immobile for a moment with the sound of the still raining water as the baseline to our hearts beating as one. Ophelia suddenly stiffening snapped me out of my blissful daze.

"Don't stop!" she exclaimed in a pleading voice.

I lifted my head to look at her with confusion. "Don't stop what?"

"You were purring," she said piteously. "It was beautiful."

I gaped at her for a moment, trying to remember myself doing it. Then I smiled, my heart melting with a tender emotion.

"I don't recall doing it, but I could see it happening for you. Sadly, as I mentioned before, it cannot be ordered. It must be earned," I said teasingly.

Ophelia scrunched her face at me and mumbled something unintelligible that made me chuckle. She then glanced down between us before looking back up at me with a falsely disapproving look.

"We just finished washing. And now you've made a mess again!"

"I did," I concurred, unrepentant. "But since we're already in the shower, I say we get a little dirtier still and then wash it off when we're done."

She grinned and gently bit my bottom lip. "I like the way you think. By all means, show me how dirty you can get, especially if it ends with some more purring," she quipped, making me instantly hard again.

And show her, I did.

CHAPTER 15
OPHELIA

We spent the next couple of days scouting the land in search of our new home. Things were a little complicated as Gaelec still needed to work during the day. Obviously, we couldn't broadcast our intentions and played it off as if we were just going on romantic escapades while my mate showed me my new home world.

A part of me felt guilty about using the Pride's shuttle and speeders to plan our departure. At the same time, it was only fair considering the measly wages my husband received for the long hours of work he put in daily.

Granted, in comparison to the city, prices within the Pride were extremely low. Most goods would be traded amongst them in exchange for another item or for labor. People didn't have to shop for food as all meals were communal. Even for couples who ate privately at home instead of with everyone else in the Great Hall, they only had to go pick up whatever ingredients they needed from the larder and shared food storage.

As overwhelming as our plans somewhat felt, I was truly excited about embarking on that adventure with Gaelec. Melelyn was a stunning planet. The region we lived in also had the perfect weather. There was no winter here. This area compared to the Caribbean on Earth. With sunny skies year-round, warm weather, little humidity, and no tornadoes or hurricanes, what more could we want?

We stopped in various sectors that were deemed fair game. They were easily identifiable as claimed land had a marker warning wandering people that they were on the verge of trespassing. The specific boundaries of claimed territory would show up on their version of a GPS. They also had motion detectors and beacons set specifically to issue a warning whenever strangers entered that land. Furthermore, like cats, Nazhrals possessed scent glands under their paws that allowed them to mark their territory.

It turned out to be even more complicated than buying a house. So many things needed to be taken into consideration beyond the mere availability of resources nearby. Yes, we wanted highly populated hunting grounds, fertile land to grow some of our own produce or breed some animals, a good water source, easily defensible positions, and reasonable accessibility to nearby villages for trade, and to the city to be able to hook up to their network... among others.

Many of the places that we visited lacked one or more of those things. The first abandoned nomad camp that we stumbled on got me excited. But it quickly became obvious why they gave up on it. The soil was too hard with some kind of really dense rocks that would make it extremely costly and time consuming to dig a proper sewer system. It also sat open on every side, making it extremely difficult to protect. We didn't fear attacks from other Prides, but roaming animals could prove problematic, especially during mating season.

It was only on the fourth day that we found the one. Another abandoned roaming males' camp. Located on the Gyota Plateau, the place was stunning. I wasn't quite certain why they called it a plateau when it was in fact a bay surrounded by tall rock outcroppings that provided the natural defenses we sought. A beautiful waterfall on the left side gave it a lost paradise feel. A short distance away, the plateau gradually turned into a forest teeming with life, but nothing too fearsome or dangerous.

The best part of it all was that a basic sewer system had already been set up on top of a well for fresh water. The latter surprised me as Nazhrals, like most cats, could drink seawater. Unlike humans, their kidneys were able to filter salt out of the water. This was great news as it reduced the burden of making this place more welcoming for me. The handful of buildings that once served as houses would need to be razed to the ground. At a glance, this place had been deserted for several years.

"Why was it abandoned?" I asked, baffled as to why they did all this work only to call it quits.

"I can only speculate," Gaelec said pensively as he examined our surroundings. "I don't see any functional energy or communication systems. If they failed to set proper ones, their camp would never have thrived in the long run. They had to have had something energy-wise, if only to dig the sewer system. But I suspect they might have had a generator, which gets extremely costly and isn't a viable permanent solution."

"Won't we have the same issue?" I asked, worried.

He shook his head and smiled smugly. "Energy efficiency is my specialty. This place is perfect for us to set up a geothermal energy system. It is going to be our most costly investment, but it will make our lives infinitely better down the road. As for coms, we'll have to get ourselves a tower with a signal booster. It will be a lot of work, but I'm thrilled at the prospect. If those charitable organizations you spoke about can help us find discounted electronics, it will allow me to stretch my funds to the fullest. For most everything else, we can gather the materials ourselves to save on cost."

"And my funds as well," I reminded him in a slightly chastising tone.

He smiled and nodded, although I suspected that, as much as possible, he would try to keep my own savings for last.

"Any chance your brother would join us?" I asked as we walked around the area, trying to plan the rough layout of what our village could eventually look like.

He pursed his lips with a dubious expression. "Kazaer and Ylis are growing extremely close. I'm certain she will claim him."

"Exactly!" I exclaimed enthusiastically. "Having them both here would be perfect."

He gave me an indulgent smile. "You forget that Ylis is in a very strong position at the Pride. I suspect she will become the Head Huntress in the not-too-distant future in spite of Oluina's plotting and scheming. Life here in Gyota will be hard for the first few years. For me, it will be no different than my time on Molvi. For them, it will be brutal."

He cast a concerned look my way, his wheels spinning as he further pondered the matter.

"I know you said you're used to roughing things. But I fear that it might be difficult for you as well."

"Don't worry about me. So far, I've seen nothing that makes me freak out," I said in all sincerity. "I've helped rebuild entire villages from scratch after they got devastated by a natural disaster. Granted, we had some additional support and decent equipment from the charitable organizations I worked for. But like I said, I've been looking into what kind of aid and programs we might get some help with. I think we'll be fine. The challenge will be getting a few more hands on deck. It will be harder to get aid for only two people."

He nodded, a serious expression on his face as he reflected on my words. "We will have a few people with us. I'm not worried about that. And once the word spreads, I wouldn't be surprised if we start benefiting from the presence of a few older males who just got evicted. They will be only too happy to find a new permanent home where they can thrive."

I returned his smile despite the sliver of worry that sparked deep within. I didn't know and understand his people well enough just yet to truly know what to expect of roaming males. In my mind, all I pictured were a bunch of raiders and poachers, ready to descend upon us and appropriate everything we would build here.

We would need to further discuss the matter based on how many people ended up choosing to join us, whether from our current Pride or elsewhere. The prospect of being the sole woman among a whole bunch of single males who'd been discarded by their previous females didn't exactly make me feel safe. No matter how badass a fighter Gaelec was, if everyone else turned on us, there wouldn't be much he could do. I could fire a mean blaster, but seeing how fast those Nazhrals moved, I could only take out so many attackers before I became over-whelmed.

Casting out those grim thoughts, I refocused on the task at hand as we finished plotting out our new village.

The next evening, we flew to the capital city, once again under the pretense of Gaelec giving me a tour. In reality, we wanted to shop around for base materials, equipment, tools, and check out what governmental services might be available for Prides.

To our shock, there turned out to be quite a few, including some aimed at providing advanced education focused on new technology.

"I wonder if the Matriarchs know about this," Gaelec mused aloud.

I chewed my bottom lip while reflecting on it. Simply navigating the interface of the self-serve kiosk in the Office of Citizens Services was super complicated. Someone as resistant to change as Rozel was might have been turned off by this—assuming she ever even saw any of this.

"I don't know," I replied at last. "Governmental programs like these are often needlessly complicated. Applying is a headache, meeting the qualifications can be quite a challenge, and getting proper assistance navigating the process is nearly impossible. On Earth, some of our leaders would create similar programs purely for political gain and as a nice talking point. They would brag about all the things they did for us. But at the end of the day, they made them extremely hard to access specifically so that they would never have to spend any budget on it."

"That's rather devious," Gaelec said with a frown.

"That's politicians for you," I said, my voice making it clear I didn't have too high an opinion of people in that field. "I've filled in these kinds of forms in the past. So I have no problem playing with it."

We left the governmental office and returned to our shopping —although it was simply browsing to get an idea of what kind of dent our budget would suffer once we were ready to make the move. By the time we were done, I was beyond ready to get the hell out of the city.

The capital was your typical metropolis. Everything was too big, too busy, too noisy, and especially too flashy. I was surprised I didn't have a seizure from all the blinking lights and animations from the giant screens everywhere trying to draw people's attention. Even the signs outside the various businesses and venues felt like they were screaming at me.

Although I wasn't clinically diagnosed with agoraphobia, being surrounded by so many people rushing in every direction made me dizzy, almost nauseous. I didn't understand how people could enjoy that life where they all looked constantly stressed and either running after something or being chased by someone. I felt exhausted just observing the city dwellers' interactions.

Flying back out to the Nevian Valley felt like stepping into another world. It was insane the drastic difference in lifestyle between two classes of the same species. The Capital City might have been anywhere on any other advanced planet, with a diverse population from countless other worlds and high-tech galore.

As much as I disliked the current Pride we were living in, I would pick that life any day over drowning in the glitz and whirlwind of that urban jungle.

Struck by an idea, as soon as we got home, I sent inquiries about any available UPO support programs for developing member planets. Even though the Nazhrals' home world sat high on the naughty list, they remained official members of the organization, and therefore were entitled to some benefits.

Three days later, after we returned home from one of the few times we participated in the communal meals to help hide what we were planning, my com beeped with a new message.

"Oh putain!" I exclaimed when I saw the name of the sender.

"What is it?" Gaelec asked, immediately tense.

"It's from Kayog," I replied. "He wants us to have a call in twenty minutes, if possible."

Gaelec immediately frowned, his almost angry expression taking me aback.

"What's wrong?" I asked, wondering what might have happened between them since our marriage that would have prompted such a negative reaction.

"You are already mated," Gaelec snarled. "You're mine, *my* soulmate. The Temern doesn't get to change his mind."

I gaped at him for a second before bursting out laughing. He was so stinking cute, even as he stared at me with an expression equally hurt and outraged that I hadn't instantly sided with him.

"Oh, sweetie, whatever Kayog is messaging me about, I assure you it's not to try and hook me up with someone else.

He's never wrong, remember? He already paired the two of us, and I don't want anyone else but you."

Gaelec scrunched his face, feeling equally silly for his over-reaction and touched by my words. I walked up to him and slipped my arms around his waist.

"You're cute when you're jealous. But you have no reason to be."

He harrumphed and then leaned forward to kiss me. It was far too brief for my liking. At the same time, if we indulged further, I would undoubtedly miss the call with the Temern.

"Give me a second to confirm," I said, brushing my lips against his before pulling out of his embrace.

"You let him know I will attend as well," he grumbled.

I snorted but nodded and quickly typed the response on my com.

"By the way, what was that word you said when you received the message?" Gaelec asked.

I blinked, unsure what he meant. "What word?"

"Pootain, or something along those lines," he said.

My cheeks immediately felt on the verge of bursting into flames. I had quite the potty mouth at times. The worst part was that I often didn't even realize I was using questionable words.

"It's a French swear word," I admitted sheepishly. "French is one of many languages on Earth. Doesn't your translation implant have that module included?"

"I don't have a translation implant. Only the people raised in the cities do. Pride members don't get them at birth. As we don't really interact with off-worlders, it's not necessary," he explained. "We learn Universal, which is enough to meet our needs on the rare occasions some of us go on missions or in the city."

"Fair enough," I conceded.

Learning Universal as a secondary language was compulsory for every member of the United Planets Organization. Even species that weren't part of the alliance—but who had achieved light travel—also learned it as it was the one language that allowed for intergalactic communication.

"So what does it mean? That word and the other strange things you say sometimes? Like..." He hesitated, his eyes tilting up and to the right as he searched his memory. "Board hell?"

I squirmed and glanced at my watch, hoping the twenty minutes were up, but we still had plenty of time left.

"It can't be that bad?" he insisted, now looking extremely curious in light of my reluctance.

I heaved a sigh and just went for it. "It's not Pootain, but *Putain*. Literally, it means prostitute," I said, heat creeping back up on my cheeks at his stunned expression. "But in practice, it's mostly used almost the exact same way we use fuck. So it can express amazement, anger, confusion, or excitement."

"What a strange term for that," he said, looking baffled.

I shrugged. "No stranger than fuck. After all it means penetrative sex. So when you think about it, saying 'I don't fucking know' makes absolutely no sense if you take the word literally."

He nodded. "Good point. And what about the other?"

"*Bordel* means whorehouse," I said, embarrassed. "And it's pretty much used the same way as *putain*, with subtle nuances. And it will often come accompanied by a couple of extra words like for reinforcement, usually when angry. Like *bordel de merde*, which would literally translate as whorehouse of shit."

I couldn't help but chuckle like a schoolgirl just listening to myself say the words.

He snorted, amusement creeping in on his features. "Merrde. That's another one I heard you say quite a few times. So I'm assuming that means feces?"

I nodded, a silly grin plastered on my face, not only over the fact that I was teaching him French swear words, but also at his ridiculously adorable accent.

"And when you truly want to go all out, you can say *putain de bordel de saloperie de merde!'* right before you flip a table or something."

He laughed. "Would it be fair to presume that *salop*... whatever that word was is also sex trade related?" he asked with a smile in his voice.

"Kind of. *Salope* is another vulgar term for a whore—though it could also refer to a slob—but it's truly used as an insult. And *saloperie* is a noun derived from it meaning something extremely crappy and vulgar."

"Are all French swear words related to prostitution?!" he asked, laughing.

"Not prostitution, specifically. But to sex in general, yeah."

For half a beat, I considered just stringing a whole bunch of them just to see how much I could traumatize him. But just as I was starting to think better of it, my com went off, informing me of an incoming call.

"*Oh merde!*" I exclaimed.

Gaelec laughed behind me as I rushed to the vidscreen. I accepted the call before casting it onto the large device while settling down on the couch. My mate sat next to me. The possessive, almost defiant way in which he placed his hand on my lap to clearly mark me as his cracked me up. I bit the inside of my cheeks to repress a smile. His insecurity was both silly and incredibly endearing. The fool didn't realize how hard I'd been falling for him over the past few days.

"Hello, Ophelia and Gaelec," Kayog said with his legendary enthusiasm.

"Hello, Kayog," I said in a similarly cheerful tone.

Gaelec gave him a polite, if somewhat stiff nod.

The Temern's silver eyes flicked to my mate's hand on my lap, and the subtle quirking of the stiff corners of his beak seemed to hint he'd guessed the meaning of that possessive display. Obviously, he couldn't read emotions through a vidscreen, but I bet he was a master at reading body language.

"Marriage seems to agree with the both of you," Kayog continued. "I'm assuming things are going well?"

"Perfectly well," Gaelec replied, sounding slightly belligerent.

I barely kept myself from rolling my eyes while Kayog's smile broadened to the extent his beak allowed.

"Unsurprising. After all, I'm never wrong," he said smugly.

I snorted, not so much because of the shameless boasting, but because my gut told me with a certainty I couldn't explain that the comment had been directly aimed at my husband to tell him to stop being so silly. And it worked like a charm. Gaelec immediately relaxed. I gave him a mocking sideways glance, to which he replied by scrunching his face.

"What can we do for you, Master Voln?" Gaelec asked, a bit of grumpiness lingering in his voice.

"Actually, I'm calling to tell you what *I* can do for *you*!" he said with a grin.

Gaelec and I exchanged a confused look before glancing back at the Temern.

"What *you* can do for *us*?" I repeated.

He nodded. "If you recall, before leaving the spaceport, I mentioned that I would be late sending your wedding present."

"Oh, wow! Right. I forgot about that," I said sheepishly. "But you don't have to give us anything. Pairing us was already the best present you could have come up with."

My throat constricted at the sweet and paternal expression that descended over his features when I said those words.

"Oh, my dear… While your words touch me deeply, and although I couldn't agree with them more, reuniting two soulmates is only indirectly a gift to them. It's an even greater one to myself. Which means I still owe you a present. And from what I hear, it would come in extremely handy to the two of you."

I blinked, taken aback by that last comment. Gaelec and I exchanged another confused look, laced with the same curiosity.

"Okay, color me intrigued," I said.

"I heard about your request to the UPO," he explained, his face suddenly taking on an unusually serious expression. "As the UPO has a vested interest in the type of changes your plan could help bring about for your people, I can be significantly more generous in the type of presents I can offer."

My heart skipped a beat. My eyes still glued to the screen, I blindly reached for Gaelec's hand, squeezing it tightly. He placed his other hand on top of mine, giving it a soothing caress even as he also continued to stare at the Temern with the same anticipatory tension I felt.

"As you may know, my agency has a discretionary budget for presents to newlyweds. On rare occasions, the UPO will give us the green light to increase it, which was the case for you."

"Why?" Gaelec asked, suspicion seeping into his voice.

"Your success could have the type of domino effect that the UPO and the Enforcers are looking for," Kayog explained. "For them, this constitutes a long-term investment without them having to send in off-worlders to meddle daily with the local population—which usually doesn't go too well."

"What's the catch?" Gaelec insisted, his suspicion cranking up another notch.

Although taken aback by his reaction, I couldn't deny the validity of his inquiry. Having always worked under the umbrella of large charities, I never really bothered with the politics behind the funding we received. I was just happy to get my hands dirty and see how my work helped improve the lives of people facing hardships. But now, I realized I could be a little naive as my brain started listing all the things that could indeed be problematic for my husband. I didn't go into law because I couldn't be bothered with the fine print. Yet that was the most important as it was how they always screwed you over.

"The requirements are that everything you will receive must be used exclusively for your new Pride, not be resold or traded to a third party. Your Pride must commit not to engage in crimes or piracy and pledge to expel any member who breaks that commitment. The UPO will also want some oversight on—"

"No!" Gaelec said in a tone that brooked no argument, interrupting him halfway through that last sentence. "The first two requests are entirely acceptable. Giving away whatever technology you share with us would be stupid, and the whole point of leaving Nevian Pride is specifically because we no longer want to be forced into committing crimes. But the last demand is a deal breaker. The UPO will not get to dictate anything that happens here. We will be our own people, with our own rules, not puppets to be controlled and manipulated according to the whims of some overseer."

To my shock, Kayog didn't launch into a vehement argument as to why it is entirely reasonable for the UPO to want to have some sort of say, considering the substantial investment they might make in us. Instead, he gave Gaelec a mysterious smile. In that instant, I realized he not only approved of his response, but he likely also hoped my husband would have shut him down on that point.

"Expect them to try to push," Kayog said in a slightly teasing tone.

Gaelec shrugged. "They can push all they want. The answer will remain no."

The Temern's smile broadened. This time, whatever doubt I might still have that he wanted my mate to stand firm against the UPO fully vanished. In fact, I believed this had been a test and that, had Gaelec answered the wrong way, Kayog might have tried to coach him into taking a different stance.

"You have a difficult journey ahead," Kayog continued, sobering. "But no challenge is too great with the right partner. Rely on each other, and I have no doubt you will accomplish great things. I cannot stay much longer as duty calls me away. But I will forward to your com the list of items the PMA will personally gift to you. The UPO—although I suspect it will be the Enforcers—will directly contact you in the upcoming days to let you know what programs you are eligible for. I wish you the very best of success and happiness."

"Thank you, Kayog," I said, my heart filling with gratitude.

"Yes, thank you, Master Voln," Gaelec echoed.

The Temern winked at us and then terminated the communication.

Seconds later, my com went off with an incoming message. Before I even opened it, I knew it would be the list he mentioned. I cast it onto the vidscreen so that we could both browse it at the same time.

My jaw dropped as soon as it came into focus.

"By the Gods!" Gaelec whispered, shock, awe, and something else I couldn't describe filling his voice.

But I didn't need to read minds to know what powerful emotion was coursing through him. My own throat felt constricted as I read some of the biggest expenses we would have to juggle being listed as gifts. The major one, which would have eaten more than half of Gaelec's savings was a state-of-the-art geothermal energy system. The other notable elements included a high-end com system booster, two advanced medical pods, five self-deployable buildings, two speeders, and one-rent-to-buy shuttle.

Although the latter would require for us to shell out some credits, it was the best possible option for us as this type of rental came with full maintenance and repair services, including replacement if it became unusable. Under the circumstances, the chances of us passing the credit approval for a lease on our own would have been slim to none.

Happy tears pricked my eyes as I turned to look at Gaelec. Seeing his eyes overly bright as his own happy tears threatened to well utterly wrecked me.

"We're going to do this," I said, my voice thick with

emotion. "We're going to succeed beyond anything we ever hoped for."

"We are," Gaelec replied before crushing my lips in a passionate kiss devoid of lust.

A yelp escaped me, interrupting our kiss when the sound of a loud banging rattled the front door. Startled, my mate and I exchanged a confused and slightly worried look as to what this could be about.

"Gaelec Sulwyn, open the door immediately!" Moriak's voice shouted from outside. "You and your human are to stand immediately before the Matriarchs for treason!"

CHAPTER 16
GAELEC

My blood boiled with rage as we were all but dragged to the Great Hall by Moriak and his usual minions—Latsa and Olmar—like a pair of vulgar criminals. I didn't care so much about their treatment of me, but the disrespect to my woman was unacceptable. Had I not already decided to leave the Pride, this would have been the final strike.

We entered the Hall and already found it packed, the few stragglers hurrying in behind us. How did the word spread so far and wide in the short time it took them to lay that accusation and fetch us? As the communal meal ended more than an hour ago, people should have been at home minding their own business.

The usual suspects were sitting on the dais. Rozel looked furious. Oluina grinned with an air of triumphant malice. But it was the worried look on Ylis's face that unsettled me. Although the accusation was serious, her reaction hinted that things might be worse than I feared.

"You lied to us about your visit to the city and around the land," Rozel hissed in lieu of greeting as soon as we stopped in front of her.

Although we weren't handcuffed or otherwise restrained,

Moriak and the two guards continued flanking us, ready to intervene at the first sign of trouble. For all that, Latsa and Olmar didn't seem particularly happy to be performing that duty.

"How did I lie?" I challenged, my voice frosty. "You can check the tracker on the shuttle and on the speeders which will confirm that we have indeed been to the city and the surrounding lands. How does that get my mate and me slandered with the label of traitors?"

"Because they weren't purely for touristic reasons, like you pretended. You did so because you're planning on leaving!" she snarled.

I lifted a defiant chin, and stared at her in a way that made it clear I didn't see how that was a problem.

"I did take my mate on a touristic exploration of her new home world, but I also seized the opportunity to assess our options."

"That's treason!" Rozel shouted over the shocked murmurs of the crowd around us.

"How is that treason?" I demanded, undaunted. "From the day I returned, and even more so since my mate's arrival, you've done nothing but constantly threaten us with eviction. What did you expect us to do? Sit by idly with hopes and prayers while waiting for you to reach a verdict? What would happen if you decided to kick us out, and we didn't plan for an alternative place for us to go? You may be dismissive of our fate, but I have a mate to care for. It is my duty to plan for her comfort and welfare, whatever the ultimate outcome."

Rozel huffed and waved her hand with disdain. "That's irrelevant. Granted, we can't begrudge you looking for a backup plan, but your top priority should have been to make every reasonable effort to convince us to keep you. You have shown no devotion, no commitment."

"Convince you how?" I asked, throwing my hands up in exasperated disbelief. "Do I not contribute every day? Did I not pass a test that very few could boast about being even able to survive? Did I not go out of my way to warn you of all the potential dangers to this Pride? Have I not offered time and time again to upgrade the village's infrastructure and optimize our systems—all of which *you* declined? What more do you want from me?"

"Commitment!" she yelled.

I huffed, making no effort to hide the contempt I felt. "No, Matriarch. It's not a commitment you want. You just want me to grovel. This entire time, you've made it a point to remind me how my mate and I were only here by your grace, that we could easily be dismissed on your whim. You wanted us to feel insecure and helpless. Desperate people accept anything."

"I never asked you to grovel!" Rozel exclaimed in outrage.

"You never ask for it in so many words, but your actions demanded no less. This tactic may work with others—and it used to work with me as well when I was young and naïve—but no more," I continued, my voice harsh and unyielding. "Now, I make sure to never place myself in a situation where I'll be so desperate as to find myself at someone else's mercy. So yes, we've been planning our departure. I will not beg for acceptance. We have laid before you all that we could offer, but nothing ever seems to be enough. If you do not see my worth, then that's your loss."

She made another dismissive gesture, her eyes burning with anger—although I suspected that it was more aimed at my defiance and lack of submission than at my words themselves.

"Whatever talents you may possess mean nothing without loyalty," she argued.

"Loyalty?" I echoed with disbelief before waving a hand at Moriak. "Is *that* your glowing example of what a loyal male should be? Because by my definition, this is what I call self-serving ambition. You used to have the best Pride in the entire county. Why do you think I came here as soon as I reached maturity instead of the many other Prides closer to my birthplace? But over the years, this aging fool you call your Alpha keeps culling all the prime males who tried to join you to save his position."

Moriak started sputtering in outrage at the offense, but I ignored him to point an accusing finger at Oluina.

"Your own daughter, your Head Huntress, only half-trains your younger females for fear they will surpass her in time. I consented to train Ylis when she approached me about it, once I noticed how lacking the current program was. There's a reason she's the best one you have today."

"That's a lie!" Oluina shouted, abruptly standing up, her hands fisted on each side of her body.

"It *is* true!" Ylis interjected. "We have lost too many hunts that we shouldn't have due to poor training. Ask our younglings how many times you've told them that some techniques are pointless."

"Because they are!" Oluina snapped defensively.

I made a disgusted sound while a troubled expression descended over Rozel's features.

"See? Even your females can see the problems. You are letting your village become antiquated because you're afraid to adapt and to evolve. So yes, I *am* looking to leave. Life is too short to waste it being used by ungrateful and calculating people," I said, throwing all caution to the wind.

I realized how I had allowed myself to get carried away when Ophelia slipped her hand in mine. My head jerked towards her. The guilt wanting to surge within me instantly faded when I found her staring defiantly at the Matriarch. She wasn't distressed by how I had handled it but clearly supported it. My heart once again filled with affection for my little human. She was truly my soulmate.

"Then leave now!" Rozel yelled, jumping to her paws.

"As you wish," I replied, sounding almost pleased in my anger.

"Gaelec!" Ylis exclaimed, standing up as well with a disbelieving expression.

I gave her an apologetic look. "It's okay, Ylis. It was inevitable and obvious from day one. Be safe, and I'm sure we'll talk again at some point."

Holding my woman's hand, I turned around to leave the Hall under the flabbergasted murmurs of the crowd.

"Do not use our shuttles or speeders!" Rozel shouted behind us, her voice bitter and filled with venom. "You have two hours to be gone or face our wrath!"

I didn't turn to acknowledge her and merely kept walking. Ophelia cast a slightly worried glance my way. I squeezed her hand and gave her a reassuring smile. Despite her fury, the Matriarch would not do us harm without seriously jeopardizing her own standing within the Pride—not that I believed she would stoop so low. That excessive reaction was due to a bruised ego. She'd never been thus publicly rejected. This was her humiliation speaking.

Two hours would be extremely tight to pack everything and be gone, especially without a shuttle. I whipped out my com from my belt and tapped a few instructions to call a city shuttle. The earliest one would be here in twenty-five minutes. Not wanting to waste more credits than necessary as it idled outside, I booked it to be here in an hour. If we hurried, we could have our most important things packed and ready to load by the time it arrived.

Wasting no time, we went straight for the essentials, which mainly revolved around clothes for my mate, our computers, my tools, and everything necessary to cook and hunt. Barely ten minutes in, a loud banging on the door resonated, startling us. Ophelia ran out of the bedroom, where she had been packing her stuff to cast a panicked look towards the front door and then towards me. I raised my hand in an appeasing gesture before heading for the door.

"Gaelec! It's me, Ylis!"

A wave of relief flooded through me upon hearing the muffled sound of the huntress' voice. She barged inside the house as soon as I opened the door. She was carrying a few large, empty travel bags.

"What can I help with?" she demanded, her eyes flicking left and right to assess the amount of things to be packed.

My heart filled with affection for the young female. We didn't share blood, but she truly was the sister of my heart.

"The bedroom," I said, gesturing towards it.

Her palm pressed to her chest, Ophelia was staring at Ylis with a trembling smile filled with gratitude. The same affection shone in her eyes as we headed towards her.

Thankfully, as I returned to the Pride barely a month ago, I hadn't had a chance to acquire too many new things beyond the personal belongings I brought back from the prison planet. Ophelia had the largest number of items, many of which we worked swiftly to organize in the original crates she brought them in. While the two females worked on that, I threw my own stuff into a separate bag.

"Why did you have to be so harsh?" Ylis asked, her voice filled with disapproval and confusion. "Why not keep the peace? She wouldn't have cast you out. Too many of us had already voted in both your favor."

"I won't be a servant, Ylis," I said firmly. "And I certainly will not tolerate my mate being constantly disrespected and facing intimidation attempts. And we both want younglings that we refuse to see treated the way they currently are in this Pride."

"I get that, but you barely got here!" Ylis exclaimed as if she found me irrational. "You haven't had a chance to get your bearings, and Ophelia still barely knows our world. Where will you go? You know they will try to exploit you in the city."

I nodded and gave her a gentle smile while picking my weapons from the bottom drawer.

"Like I told Rozel, we've been planning for the eventuality that we would be kicked out. We already found a place. And it's definitely not the city."

Ylis perked up. "Oh? Where are you going? Are you planning to join the Osuan Pride?"

I snorted and shook my head. "Although I did consider it, and as much as I like the more modern approach that they're taking with how they run their village, we have decided to start our own Pride, or rather camp, as that would be a more accurate term. We will settle in the Gyota Plateau."

"The abandoned nomad camp?!"

I nodded. Her eyes flicked from side to side as she heavily reflected on the matter. She was likely cycling through what memories she had of the place and assessing its viability.

"It is a beautiful place with good hunting," Ylis conceded carefully, "but it is pretty bare there. The infrastructure is super basic."

I nodded again. "It is, but it also has a pretty good foundation for us to build on, and we already have quite a few things in motion that should have us in a great position fairly quickly."

"I'm glad to hear it," she said, her tone somewhat relieved despite the lingering uncertainty. "You will need help. A lot of the older males here have a great deal of respect for you. They would certainly be relieved to hear that there was a place that might welcome them when Rozel begins the evictions in the upcoming weeks."

I snorted and smiled in a non-committal fashion. "The respect for them is mutual. So long as they were willing to abide by the rules we will set, I would be happy to have them."

She smiled, looking further relieved. A part of me wanted to tell her that I already broached the topic with a few of those males who expressed their enthusiasm at tagging along. But now that this whole thing was becoming a reality, I had to account for the possibility that they might get nervous at the last minute and bow out. Outing them before they were fully committed didn't feel right.

"Take Kazaer with you," Ylis said in a tone that brooked no argument.

Ophelia's face reflected the shock I felt upon hearing those words.

"Really?" my mate asked hesitantly. "You don't want him to stay here? I doubt he'll want to go anywhere that you're not."

Ylis's face heated in the most adorable fashion, that instantly had some of my tension lessen. She gave her a timid but strained smile.

"Of course, I want him here. But this place is a complete mess right now. No one in their right mind should join us until all the internal conflicts are sorted out," she said, looking dejected.

"Then maybe you should join us," Ophelia said with a shameless grin.

"Ophelia!" I exclaimed in a disapproving tone.

"What?!" she asked with an exaggerated innocent expression. "You're thinking it, too!"

"Be that as it may, we cannot put this kind of pressure on her," I said in a chastising tone.

"It's okay, Gaelec. Honestly, I would have been offended had neither of you offered," Ylis said with a stiff smile. "But things are complicated. If I leave, many of the young females will want to follow. They do not want to be under Oluina's lead."

"That's perfect!" Ophelia exclaimed, her excitement palpable.

I hated dampening her joy, but a few facts needed to be stated, and expectations properly managed to avoid future disappointments and conflicts.

"Ylis, do not doubt that I would love nothing more than to have you and some of the other females with us. But you must understand that we're *not* building another Nevian Pride. We are done being used and abused," I explained gently but firmly. "Females who join us will not have dominion over us. Everyone will be treated as equals, and no one will live on borrowed time based on the whims of one group. That is the main reason we're currently not looking at inviting females. Their expectations would be unrealistic, based on traditions."

"Maybe some of them would agree to these new rules," Ophelia offered gently. "It's unfair to assume that none of them might be open to this. I think we should give them a chance to refuse, while hoping some would agree."

"I wouldn't have a problem with it," Ylis said without hesitation.

I chuckled affectionately while closing the bag I'd put most of my weapons within.

"*You* wouldn't, but how many others?" I challenged.

She pursed her lips, reflecting on my words as she finished stuffing one last pile of clothes in the biggest crate.

"That's food for thought," she conceded. "But like Ophelia said, I think you should give us a chance. I cannot speak for other Prides, but I can tell you that many of the younger females are not happy with how things are going. We're especially disgruntled with Moriak's behavior towards the candidates. Things are changing. You've given us much to reflect on since your return. And that's why I wished you had stayed with us longer. Do not sell us short. You've had a greater impact than you realize."

"Your words flatter me, Ylis," I said, genuinely touched. "But staying here truly was no longer viable."

She frowned and nodded. "It is indeed not viable for any male that Moriak perceives as a threat. He's grown more paranoid than ever since he put you through that 'test' the other day. And that's specifically why you need to take Kazaer with you to your camp. I really like him, and I cannot risk him getting harmed by Moriak."

"Then claim him!" I said in a self-evident tone.

She shook her head even as she started filling a second crate. "Moriak demands that anyone who wishes to join us participates in the upcoming Levendoc mission. The crew is set to depart in two days from now."

I bared my teeth, and a series of foul expletives tumbled out of my mouth.

"Kazaer can't go," Ophelia said, her voice tense.

"I know," Ylis said. "If he remains in the nomad camp outside instead of joining the mission, he will automatically be banned from joining our Pride under the pretext that he's a coward, not devoted enough to the Pride, and too rebellious to follow the Alpha's lead."

"That's such nonsense! That's just bullying and intimidation to try and coerce them into doing his bidding!" Ophelia exclaimed. "Is he seriously expecting every single one of these young males to go on a mission that is a trap from all indications?! Is Rozel truly okay with condemning these innocent candidates just because her sorry excuse of an Alpha is getting nervous?!"

"Like I said, it's complicated. Things were already slowly coming to a head. You two just precipitated the inevitable. Something will have to give, one way or the other," Ylis said with determination. "Just keep Kazaer safe for me while we sort things out here."

"I will," I promised.

She smiled gratefully. Having finished gathering my things in the bedroom, I left the two females to finish packing Ophelia's belongings and swiftly went through the other rooms where they joined me shortly afterwards.

The shuttle arrived ten minutes later than scheduled, which served us just fine in the end as it gave us the little extra time necessary to finish packing. As we loaded everything into our transport, a small crowd gathered outside our dwelling. They didn't speak. Some faces looked sad, others troubled, and the last group glared with unrepressed anger. It boggled my mind that they could truly be angry at me and deem me a traitor.

Then again, Ylis's words replayed in my mind. If my actions had indeed triggered a fundamental questioning of how things were run here, I could understand their resentment. Some people only wanted the comfort and safety of their routine. Anything that threatened it would be deemed as an assault. Change was a scary thing for many, even though it might be desperately needed.

We exchanged hugs with Ylis.

"You are welcome to visit us anytime," I said before releasing her from my embrace.

"Count on it," she replied, her voice thick with emotion.

I caressed her cheek, then turned to my mate to help her inside the shuttle, and then climbed on board. As the shuttle took off, I looked back down at the village that had so radically changed my life twice, first by sending me to prison, and now by setting me onto a new uncharted path.

Fear should have me nearly paralyzed, but as I glanced back at my mate's beautiful face, it was hope and excitement that filled my heart.

CHAPTER 17
OPHELIA

Despite the impromptu fashion in which we ended up moving into our new place, our first evening in Gyota was quite nice. While I cleaned up the biggest cabin with a breathtaking view of the river, Gaelec went hunting for something for us to eat. At the same time, he placed some motion detectors around a wide radius of our fledgling village. It was one of the few expenses we had done in the city.

They were a bit more advanced than the standard perimeter defense their people used whenever they would go on long hunts that could span a few days, requiring them to sleep in the wild. Roaming males and nomads also used something similar. It could identify whether the detected presence was a person or an animal.

If the former, we would receive a warning on our com system of an approaching intruder. In turn, that person would receive a warning of their own that they had just trespassed into claimed territory.

If the latter, the detector would emit either an audio or visual signal specifically adapted to the creature to scare it away, if necessary. Inoffensive creatures would be ignored, but predators would be chased.

We ended up having a rather romantic dinner on the beach, with roasted meat and some of the vegetables I had packed from the house. We slept on my extremely comfortable inflatable mattress. The intelligent foam inflated with a simple pressure from a button into a queen-size mattress. And in the morning, you only had to press that button again for it to deflate into a compact square shape the size of a folded blanket for easy storage.

It had been one of the perks provided by the charitable organizations for which I worked over the years. Unfortunately, as comfortable as it was, I often chose not to use it simply because some of the primitive tribes with which I worked frowned at me for not emulating their rougher lifestyles.

For the first half of the next day, we destroyed and cleaned everythings that had to go or could present a hazard. A little after lunch, the motion detector went off, informing us of four males approaching. Seconds later, Gaelec received a message from his brother reassuring him that he was the one who breached the perimeter with three companions.

My heart soared, not only that Kazaer agreed to join us—at least for now—but that he apparently succeeded in convincing a few of the other males camping with him outside the Nevian Village to also tag along.

As soon as they arrived, I immediately recognized the others from the feast. They had been among those who caught my attention by their impressive performance. Therefore, it wasn't surprising that Moriak wanted to get rid of them before they became an issue for him.

After quick formal introductions, Gaelec went over his vision for our village with them. Over the past week since we'd started getting this whole thing in motion, he had only given Kazaer a high-level description of what he intended to do on the rare occasions he went to visit him in the camp. Between his work during the day, and our scouting and plotting in the evening, there hadn't been much time for socializing, especially with these young males being forced to stay a fair distance away from the village in their makeshift camp.

Things were awkward at first. Considering the extent of the work that awaited us, they visibly questioned if that entire project actually had a leg to stand on. A part of me wished Gaelec would tell them about the amazing promise both Kayog and the UPO had given us, but the other was grateful he didn't. Although we had no reason to believe they might renege on any of it, it was better not to get the newcomers' hopes up only for them to be crushed if things fell through. But I also realized that my husband was testing their commitment to this project for its own merits, and not for easy access to the high-end technology that could arrive soon.

My gut told me that what would happen tomorrow or in the following days with that Levendoc mission would seriously impact these young males' desire to stay or leave. I felt horrible for wanting that mission to be over and to utterly fail so that my husband could be vindicated. Because that also meant the naïve candidates who chose to believe Moriak would be the ones paying the steep price.

Still, with these extra hands—who also happened to be quite strong—we got an insane amount of work done in record time. My mate being a natural leader, and a charismatic one at that, had no problem getting them to follow his instructions. His visible knowledge in a variety of fields further earned their respect.

But we had no illusions about them sticking around for long. They were young and healthy males who would soon want to seek out females to partner with. For now, I was just grateful for the help, and to know that their presence here meant they would be spared whatever awaited the others.

Like Gaelec and I did, they patched up one of the less damaged cabins which the four of them shared that night.

The next morning, four more males joined us, all of them older. I recognized Danel, the supervisor at the fishing plant. I didn't know the other three, except from seeing them in passing in the village.

He gave Gaelec a manly embrace that took me by surprise. I had not expected them to act with an almost brotherly familiarity. But as I observed the interaction between them, it dawned on me that this had been an instinctive reaction fueled by relief from Danel.

"I hope you still have room for us," Danel said with a slightly nervous laugh.

By human standards, at forty-two, he was still a young male. But for a Nazhral, he was deemed past his prime. It was all the more infuriating that they had a lifespan of a hundred and forty years, although males usually lasted less than half that due to the difficult lives they led.

"Of course, my friend," Gaelec said warmly. "There's plenty of room for people of goodwill and not afraid to get their hands dirty."

"That's definitely us," he replied, waving at his other companions. "As you can imagine, we were asked to join that ridiculous mission that seems to be a secret to no one. The four of us refused, so we were given an ultimatum. Either we participated or we would get kicked out. I'll let you guess which choice we made."

Gaelec chuckled. "Moriak must be livid to yet again have his authority challenged."

"That's quite the understatement, my friend," Danel said with a chuckle, before sobering. "Truth be told, if not for you, we probably would have caved in. We had no other option. Even with our skills, no Pride would want us when they can have younger males. Between roaming aimlessly until death claims us or taking our chances with a mission that would ensure our position in the Pride for a while longer, one seemed less terrible than the other."

"Getting caught during that mission—and that is a guarantee—would have landed you in a far worse situation than becoming a nomad. But I'm glad you're here. We can use your skills. As you can see, we are in a prime fishing location. You can help us set up the perfect fish plant taking into account all the things you wish you could have changed or improved back in Nevian."

"That sounds like a plan!" he replied enthusiastically.

Like Gaelec did, each of the males came with their tools and some equipment. They quickly got to work, a lot of it coming down to gathering the basic construction material needed to start building in earnest. Throughout the day, we checked for any news about the mission, but it was complete radio silence.

The next morning, we were all having breakfast gathered around a bonfire on the beach when the sound of thunderclap resonated above us followed by the opening of a giant portal in the sky. I nearly peed myself in fright. Our collective panic turned into awe when an Enforcer transport ship came right out of the giant black vortex and landed a short distance away on a large, unencumbered section of the beach.

Standing on wobbly legs, my heart still trying to beat its way out of my chest, I couldn't decide whether to keep gaping at the portal or shift my attention to the human man descending from the vessel. That was quickly sorted out for me as the portal vanished with a woosh.

"By the Gods! What is that?" Danel asked, seeming as unsure as the others if they should go into a defensive stance.

"It's the PMA and the UPO!" Kazaer replied, his voice bubbling with excitement. "They kept their promise!"

"What promise?" Danel asked.

"You'll see," Gaelec replied, a triumphant grin stretching his lips.

He marched towards the human with determined steps that went a long way to appeasing our companions, who were still somewhat frazzled by what we'd just witnessed. I was freaked out, too. But over the years, I'd grown to accept that all kinds of insane technology existed out there, some of which defied anything we could imagine. Nevertheless, it disturbed me that they should possess the ability to basically teleport a ship—and probably even an entire fleet—to a specific location on a whim. If they decided to perform a raid on us, we would never see them coming in time and let alone have any means to defend against it.

"Hello, Gaelec. I'm Tedrick Wilson, a senior officer with the Enforcers," the man said in a polite and friendly voice as he stopped a meter in front of us.

"Greetings, Tedrick," Gaelec replied in a similar fashion.

Tedrick turned to me with the same demeanor. "Ms. Moreau, it's a pleasure to meet you as well."

"The pleasure is mine. But please call me Ophelia," I replied, warmly.

Under different circumstances, one might have assumed it was a lack of respect for him to immediately use my husband's first name instead of more formally addressing him by his surname, like he did with me. But during my short stay among the Nazhrals so far, I learned that, in their culture, addressing someone by their last name was not a good thing. It usually implied that they were in trouble—like when your mother would call you by your full name—or that you either didn't deem them an equal or wanted to establish a clear distance between the two of you. Using someone's first name meant that you considered them as your peer.

"Gladly," the Enforcer replied, "but only if you call me Tedrick!"

Even as I smiled in response, I didn't miss the confused looks on our males' faces in light of that exchange. With their limited interactions with off-worlders, they didn't know much about the ridiculous number of hoops humans jumped through for no real reason, and in the name of propriety. Although they gathered to see what was going on, they kept a reasonable distance as to not be overly intrusive or coming across as threatening.

"That was quite the entrance you made," Gaelec said, his only semi-playful tone making it clear he wasn't necessarily comfortable with it.

A strange glimmer flashed through Tedrick's gray eyes.

"It was," the Enforcer conceded. "We're only allowed to use this fast-travel method under very strict guidelines, and fairly rarely for reasons I'm sure you understand."

"What allowed us benefit of this exception?" Gaelec asked.

"We figured it would be best to have you comfortably set up as quickly as possible, especially in light of some of the news that will be breaking soon regarding a certain mission," Tedrick replied, his gaze intense as he spoke those words.

"So things didn't go well?" I asked, my heart breaking for all the people who had taken part in it.

"That's a matter of perspective. For the pirates, you would be totally correct. For us, it was a resounding success."

Behind us, our males murmured, probably expressing their dismay or sadness. A glance over my shoulder confirmed it, some faces also displaying an odd mix of guilt and relief that they'd made the right decision and been spared that terrible outcome.

"But you will hear more about it soon. For now, we come bearing gifts from the PMA and the UPO," Tedrick said, shifting his attention back to my husband. "My men could use some help unloading while you and I go over a few details. We also have a couple of experts to assist with setup, if needed."

"Of course," Gaelec replied, gesturing at Kazaer and a couple other males to come forward.

Five Enforcers—two women, two men, and an Edocit male —walked out of the large ship and smiled warmly at our males as they watched them approach. I met a few Edocits before, and they still fascinated me. Everyone in that dryad-like species was gorgeous. That male seemed to be in his late twenties, with shoulder length dark-brown hair. A few white flowers had bloomed in the elegant vines intertwined with his locks. This meant he was happy, which was a good sign for us.

A heavy ramp lowered, and a series of massive hovering platforms glided out, laden with huge crates, and the type of equipment that had our collective eyes popping out of our heads. My throat tightened with emotion at the air of pure awe on the faces of our Pride members. But that emotion turned to amusement as I watched them stare in disbelief at what they likely interpreted as being some sort of armored tank rolling out of the ship. It was in fact the deployable buildings.

Those wonders of technology could travel through some of the most challenging terrains, and even had an amphibian mode that allowed them to cross shallow rivers if needed to reach their destination. Once in position, you only had a button to push for them to unfold, transforming into a fully functional building, with every amenity required, including basic hygiene features like a toilet, bath or shower—depending on the model—kitchen, and even a laundry room. Those buildings were designed so that they could be easily linked to a local sewer system, freshwater system, and power grid. Otherwise, they came by default with chemical waste management.

Our companions' jaws dropped even more when five such 'tanks' rolled out one by one from the ship. Jumping into action, Kazaer indicated where each one was to be positioned, based on the instructions Gaelec previously communicated to him. But it was seeing the state-of-the-art geothermal system being brought out that nearly undid them. I blinked to stem the tears that wanted to prick my eyes at the way everyone looked at my husband.

These males had taken a huge gamble turning back on what had been centuries old customs to follow someone they barely knew. Finding out the raid had indeed occurred as he warned silenced some of the second guessing that had been growing amongst them since their arrival here. But seeing what he had been able to secure for this fledgling Pride in such record time made them look at him with new eyes. Just like I was, they were realizing that we were now part of something greater than any of us imagined.

"We ended up scraping a few extra things to throw into your package," Tedrick said, reclaiming our attention. "You see those red crates on that platform over there?" he added, pointing at it. "It contains a series of non-military grade weapons."

As one, Gaelec and I recoiled.

"Why in the world would you bring us weapons?" Gaelec asked, outrage and confusion filling his voice.

"Like I said, they are common and non-military grade weapons," Tedrick repeated, his face serious. "You are currently receiving goods and technology that totals a little over a million credits. Word will spread quickly, even faster than the one of your departure from Nevian to create your own Pride, and the reasons why you did so. The other Prides are already abuzz about a male creating his own, which is unheard of. Once they hear the outcome of the mission, and how your warnings were ignored, you will generate even more curiosity. And when they see what you have, they will want to appropriate it. You will need deterrents."

My stomach dropped a bit more with each word. I wanted to kick myself for not even contemplating the likelihood of people trying to take over the village we were building. Gaelec frequently mentioned that Prides respected each other's territories. Occasionally, the only troublemakers were roaming males.

But I could see this equipment drawing far more people. My next thought shamed me, but I couldn't help remembering that many of his people made a living by stealing from others. Granted, they normally stole from off-worlders. As all of this came from strangers, would they deem it fair game?

"I have no intention of shooting my own people," Gaelec growled, although I didn't miss the sliver of worry in his blue eyes.

"Nor am I asking you to," Tedrick said in an appeasing tone. "Most advanced planets pursue research into extremely powerful weapons, but specifically with the intent of never having to use them. Flaunting the fact that you have them is usually enough for potential aggressors to think twice before doing anything stupid. Frankly, I pray that you never have to use them as it could cause a galactic conflict. We wouldn't want your government to accuse us of arming rebel militias in their midst."

Gaelec snorted, but didn't challenge his words.

"We've also included a set of advanced perimeter security," Tedrick continued. "Our scanners indicate you have done a pretty good job with the basic models you already set up. These offer a lot more features that you will enjoy a great deal, on top of them coming with integrated camera systems."

This time, it was my turn to frown. "This is all starting to sound a little excessive," I said, suspicion seeping into my voice. "Is there something else you're not telling us? Both the UPO and especially the Enforcers are renowned for being extremely stingy and reluctant when it comes to arming anyone, especially on a planet like Melelyn. Right now, you sound like you are doing exactly what you claim not to want to be accused of."

Gaelec nodded in agreement, his eyes narrowing on the senior officer with the same suspicion I felt. To my surprise, instead of going on the defensive, Tedrick smiled with a glimmer of approval.

"Suspicion is always good whenever strangers come

offering extremely valuable gifts while asking for very little in return. But once you open the crates, you will see that there is nothing illegal or problematic in what we have brought in terms of weapons. They are comparable to the ones your Prides already use, and easily purchased in any city," Tedrick explained.

He turned to look at one of the first deployable houses currently unfolding near the beach, but at a safe enough distance from the water.

"We're not violating the Prime Directive," Tedrick continued pensively. "Although the lifestyle of the Prides would be deemed primitive by most galactic standards, the tribes within a species do not define their entire people's evolution status. Your industrialized cities and regions are on par with most other worlds. But culturally, Nazhrals are on the verge of a major clash with the rest of the galaxy."

He stared back at my husband, studying his features while a million thoughts fleeted over his face.

"You were wise not to join that raid. Within the next hour, you will start hearing the details of what happened. As bad as it will be, understand that it is nothing compared to the even more vicious crackdowns that we have coming. UPO members are beyond fed up."

"Why leak that information, then?" Gaelec asked, echoing the question I'd also been wondering about.

"Because it sends a louder message. Many doubted you. It will be an even harder blow once they realize you were right. If your warning about this was accurate, then the one about our even fiercer attacks against pirates will hold a lot more weight and will have more people think twice before crossing the line," Tedrick explained.

"Fair enough. But it still doesn't explain why you are showering us with so much expensive equipment," I insisted, my suspicion still obvious.

He gave me an indulgent smile. "If you worry that we're trying to buy your loyalty, you can cast that thought out."

My stupid cheeks heated. It was indeed what I'd been implying. I just hated that my face would give off the impression I was embarrassed to have thought it as it was a fair question to ask.

"What you need to understand is that at the end of the day, as we say on Earth, money talks and bullshit walks. This piracy business costs a lot of people a lot of credits. The cruise ship you arrived here on now spends nearly three million credits a year just to keep its ships safe from attacks like the one you faced. Every single year. And that's one company. Tens of thousands of companies, many a lot smaller that cannot afford this type of defensive budgets, have to contend with the same issue. I'll let you take a wild guess what kind of costs, both in protection and in lost goods this creates."

I pursed my lips and nodded slowly. He didn't have to tell me any specific numbers, but we were easily talking about billions of credits every year. And that was without even mentioning the lives lost on all sides.

"So a million credits here to set you up is but a drop in the ocean," Tedrick explained. "This is an investment for the future so they can significantly reduce these avoidable expenses. Obviously, Nazhrals aren't the only pirates, but you represent a big percentage of them. People are rarely born criminals. It is their circumstances, usually the lack of opportunities and education that forces them into those dark paths. Young Nazhrals from your Prides are the perfect victims to be exploited by unscrupulous people. If we cut the problem at the root by helping them get the stability and security they need, they will not be lured into these so-called missions."

"I couldn't agree more," Gaelec said. "I'm just confused as to why you waited for me to leave my Pride instead of approaching existing ones with this kind of offer."

"Because this type of fundamental change must come from

within. We cannot come here and try to indoctrinate your people into adopting our ways. All we can do is have the opportunities available and hope the right people will seize them. You do not realize how important it is for us to see you succeed and thrive. You're exactly the champion we needed for this entire project to be set in motion. Obviously, we don't expect you to perform any type of overnight miracle. But you're that strong seed of change that we will help blossom so that your roots will hopefully spread far and wide."

"I still don't understand," Gaelec argued. "The Osuan Pride has been pushing for a more modern and egalitarian approach. Did you not approach them?"

He nodded. "We have had talks with them and have provided some support. But your situations are extremely different. They remain a matriarchy that is simply more protective of its males. But in the end, they still cast their males out, most of whom end up either moving to the city or flat out going off-world. It doesn't solve the problem. We need the males from every Pride to have a reason to stay home and help elevate the living conditions of every other male on Melelyn. Which is exactly what you're doing."

This time, Gaelec's face lit up with understanding, as did mine. It had been a frequent issue back when I performed charity work. The brain exodus from rural areas and tribal villages was a real thing. Changes needed to be brought about by locals for locals. And what better champion than my man?

"For the record, any other new Pride similar to yours that will form isn't likely to get as generous an assistance as you are," Tedrick warned. "Or at least, they will have to jump through hoops to earn it. You passed three separate tests with flying colors. This is why you are receiving all this with very little required in exchange."

"Three tests?" I asked before Gaelec could, although his face displayed the same confusion I felt.

"The first one lasted twelve years on Molvi. Your final evaluation report from Lord Amreth was stellar. He's a good and fair male, but not one to sugarcoat. His high recommendation is far more powerful than you can ever imagine," Tedrick explained.

Gaelec smiled, his eyes going slightly out of focus as he probably thought back on his time on Molvi or on his interactions with his former Warden.

"It does mean a lot. Lord Amreth was strict but fair. He not only gave us every opportunity to improve ourselves to build a better future once we left, but he also highly encouraged it. I owe him a great deal."

"You owe yourself," Tedrick corrected. "Thousands of inmates end up on Molvi every year. Very few of them seize the opportunities like you did. And his evaluation of you was confirmed by Kayog, long before you even completed your sentence. As one of the most powerful Temerns alive, Master Voln can see things about a person that others can't. In his own initial report after seeing you on Molvi, Kayog vouched for your character. So you know, he doesn't match anyone with questionable morals."

Gaelec and I exchanged a look and then a smile. I found myself melting against his side while he slipped a possessive arm around me. Without Kayog, we never would have found each other.

"They're both right. My husband is a good male with great morals," I whispered, eyes still locked with Gaelec.

The tenderness in his eyes turned me upside down as he leaned forward to kiss me. If not for the clanging sound from the people unloading more of our new equipment, my mate and I would likely still be lost in each other. We turned back to look at the Enforcer, my cheeks turning red again.

There was something almost paternal to the amused look he gave us. It was funny that this was the adjective that came to mind considering he looked barely ten years older than I was.

"Last but not least, you actually made the move we hoped you would by leaving and starting this Pride," Tedrick said. "You're not going to have an easy journey ahead. You're creating a brand-new social structure for your people. These types of fundamental changes take years, sometimes generations. But we will assist in any way we can."

"We do not want interference," Gaelec interjected, his tone immediately hardening.

Tedrick raised his palms in an appeasing gesture. "Nor do we intend to. Like I said, for this to work, it must come from you, not us. So long as you stay the course, the head of our outreach program will inform you of whatever new programs or services may arise that could be beneficial to you. Just know that there are some security measures embedded in the most valuable pieces of equipment that we gave you."

"Like what?" Gaelec asked, his back stiffening.

"Nothing intrusive," Tedrick replied in a slightly mocking tone. "But we want to make sure you remain in control of all of this. Therefore, all the deployable buildings, com system, geothermal system, speeders and shuttle have biometric locks configured specifically for you and Ophelia. Should anyone attempt to steal them, you can remotely shut them down, and no one will have access to them again until you reactivate them."

"This, I approve of," Gaelec replied with a shit-eating grin.

With this, he gave us a quick overview of some of the security features included with the equipment provided, followed by two solid hours of their female engineer working with Gaelec to set up the geothermal system. The atmosphere and mood in our budding village was electric—pun intended.

By the time the Enforcers left, all five buildings had been deployed, hooked to our new electrical grid, and to both our water and sewer systems. The latter two would require significant upgrading to optimize their function, especially to help support what we hoped would soon be a growing population. But for tonight, it would give us a similar comfort level to what we previously had in Nevian.

That first night, we celebrated with a big feast on the beach. We agreed to temporarily use three of the deployable buildings as dwellings. Gaelec and I would use one, Kazaer and the three young males who had followed him would share another, and the four older males from Nevian would share the third. The remaining would be used for more official functions. One of them would be focused on everything food-related, like both our fish plant and larder. The other would serve for crafting.

Once we finished building proper dwellings from scratch, we would gradually shift the other three deployable buildings to more specialized functions such as a school and medical clinic. After moving our 'mattress' and belongings into our new home, Gaelec and I went all out baptizing every room and every surface in the naughtiest way possible.

Life was good.

CHAPTER 18
GAELEC

Contrary to what Tedrick implied, we didn't get the news about the raid until the next day. Then again, we'd been a little too busy playing with our new toys to really devote much time tracking down any tidbits of information we could get.

For all the relief we felt for having wisely steered clear of it, reading the fate that befell those who went out of stubbornness—but especially those who did out of desperation—broke our hearts. The Enforcer didn't exaggerate by saying they wanted to make a statement with this. Nearly two hundred males from various Prides were caught alive. Fifty-six lost their lives trying to escape or resist. Twenty-three were injured, some seriously maimed. Every single survivor, injured or not, was guaranteed a minimum of fifteen years in a Q2 or Q3 on Molvi. For most of them, it was a death sentence.

On top of that, their Prides were fined a flat amount for each of their members as punitive damage for their part in encouraging or coercing them to participate. It would be a severe blow to a lot of them, as most Prides pushed their males to participate in those missions to bring back desperately needed extra income. They likely wouldn't have the credits to pay.

Naturally, our government would challenge that sanction, claiming that the Enforcers had no jurisdiction on our people. My gut told me that the UPO was hoping specifically for that response so that they could then put the burden on our government to take steps to eradicate piracy. Obviously they never would. Too many of our major corporations and wealthy preyed on our males intentionally to do their dirty work. Most of Melelyn's technology was stolen during those raids. The firms who funded these missions would then reverse engineer and sell their knock-off versions of the same technology.

In all probability, once the UPO either threatened or applied sanctions against Melelyn due to our government's lack of cooperation, our leaders would likely simply pay the fines or negotiate a lesser amount, promising to instate some sort of educational programs to help fight crime and crack down on recruiters.

All of which would conveniently meet one hurdle after another until it was simply abandoned before it ever truly took place.

Despite how devastated we were by the news, especially since most of us knew at least one person or more from the list of names that was made public, we needed to focus on our own future. Anyway, we still had tons of work to do building our new home.

The next five days flew by in a whirlwind of activity. The village was coming along nicely. Thanks to all the gifts we received, my original budget remained intact. We were debating whether to buy a small fishing ship or build our own. With the fancy tools we now possessed, we could make something pretty impressive in a relatively short amount of time. However, considering all the other work we needed to do, we had to carefully weigh what made the most sense for us.

The biggest issue was the need to bring in credits. Without the shuttle, we would have had a bit more time. But as we had to pay the lease on it, we had to bring in some form of income. Fishing was the fastest thing we could do on that front... which required a boat. On the other hand, if I didn't spend my credits buying that ship, we could use them to pay the lease, which would keep us covered for several months. If we had more people helping us build everything, then it would have been a non-issue.

And that was the crux of it.

I didn't know how I felt about the fact that, contrary to Tedrick's warning, no one had come knocking to join us or even attempt to take over what we were building here. Although relieved that we could continue building our new home in peace, a part of me felt a little hurt and even slightly depressed that no one seemed interested in what we had to offer. In truth, I expected the floodgates to open the minute people heard what a failure the mission had been. Was I truly so out of touch with my people that I still completely misinterpreted what other males might want?

And then the tsunami hit.

Exactly seven days after we received those gifts, and ten days after leaving the Nevian Village, the one person I truly hoped to see showed up. My brother's happy shouts alerted me as to the identity of the intruder announced by the perimeter motion detector.

I rushed out of the house we'd been working on only to see Kazaer running towards the forest. It was silly considering she was still a few minutes away. But she also wasn't alone. Based on the security system, three more females were tagging along. I didn't quite know how I felt about it. It could both be great and seriously problematic.

Walking hand in hand with my mate, we approached the entrance of the village, our other males, especially the younger ones, perking up. My stomach knotted with apprehension. Although they'd not been with us for very long, I'd seriously grown attached to all the members of my Pride. They were good, hard-working males, and had so far shown themselves to be respectable and honorable. Without bringing females into our village, they would eventually have no choice but to leave. I couldn't expect them to remain celibate through their prime years while personally enjoying the companionship of my own mate.

The newcomers finally cleared the forest. My chest warmed at seeing Ylis and Kazaer entering the village, their hands clasped, and their eyes filled with the joy of being reunited. Despite us having established our com system, my brother complained about her going radio silent since he joined us.

At first, he acknowledged that things were probably shaking up so much over there that she had her hands too full to contact him. But as more and more days went by without a word from her or any response to his messages, Kazaer started convincing himself that she never truly wanted a future with him and had used my project of starting my own village as an excuse to get rid of him.

Although I went out of my way to reassure him that he was being silly, I couldn't deny feeling relieved she was finally here, confirming that she had not been leading him on.

Her dreamy smile faded to give way to complete shock and wonder as she took in the appearance of our village. Her companions, all young huntresses in their early twenties, looked just as stupefied. I didn't need to look at our males to know they were bubbling with excitement.

"By the Gods, Gaelec! This is incredible!" Ylis whispered, transfixed as she closed the distance between us.

"Thank you, Ylis. And welcome to Gyota Village," I said, my tone friendly although a little guarded.

She immediately picked up on my reservation, subtle though it was. Her gaze flicked back to me, ending her mesmerized examination of our surroundings. A sliver of worry flitted over her lovely features as she studied me.

"Are we… welcome?" she asked in a soft voice.

"Of course you are!" Kazaer exclaimed as if she had said something silly.

When she continued to stare at me, my brother turned his attention to me, his brow creased in a frown.

"Gaelec, tell her!" he said, looking confused.

"You are always welcome to visit. But am I to understand you and your companions are thinking of something a bit more permanent?" I asked in a gentle tone.

The females shifted uneasily on their paws, their eyes flicking towards Ylis before eyeing me warily. I hated to put them in the same type of uncertainty Rozel subjected me to when I first returned. However, even though I didn't plan on dragging this on unnecessarily, I needed to make sure we were all on the same wavelength before opening the door to what could spell disaster down the road.

"Yes, we would be interested in something more permanent, or at least temporary," she added, glancing at her companions.

"I'm listening," I said, intrigued.

"Things are a complete mess back home… or rather what used to be our home," Ylis explained. "You probably heard what a tragedy that mission turned out to be. Arys and Izana both lost the visiting males they'd hoped to pair with to that raid," she added, waving at two of the young huntresses. "And Andrane is one of the young Queens who was supposed to leave with some of her sisters in two years from now to form their own Pride. But none of us wish to remain under Rozel's tyranny."

"Tyranny?" I repeated, shocked by that extreme choice of word.

"There are a lot of people talking about leaving. After what happened, when she blatantly ignored the warnings that you gave and that many of us told her to heed, the Queens and huntresses asked Rozel to step down as Head Matriarch and to let my mother take over. Naturally, Rozel refused. She even refused to depose Moriak. Unfortunately, you know the rule. None of the younger females can issue a challenge to the Head Matriarch unless she be labeled a pariah. The only people who can are the other two Matriarchs, meaning my mother and my aunt."

"Pryia and Jilam will never challenge their sister to a duel," I said with conviction.

"Exactly. Which means we either accept it or leave. We have chosen to leave," Ylis said, before running a frustrated hand through her mane. "A third of our males have left."

"WHAT?!" I exclaimed, my shock reflected on every face.

"The younger ones are looking for a new Pride to join with a more reasonable Head Matriarch," she continued grimly. "Some of the others are roaming together while trying to assess what their next move will be. And then you have a few more who are considering joining you, if you will have them. They're waiting to see whether we will be welcome before taking their chances."

"Why would they want to wait after you tried? You are females, they are males. The criteria for acceptance are extremely different," I said, baffled.

"They figure if you refuse the person you treated like your baby sister since you joined us, then they will not stand a chance," she said with a shrug.

Her pretend nonchalance didn't fool me. I could feel her underlying tension. "That is a completely flawed assumption. The bar for a male joining us is much lower than for females."

She instantly stiffened, as did the others, my brother included. I gave her a reassuring smile.

"I explained my rules to you before I left. Like you said, you've been like a little sister to me from the moment we met. And now, you could officially be one," I continued, gesturing at my brother with my chin. "Nothing would make me happier, so long as you understand that no female will come here to dominate and rule the males."

She gave me a firm nod, as did the other three females. "We fully understand. I made sure to explain it to them, and we're all in agreement. Arys and Izana are looking for a permanent home with all of you, as am I. Andrane wants to keep her options open. Her sisters, with whom she was meant to start her own Pride, are still uncertain as to what they want to do. But they definitely don't want to repeat the disaster that Rozel made of Nevian, and they don't want to see more young males meeting the fate of their young brother. Living among you with this new structure would be a great experience allowing her to see if this is something they could implement in their own Pride."

"That seems like a good idea," Ophelia said timidly.

I glanced at her and found her staring at me with almost pleading eyes. I smiled and caressed her cheek.

"Yes, it does seem like a good idea. It is wise to try things first when given the opportunity before making a permanent commitment. Therefore, unless anyone else objects, I'm happy to welcome all four of you to the Gyota Pride."

"Fuck yeah!" Kazaer exclaimed, making us all laugh.

He scooped Ylis into his arms, effortlessly lifting her, and twirled while she laughed.

We spent the next little while giving the females a tour. No words could express the extent of the pride I felt seeing their reaction to what we'd accomplished. To my surprise, Izana left, accompanied by Danel to fetch the couple of hover carts they had hidden a short distance outside our security perimeter and which contained most of the belongings they simply couldn't part with. They initially planned on using a city shuttle to get the rest of their stuff once they received confirmation that we would welcome them. But seeing the fancy shuttle we now possessed had them fanning themselves.

On the following day, six more males from Nevian—the ones

who had been waiting to see how Ylis and the other three females would be received—also came to join us. Things turned quite awkward when I rejected two of them. They'd been problematic in their work ethics, performance, and general attitude. I laughed at their pathetic attempt to make a stink about it, calling me an elitist. But in the end, they had no choice but to go back on their way.

The other four gladly stayed.

It triggered a longer debate among us as to our criteria of acceptance for newcomers, as well as the maximum population we sought, and at which pace we could welcome them. Even with these extra hands helping, it took time to build entire houses from scratch. All these people also required necessities such as beds, mattresses, and blankets. And all of that required credits that were not coming in as we weren't set up yet to weave our own fabrics and craft various other things.

"Don't fret so much about it, Brother," Kazaer said in a reassuring tone. "You warned us the first few months—and maybe even the first couple of years—wouldn't be an easy ride. But what we're building here exceeds anything I could have hoped for. We have solid roofs over our heads, food in our bellies, and wonderful companions to rely upon."

Everyone nodded.

"You've given us safety and a place to call home, Alpha," Faran said, one of the young males who joined us with Kazaer. "None of us fear hardship. We expected much worse as nomads. The question for us isn't how much work will be required to get this place to where it needs to be, but whether it will always be our home should we temporarily go away."

My chest warmed with the oddly paternal emotion I increasingly felt towards the younger males. It was all the sillier that we barely had ten years difference.

"You're a member of this Pride now, Faran. You're young and in your prime. It's normal for you to feel the call to roam and find a mate," I said gently. "When the time for you to set off comes, we'll be sad to see you go. But know that we'll wait for you with open arms the day you decide to come back home."

The air of deep gratitude and affection that burned in every males' eyes warmed my chest. The thought that I would one day have a similar conversation with the sons I hoped to have filled me with a joy I could barely contain.

"Thank you, Alpha. But don't think you will be rid of me anytime soon," Faran said with a grin. "I will see this village properly built and surpass every other in the realm. The day I and any of our males go roaming, the Prides we visit will be the ones begging for the attention of one of the sons of Gyota."

Cheers welcomed his words.

Sadly, that optimistic mood was dampened the following day, first by a group of roaming males who tried to challenge me as the new Alpha of our Pride. Although I made mincemeat out of their leader, it only marked the beginning of an endless string of random people showing up, acting as if being welcomed in was their due.

The most infuriating case was when a pack of ten females showed up, claiming our village as theirs and demanding to be instated as our Matriarchs and huntresses. They even had the nerve to demand we expel Ylis and her three relatives who followed her here. My blood still boiled at the sheer entitlement. It boggled my mind that they genuinely believed they were doing us a favor—if not an honor—by settling among us and allowing a bunch of males they had not personally vetted first to stay.

Needless to say we sent them packing quickly. Their wretched leader tried to challenge my mate as new Head Matriarch, thinking it would be an easy win. Watching Ylis giving her the trouncing of the century still had me grinning from ear to ear.

As infuriating as these intrusions were, they achieved something that otherwise might have taken a very long time. It brought us all closer, deepened our mutual loyalty, but above all gave every member of our Pride a sense of ownership. They weren't just helping me build *my* village. We were building *our* home, and we wouldn't let anyone take that away from us.

By the fourth week, with a sufficient number of homes for everyone, and our first trade workshop functional, things finally felt like they were settling down. Through her contacts, Ophelia found us a used fishing ship in prime condition. The cost of getting it delivered to us was a fraction of what it would have cost to buy a new one or even to build it from scratch. That day, when the motion detectors went off, we assumed our ship had finally arrived.

The reality couldn't have been farther from the truth.

The alarmed voices outside echoed the shock I felt upon seeing Oluina and two of her huntresses, followed by Moriak, Latsa, and Olmar quickly approaching on their speeders.

I ran to our dwelling to grab my staff. Ophelia—who had been tanning the leather from the creatures our huntresses had brought back—ran towards me with an air of panic. I caressed her cheek in a reassuring fashion.

"All will be well, my mate. They have no jurisdiction here and no power over us," I said in a soft voice.

She nodded, her expression still troubled. It bothered me to see her absent-mindedly touch her blaster. I wanted us to reach a point where she no longer felt the need to stay armed at all times. We'd had a few close calls in the past couple of weeks, but nothing that actually required her to shoot. I just wished people would leave us alone.

We headed towards the entrance of the village, the rest of our Pride also gathering around us. Their timing couldn't have been more rotten as Ylis and our other females were out hunting. As they would have received the intruder warning, I didn't doubt they were rushing back home in all haste.

I didn't believe things would devolve into a physical altercation. However, if things got heated, no male wanted to be forced to manhandle a female. While we were undeniably stronger, our females were faster. Except for duels, they usually fought as a pack, thus easily overwhelming their target. This meant, should things get ugly, many of us would have to jump in if Oluina and her companions charged us.

I could only hope Moriak would be the one to issue a challenge. My claws had been itching for a long time to give him a new look.

A burning contempt surged within me upon seeing their wretched faces. It baffled me that I had once thought her the sweetest, loveliest, and most beautiful female in the world. As a naïve cub, I truly believed myself in love with her. And yet, in retrospect, all the signs had been there. She didn't change into someone despicable. I simply no longer was blind to her true personality. And that made her ugly.

As for Moriak, if not for how many lives he had destroyed in his malicious attempts at securing his position, I would feel pity for him. He was only seven or eight years older than I was, but the past few weeks had aged him before his time. His features were strained, his eyes a bit haggard as if from lack of sleep. I heard of Nevian's steady decline since our departure. The failed mission had been a major blow that nearly got him evicted. I strongly suspected that he was still on borrowed time over it.

The saddest part was that I genuinely believed that he'd trusted Ranor as to the partial safety of the mission. He likely thought only a handful of people would be caught or harmed. After all, they'd sent a little over three hundred males. With a crew this size, he couldn't have imagined most wouldn't make it out.

However, it was the incredulous look on their faces as they took in our village that affected me the most. I should be ashamed of the malicious glee their devastated expressions stirred within me. Even halfway built as it was, anyone with eyes could see that it by far surpassed what they currently had. For all its qualities, their village was dated because of their stubborn refusal to update it.

They had expected us to utterly fail and come groveling back for mercy. Instead, they started reaching out to us—or more specifically to me—over the past ten days. I ignored every single one of their messages.

"What are you doing here, Oluina? What do you want?" I demanded, my voice frosty.

She lifted her chin defiantly, instantly angered by my hostile stance. Where before I would have forced myself to be a bit more diplomatic and less confrontational, now I no longer cared if she got riled up. She had no power, here in our Pride.

"You have not responded to Rozel's summons. We would know the reason for such rudeness," she said in a haughty tone.

I snorted in disbelief, my reaction echoed by the members of my Pride.

"Why would I? I'm not her servant or employee. I'm no longer a member of your Pride that she should have any authority over me. She is nothing to me anymore... as are the rest of you."

"Do not be disrespectful," she snarled. "You've made your point. You were right about the mission, and we acknowledge that we need to update our village to be more modern and efficient. Now let us stop this nonsense. You can apologize to my mother and return to the Pride."

I burst out laughing, while my mate and our companions emitted various incredulous sounds, some of them joining their laughter to mine.

"Fuck that!" Ophelia said, looking at her like she had lost her mind. "If anyone owes anyone else an apology it's your mother, you, and that fool you call your Alpha!"

"Do not meddle in Nazhral affairs, human!" Oluina hissed.

"You watch how you address my mate!" I snarled. "This is

her home, not yours. You will show her the proper respect or leave at once."

Oluina clenched her teeth, fury burning in her green eyes.

"We will never return to Nevian. If you want to establish business trades with us, tell us what you have to offer, and we will assess if we want any of it. Otherwise, I will ask you to leave. You are not welcome here," I said sternly.

"What we have to offer?!" she exclaimed angrily. "We took you in! You *owe* us!"

"I owe you *nothing*!" I ground between my teeth. "If anyone is indebted, it is your Pride towards me. My credits during my incarceration and the extra labor I performed upon my return are the last things you will have ever gotten from me. You wanted us gone, we are."

"In light of the recent events, we've changed our minds on that front," Oluina said, the words appearing to scorch her lips.

"That's just too bad. As you can see, we've set a pretty good life for ourselves here, without you and your mother's toxicity," I said mockingly while waving at our village.

"It is a pretty decent village," she conceded, the malicious glimmer in her eyes immediately setting all my senses on high alert. "Such a nice place will need a proper hand to manage it. Therefore, if you will not return home where you belong, then I will have to challenge your Queen to take over your Pride."

The same incredulous sounds resonated from everyone.

"We don't do that here, you stupid female!" I said, laughing disdainfully at her.

"It is the law!" she exclaimed.

"It is *your* law!" I corrected. "This is *our* Pride, and we follow *our* own rules. Now fuck off!"

"You cannot do this!" she shouted.

"*Oh, putain!* Won't you ever learn?!" Ophelia exclaimed, exasperated. "What did I tell you about showing some self-respect and not throwing yourself at someone who doesn't want you? We all left because life in your Pride was toxic. We've moved on. How about you try and do the same? Nobody wants you here. None of us would follow your lead. So what are you trying to accomplish? Just fuck off already!"

"Fight me!" Oluina hissed, taking a menacing step forward.

I instinctively raised my arm protectively in front of my mate, pushing her back slightly to get in the way of Oluina's line of sight.

"I already told you that we do not do that here!" I growled.

"You do not get to rewrite the law because you chose to lie with a weak female!" Oluina said, taking yet another step forward. "I demand—"

"You demand nothing!" Ylis shouted in the distance.

My heart soared upon seeing her coming out of the forest, our other females in tow.

"If you're itching so badly for a fight, you fight me!" Ylis said as she stopped her speeder halfway between her cousin and us.

"You would turn on your own family and fight your own blood?!" Oluina exclaimed as she watched her cousin dismount.

"You're the one who turned on our family years ago," Ylis said, her tone sharp enough to cut through metal. "You were warned and stubbornly chose this path. Now you reap what you sowed. That pathetic Alpha of yours drove off every good male the Pride ever had, got them killed or incarcerated. Now you don't get to crawl over here trying to get back the truest Alpha we've ever had. There's a reason why your last feast drew absolutely no one."

She turned to stare at Moriak, examining him from top to bottom with an air of pure disgust. She waved at him before turning to her cousin.

"This is what you put above the welfare of a Pride that had endured for generations. And today, no male will want to put their lives at the mercy of that fool. Good luck attracting new blood to Nevian with your poorly trained huntresses, this sorry excuse of an Alpha, and your outdated village," Ylis hissed. "You made the place so foul we left our home. Now leave and never come back. We both know the outcome of a duel between us."

For the first time, I felt true pity for Oluina. In many ways, her mother turned her into this spoiled and entitled brat. According to rumors—apparently confirmed by the fact she didn't argue Ylis's statement—not a single male showed up at the feast they held a week after the outcome of the disastrous raid had gone public. It was rare for a Pride to be blacklisted. But it was now Nevian's case. Unlike the other villages who had lost many males, our Alpha had known about the trap and deliberately chose to ignore it and not warn the others.

No wonder Rozel was desperate for me to return. Forgiveness from me would signal to others that the village deserved a second chance, and that maybe the rumors about their criminal negligence in this disaster were in fact exaggerated.

Eyes brimming with tears of helpless rage, Oluina cast one last glance filled with hatred at my mate, then one of betrayal at her cousin before turning around and walking away. Tension slowly bled out of my shoulders as I cast a grateful smile at Ylis.

Behind her, Moriak drew my attention. He was staring in turn at me and at the village with seething rage. I didn't need to read minds to know he believed this place should be his to lead. Unable to resist, I gave him a taunting smile before winking at him. He bared his teeth at me, and I held this gaze, daring him to issue the challenge I was praying for.

I could see him genuinely considering it. He blamed me for how his life had been upended. Moriak was too much of a narcissist to acknowledge how his own actions and choices led him to this moment. At the same time, his survival instincts told him not to be even more foolish than he'd already been. A defeat at my hands before so many witnesses, especially the top huntresses of what was left of their Pride would be the final blow to his already crumbling future.

Just when he looked about to choose the wiser path and go back to Nevian with his tail between his legs, movement at the edge of my vision drew my attention. As if in slow motion, I watched Oluina spin around and throw something in our direction. Alarmed shouts resonated all around us as I stared in horror at a sharp dagger flying straight for my woman. On instinct, I shoved Ophelia out of the way half a second before the blade would have embedded itself in her neck.

I hissed at the burning sensation of the blade slicing through the skin and muscle of my upper arm. It wasn't a critical wound, but deep enough that it would likely require a few stitches. But a blind rage took over me. I raced towards Oluina, who was pulling out a second dagger. Simultaneously, Moriak burst into action. Their companions appeared frozen in shock and disbelief.

And then mayhem broke out.

CHAPTER 19
OPHELIA

I had never been the violent type, but for the first time in my life I truly wanted to harm someone in the most vicious fashion. The mere thought of my fist connecting repeatedly with that wretched female's face was literally orgasmic. The absolute gall of Oluina and her mother just blew my mind. In what world would Gaelec apologize to them or even consider returning to the life of near servitude and helplessness they had trapped him in? Especially considering what he had now…

But it was also her shameless cowardice that she would try to duel me that made her all the more despicable. Even the two huntresses who had accompanied her looked increasingly disgusted with her behavior. The stupid bitch didn't know when to quit. She just kept digging her grave deeper and deeper. Although they were all relatives, I could see these two females either demanding that she step down as Head Huntress or for them to decide to leave the Pride as well.

As relieved as I felt to see Ylis return just in time to send that foul lot back from whence they came, I had not actually feared for my own safety. The entire village would have stepped in to keep her from assaulting me. It would have simply sucked to have the story going around about how all the males of the Gyota Pride ganged up on a huntress, beating her into submission before casting her out merely because she had wanted to challenge their Matriarch. It didn't take much to destroy a reputation. Sadly, a mere whisper often sufficed as people were usually far too lazy to actually investigate the truth and facts behind the rumors they heard.

The smile stretching my lips as I watched Gaelec silently taunt Moriak when Oluina finally decided to leave turned to shock and then horror when my mate suddenly shoved me out of the way. It was only as I fell back from the strength of the push that I finally understood what had prompted what looked like an unprovoked attack. Almost in a blur, I saw a blade flash by, right where my face had been but seconds prior, slicing through my husband's arm in the process.

A painful gasp escaped me half a beat later as I landed hard on my butt, and a lancing pain radiated through my leg. But I cast the pain right out of my mind. Fueled by adrenaline, I jumped back onto my feet and whipped out my blaster while everyone around us appeared to burst into action. My surroundings faded, my whole world entirely focused on my nemesis as I watched her yanking out a second dagger from her weapons belt. Before it even had a chance to leave her hand, I had my blaster trained on her, and I fired without hesitation.

The shot struck her straight in the chest. The way she flew back before landing hard on the ground, you'd think she'd been hit by a battering ram. It was somewhat accurate. Her entire body began to shake, rocked by violent spasms of the powerful electric discharge from my blaster set to maximum Taser mode. I silently thanked all the powers that be that I had opened the latch that kept my blaster secured in its holster on my hips as soon as I realized who was coming.

I liked being ready in case of foul play. And today, that might have saved a life.

Ylis and the other females of our Pride—who had been rushing towards Oluina to intercept her after her initial attack—shifted as one with an eerie level of synchronism to tackle the other two females who had come with her cousin.

But I only had eyes for my husband. Like our females, seeing Oluina out of commission, he instantly switched his attention to Moriak, who was coming at him with his spear raised. That angered me far more than it freaked me out. Having seen my mate battle the idiots who had sought to depose him, I had no worries about his skills on that front. However, duels never involved piercing weapons as they were not to the death. He should be using a staff, like Gaelec was, or settle for a fist fight should the proper type of weapon not be available. Granted, he was visibly acting on instinct to seeing his Head Huntress knocked out.

But that fight literally ended in less than a minute.

The two males, approximately ten meters apart, ran towards each other. Kazaer, Faran, and Danel were rushing Latsa and Olmar, who immediately raised their hands in surrender.

Gaelec only ran three steps towards Moriak before leaping forward like a jaguar. I'd read about Nazhrals being similar to many felines in their abilities to jump five to six times their own height. But this blew my mind. My mate shot forward like a bullet, taking his opponent by surprise, who then attempted to jump over him.

Mid-air, Gaelec twisted around, slamming Moriak's legs with his staff just as he was leaping over him. The latter cried out as he was sent crashing onto the ground, face first. His attempt at twisting into landing on all fours failed miserably. But my man, carried by his momentum, landed into a roll and directly back onto his paws. He raced back to his rival, who was scrambling to get up. Another savage blow of Gaelec's staff on the back of his legs had him roaring in pain.

Pressing his knee on the small of his back, my mate yanked

Moriak's head back by his mane and swiped his right hand in front of his throat. For half a beat, I thought he'd slit the fool's throat. To my relief, his hand stopped but a few centimeters from his neck, vicious claws extruded, ready to finish him.

"I yield!" Moriak shouted, his voice filled with pain and panic.

A slow, steady growl flowed out of my man as he continued to hold his nemesis' head back, making him bend backward at an angle that had to be excruciating. Judging by the force with which Gaelec fisted his hair on his nape, I was surprised a clump hadn't been torn right off.

For a scary moment, my husband appeared to fight the urge to kill anyway, or at least to beat him to a pulp. The whirlwind of emotion that flashed over his features told a story of grief, rage, loss, and hatred. Moriak destroyed so many lives, stole his youth, and enabled the downfall of one of Melelyn's long-standing Prides. I couldn't fault my mate for wanting to exact revenge.

But he couldn't go down that path.

A muscle ticked on his temple, and he pulled his upper lip into a snarl. A part of me felt this was a battle he needed to win on his own. Yet another screamed that, as his partner, it was my duty to draw him back into the light when he began to stray.

The latter won.

"Gaelec, my love, he's not worth it," I said in a soft voice.

A violent shudder coursed through him. His steady growling stopped abruptly, and he blinked as if emerging from a trance. Despite that, he didn't release him right away, but he lowered the hand that had been hovering in front of Moriak's throat, ready to shred it to pieces. His claws retracted, and he stared at the back of the older male's head with a mix of hatred and contempt. The whole time, the pathetic Alpha kept pleading to be released while apparently struggling to breathe.

Suddenly, Gaelec smashed his face into the dirt, although nowhere near hard enough to cause any real harm. Maintaining his face pressed to the ground, my husband leaned forward to speak into his opponent's ear.

"It took me mere seconds to knock you down and make you snivel and whimper like a wounded cub. Don't ever come back to my lands again. Don't ever show your face to me, to my mate, or to anyone that I value. Should we cross paths, no amount of pleading and begging will spare you. Next time, I will break every single bone in your body before I gut you like the animal you are."

He released him just as brutally and got off him with an air of pure disgust on his face. His almost feral look, with his fangs bared, was both terrifying as hell and sexy as fuck. He took a couple of steps back while watching his defeated foe spit out the dirt and rocks that had gotten into his mouth when Gaelec shoved his face into the ground. Head bowed, Moriak clumsily got back up before limping towards the exit.

Oluina—who had been painfully recovering—stared at her defeated Alpha with burning resentment. She turned to us and started yelling a bunch of foul words.

I had zero time for that shit.

"Oh, shut the fuck up, *pétasse*!" I snapped before zapping her again with a second electric jolt.

She fell back down from her sitting position, her body shaken by spams again.

I turned to her companions, the anger I felt visible on my face. "You pick up that trash and take her back to your village. And make sure to warn her that the next time she comes here or tries to mess with me, I won't be zapping her ass, I'll put a fucking hole through her. I can't fight like you Nazhral can, but when I shoot, I don't miss. She picked the wrong woman to mess with. Get her the fuck out of here."

They didn't say a word or even appear to want to argue. Hooking a hand under each of her armpits, her two companions started dragging her towards their speeders.

"Remember well, Moriak, not to ever show your face here again," Gaelec warned in a tone that brooked no argument, before glaring at Latsa and Olmar who were staring at the whole scene in shock. "And that applies for you both as well. For the record, know that even had you succeeded—which obviously wouldn't happen—you could never get your greedy hands on any of this advanced technology. The day I leave Gyota, all this leaves with me, as per my agreement with the UPO."

He waved at the beautiful village we had steadily been erecting.

"You want something like this? Earn it instead of trying to leech off the work of others. Now get out of my village," Gaelec spat.

"*Enculé*!" I muttered at the idiot as he clumsily got back onto his speeder.

One of the females shared a speeder with Oluina, who seemed too out of it to ride on her own. They set her own speeder to follow and left under the jeers and mockery of the rest of our Pride.

Although they all stated that they would not follow another Alpha should Gaelec ever be defeated, I still hated that this possibility existed. Clearly, my man was badass. But where will things stand twenty years from now? Granted, an Alpha wasn't technically obligated to accept a challenge. A would-be usurper could simply be driven out of the village by everyone. I wanted to believe that this would be the stance he adopted going forward.

Gaelec turned to look at me with an amused expression. "What did you just call him? Is that the word for male prostitute?"

I snorted and shook my head. "No. Generally, it would be like calling someone an asshole or motherfucker. But the literal translation for this one means a person who got fucked in the ass," I admitted sheepishly.

He burst out laughing and shook his head as if I was a hope-less case. But considering what just went down, I believed the epithet was more than appropriate.

"You're wounded," I said, grabbing his wrist to look at the cut on his forearm.

"It's nothing, my mate. Those fancy medical pods Kayog sent us will have me as good as new in minutes," Gaelec said reassuringly.

I still took a moment to have a closer look to make sure it didn't require an urgent intervention. Only then did I look at him with the depth of emotions he awakened in me.

"You saved my life, just now," I said, my throat constricting with emotion.

"I did half the job, you did the other," he said. "Although you let her off easy."

"Not really…"

"Yes, you did," Ylis interjected. "This was a murder attempt that nearly succeeded. She spilled blood after trespassing on another Pride's lands. Based on our laws, her actions warrant her execution."

"Maybe so, but ultimately, no one died," I argued. "At the end of the day, I don't want her blood on my hands. You've seen how the other huntresses and the two males who accompanied them looked at Oluina and Moriak. I may not be an expert in Prides, but I am certain these two will be demoted when they return home."

"Moriak will be cast out," Danel said with conviction. "He was defeated in thirty seconds and squealed like a swine for mercy. The huntresses will demand his removal and eviction."

Ylis nodded. "Moriak is done for. As for Oluina, if Rozel doesn't demote her, they will both fall."

"Well, that's no longer our problem. We have an amazing new home, and an even more amazing Pride. Let's not give those idiots any more of our time," I said.

After a few more cheers, everyone scattered to get back to their work, except for Faran and Kazaer who headed into the forest to make sure the intruders were indeed going back to their own village.

"Now let's go patch you up," I said, rubbing my nose against his.

It immediately began to twitch, his whiskers flailing as he fought the urge to sneeze. I burst out laughing before I kissed his lips.

EPILOGUE
OPHELIA

That evening, as had become our habit, we settled around the bonfire on the beach where we held our communal meals. The females had made it a point of going back hunting for the best possible celebration feast tonight. Although I would stuff my face with my share of meat, I also prepared a small portion of salad for myself.

Being predominantly carnivores, the Nazhrals often only ate meat, which naturally didn't meet my dietary needs. The occasional side dishes they had mostly consisted of starch and carbs. I needed my greens. Normally, I would steam some veggies in the kitchen or grill some of them next to the spit. But tonight, I was in the mood for something different.

I quickly whipped up a traditional chef salad with their equivalent of lettuce—although it was more like spinach—tomatoes, a purple thing that tasted like slightly sweet cucumber, grated carrots, and a few green olives from the stash I'd brought with me. To my delight, I found out I could get more olives delivered to Melelyn, as they were not naturally produced here.

I hastened back to the beach. Before I even settled down next to Gaelec, every head turned my way, their nostrils flaring, and the oddest expression descending over their features.

I glanced down at myself, wondering if I had spilled something on me or was somehow suffering a wardrobe malfunction. But nothing looked out of place.

"What's wrong?" I asked, baffled.

They sniffed the air, and Gaelec's eyes darkened, looking slightly glazed over as he leaned towards my salad.

"What is that?" he asked, his voice dropping an octave.

"A salad?" I said, sounding both uncertain and as if it should be obvious.

"I've seen those vegetables before, but not those green things," he said, looking a bit more restless.

"That?" I asked, pointing at one of the olives. "I've eaten them frequently at the house," I said, still just as confused.

And then it dawned on me that I normally ate them during the day when he was off working.

"Do you want to try one, or does this smell bother you?"

"I would try one!"

The eagerness with which he replied threw me for a loop. Judging by their collective weird reaction, I had expected them to tell me to get rid of it, and that it smelled foul to their particularly sensitive noses. Relieved, I happily gave him one.

"I wouldn't mind trying one as well," Kazaer said, everyone else nodding with the same hopeful glances. "It smells amazing!"

Although stunned, I agreed and started spreading them around. Thankfully, as I previously cut them in half, there was just enough for everyone with a couple left in my bowl. But the spectacle that followed initially had me on the verge of panic before I ended up nearly laughing my ass off.

Their collective eyes glazed over, and they started moaning and purring, some of them even slightly twitching. I almost expected them to start rolling on the ground. To my shock, they didn't flat out chew and swallow, but most of them were just sucking on the small piece, half chewing in that playful way one would pretend to bite someone else.

They all looked high…

However, and to my utter relief, it wasn't in the scary way of a junkie or someone who got utterly wasted. They struck me more like someone having a nice buzz after a couple of drinks, but still very functional and aware.

As I vaguely recalled something about cats and olives, I whipped out my com to do a quick search only to have it confirmed. It turned out that olives shared some of the chemical compounds found in catnip, especially nepetalactone. Cats could detect those chemicals with the receptors in their noses and mouths. That explained why their noses started twitching the minute I showed up with my salad, and why they were making the pleasure last by not swallowing right away.

For the next thirty minutes, I just watched my entire Pride having a blast over such a simple ingredient before fully recovering from it. Thankfully, olives were not harmful to felines. We needed to confirm that the same would apply to Nazhrals.

I already discovered that, like cats, Nazhrals couldn't taste sweetness. Due to genetic mutations that affected their taste receptors, felines couldn't enjoy the unique taste of anything sugary. So much for the chocolate croissants, cakes, and other pastries I had planned on making to introduce them to some human dishes. It was even more disturbing that I didn't know how the final taste would come across to them.

Naturally, they not only made sure I would order more olives in the future, but they also discussed the possibility of growing them right here on Melelyn. It currently was an untapped market that could possibly give us the financial independence we needed. Obviously, it would require a bit more investigation to make sure it was not only safe for the population, but also that introducing these trees to their home world's ecosystem wouldn't be harmful.

GAELEC

In the week that followed, a major overhaul occurred in Nevian Valley. As expected, Rozel was forced to step down from her role as Head Matriarch in favor of her sister Pryia. It was unfortunate that it took so long for this to happen. Ylis's mother had always been the better choice. It would take a long time for them to rebuild, but evicting Moriak was the first step in the right direction.

That, too, had been rather tragic. When he refused to leave, the females turned on him and drove him out of the village with deep cuts and lacerations instead of peacefully with his bags. Injured, without weapons or provisions, he roamed the forest for a couple of weeks during which every village he approached turned him away. That some of his wounds had begun to fester only made matters worse. No Pride would want to shelter a sick male.

Three days after his last rejection, huntresses found him nearly dead, being ravaged by a Sikkal. They killed the beast and called a city shuttle to have him brought to a hospital in the capital. Although he survived, he lost a leg and a couple fingers, on top of being permanently disfigured by vicious claw marks. With today's advanced technology, he could have been mostly mended, but he didn't have the credits for it. Considering all the wealth he'd acquired by selling us off to his recruiter buddy, he should have been able to cover the cost. However, he apparently blew all of it to buy the Matriarchs' clemency after the disastrous

Levendoc mission. Naturally, Rozel had gladly taken everything he had. He should have known that it wouldn't save him if he made a single other mistake, especially once he ran out of credits.

The fool should have left with his wealth while he still could. Instead, broke, disfigured, amputated, and with little professional education, he failed to find a decent job in the city. In desperation, he turned to Ranor to find him one of those safe missions he had shunned for the rest of us. Ranor totally found him a mission. It turned out not to be as safe as he claimed. Last I heard, he'd in fact given Moriak a one-way ticket to Molvi.

It shamed me to rejoice at his downfall. And yet, he deserved to get a proper taste of the pain he subjected others to. It just saddened me that he was sent to a Gray Quadrant as, in his current state, he probably wouldn't last more than a week. He should have served twelve plus years in a Light Quadrant to fully pay for his crimes.

But I refused to waste any additional mental energy on him.

Oluina fell into a deep depression. She attempted to join a different Pride only to be soundly rejected by every single one of them. Word of her attack on my mate spread far and wide. As I didn't believe the Nevian females would have further harmed their reputation by leaking that information, I assumed one of our males—most probably the younger ones—shared that info. I couldn't blame them for it. After how she and Moriak caused the deaths of so many innocent young males, they would want to protect each other from someone like her.

As for us, we were steadily thriving. Despite the scarcity of funds, we had a comfortable life, and all our basic needs were met. With the arrival of the fishing ship, we finally started getting a steady stream of credits. We wouldn't get rich off it, but it allowed us to acquire some of the creature comforts we lacked.

Andrane proved to be a real blessing. Even though she had

no intention of remaining with us for the long haul, she took getting our village off on the right foot extremely seriously. For her, this was a live rehearsal for when she would start her own Pride with her sisters. Thanks to the more advanced administrative training she received specifically for that purpose, she helped set all that management side of things.

She ended up being the one training Ophelia, sharing her contacts and procedure for acquiring supplies from the capital, inventory management, taxes and finances, etc.

In parallel, Ophelia and Andrane both worked with my mate's contacts with the charities, the UPO, and the Obosian carceral education teams to build the list of programs we would be offering our males. This whole thing ended up blowing up into something much bigger.

My mate had the brilliant idea of opening access to those programs to other Prides. Every day, the teenagers from various Prides would attend a weekly class with hands-on training in the integrated holodeck of our largest deployable building. As they could never access that technology in the near future, many of our neighbors gladly participated. In exchange, they compensated us with credits—for those who could afford it—or with the crafted goods we sorely needed.

Although quite a few young females joined the training, the overwhelming majority of participants were males, specifically acquiring the trade skills that would open safer opportunities for them in the future.

On that front, the Enforcers came through for us even more than the charitable organizations. They paired us with a recruitment agent who found us some of the most lucrative temporary off-world jobs. As we couldn't really afford to send our own males off on most of those missions, which lasted on average three to six months, Kazaer suggested that we operate as what my mate called a middle-man.

The principle was quite simple. The Enforcer agent sent us regular lists of jobs to be filled. We narrowed down suitable candidates. Once they got a job, they received their full wages, and the employer paid us a finder's fee of ten percent of their salaries. It was a huge incentive for the participants as Prides normally took twenty-five to forty percent of the males' wages, and that didn't guarantee they would still have a place in their village when they returned.

Although we remained extremely picky as to who we allowed to become permanent members of our Pride, we set up a comfortable camp at the edge of our territory where those temporary workers could return and stay in-between contracts. It was connected to our power grid and com system, providing them with greater comfort than most nomad camps, with proper dormitories, hygiene facilities, and discounted cost on food.

It turned out that olives were already a thing in the capital but were considered a gourmet delicacy that only the rich got to enjoy. Ophelia got us all the legal and agricultural approvals necessary to buy a dozen already mature olive trees to plant here. They became our biggest source of income.

We ran into a few hiccups along the way and expected to face many more hurdles in the future, but things were looking up. It would take years to iron out all the kinks, and we would continue to redefine ourselves over time.

We also understood that what we were creating was an anomaly. I initially had the crazy idea that more villages like ours would pop up in the future, but it was too fundamental a change to our way of life. Our people weren't ready for it, and frankly most didn't want it, not even our males. Andrane helped open my eyes on that front.

We were a matriarchal society, and our males actually had the instinctive—not to say genetic—need to roam. In truth, I had a happy youth and been excited about setting off. Losing her eighteen-year-old brother to the raid against Ophelia's vessel convinced Andrane that she didn't want her sons and the males in her future Pride to meet a similar fate. Working with her helped us better refine the services we were offering to keep our traditional Prides thriving and our males of all ages safe and prospering.

As I gazed upon my Pride, gathering on the beach for the evening communal meal, I couldn't help a smile. We started off a handful, and now fifty-four people—twelve of them females—were happily bringing the seasoned meat to the spit.

A week ago, Ylis gave birth to two cubs, a male named Kaden after Ylis's sire, and a female named Lia, after my mate. Even now, Ophelia was standing outside our house, cooing at her namesake. I walked up to her and drew her into my embrace. I kissed Lia's little forehead before kissing my mate.

"Someone is quite fond of her niece," I said teasingly.

"Someone most definitely is. In fact, someone was thinking she should get rid of her contraceptive implant," my mate deadpanned, although I didn't miss the slight tension in her voice.

My heart leapt in my chest. Since Ylis and Kazaer announced they were expecting, I'd been burning with the desire for us to start our own family. But as we'd just completed our trial period, and with still so much work to do building our new village, I had been reluctant to add that pressure on her.

"The little ones could certainly use more friends to play with. So I would tend to agree with that idea," I said tenderly.

"Really?!" Ophelia exclaimed, her eyes sparkling with joy.

I chuckled and nodded. "Yes, my Ophelia. I love you. I want everything with you, including a family."

"I love you, too, Gaelec," she said, her eyes misting. "Believe me, I've been ready for a while now. We said for better or for worse. The worst is behind us. Every day since with you, with our Pride, has only gotten better."

"Then let's do it. For better or for worse, so long as we're together, no challenge will ever be too great."

And yes, many more challenges awaited us. But all that mattered was that we were together. We were free. We were safe. We were home.

THE END

ALSO BY REGINE ABEL

THE VEREDIAN CHRONICLES
Escaping Fate
Blind Fate
Raising Amalia
Twist of Fate
Hands of Fate
Defying Fate
Imperial Fate

BRAXIANS
Anton's Grace
Ravik's Mercy
Krygor's Hope
Keran's Dawn

XIAN WARRIORS
Doom
Legion
Raven
Bane
Chaos
Varnog
Reaper
Wrath
Xenon
Nevrik
Rogue

PRIME MATING AGENCY
I Married A Lizardman

ABOUT REGINE

USA Today bestselling author Regine Abel is a fantasy, paranormal and sci-fi junkie. Anything with a bit of magic, a touch of the unusual, and a lot of romance will have her jumping for joy. She loves creating hot alien warriors and no-nonsense, kick-ass heroines that evolve in fantastic new worlds while embarking on action-packed adventures filled with mystery and the twists you never saw coming.

Before devoting herself as a full-time writer, Regine had surrendered to her other passions: music and video games! After a decade working as a Sound Engineer in movie dubbing and live concerts, Regine became a professional Game Designer and Creative Director, a career that has led her from her home in Canada to the US and various countries in Europe and Asia.

Facebook

https://www.facebook.com/regine.abel.author/

Website

https://regineabel.com

Regine's Rebels Reader Group

https://www.facebook.com/groups/ReginesRebels/

Newsletter

http://smarturl.it/RA_Newsletter

Goodreads

http://smarturl.it/RA_Goodreads

Bookbub

https://www.bookbub.com/profile/regine-abel

Amazon

http://smarturl.it/AuthorAMS